The Girls from See Saw Lane

The Girls from See Saw Lane

SANDY TAYLOR

bookouture

Published by Bookouture
An imprint of StoryFire Ltd.
23 Sussex Road, Ickenham, UB10 8PN
United Kingdom

www.bookouture.com

ISBN: 978-1-910751-59-6

*This book is dedicated to the memory of
my dear friend Carol Faithful, who was taken from us far too soon.
Carol, I wish you could have read my book.*

Prologue

Brighton
1965

You watch your feet as they walk along the hospital corridor, your heels clicking on the floor. Behind you, outside the heavy swing doors, is a sunny July day and Brighton is in full swing. It is bright and breezy, full of holidaymakers and people enjoying the sunshine. Children are playing on the beach, adults are sitting on deckchairs reading newspapers and eating ice cream, having a laugh. The vendors are doing great trade, selling coloured windmills and buckets and spades, candyfloss and paper boxes of cockles and whelks. Music sings out of the record shops and the cafés and the fairground at the end of the pier, and the dry, sharp sugar-smell of candyfloss mingles with the salt air of the sea and the pinching aroma of hot chip fat – even thinking of the smell makes your stomach clench with pleasure.

Inside the hospital, it is always the same; it is always dark brown. It smells of disinfectant, floor-polish and of dying flowers and tears. Your heart sinks a little further every time you visit.

You don't have to think about where you are going anymore; you've been so many times that you somehow arrive at the ward doors without noticing how you got there. They were very strict about visiting times at the hospital but in the past week or so nobody has said anything to you when you arrived a little early.

The slender nurse with the beehive hair puts down her knitting and smiles at you as you turn into the ward. You call her Audrey Hepburn.

'You're her friend, aren't you?'

You nod.

'Wait here a minute, dear,' she says.

You stand still, looking down. If you look up you will see the faces of the people in the beds and you never know how to look at them. It seems wrong to smile, but what else is there? So you look down at the roses in your hands. They are yellow, with a pinkish stain at the edge of the petals.

You hold the flowers up so that you can catch their scent. It is sweet and warm and it reminds you of home and of your mum and dad. And you stay like that, holding the flowers up to your chest until the nurse returns.

She puts a hand on your arm.

'She's not had a good day,' the nurse says gently. 'She's very tired. Do you understand?'

You nod.

The nurse smiles at you. She leans forward and brushes the hair out of your eyes.

'You're being very brave,' she says. 'She's lucky to have a friend like you.'

But the nurse doesn't know what you've done, how you betrayed her. She doesn't know the truth.

This Book Belongs To Mary Pickles

46 See Saw Lane

Brighton

The World.

This is my secret diery. No one is alowed to look at it on payn of deth or wors.

Dear Diery

I am going to right in you evry day

or just somtimes.

I used to live in London

now I live in See Saw LAane. I like it in See Saw Lane.

from

Mary Pickles

Aged 8 and two weeks.

Chapter One

1963

Mary Pickles and I walked along the street with our arms linked, looking in the shop windows. The sun was shining, dazzling off the bonnets of the holidaymakers' cars, and Brighton was buzzing like it always is in the summer. We were walking fast, perfectly in step with each other and my heart felt fizzy with all the potential that a day off work could bring. Every now and then Mary glanced towards me and smiled, and I smiled back at her, and I think we both felt the same; we were best friends and together we were invincible.

It was a Saturday, and me and Mary Pickles had managed to get the same day off work. It was almost a miracle. Normally at least one of us, and usually both of us, had to work Saturdays, but our supervisor Sally was in a particularly good mood because she'd been talent-spotted in Marks and Spencer's and asked to go in for the Miss Brighton competition. Because of this, and because she liked us, Sally said we could both have that summer Saturday off.

So there we were, in Brighton, with nothing much to do except enjoy ourselves, walking up and down the high street, looking in the shop windows, watching the boys. Mary kept looking at her reflection in the glass and smiling at what she saw. Her dark hair was tied back into a ponytail with a yellow ribbon; she looked neat and pretty. We stopped outside Woolworths, which had the biggest window on the high street. This was where we both worked.

Usually I was on cosmetics and Mary was on sweets, because Sally said she was too small to be on cosmetics. Mary was more than a bit miffed about this, but I thought Sally had a point. Mary was so small; it would look like there was no one serving if she stood behind the racks of lipsticks and eye shadows on the cosmetics counter. I didn't tell Mary that, because she was very sensitive about her height. She was even more sensitive about her height than I was about my weight and that's saying something.

That Saturday, we could see that Woollies was packed with shoppers, women with shopping bags holding the hands of little children and men buying paint and newspapers. Mary pulled faces at the back of Mr Rankworthy, who managed the DIY section, but the moment he came towards the window, she smiled and waved and you could see his heart melt.

Mary had that effect on people.

Mr Rankworthy came outside, and lit a cigarette.

'What are you doing here on your day off?' he asked, looking at Mary's chest. She was wearing a tight, short-sleeved top that made her look amazing. 'Haven't you got anywhere better to be of a Saturday? No boyfriend?'

He talked to Mary as if I wasn't there. That was the effect *I* had on people.

Mary smiled. 'Why do you want to know about my boyfriend, Jeffrey?' she asked. She licked her lips and made her eyes wide and Mr Rankworthy tugged at the collar of his overalls.

'Come on,' I said, tugging at her arm. I didn't like Mr Rankworthy. I didn't like the way his face went red and sweaty when he looked at Mary. And anyway, it seemed daft to spend our one proper day off in the whole week standing outside the place where we worked!

Not that I was ungrateful or anything.

Woolworths was one of the best places to work in Brighton, everyone knew that. There were plenty of summer jobs going in the town in the amusement arcades and the sweet shops and the beach kiosks, which was fine for the holiday season, but most of those places closed down during the winter months. Woolworths was one of the few shops that was busy all year round, the pay was good, the uniform wasn't bad, and a lively, mostly young team of staff worked there. The shop was almost always full of young people too, coming in to browse and to chat. Mary and I had been at Woolworths since we left school and although we complained about having to spend most of our days there, the truth was I loved it. It was like being in a youth club and being paid for it.

I loved it, but Woolworths was never enough for Mary. Her heart was in Paris.

As we walked away from the shop that day, Mary sighed theatrically.

'Oh well,' she said. 'At least I won't have to put up with Mr Rankworthy for much longer.'

'Why not?' I asked. 'Is he leaving?'

'No,' Mary laughed, 'he'll be there until he's ancient. No, I'm the one who'll be leaving, off to L'Institut d'Art.'

She beamed at me like this was good news and I said: 'Oh yeah.'

Mary put her hands on her hips. 'Oh, Dottie,' she said, 'couldn't you just try to be a bit more enthusiastic?'

'I could try,' I said, but I knew I wouldn't succeed because Mary going away was not something I felt the slightest bit enthusiastic about.

Mary had a plan. She'd had the same plan since school. She wanted to be an artist. She wanted to travel the world and paint. The first step of this plan was going to art school in Paris. It was a special school, only the best young artists could go there, the ones who were serious about their work. Mary wanted to go to Paris and live there for three years while she studied at the Institute. I couldn't understand why she'd want to leave Brighton. It wasn't as if there wasn't enough things to paint right where we were, and it had a good art school. But no, Mary's heart was in Paris.

We turned the corner into one of the side roads and headed towards the seafront. Music was playing in the amusement arcades and the pavements were packed with people, most of them smiling, all of them in their summer clothes.

'You have to come with me when I go,' Mary said. 'We'd have the best time together! Imagine you and me sitting on the banks of the Seine or climbing to the top of the Eiffel Tower. Imagine living in Paris, Dottie, that beautiful city! It would turn the world into our oyster.'

'I don't like oysters!'

'Very funny.'

'Anyway,' I said, 'people like us don't go to places like that.'

'What do you mean, people like *us*?'

'Well,' I said, 'people that live on council estates. People who work in Woolworths.'

Mary rolled her eyes. 'I don't believe you sometimes.'

'What?'

'Where you *live* and where you *work* doesn't make you who you *are*. Growing up on a council estate didn't stop Paul McCartney, did it? I'm Mary Pickles and you're Dottie Perks and we're just as good as anyone else, and if we want to climb to the top of the Eiffel Tower we jolly well will.'

I didn't doubt for one second that Mary would climb the tower one day. Perhaps not me though. I didn't want to leave Brighton, I liked it there. I liked living on the estate and working in Woolworths. I wanted to be like my mum, get married one day, and have kids. I didn't want anything more than that.

Mary must have been reading my thoughts. 'The world doesn't begin and end with Brighton, you know.'

'I know. But I don't like the thought of going away. Maybe when I'm older. After I've been married and my children are grown up.'

Mary snorted. 'You'll be too old to enjoy it then. I'm not getting married until I'm at least thirty and I definitely don't want kids.'

'What, never?'

'Never!'

'Golly,' I said.

'And you can't have any either.'

'Can't I?'

'Not till you're a lot older, because I can't be fabulous on my own, I need you with me.'

'Okay,' I said.

'Good,' Mary said. She squeezed my arm. 'And one day I am going to be a world-famous artist and I'm going to stand at the top of the Eiffel Tower with the boy that I love.'

'You'll have to find him first.'

'I will,' she said, smiling.

Chapter Two

After we'd walked up and down the high street a few times, Mary and I went and sat on the railings by the seafront and watched the light bouncing off the waves that came rolling in, rattling the pebbles on the beach. Behind us, buses trundled by. We talked about the people at work. We were both pretty impressed about Sally being in the beauty show, which was about the biggest thing that ever happened in our part of the world. Even if she didn't win, she'd still get her picture in the *Argus* and she'd meet Ken Dodd, who was going to be one of the judges. Girls who did well in the Miss Brighton competition were like superstars to the rest of us.

'Ken Dodd! Can you believe it?' said Mary. She was trying to hold the hem of her skirt down with her hands but the breeze kept picking it up and riffling its edges like a fan. I was wearing pale pink pedal pushers and regretting it because they were a bit tight at the seams and they were making my thighs look even bigger than they already were.

'If she wins she'll go on to the Miss Sussex contest,' I said, hitching at my waistband to make a bit more room. 'Then Miss England, then Miss United Kingdom and then Miss Europe and then Miss World. Imagine! We'll know somebody famous.'

'Shhh…' Mary hissed pulling an exaggerated face. 'Behind you.'

I peered at Mary over the top of my sunglasses.

'Boys!' she whispered.

I looked over my shoulder and sure enough a small gang of boys were coming along the seafront, all jostling their elbows and smoking and talking too loudly, like boys do.

Mary and I immediately crossed our legs and adopted bored-to-death expressions. I chewed my gum very obviously and she examined her fingernails. We could actually feel the boys looking us up and down as they went past.

'Morning, darlin'!' one of them said to Mary.

'I'm not your darling,' said Mary.

'You don't know what you're missing, love,' said the boy.

'Ignore him,' I said, but I may as well have saved my breath.

'What would that be, then?' said Mary, smiling sweetly. 'Your scintillating conversation or the tidemark round your neck?'

'Leave her,' said one of the boys. 'She only looks about ten.' The rest of them started laughing.

Mary jumped off the railings.

I stepped down as elegantly as I could, which wasn't very, and took hold of Mary's elbow.

'Come on, Mary, they're only boys, they're not worth it,' I said haughtily. 'Let's go to the record shop.'

'Yes, let's. We might meet some *men* there.'

We linked arms and walked back into town, heading for the In-A-Spin record shop. We went there whenever we had a day off together. I didn't like going on my own. It was much more fun when Mary was there. The young people went there to look at one another as much as to look at the records. There was a very hip boy who worked behind the counter. He wore winkle-pickers and sweaters and he was very slouchy. He always looked bored, except when he was talking to other young men about the latest musical trends, and then he got quite chatty and animated. He gave the impression of knowing absolutely everything there was to know, about all the latest bands. There was always a cigarette burning in the ashtray on the counter and he always seemed to have a cup of coffee on the go.

The shop walls were covered in posters and the records were all stacked in racks, the Top Twenty singles at the front of the shop, and the LPs arranged by artist. We never had enough money for LPs, but we liked buying singles.

Me and Mary were totally in love with a Liverpool band called The Beatles and I had a huge crush on one of the lads, Paul McCartney. Mary was crazy about John Lennon. My sister Rita had given me a poster of The Beatles that I stuck behind my bed. Rita preferred The Dave Clark Five.

Mary picked up a single, *From Me to You*. She danced over to me, holding it up in front of her for me to see.

'I'm going to listen to this!' she announced. 'How about you?'

I grinned. '*Please, Please Me,*' I told her.

'Okay,' said Mary. 'We can swap when we've finished listening to them.'

We told the boy behind the counter which records we wanted to listen to and went into adjoining booths. The booths were made of glass, so we could still see each other.

We put on the headphones and I was soon being carried away by Paul. Even though there were three other boys in the band, I could still pick out Paul's voice. He had the dreamiest voice in the whole world, and if I closed my eyes I could imagine that he was singing just to me. I loved him so much. I would have done anything for Paul McCartney, anything at all.

When I opened my eyes again, Mary seemed to be having some sort of fit in the next-door booth. She was waving her arms about and jumping up and down and she was all bright-eyed and red in the face. She must be really enjoying the record. I waved back at her and carried on listening to Paul. Next thing I knew Mary was banging on the glass and waving urgently.

'What?' I mouthed. She mouthed something back but I couldn't understand what she was saying, so I took off my headphones and put my head into her booth.

'What?'

'Look there! In the shop!' she squeaked, bouncing up and down on the soles of her feet.

I looked at where she was pointing, and standing at the counter was a skinny boy. He seemed much taller than last time we'd seen him. I suppose he was good-looking, that is if you like boys with long necks and tight trousers. He kept flicking back his hair and gazing at everyone in a slightly superior way. Yes, it was Elton Briggs, the boy whom Mary had always adored when we were at school, and standing next to him was Ralph Bennett. My heart gave a little flip and I could feel my face going red. Mary was now out of the booth, brushing down her skirt and tossing her ponytail. I grabbed my bag and followed her. She hung onto my arm and whispered: 'Doesn't he look amazing?'

But I wasn't looking at Elton. I was looking at Ralph.

'Go over and say hello,' said Mary, giving me a little push.

'*You* go over and say hello,' I said.

'Don't be mean,' said Mary. 'You know what Elton means to me!'

'*Meant,*' I said. 'The last time you saw him he had his tongue halfway down Beverly Johnson's throat.'

'It wasn't our time then, but it is now, Dottie, I just know it is.'

Sometimes I thought Mary would have done quite well on the stage. She sounded like some kind of film star, all desperate and tragic.

'Please, Dottie,' she wheedled and her little face looked all screwed up and sad, so I did what I always did when Mary was sad: I gave in.

'Okay,' I said. 'But what's the betting they won't even remember us?'

'Thanks,' said Mary, miraculously cheering up and immediately fishing in her bag for her compact so she could check her face.

I went up to the counter and stood next to Elton. I looked at the hairs on the back of his neck and cleared my throat. He completely ignored me.

'Have you got *Telstar* by The Tornados?' he asked the boy behind the counter.

'Now that,' said the hip boy taking a swig of his coffee, 'is a very good choice. They recorded that track in their agent's front room.' And Elton got all puffed up with importance like it was *him* that had recorded *Telstar* in *his* front room.

'Hello,' I said.

Elton turned slowly and frowned at me as if I'd just crawled out from under a log. I smiled at him hopefully. He was wearing aftershave that made him smell like a car smells, of leather and petrol. He looked me up and down very slowly but didn't speak.

'Hello Dottie,' said Ralph, smiling around Elton.

I smiled gratefully at Ralph. He smiled back at me. I smiled some more. Elton made a bit of a sneery face and I remembered what I was supposed to be doing.

'I'm with Mary,' I said. 'Mary Pickles.' I glanced over my shoulder. Mary was hiding behind one of the record racks out of Elton's sight. She had crossed the first two fingers on each hand and was holding them up to me, nodding her head in encouragement.

'You two were always together at school,' said Ralph. His voice was soft and deep, more like a man than the boy I remembered.

'So were you two,' I said.

'Blast from the past,' said Ralph, smiling.

'Yeah,' I said, smiling back. We couldn't stop smiling at one another.

Elton rolled his eyes, turned away and started to flick through the bargain records in the rack by the counter. He didn't seem in the least bit interested in the conversation. Ralph might have changed but Elton was exactly the same: arrogant and kind of pompous.

Mary must have given up on me. She came over to stand by us. She squeezed in between me and Elton and gazed up at him like a lovesick puppy. He didn't take a blind bit of notice of her; he just continued looking through the records.

I didn't know what else to say and I was beginning to feel a bit stupid just standing there.

'Aren't you going to get a record?' Elton asked Ralph.

'In a minute,' Ralph answered. There was a red rash creeping up from the collar of his shirt and making its way up his neck. Suddenly he blurted out: 'Fancy a coffee?'

'There's a good café opposite the Palace Pier,' said Mary. She was speaking very fast and in a very high voice, and her smile was nearly splitting her face. 'It's called *Dells*. They've got a jukebox and a football table.'

'And they do really good coffees,' I said. I needed a drink. My mouth felt like the bottom of a baby's pram, all fluff and biscuits.

'Great,' said Ralph. He glanced at Elton, who was still ignoring us. 'Why don't we meet you there in about twenty minutes? That all right with you, Elton?'

Elton looked at me and Mary as if he'd only just noticed us. 'Don't mind,' he said, in a bored sort of voice.

Beside me I could sense Mary nearly fainting with exitement.

'That's settled then,' said Ralph. 'See you in twenty minutes.'

Me and Mary paid for our records and the hip boy put them in paper bags and passed them back to us, and all the time I was really conscious of Ralph watching, and it was strange, because it was only old Ralph Bennett. It wasn't like he was somebody new and yet, in a strange sort of way, it *was*. I was quite relieved when Mary and I went out of the shop and headed to the café.

Dear Diary,

Me and Dottie could have gone to the record shop any day but we went today. I call that fate it was definiately meant to be. I have been waiting for this moment all my life

Oh Elton, Elton, Elton

Mary Pickles

loves

Elton Briggs

She really does!!!!!

Love Mary Pickles

Aged seventeen.

Chapter Three

Me and Mary hadn't seen Elton and Ralph since we'd left school two years ago and now here they were in our record shop.

'I think I'm going to faint,' said Mary, going all dramatic.

'Well, don't faint all over me,' I said.

'Did you see the way he looked at me?'

'I did actually. He looked at you as if you'd just crawled out from under the same log that I'd crawled out from.'

'Elton always looks like that, he's just really cool.'

'Positively arctic,' I said.

'Dottie, this is really important to me. This could be the most important day of my life.'

I smiled. 'Yes, I suppose it could.'

'I want to run.'

'What?'

'I want to run and run and run.'

'Couldn't we just walk fast?'

'Oh you, Dottie Perks.'

'Oh you, Mary Pickles.'

'I've never forgotten Elton, you know.'

'Well I can see that now, but I kind of hoped you had. You haven't exactly gone on about him since we left school.'

'That's because I knew you didn't like him.'

'I don't *know* him. All I know is that he was always upsetting you.'

'That's part of being in love, Dottie. You always hurt the one you love.'

'Is that a fact?'

'Well, that's what Clarence Frogmore Henry said.'

'Who the heck's Clarence Frogmore Henry?'

'He's the bloke that sang the song.'

'Well, I don't think you have to hurt the one you love. I think it makes more sense to be nice to the one you love.'

'You've got a lot to learn about love,' she said, catching hold of my hand and starting to run.

'I don't think I'll bother,' I shouted, stumbling behind her.

We had only run a short distance when I let go of her hand and leant against a wall.

Mary ran back to me.

I took the puffer out of my pocket, inhaling the medicine and holding my breath.

'I forgot,' said Mary.

'I know.'

'I'm always forgetting.'

'I know.'

'We'll walk really slowly,' she said. 'In fact we'll crawl, and if anyone says anything, we'll tell them to take a long run off a short pier.'

'You're daft, you are.'

'I know, it's endearing, isn't it?'

'That's one word for it.'

'Feeling better?'

'Much.'

We walked slowly down West Street and on to the seafront. There were crowds of people milling around the aquarium and the little shops, whose windows were full of pink shiny Brighton rock wrapped in cellophane and plastic windmills for the children to hold in the wind. We were used to all the holidaymakers who arrived in the summer with their umbrellas and their plastic mats and their noisy children. The rock in the sweet shops was for them. Me and Mary had never bought the rock and we'd never visited the aquarium. When I was a kid, my mum said if I ever ate it I'd end up with no teeth. My sister Rita said that in my case that could only be an improvement. She's very sweet, my sister. Not.

'How do I look?' asked Mary.

'You look nice.'

'What do you mean I look nice? I need to look more than nice, nice is ordinary, I have to look better than ordinary. I have to look extraordinary.'

'You look fab,' I said. 'Really, you do.'

'Have you got any lippy on you?'

'Haven't you got any, then?'

'I wouldn't be asking you if I had any would I?'

'Well you usually do.'

'For heaven's sake, have you got any or not?'

'A bit but you'll have to dig it out with a match.'

'Have you got a match?'

'I don't think so.'

'Do you know how irritating you can be at times?'

'It has been mentioned. I've got a hairgrip, that should do it.'

'What colour is it?' she said.

'What the hairgrip?'

'No, stupid, the lippy.'

'It's called Corn Silk. It's a kind of apricot colour. It will go nicely with your jumper.'

Before we went into the café, we went across the road to the Flick 'n' Curl hairdressers, 'cos they had this big mirror in the window and Mary could put the lippy on.

I found the hairgrip, managed to get the lippy out and smeared some on Mary's lips. She tucked them into her mouth to spread it about a bit. She stood in front of me holding her face up like a child. I licked the corner of my handkerchief and tidied the edges up for her.

'Do I look all right?' she said again.

'You look fab!' I said, smiling at her.

Dells café was full of people. Its windows were covered with posters and notices advertising gigs and what films were on at the Regent Cinema, and there was a lovely smell, a combination of coffee and that hot, sugary scent of fresh doughnuts. Mary and I went in and the first person we saw was Christine Smith, leaning against the jukebox. Her best friend Angie Brown was over by the counter. They both worked in the sack factory and they had this permanent smell of fish about them. I don't know why working in a sack factory made them smell of fish, but it did.

'All right?' asked Christine when we walked in. Her face was red and damp in the heat. She popped the last piece of a hot dog into her mouth and wiped her lips with the back of her hand.

'Yes, we're fine thanks,' I said.

'Still working in Woollies?'

I nodded. 'You still working in the sack factory?' As if you couldn't tell, I thought.

'Of course we are,' Christine said as if it was a daft question. 'What are Woollies paying now?'

'Three pounds five shillings,' I said.

'You're mad,' said Christine. 'Me and Angie bring home five pounds a week.'

'Five pounds!' said Mary.

'Blimey!' I said. We were both pretty impressed. Five pounds would buy you a lot of clothes and make-up and records.

'And we don't have to work on a Saturday,' said Christine. 'Never.' She was starting to show off a bit now. Never mind all that, I thought, at least Mary and me didn't smell of smoked haddock.

Christine called to Angie who came over, sipping Coca-Cola through a straw from the bottle.

'I was just telling these two, they must be mad working in Woollies. They only get three pound five a week and they have to work on a Saturday.'

'You wouldn't catch me working on a Saturday,' said Angie.

'It's not so bad,' I said. 'We've both had today off.'

'You wouldn't catch me working *any* Saturday.'

So you just said, I thought.

'You ought to come and work with the sacks,' said Angie. 'It's a good laugh.'

'Don't you mind the smell?' asked Mary with an innocent look on her face. Mary never meant to be rude, but sometimes she accidentally was.

'What smell?' asked Christine. She looked genuinely confused, and wrinkled up her nose and sniffed at her arm.

'That sort of fishy smell.' said Mary.

'Are you saying we smell of fish?' said Christine.

'No,' I said quickly. '*You* don't smell of fish, it just smells a bit fishy when you walk past the factory.'

'I hadn't noticed,' she said. 'Have you noticed, Angie?'

'Noticed what?'

'That the factory smells of fish.'

'Can't say I have.'

'Anyway,' said Christine, 'they wouldn't take Mary on, she'd be too small to stack the sacks up. They've got a height restriction.'

'I never knew that,' said Angie, frowning.

'Well, it's true,' said Christine, glaring at her.

'But what about Brenda Cooper?' I said. 'She's not much bigger than Mary and she...'

'Fancy a go on the football table?' said Christine, butting in.

'If you like,' said Angie.

Christine whispered something in Angie's ear and they walked away giggling.

'Blooming cheek,' said Mary. She pulled out a chair and sat down at a table. I sat down next to her. Shafts of light fell across its surface. Mary took a packet of sugar cubes from the bowl on the table, unwrapped the paper and put both cubes into her mouth and began to crunch furiously.

'I shouldn't worry about it,' I said.

'I'm not,' she replied.

But I knew she was. Mary got embarrassed when people went on about her height. I sat there not knowing what to say. I took my record out of the bag, there was something about the feel of a new record, it reminded me of when I was a kid and I found a Famous Five book at the library that I hadn't read before. The word 'Parlophone' was printed on the record sleeve. I traced it with my finger. I wished the boys would hurry up.

As if on cue, the door banged against the bin and Elton and Ralph came into the coffee bar. We were sitting more or less by the door, so they saw us straight away. Mary sat up and made a big effort to swallow the sugar and to try to look composed. Elton winked at her, slicked back his hair with his fingers and walked straight past. Mary looked at me to see if I'd noticed the wink, but I couldn't pay her any attention right then because Ralph was standing just in front of me and I noticed for the first time, properly, how tall he was now, and how wide his shoulders were, and how grown-up he seemed.

'Hello again,' Ralph smiled. It felt as if he was smiling at me, just me. I wriggled in my seat a little and tried to pull my pedal pushers further down my legs.

'Hello,' I said, trying not to look as pleased as I was. After that I couldn't think of anything to say. My mind was as empty as the beach on a school day. It was like an empty space with the wind blowing through it. It was like the streets of our estate when everyone's gone to bed.

After I hadn't said anything for about a minute and a half, Ralph cleared his throat. 'Frothy coffees all round then?' he asked.

'Thanks very much,' I said gratefully.

'Yeah, thanks,' said Mary.

Ralph went to the counter to order the drinks and I followed Mary's eyes back to Elton. He was chatting to Christine by the table football. Either he was downwind of her, or he had no sense of smell. Christine was wearing a gingham dress with buttons down the front and matching sandals, and she did look pretty, in an obvious sort of way.

'Isn't Elton dreamy?' said Mary.

'I suppose so,' I said. I can't have sounded very enthusiastic because Mary immediately responded.

'What do you mean, you *suppose* so?'

I looked at Elton. He *was* good-looking, with his pointed boots and his tight trousers and his sharp haircut, but that was all he was. I didn't exactly have much experience, but I'd met boys like him in Woolworths. They were always flirting, they'd smile and say something nice to you and make you feel as if you were special, and the next second, some other girl would catch their eye and they'd move on without a second thought. My Aunty Brenda said boys like that were 'all trousers and no braces.'

Mary was staring at me, waiting for my answer.

'Elton's just not my type,' I mumbled. 'We can't all fancy the same type, can we?'

'But Dottie, he looks like Mick Jagger.'

'*He's* not my type either!'

She looked at me as if I was mad.

'So who is your type? Ralph Bennett?'

She meant it as a joke.

'Why not?' I said.

'Ralph Bennett!!!' said Mary, screwing up her nose like there was a bad smell under it. I glanced at Ralph. He was paying for our coffees at the counter. I was relieved to see he had his back to us.

'He's nice,' I said. 'At least he talks to us! At least he shows an interest!'

'Talks to *you*,' Mary corrected. 'And anyway, he's got ginger hair!'

'That bloke from Wagon Train's got ginger hair and you used to belong to his fan club! And anyway there's nothing wrong with ginger hair.'

'I know,' said Mary. 'But Ralph Bennett!!'

'Well I think he's turned out nice. Sssh,' I said, 'he's coming back.'

'Here you go, frothy coffees,' said Ralph, putting a tray with four coffees down on the table in front of us.

Elton noticed his return, said something to Christine that made her laugh very loudly and in a very obvious way, and he sauntered across to us. He pulled up a chair and sat down, stretching his legs out in front of him and crossing them at the ankle so that he took up an awful lot of space. He was probably trying to show off how skinny and long his legs were. They didn't do anything for me, but I could see Mary noticing them. Elton did look a little like Mick Jagger. He had the same sort of swagger about him. He took a red Embassy box out of the pocket of his jacket, tapped it on the table, flicked open the lid, and shook out a cigarette. He offered it to Mary, and then to me, and when we both shook our heads. He put the cigarette into the corner of his mouth, struck a match, and cupped the end of the cigarette in his two hands as he sucked on it until the tobacco caught. Mary was trying not to stare, but he caught her eye and I saw him look at her for a few seconds. It was a very intense look. It wasn't even me he was looking at but it made me feel a bit hot and uncomfortable. Mary blushed and turned away. She played with the end of her ponytail.

'So…' said Ralph, 'what have you been up to since school?'

I concentrated on stirring my coffee.

'We're working in Woollies,' I said. 'How about you?'

'Well I worked on the railways for a while, but now I'm an apprentice plumber,' said Ralph with some pride. 'It doesn't pay much while I'm training, but the money should be pretty good once I'm qualified. Then I'm going to get a van and work for myself.'

'So if you ever get a leak, Ralph's your man,' said Elton.

Mary giggled, and Elton grinned at her. 'You'd never catch me with my head under a sink!' he said.

That's because your head's too big to *fit* under a sink, I thought. I sipped my coffee. It was milky and sweet and delicious.

'What are *you* doing now, Elton?' Mary asked, holding her cup in both hands and blinking at Elton. There was a tiny, pale moustache of froth on her upper lip.

'I work in the offices at the cake factory, but it's just a stopgap.'

'Our Elton's going to be a rock star,' said Ralph.

'A rock star!' said Mary, her eyes nearly popping out of her head. Some of her coffee slopped over the rim of her cup and went onto the table, but she didn't even notice.

Elton ignored this. He was trying to look cool, but you could tell he was enjoying the attention.

'I'm in a band,' he said. 'We're called Brainless.'

Figures, I thought.

'I remember when you won that talent show at the Dome,' said Mary.

'He came third,' I said.

'Well, you should have won,' said Mary. 'You were the best one there by a mile.'

Sometimes Mary said things that hurt me. I knew she didn't mean to and I really tried not to mind, but sometimes it was difficult. That day, she seemed to have forgotten that I was in that very same talent show, and I had only entered the contest because Mary wanted to get to know Elton better. As it happened, he was pretty good, but he was beaten into third place by The Betty Bounce Dance Academy doing a piece called *Woodland Frolics* and a fat girl singing *Jesus Wants Me for a Sunbeam*. Personally I thought she would have made a better planet. I got highly commended for singing *The Merry Merry Pipes of Pan* unaccompanied.

'You're right,' said Elton. 'I should have won. I thought at the time it was a fix.'

'You were amazing!' said Mary.

'Thanks,' said Elton. He was relaxing and smiling at Mary now she was telling him how great he was and she was almost fainting with the effort of trying not to show how pleased she was. She kept glancing at me under her fringe to see if I had noticed that he was looking at her.

'The band's playing at the Whisky A Go Go on Saturday night,' said Ralph. 'Would you like to come and see them?'

'We'd love to come,' said Mary. 'Wouldn't we, Dottie?'

I wanted to see more of Ralph, I knew that, but I knew my mum wouldn't like me going into a nightclub – especially not the Whisky A Go Go. It had a reputation. Things went on in there that were sometimes hinted at in the newspapers. In fact, only a year earlier, the owner of the club murdered his wife. I didn't have to tell her I was going of course, but me and Mum were very close and I didn't like going behind her back.

Ralph noticed my hesitation.

'You could think about it, Dottie,' he said. 'You don't have to decide right now.'

'She doesn't have to think about it,' said Mary. 'We're going.'

I frowned at her. She pulled a face back at me.

'Are you mods or rockers?' said Elton, leaning back in his chair so that it balanced precariously on two legs.

'We're neither,' said Mary.

'Well, you must be one or the other,' said Elton.

'Why?' asked Mary.

Elton righted the chair, banging it against the table as it landed back on four legs so that all our coffees slopped onto the saucers.

You could see that Elton was lost for words. 'Because everyone is,' he mumbled.

'Well that's the whole trouble,' said Mary. 'We don't want to be like everyone else. Me and Dottie are individualists.'

This was news to me, but I liked the idea of being an individualist and I was really proud of Mary for saying it instead of trying to impress Elton.

'What are *you* then?' said Mary.

'A rocker, of course. You wouldn't catch me dead wearing those poofy mod clothes and riding those pathetic excuses for bikes.'

I looked at Ralph. 'How about you?'

'Oh, I can't afford to be either.'

'He's a rocker in his heart,' said Elton, draping his arm around Ralph's shoulder.

'I just can't afford the uniform,' said Ralph sticking out his bottom lip and trying to look pathetic. We all laughed, even Elton, which made him look friendlier. 'So, what clubs do you go to?' said Elton.

'We don't,' I said. 'We just come down here to the café.'

'Not very with it then.'

'We'd sooner be without it, thanks,' said Mary.

'But you'll try to come to the Whisky on Saturday?'

'Why not?' said Mary.

'And you, Dottie?' asked Ralph. 'Are you ready to branch out?'

'Of course she is,' said Mary. 'If anyone is in need of a bit of branching out, it's Dottie.'

'Good,' said Ralph, smiling at me.

I smiled back and my heart gave a little jump. I felt my cheeks flushing with heat, and had to stare down into my cup, but I couldn't stop the happy feeling bubbling up inside me.

'Can anyone smell fish?' asked Elton.

Dear Diery

Today I met a girl called Dotty. Shes got a rownd face and rownd glasses She shared her sweets with me

She is going to be my bestest frend forever and ever till the day I die

I am not going to die for a long time I mite be a hundred

Tatty bye diery

Mary Pickles

Aged 8 and a half.

Chapter Four

I'd been Mary's best friend and she'd been mine since we were both little girls. People used to laugh at us, the big fat kid in the glasses and the tiny little one who looked like butter wouldn't melt. I was usually described as 'no oil painting' and Mary was so pretty that complete strangers used to come up to her and tweak her cheeks and call her a 'little angel!'

The differences between us never bothered Mary and me. We never even thought about them. It was like that from the first day we met.

It was the start of the summer holidays and my dad had given me a handful of coins and sent me off to the rank of shops on the edge of the estate to buy a packet of Woodbines for him. He'd said I could get myself some sweets or a comic with the change. I was jingling the coins in my pocket and skipping a bit and thinking about what to buy with my windfall. I'd just got to the top of the twitten, which is the alleyway that runs between our road and the road that backs onto it, when I saw this girl hanging upside down on the railings. I couldn't actually see her face because it was covered by her skirt; all I could see were two skinny legs and a pair of navy blue knickers.

'What are you staring at?' she said. I looked around to see who she was talking to and realised that I was the only one there.

'Are you talking to me?'

'Well, I can only see one pair of shoes. Unless you've got a couple of kids on your back.'

'No, it's just me,' I said.

She suddenly swung down from the bars, and when she was the right way up, I found myself looking into the bluest pair of eyes I had ever seen. I'd lived on See Saw Lane all my life and I'd never seen her before. The girl rubbed the bridge of her nose with her finger and said: 'I'm Mary Pickles, what's your name?'

'Dorothy Perks,' I said. 'My mum named me after Dorothy in the Wizard of Oz, but everyone calls me Dottie.'

The girl stared at me and then said, 'Do you wanna be best friends?'

I'd never had a best friend in my whole life. I'd always been what you'd call a hanger-on. I sort of hung around on the edge, hoping someone would ask me to join in their game, and most of the time they didn't. I prayed every night for a best friend. Well, that and a rocking horse. I had kind of accepted that I would never get a rocking horse, but here was this pretty little girl saying we could be best friends.

'Yes, please,' I said.

'What school do you go to?'

'Whitehawk,' I said.

'That's where I'm going,' she said. 'I expect we'll be in the same class.'

'How old are you?' I asked.

'Eight and a half " she said, taking two gobstoppers out of her pocket and handing me one. 'I've only sucked that one a couple of times, it's still got a lot of sucking left in it.'

'Thanks,' I said, putting it in my mouth. I had a good suck and then said, 'I haven't seen you round here before.'

'That's cos we've only just moved here.'

'Oh.'

'What's it like?'

'What, round here?'

'No, school.'

I didn't know what to say to her. I mean, it was just school, and you had to go there every day whether you wanted to or not.

'Well?'

'It's okay, I suppose.'

'That bad eh?'

'I get teased.'

'Why?'

'Cos I'm fat.'

'Well they won't tease you any more, Dottie Perks,' she said, grinning.

'Won't they?'

'Not if I've got anything to do with it.'

We smiled at each other, and in that moment it was as if we both knew that something wonderful and special had just happened.

'I'd better get my dad's fags,' I said.

'Okay,' she said. 'See you in a minute.'

I ran over to the shop to get Dad's ciggies and choose my sweets. I had a whole threepence to spend and you could get a lot of sweets for threepence, so I was humming and hawing about what to buy. Black Jacks made your tongue all gooey and black, but gobstoppers lasted for ages. The people in the queue behind me started tutting, But Mr Orme said: 'The child is a paying customer the same as you ladies, and she has every right to choose her purchases carefully.'

I gave him a big grin and settled on a mixture of Black Jacks and gobstoppers.

'Could you put them in two bags please?' I said.

'Certainly, madam,' said Mr Orme, winking at me.

I stuffed Dad's fags in my pocket and walked back to the top of the alley, where Mary was still hanging off the railings.

'I bought you some sweets,' I said shyly. Mary swung back up and perched herself on the top bar.

'Thanks,' she said. She dived into the bag, pulled out a Black Jack, and unwrapped it. She concentrated hard on chewing for a bit, then said: 'Do you want to hang upside down next to me? There's plenty of room if I shift along a bit.'

I looked at the railings and tried to imagine what it would feel like. 'No, thanks,' I said.

'Why not?'

'My legs are too fat, I'd fall off.'

'You ought to try it.'

'Why?'

'Because it's like looking at the world from an upside down sort of place.'

'I'd just as soon look at it the right way up,' I said.

'You don't know what you're missing.'

I did a bit of hopscotch on the pavement to change the subject. 'I'd better go,' I said. 'My dad will be wanting his ciggies.'

'I'll call for you later if you like. What number do you live at?'

'Fifteen See Saw Lane.'

'I live at number forty six.'

'See you later,' I said and ran down the twitten. I had a little bubble of excitement in my tummy because suddenly the world seemed brighter and happier and more fun. I was halfway down the alley when I heard Mary calling my name.

'Dottie!'

I called back: 'Mary!' and we continued to call to each other until I was at the other end.

'Dottie!'

'Mary!'

'Dottie!'

'Mary!'

'Dottie!'

We called to each other for the rest of our lives.

Dear Diery,

When I grow up I am going to be a famus artist

I am reely good at drawrin.

I like my old skool better than my new one.

The only thing I like about my new one is sittin next to my best friend Dotty Perks.

The art teecher is bonkers

so is the gografy teecher.

Tatty bye diery

Love from

Mary Pickles

Aged 8 and a half ish.

Chapter Five

Mary Pickles didn't like school. Well, I didn't like it much either. In fact, I didn't know anyone who liked it, except perhaps Betty Baxter who was teacher's pet and ate sandwiches with the crusts cut off. Mary was really good at art but she didn't like the art teacher. Miss Philips brought in some tatty old jug from home, stuck a few weeds in it and told us to draw it, then leant back in her chair and read a magazine and ate sweets that she kept in her drawer. Every November we had to do a painting of bonfire night.

One rainy afternoon I was happily engrossed, using every colour in the paint pots, trying to create something that vaguely resembled a bonfire. I was concentrating really hard on getting just the right mix of colours to shoot up into the night sky.

By the time I had finished it, I thought it wasn't half bad; I might have overdone it on the red paint, but Mary had hogged the orange, so I didn't have much choice.

'What do you think?' I said, pushing my masterpiece across the desk.

'How many times have you drawn that exact same picture?' said Mary.

'What are you talking about?'

'That picture. How many times have you painted it?'

'I don't know.'

'Well, I do,' she said. 'You've painted it every bloody bonfire night for the last four years.'

'I suppose I have,' I said, giggling. 'What have you painted then?'

She pushed her paper across to me.

I stared at the painting and then at Mary. 'It's a plate of beans on toast,' I said.

'That's what I had for my tea on bonfire night.'

Well that explained the orange paint. 'She's going to murder you.'

'Shouldn't think she even looks at them. I bet that as soon as we leave the room she throws the whole lot in the bin.'

'Not Betty Baxter's, she sticks hers on the wall.'

'Betty Baxter can't paint for toffee.'

That really surprised me, because one whole wall in our classroom looked like a Betty Baxter private art collection.

I peered at Mary through my paint-spattered glasses, 'You're a very strange girl, do you know that?'

'Oh, I do hope so,' she said, smiling.

❋ ❋ ❋

And then there was geography, Mary's second favourite subject.

One day after a particularly boring lesson, me and Mary were sitting in our favourite spot, under the big tree on the school field. Mary was in a bad mood.

'I want to learn about countries,' she said. 'Not bloody rocks.'

'What are you on about?'

'I'm on about bloody rocks, it's all she ever goes on about. Big rocks, little rocks, black rocks, red rocks, blah, blah, blah. I'm going to travel round the world one day, Dottie, and I want to learn more about countries than what bloody rocks they've got.'

I had never really thought much about lessons. I just went into the classroom and did whatever I was told to do, then I forgot all about it. I'd never once thought, Oh, I wish she had taught us about this, or that. I had never met anyone like Mary before. She was still going on.

'I mean, if I wanted to be some kind of rockologist, then I'd have a head start wouldn't I? And when I wrote my first book about rocks, I'd give her a mention and say I couldn't have done it without her.'

Mary was twisting her hair round and round her fingers. 'You're gonna get your hair all tangled up doing that,' I said.

'But I don't want to be a rockologist do I?'

'What do you want to be then?'

'A travelling artist.'

'What's that?'

Mary gave me one of her withering looks. 'Think about it, Dottie.'

           ❋ ❋ ❋

One day Mary put her hand up and said, 'Miss? When did the Italian civil war start?'

'That's history, not geography, Mary,' said Miss Flowers. 'Get back to drawing your rocks.'

Mary leaned over and whispered in my ear, 'I bet if I asked her how many rocks were thrown during the fighting, she'd know down to the last piece of grit.'

           ❋ ❋ ❋

You see, Mary knew all about stuff like that, because she went down to the library every Saturday morning. I started going with her and I loved it there. It was only a small library, but it was really nice. It smelt kind of musty and it had a couple of old sofas in the children's bit that you could curl up in and read the books. I always read the Famous Five books. 'Five on a Treasure Island' and 'Five get into Trouble' and the Malory Towers books about girls at boarding school. I couldn't imagine sleeping at school instead of going home.

Mary said she'd outgrown the children's section and asked the lady behind the desk if she could borrow some of the grown-up books. The lady said certainly not and batted her away as if she was some sort of annoying little fly.

'People!' said Mary.

'Yes, people,' I said, giggling.

'Shush!' said the lady behind the desk.

✻ ✻ ✻

Mary was a really fast runner and she became sports captain for 'Campian House'. She also played centre in netball. I couldn't play any kind of sports because of my breathing, so I had to give out the balls and hoops and beanbags then clear up afterwards. That was what the bullying was all about. That and the fact that the medicine I had to take made me a bit on the plump side. All the bullying stopped once Mary became sports captain, because they knew that if they bullied me, Mary wouldn't pick them for the team.

From the moment we met, Mary and I were inseparable; either she was at my house, or I was at hers. There wasn't a lot of space at Mary's house because she had six brothers, but, unlike me, she had her own room. It was only small, but it was all hers. Mary said her brothers were jealous because they were all crammed into two bedrooms. She put a sign on her door that said, 'Private, GIRLS ONLY', which annoyed them even more.

Mary's mum stayed at home to look after the house and do all the cooking and her dad worked on the bins. I think they spoiled her a bit because she was the only girl, which suited Mary fine.

Her brothers were all older than her. There was Winston, Warren, Wesley, Wayne, and the twins William and Wallace. I got used to the hustle and bustle at Mary's house and was soon just one of the family.

One afternoon, when I was sitting on her bed and Mary was underneath it looking for the snakes and ladders, I said, 'Why do all your brothers' names begin with W?'

'Because my dad's a big West Ham supporter,' she said.

'Why doesn't he support Brighton and Hove Albion?'

'Because he was brought up in London and all his family are West Ham supporters. I'm sure that game's under here.'

'How come your name doesn't begin with a W then?' I asked.

'Got it,' she said, crawling out from under the bed. 'What did you say?'

'I said why doesn't your name begin with a W?'

'Because Dad had always promised Mum that if they ever had a girl then Mum should name her, which was fair enough, as she had to have six boys before she finally got me.' She took the board out of the box and opened it out on the bed. She passed me the red counter and took the yellow one, her favourite colour.

'Mary's a pretty name though,' I said, 'better than Dorothy, anyway.'

'I'm named after the virgin.'

'What virgin?'

'The Virgin Mary.' She shook the dice and then threw a six. 'I start,' she shouted.

'Why?' I said.

'Because I threw six.'

'No, I mean why did she call you after the Virgin Mary? You're not Catholics, are you?'

'No, it's just that every time Mum got pregnant, she prayed to a saint to have a girl. She'd done all the Church of England ones, so she thought she'd go straight to the top and have a word with the Virgin, because as she said, the Virgin Mary was a mother herself who had never managed to have a girl, so she might be more understanding than saints like Saint Andrew and Saint George, and it paid off, so she called me Mary as a sort of thank you.'

I smiled at her. 'I think that's a really nice story.'

I threw five and landed on a ladder and nearly got to the top of the board.

❆ ❆ ❆

When me and Mary weren't at her house or mine, we would be on Brighton beach. That first summer that we met seemed to go on forever, the sky was always blue and the sun shone for the whole six weeks. We spent every day down on the pebbly beach, skimming stones on the water and paddling in the icy sea. Mary always had a sketch pad with her. She loved to draw the sea, especially when the sky was full of dark clouds and the sea was wild and choppy and racing over the pebbles, thundering into the sea wall and splashing white foam and spray onto the prom. We went to the arcade on the Palace Pier and searched under the slot machines for pennies, then fed them into the sweet machines and filled our pockets with gobstoppers which lasted for hours. When the tide was out, we dug for worms and took them back to the estate to give to Mr Parish, who collected them for his fishing. We bought fish and chips with the money he gave us and sat on the wooden groyne eating them out of the paper with our fingers, washing the grease off in the rock pools. We would go home at the end of the day, two eight-year-olds, hot and tired, Mary as brown as a berry and me covered in freckles.

One day, Mary climbed up onto the groyne and started walking along it.

'Don't,' I shouted, 'you might fall off.'

She looked down at me grinning, 'I might,' she said.

'Why are you doing it then?'

'Because I might not, I don't always.' She held her hand out towards me. 'Come on, give it a try.'

'It's all slippery,' I said, 'I'll fall.'

'Okay you might fall,' she said, 'but think how great you'll feel if you don't.'

'I know I'll fall.'

'No, you don't, that's the exciting bit. What's the point in doing something if you always know how it's going to turn out?'

I stood looking up at her, her hair was blowing across her face and she was grinning. She looked so brave and strong that it made me want to be brave too. It made me want to be just like my friend Mary Pickles.

I was still feeling a bit unsure, but I sat down on the pebbles and took off my sandals. I lined them up neatly, side by side. Mary held out her hand towards me and helped me up onto the groyne. The wood was thick and old. It had been there for centuries, with the tide coming in and out over it. It felt very solid beneath my feet. Very slowly, I stood up, wobbled a bit and then managed to balance. I reached out towards Mary, and she took hold of my hand. She gave me a little smile and squeezed my fingers.

'Come on then,' she said. Slowly, we started to walk along the wooden structure. I was watching my bare feet, treading very carefully. Once or twice I thought I was going to fall, but I didn't. We balanced all the way down to the water's edge, then jumped down onto the pebbles.

'You did it,' she said, swinging me round. 'She did it!' Mary shouted into the wind.

'I did, didn't I?' I said, grinning.

'Wanna do it again?' she said.

'Not on your Nellie,' I replied, walking up the beach laughing.

Mary caught up with me and pulled me down onto the stones, where we lay side by side, staring up at the endless blue sky and listening to the water rattling over the pebbles, then the soft whoosh as the tide dragged them back into the sea.

Mary and I were inseparable. We were like two people living the same life. Whenever I was worried or sad, I would think of something that we had done together and it would always make me smile.

I remembered one particular Saturday morning, the morning Dad burnt down the garden shed. Me and Mary Pickles were about nine at the time.

My sister Rita, who was a pain-in-the-neck teenager, had spent the morning crying because she'd read in *lush* magazine that you had to be 5'10" to be a model and she'd be lucky if she reached 5'4"!

She'd locked herself in the bedroom and no one could get her to come out, which wouldn't have bothered me in the least if it wasn't for the fact that half the bedroom's mine. I was still in my pyjamas and Mary and me were going to Saturday morning pictures that started at eleven o'clock. Last week's episode of *Flash Gordon* ended where Ming the Merciless, the ruler of the planet Mongo, was lowering Flash Gordon down into a vat of boiling oil and we'd been waiting all week to see if he was going to be saved by the forces of good. As it happened, he was saved every week, but as Mary said, this could be the one week when he wasn't, so we had to get there on time. Plus the dreaded Mr Barclay in the ticket office wouldn't let you in if you were late. He said it interfered with the viewing of the kids that had turned up on time. Not that he cared, if you ask me, he hated kids. Anyway, there I was in my pyjamas on the wrong side of the door when I needed to get dressed. Mum was kneeling on the landing trying to persuade Rita to come out.

'You may not be 5'10',' Mum coaxed through the keyhole, 'but you're perfectly formed!'

This got no response, so Mum tried again. 'You nearly won the "most beautiful baby in Brighton" contest,' she said. 'That Baxter baby had sticky-out ears – he only won because it was rumoured that the judge might have been the Baxter baby's father, on account of the fact that his ears stuck out as well and he used to give Mrs Baxter marrows off his allotment.'

Still no response. Then Dad came upstairs.

'What's going on?' he asked. Mum told him and he shouted through the keyhole that modelling was a daft job, and why couldn't she do something useful, like nursing? That certainly got a response from Rita, and she started throwing things around the room. I decided to keep well out of it.

Dad said he was going out to his shed and he went downstairs, mumbling about hysterical women.

It had gone all quiet inside the bedroom, so Mum laid flat on the floor and peered under the door. 'I can't see her,' she said to me. 'Do you think she's all right?'

'She sounded all right just now,' I said.

All the noise had woken Clark up and he came out of his bedroom, stepped over Mum, and went downstairs.

'Clark, go and tell your Aunty Brenda to come over,' said Mum. 'She'll know what to do. Dottie, you stay here and listen.'

There was nothing to listen to, so I went into Clark's room. His Dennis the Menace clock said it was 9.15. Mary was going to kill me if I was late.

Mum came back upstairs: 'Don't worry,' she said. 'Your Aunty Brenda will be here soon.'

'I hope so,' I said. 'Mary will be round soon, and I need to get dressed.'

'Where are you going?' said Mum.

'Saturday morning pictures.'

'That's nice.'

Clark returned all red-faced and out of breath and suggested we kicked the door down. Actually, I thought that was a pretty good idea, but Mum said if Clark went anywhere near the door, he wouldn't be able to sit down for a month.

Just then Aunty Brenda came running up the stairs.

'Thank goodness you're here, Brenda!' said Mum. 'Perhaps you can talk some sense into her.'

'I'll do my best,' said Aunty Brenda, and she put her ear to the door.

'Dottie, get your Aunty Brenda a cup of tea.'

I went downstairs, put the kettle on and sat down at the kitchen table. Clark was shovelling cornflakes into his mouth as if he hadn't eaten for a year.

I made the tea and went back upstairs. Aunty Brenda was half-way through the tale of the Baxter baby's sticky-out ears and the judge's marrows when Rita started screaming that her career was in ruins and why couldn't Mum have married someone taller. Mum said that Dad *was* taller when she'd married him, but he'd shrunk.

Rita said she was going to stay in there forever, and fade away, and that we'd all be sorry. Well, I reckoned I was the only one that would be sorry, because dead bodies smell after a bit, and I had to sleep in there.

Mum and Aunty Brenda were just about to resort to kicking down the door themselves when Dad set fire to the garden shed.

At the start of every New Year, my dad gives up smoking. At that point, he was two days into his hundredth attempt, and he'd gone down the shed for what my mum calls 'a sneaky one', but he'd fallen asleep, and the cigarette had dropped onto a pile of newspapers that I'd been saving in the hope that one day Mum would let me have a hamster like Mary's.

Anyway, Dad came rushing into the house screaming 'Maureen! Call the fire brigade! The shed's on fire!'

Aunty Brenda started screaming 'Women and children first', which was most of us, and Clark started turning his bedroom upside down looking for his camera. He takes action pictures whenever he can.

Mum ran next door to phone for the fire brigade, as next door was the only house in the street that had a phone, and Aunty Brenda shouted to Rita that the shed was on fire. Rita said: 'Nice try.' So Aunty Brenda hurled herself against the door, just as Rita decided to come out. They both went flying back into the room, and Rita nearly knocked herself out on the corner of the dressing table. Clark took a picture.

'Quick, Dottie! Get your mum!' screamed Aunty Brenda.

I ran downstairs. Mum and Dad were running between the kitchen sink and the shed with bowls of water.

'Aunty Brenda's nearly knocked Rita out,' I said, running beside them.

'She's done what?' said Mum.

'She pushed open the door just as Rita was coming out and Rita hit her head on the chest of drawers.'

My dad looked ever so odd, his face was all black from the smoke, which made his eyes look really white. He looked a bit like a panda.

Mum dropped the bowl she was carrying and ran back indoors.

The shed looked great, just like bonfire night, only better. Clark was getting some terrific pictures. He had climbed the apple tree to get an aerial view.

I went back upstairs. Rita was sitting propped up against the dressing table, looking a bit white, and Mum was dabbing her face with a wet cloth.

'For goodness sake, Dottie,' said Mum, looking up. 'Isn't it time you were out of those pyjamas?' The question was so unfair I couldn't think of an answer.

'Maureen!' shouted Dad from downstairs. 'Are you sure you phoned the fire brigade? The apple tree's alight now!'

'What a shame,' said Aunty Brenda. 'You've had some lovely apples off that tree.'

'Clark's in the apple tree,' I said, rummaging in the drawer for a clean pair of knickers.

'They were Worcester's,' said Mum. 'Clark's WHERE?' she screamed.

'In the apple tree,' I said. 'Taking pictures.'

'MY BABY!' shrieked Mum, dropping Rita's head on the floor.

She ran down the stairs and nearly bumped into Clark who was running up them.

'You're supposed to be in the apple tree!' yelled Mum, shaking him.

'But it's on fire!' said Clark, looking at Mum as if she'd gone mad.

Mum flopped down on the stairs and burst out crying. Aunty Brenda put her arm around her. 'What we need is a nice cup of tea,' she said, taking Mum into the kitchen. 'Dottie, be nice to your sister.'

I didn't feel a bit like being nice to my sister. The last thing in the world I felt like was being was nice to my sister. All I wanted to do was get dressed. Was that such a lot to ask?

I went into the bedroom. Everywhere was a mess. Rita was sitting on the bed looking pretty miserable. I thought I'd better try and be nice.

'Perhaps you could go to a country where they don't mind short models,' I said.

'What country?'

'I don't know, Japan or somewhere like that.'

'You don't know what you're talking about, you stupid child!'

So much for being 'nice to your sister'. I wish I hadn't bothered.

'Have you got my new scarf?' I asked.

'What would I want with your grotty scarf?' she said, gazing at herself in the mirror. She swept her hair up at the back and turned sideways: 'Do you think I look like Audrey Hepburn?'

'No, you look like Rita Perks.'

'But with my hair pushed up at the back like this, don't you think I look a bit like Audrey Hepburn?'

'No, I don't,' I said, groping under the bed for my lost scarf.

'You don't know anything,' she said. 'I don't know why I bothered asking you.' And she flounced off to the bathroom.

There was just no pleasing Rita that morning. I found my scarf under the bed and also a sherbet fountain that I'd thought Clark had pinched. Just then Mary came into the bedroom.

'The fire brigade's here,' she said. 'It only took them two squirts to put the shed out. Are you ready?'

'Just about.'

The shed looked a mess, so did the apple tree, but Mum looked a lot happier. She and Aunty Brenda were handing out cups of tea to the firemen. Dad looked a bit fed up, but then I suppose he would; if he hadn't been having a 'sneaky' one, he wouldn't have burnt the shed down.

'Perhaps now he really *will* give up smoking,' said Mary.

'I hope so,' I said, but I had my doubts.

We said goodbye to Mum and Aunty Brenda, leaving Clark interviewing the firemen and Rita moping on her bed.

Mary and I got a shilling a week pocket money, sixpence for the pictures and sixpence for sweets. We always went to the same sweet shop before going into the pictures. The woman who owned the shop was a bit strange; she always had her coat on, even in the summer when it was really hot, and she sniffed a lot. Me and Mary loved it in there. It was always packed with kids who took ages to choose their sweets. The woman behind the counter used to huff and puff and suck her cheeks in like she'd just bitten into a lemon. 'There's other people waiting, you know,' she'd grumble. 'You're not the only one in the shop.' Then she'd bully and nudge them towards making a decision like a collie dog with a load of sheep. But she was wasting her breath, because when you only had a few pennies to spend on sweets, you weren't going to be hurried. On the shelves behind her were rows and rows of jars full of pear drops, rhubarb and custards, sherbet lemons, bull's eyes, Pontefract cakes and humbugs, and on the counter were boxes of penny sweets. Black Jacks, Davy Crockett bars, flying saucers, liquorice laces and penny chews. Once we had chosen what we wanted, we went into the Regent Cinema and screamed and yelled at Ming the Merciless. We sat there glued to the screen, sticking our fingers into bags of lemonade powder so that when we came out it looked as if we were on forty fags a day.

When I got home, Mum was sitting at the kitchen table drinking a cup of tea.

'Him and his ciggies,' she said, shaking her head.

'Where's Rita?'

'She's having a little lie down in the front room,' she said quietly.

'Is she okay now?'

'She's fine,' said Mum. 'She's decided to be an actress instead.'

'Shouldn't be too difficult,' I said, smiling.

Dear Diary,

I have fallen in love with a boy called Elton Briggs

He is the most handsome boy in the school.

When I grow up I am going to marry him.

I have just got to make him fall in love with me.

I am going to ask my brother Wesley for some advice because mum says he's got a way with the girls.

Also me and Dottie saw him snogging Susan Alcorn in the park.

I passed the eleven-plus. I knew I would, because I'm dead clever. I know how long it takes five men to fill a bath if it takes two men twenty minutes. Not that I care how bloody long it took them.

Dottie is worried that we won't be best friends any more. Fat chance!!!

Tatty bye

Mary Pickles (genius)

Aged 11.

Chapter Six

'Nothing is going to change,' said Mary.

'Yes it will,' I said. 'We won't go to school on the same bus and I will have to sit next to someone I don't know and I won't have a best friend anymore.'

'We'll always be best friends, you dope.'

I could feel my eyes filling with tears and I didn't want to cry, because I was really proud that Mary had passed the exam and I didn't want her to feel guilty about going to the grammar school. 'Everything will change,' I whispered.

'No it won't,' said Mary. 'I'm not going.'

'What?'

'I'm not going.'

'But you have to go, you passed the exam.'

'It's not law, you know. There isn't some law that says, all ye who pass the eleven-plus must, on pain of death or worse, go to the bloody grammar school.'

I started to giggle: 'You're really not going?'

'I'm really not going.'

'But why?'

'Because I don't want to. It's not part of my life's plan to spend the next hundred years going to school and being told what to do and when to do it. Going to grammar school won't make the slightest bit of difference to me being an artist. In fact it might make it harder because there'll be more homework.'

This was a lot of information for me to take in all at once.

'You've got a life's plan?' I asked.

'Everyone should have one, otherwise you will end up making loads of mistakes.'

'Does that mean I need one?'

'No, you're part of mine. I'll make sure you're okay.'

'Don't your mum and dad mind you not going to the grammar school?'

'Not really. They know that I'm going to be an artist, and once I make my mind up about something, I don't usually change it.'

Mary never failed to amaze me. I could just imagine me saying to my mum, 'Oh, by the way, I passed the eleven-plus, but I've decided not to go to the grammar school, is that okay with you, Mum?'

'I think Mum was a *bit* miffed,' said Mary, 'because she would have liked to have shown off to Lady Muck who lives down the road.'

'Lady Muck?'

'Yeah, you know, the one with the mock-Tudor front door.'

'And the baldy husband?'

'That's the one. Well, according to her, her daughter Penelope is the most miraculous thing since the virgin birth, and she's always going on about how clever she is and how pretty she is, blah, blah, blah. Anyway she failed the exam, so my mum would have liked to have bragged about me.'

'Well she can still brag about you can't she, because you passed?'

'Lady Muck wouldn't believe it if I wasn't prancing round in the poncy uniform.'

'You do make me laugh, Mary Pickles.'

'I'm so glad, Dottie Perks.'

❄ ❄ ❄

I remember the day Mary told me that she had fallen in love for the first time. It was on my eleventh birthday. My Aunty Brenda had bought me a *Bunty* annual. I had the *Bunty* comic delivered to my house every Tuesday and as soon as I heard it fall through the letter box, I ran downstairs before anyone else could pick it up. 'As if,' said my sister Rita, 'anyone else would want it.'

I showed it to Mary when I got to the bus stop and she burst out laughing.

'What?' I said, staring at her.

'I can't believe you're still reading that stuff.'

'What do you mean?'

'It's kids' stuff, Dottie,' she said, screwing up her nose as if she had a bad smell under it.

'But I like it.'

'Well it's time you *stopped* liking it.'

'Why?'

'I've grown up, Dottie.'

'What, in two weeks?'

'What are you talking about?'

'I'm talking about two weeks ago when you borrowed my *Bunty* comic.'

She decided to ignore that and went on talking.

'So what's in it that you like so much?'

'I like "The Four Marys" and…'

'"The Four Marys"?' she screamed.

'And "The Dancing Life of Moira Kent".'

'"The Dancing Life of Moira Kent"!'

I was pretty confused now. 'Why are you repeating everything I'm saying?'

'Because I can't believe you're saying it.'

'Well, if you don't think I should be reading *Bunty*, what *should* I be reading?'

'Romance,' said Mary, smiling.

'Romance!' I said. 'Why would I want to read about romance?' My sister Rita was fifteen and there was enough romance floating around our house without me joining in.

'Because I've fallen in love.'

'Let me get this straight,' I said. '*You've* fallen in love and *I've* got to stop reading *Bunty*?'

'It's time you grew up. *I've* grown up, and so should you.'

'But *I* haven't fallen in love, Mary, and I don't *want* to, well not till I've read my new *Bunty* annual anyway.'

'Okay,' said Mary 'You can finish the book.'

'Thanks,' I said, grinning.

Just then the bus came round the corner, Mary and I ran up the stairs and plonked ourselves down at the front.

'Who have you fallen in love with then?' I asked, stuffing the offending book into my satchel before Mary suggested that I throw it out of the window.

'Elton Briggs,' she said. 'Who else would I be in love with?'

'Elton's not the only boy in the class, is he?' I said.

'But he's the best looking,' she said, 'and the most popular.'

Up until that point, I had never known Mary to care much about looks or popularity, it was one of the things I really liked about her, but now she had fallen in love with Elton Briggs, who although popular, wasn't always a very nice boy.

I suppose Elton *was* quite good-looking and the other boys seemed to look up to him. He was taller than most of them and he was good at things like running and football. They used to hang around him, just like the girls hung round Mary.

I had always felt a bit sorry for Elton, because his dad died when he was only nine years old. He had been called out of the classroom and then he was off school for a while. There were a lot of rumours going round. People kept asking Ralph, but when they did, Ralph sloped off with his hands in his pockets and wouldn't say anything. After a couple of days our teacher told us what had happened and asked us to be kind to Elton when he came back but not to crowd him with questions. Louise Morgan, who always seemed to have something wrong with her, went hysterical and had to be taken to the sick room.

When Elton did come back, we all tried to be extra especially kind to him, except Dominic Roberts who didn't know the meaning of the word. But Elton acted as though nothing had happened. I for one wasn't convinced, and neither was Mary, because sometimes he just stared out of the window when he should have been writing or paying attention, and Mrs Roberts our teacher never told him off. Maybe it was that vulnerable side that Mary saw, too, and not the big act that he always put on.

'I really, really love him, Dottie,' said Mary that day on the bus. 'One day I am going to marry him and we are going to travel round the world and have a fabulous life together.'

I didn't really know much about love, but it kind of made sense to me that you would probably fall in love with someone because they were nice to you and shared their sweets with you and things like that, but Elton wasn't that nice to Mary. He wasn't that nice to me either, but I wasn't the one who'd fallen in love with him so it didn't matter.

After Mary fell in love with Elton everything changed. We stopped playing exciting games and all we did was follow Elton and Ralph around the playground. Sometimes Elton paid attention to Mary and they would walk around holding hands or he'd chase her round the field; at those times Ralph Bennett and I were sort of thrown together, which was pretty embarrassing to begin with, but over time we got more comfortable with each other and we would sit on the school field talking. I learned that he'd known Elton all his life. They were born in the same hospital only days apart and the two mums had kept in touch, so they had sort of grown up together. Neither of them had brothers or sisters. Ralph was a tall, awkward-looking boy and whatever time of day it was, he looked as if he'd just fallen out of bed.

'Do you think Elton really likes Mary?' I asked him one day when we were sitting on the field.

'I dunno,' he said.

'But does he talk about Mary?'

'All Elton talks about is football and music. Perhaps if Mary had a number on her back he might take more notice of her.'

'You can be quite funny sometimes, Ralph Bennett.'

Ralph went bright red.

'It's not true love, then?' I said.

Ralph laughed. 'They're a bit young for that, don't you think?'

I thought so too, but Mary was smitten.

Sometimes Elton would completely ignore Mary and walk around the field holding Valerie Colahan's hand, or lean against the climbing frame, laughing out loud at something Beverly Johnson said, and you just knew it was all an act, because Beverly Johnson couldn't be funny if her life depended on it, added to the fact that she had the sense of humour of a gnat, and all this was done in sight of Mary.

At those times, Mary would sit with me and Ralph, looking sad and upset, and to make it worse, Ralph would then stop talking and I wouldn't know how to make things better for either of them. One day when the three of us were sitting together in silence, Mary suddenly said: 'You know what you ought to ask your mother to get you for Christmas, Ralph Bennett?'

'What?' said Ralph, looking startled.

'A tongue,' said Mary.

I thought that was a mean thing to say and I knew Mary wasn't a mean person. She was just feeling bad. Suddenly a football hit Ralph on the back of his head, a crowd of kids started laughing and one of them shouted, 'Ahh, did I hurt your little ginger bonce?'

Suddenly, Elton came racing across the field. He ran up to the boy and pushed him to the ground. 'What did you say to him?' he snarled.

The boy looked terrified. 'Nothing, Elton,' he said.

The other boys had backed away.

'I asked you what you said.' He was glaring down at the frightened boy.

'I just asked him if he was okay.'

Elton looked at us. 'What did he say?'

'Something about his ginger bonce,' said Mary.

'Leave it,' said Ralph, 'I'm okay.'

Elton pulled the boy up off the ground. 'Don't you ever say anything like that to my friend again, do you hear me?'

'I won't, Elton,' said the boy.

'Now beat it.'

The boy didn't move.

'What?' said Elton.

'Can I have my ball back?'

'What do *you* think?' said Elton, smirking.

'But I only just got it for my birthday, my dad'll kill me.' The boy looked as if he was about to cry.

Elton kicked the ball hard across the field.

'Thanks, Elton,' said the boy, looking relieved, and ran off after the ball.

'Are you all right, mate?' said Elton, sitting down next to Ralph.

Ralph was rubbing his head. 'I'll live,' he said.

'I've had more fights over your flippin' hair than I've had hot dinners,' said Elton and we all fell about laughing.

That same year someone put a Valentine's card in my desk. It had a big heart on the front surrounded by little cupids holding garlands of flowers and inside was a little poem and whoever had sent it had written: 'From your secret sweetheart'. All the girls had been really impressed when I found it. At first, I thought it was someone playing a mean trick on me, and Mary, who hadn't received a card at all that year, said it was probably someone's idea of a bad joke. I wasn't the sort of girl who got Valentine's cards, so I pretended I didn't care about the card at all. I stuffed it in my satchel and never had it on display. I still had it in my special memory box under my bed though. I had always hoped that it had come from Ralph.

Perhaps that was the day that I first fell in love, a little.

Chapter Seven

Brighton
1964

It was the day after Mary and I met Ralph and Elton in the record shop. I woke with a fizzy feeling in my stomach. It took me a moment to remember what it was and when I did, I rolled over and hugged my pillow with joy. Ralph Bennett had asked me out. He had asked *me! Dottie Perks!* Out on a *date*! It was going to be the start of something wonderful, I knew it was. I had never felt so happy, so excited; life had never seemed so full of possibilities and potential.

Ralph and I had been friends all through school. At the beginning we had been thrown together because he was Elton's best friend and I was Mary's. Soon, though, we became friends in our own right, because we wanted to be. Ralph was not a noisy, show-off boy, but one of the quieter ones, and everyone liked him, even the teachers. He always sat at the back of the class and he never said very much, but he was always smiling, always friendly. I'd seen him once or twice since we left school, but either I'd been with my mum or he'd been with someone else and so we'd never said more than 'hello' to one another. He and Elton lived in a different part of town and our paths didn't cross much.

Mary and I had been out with a few boys since leaving school. Well, Mary had been out with a few boys, I'd been stuck with their friends. Memories of spotty faces, cheese-and-onion breath and clammy hands still made me shudder. I wasn't that interested in boys. The only boy I had ever felt comfortable with was Ralph and now he was in my life again and suddenly everything seemed rather wonderful, actually.

As I was enjoying this strange and delicious feeling of anticipation, something cold and wet slapped me on the face.

'Ow!'

I sat up and removed the object. It was a flannel. My older sister Rita was standing on her side of the bedroom wrapped in a towel and smiling at me.

'What are you looking so pleased about?' she asked. 'You look like the cat that's had the cream!'

'Nothing,' I said. I threw the flannel back at her and turned over.

'Yes it is something!' Rita persisted, pulling at my covers. 'You were sighing in your sleep. You were smooching up to your pillow! It's a boy, isn't it? You've met someone, haven't you? You fancy someone! What's wrong with him? Is he desperate? Is he blind?'

'Oh go away!' I said. 'Go away forever, Rita.'

'Don't worry, I'll be out of here soon,' Rita trilled. 'Just as soon as I'm married! And while we're on the subject, don't forget Aunty Brenda's coming over later to decide on the bridesmaids' dresses.'

I had forgotten. I groaned and burrowed back down the bed.

That summer, Rita's wedding was all anyone seemed to talk about at our house. It was kind of exciting and I wasn't exactly jealous, but it was hard being Rita's younger, less attractive sister. And also it was hard because sometimes, just once in a while, it would have been nice if Rita and I could have gone shopping together or gone to the cinema, or even just walked down to the seafront for an ice cream, things we used to do together, just the two of us. I never talked to Rita like I talked to Mary, but she had always been there for me. Now it felt like I didn't have a sister any more.

Rita and I were good friends when we were younger, but since she had 'blossomed', things had started to go a bit wrong. One day she was just 'Rita' and the next she was 'Rita the beauty'. People were always saying she could have been a film star and

Rita loved that. I couldn't see it myself. She still looked exactly the same to me. We'd shared a bedroom ever since I was two, and I knew she looked pretty rotten first thing in the morning. She didn't look too great last thing at night either. She was named after Rita Hayworth and these days she acted like she expected everyone to treat her like a film star too.

I suppose Rita couldn't help being beautiful, but she always made me look worse by comparison. The most annoying aspect of this was that whatever she ate she still looked like a stick insect, whereas I only had to pass a doughnut and great blobs of fat would hurl themselves at my thighs. When I was eleven, I overheard Aunty Brenda telling Mum that she was feeding me too much starch and that I was getting very round-looking and my mum saying: 'Rubbish, it's just puppy fat, in a couple of years it will all drop off.' I told Mary and she thought that was really funny and wondered whether it would suddenly fall off me in the middle of a maths lesson, or during assembly, or whether I'd just gradually lose bits of it all over the place. Mary was great like that. She always saw the funny side of things and then you ended up seeing it as well. In the end we were both rolling around in fits of laughter, thinking of all the funny places where the fat could drop off.

Now Rita was engaged to be married to a chap called Nigel who worked in insurance. Mum was delighted because she said that with him having a proper job like that, Rita would be set up for life. Nigel had long arms. His shirtsleeves didn't quite reach to the end of them and his wrists were very bony. He tried to sell life insurance to Dad, who said if he wasn't around to get the benefit of the money then he wasn't interested. Nigel said it would give him peace of mind knowing that his loved ones could give him a proper send-off when he departed this world. Dad said he'd be quite happy in a cardboard box which shouldn't cost very much, and anyway he thought insurance was a big con and the only people who made any money out of it were the likes of Nigel. I tended to agree with him, but I did feel a tiny bit sorry for Nigel, who went all crestfallen and started scratching the back of his ear. Mum squeezed Nigel's arm and told Dad not to show his ignorance and to apologise. Dad said he had a right to say what he liked in his own home. Mum said if he felt like that she wouldn't bother with a cardboard box when he popped his clogs, she'd put him out with the rubbish. Dad just snorted and Nigel's ears went very red and you could tell he didn't know what to do with his face.

Poor Nigel. He was probably already fed up of our family and he wasn't even part of it yet. I knew how he felt. I'd been fed up of our family for years, but since Rita and Mum started planning 'The Wedding', things had become a lot worse. It was all they ever talked about, and everything reminded them of it. It was like 'The Wedding' was the most important event in the world, ever. Rita said it was. She said a wedding was the pinnacle of a girl's life. She said it was all she'd ever dreamed of since she was a little child and she was not going to let anything spoil her perfect day. It had to be absolutely, completely perfect.

I could have pointed out that she was marrying an insurance salesman and not the heir to the throne, but I didn't, because it was kind of sweet how happy she was.

The worst of it was, back then, the wedding was still *months* away. It was to be a winter wedding and we were still in the summer. It didn't stop it completely taking over our lives though. Time and time again when I wanted to be out doing something more interesting with Mary on a beautiful evening, I ended up crammed in our front room having to listen to plans for 'The Wedding'. I found the whole subject so boring. I decided that when I married, I'd do it in secret. Me and my beloved would elope. We'd get the bus to Gretna Green and after the wedding we'd have a proper wedding breakfast, bacon and egg and beans.

It would be very romantic and it would be just the two of us, me and… whoever, because that's what I knew it was supposed to be about – two people, in love.

Rita's wedding was taking place on the 23rd of November. She'd wanted a Christmas wedding but the vicar was already booked for December. He said it was usually his busiest month for dispatches, as well as the Christmas rush of people coming over all religious because they liked the carols and the candles. Rita said winter weddings were more sophisticated than summer ones. She had chosen a gown from the catalogue. It was long and white, with a hood and a fake-fur trim and it was called a 'Monroe'. The bridesmaids were me and my younger cousin Carol. Carol was my Aunty Brenda's daughter. Aunty Brenda was married to my uncle Ernie who seemed to cause her a load of grief. I once heard my mum tell my dad that Uncle Ernie was no better than he should be, whatever that meant. Every so often Mum and Aunty Brenda would open the Christmas gin and sit in the kitchen having what they called a 'good old heart-to-heart'. The day after the heart-to-heart, Mum always had a headache. I used to think it was because she and Aunty Brenda got so emotional.

Dad was a self-employed painter and decorator and sometimes months would go by when he was out of work. Mum was a dinner lady at the primary school, which didn't bring in much. Rita worked at the town hall and I was at Woollies so our wages helped, but even so, money was always a bit tight. My younger brother Clark was still at school, so he didn't bring in anything. This meant there wasn't much to spend on the bridesmaids' dresses, especially when Mum realised how much else there was that needed buying and organising to make sure Rita had the wedding she'd always wanted. As a result, Aunty Brenda was going to make the dresses for me and Carol. She was coming over to talk about what colour Rita wanted. I was going to be the one wearing the dress, but I wasn't allowed an opinion. What happened was that

Mum and Aunty Brenda spent hours in the front room holding bits of material up to my face with Rita commentating and Mary sitting behind her sketch pad drawing the scene and secretly pulling faces at me.

'What do you reckon, Bren?' asked Mum, holding something across my mouth and nose like a veil.

'You can't put her in lemon, Maureen,' said Aunty Brenda, shaking her head. 'It'll make her look pasty.'

Behind the sketch pad Mary sucked in her cheeks.

'Of course, I'm lucky with my Carol,' Aunty Brenda continued. 'She can wear anything, she has wonderful skin.'

Mary pretended to stick two fingers down her throat. I tried not to laugh.

'What do you think of this?' Mum asked Aunty Brenda, holding up a swatch of lime-green, floaty fabric. This time Rita pulled a face.

'I always think it's wise to steer clear of citrus at a wedding,' said Aunty Brenda.

Mary nodded wisely. 'Me too,' she said solemnly. Aunty Brenda smiled at her.

After what felt like hours of this, Rita settled it all by saying she wanted both bridesmaids in baby pink, which was about the only colour we hadn't tried yet.

Dad said I'd look like a giant candyfloss and started laughing, fit to bust. Rita wiped the smile off his face by telling him that he would be wearing top hat and tails, as befitted the father-of-a-bride whose groom-to-be was in insurance. Dad said he'd rather be dead than step outside his house in top hat and tails and Mum said just give her the word and she'd be delighted to arrange it.

Rita sat on the settee looking me up and down like I was a prize vegetable or something. She swung her top leg and her slipper dangled off her foot. Mary, in the opposite chair, was quietly copying her every move. I was having to hold onto my stomach to stop myself laughing.

'Stop slouching, Dottie,' Rita said.

'I'm not slouching.'

'Yes, you are. She is, isn't she, Mum, she's slouching.'

I made a sort of snorty noise as I straightened up and the laughter came out of me. This made Mary start laughing too. She clapped one hand over her mouth. I couldn't look at her.

'She'll have to lose some weight before the wedding,' said Rita. 'She'll ruin the photos otherwise.'

She was referring to me, obviously.

'Dottie's not fat,' Mary said, through her laughter. 'She's perfect!'

'Well, you would say that, wouldn't you?' said Rita. 'That's like her telling you, you're not small.'

'You're not small,' I said at once and we both went all hysterical again

'I think Dottie *has* lost weight,' Mum said thoughtfully. She squeezed the top of my arm. 'She's more podgy now than fat.'

Just then Clark came banging through the back door and into the front room.

'Have you heard the news?' he said.

'What news would that be, then?' said Rita all sarcastically.

'There's been a big robbery,' said Clark. His face was all red and sweaty with excitement. Clark was going to be a journalist when he grew up so he listened to the news a lot.

'What, round here?' said Mary.

'No,' said Clark, 'somewhere near Buckinghamshire. Someone's robbed the Royal Mail train and got away with nearly three million pounds, they think it's a gang from London.'

'Well, it would be, wouldn't it,' said Aunty Brenda 'that's where they all live.'

'My dad used to live in London,' said Mary.

'What's that got to do with anything?' asked Rita.

'Nothing, I was just saying.'

I looked across at Mary and she had crossed her eyes. I had to look away before I burst out laughing again.

'They hit the train driver over the head and he's in the hospital,' said Clark.

'Now I draw the line at that,' said Mum, 'I mean taking money is one thing, not that I approve of it, mind, but attacking a poor innocent man who was just doing his job is just plain wrong.'

Rita cleared her throat loudly. 'Excuse me, that's all very interesting, but aren't we supposed to be planning my wedding?'

'But that poor man, Rita, his family must be worried sick,' said Mum.

'Exactly, *his* family, not *ours,* now can we please get back to what is important to *our* family.'

'*You*, you mean,' said Clark.

'And why not?' said Rita. 'This is going to be my special day.'

'And don't we all know it,' I said.

'And you can shut up,' said Rita, glaring at me.

'Now now,' said Aunty Brenda. 'Let's get back to the dresses, shall we? Where were we up to?'

'Mum was just telling Dottie that she was podgy,' said Rita.

'I don't think she said it quite like that, Rita,' said Aunty Brenda.

'All I meant,' said Mum, 'is that Dottie isn't as round as she used to be. I'm sure that when she's older she'll have a beautiful figure.'

'Fat chance,' said Dad. He wasn't trying to be ironic. He doesn't know how.

'And you can shut up an' all, Nelson Perks,' said Mum. 'We all know where Dottie gets her weight from. We'll be lucky to find tails off the peg for you, with your fat belly and short legs.'

'What short legs?'

'Yours!' said Mum. 'They'll have to get a suit made specially to fit you.'

'I haven't got short legs!' said Dad. 'I've got a long body. Bloody cheek, I've got a good mind to boycott this wedding and stay at home.'

He folded his paper and picked it up and walked out of the room, slamming the door behind him.

'Don't raise our hopes!' shouted Mum.

Mary and I ran upstairs and into my bedroom and we lay on my bed side by side and laughed into the bedspread until we couldn't laugh any more.

After Mary had gone home, I went downstairs. Mum was in the living room with Rita and Aunty Brenda. I sat down beside Mum on the settee.

'Me and Mary were thinking of going to a club on Saturday night,' I said ever so casually, 'to watch a band.'

Mum pulled a face.

'I don't like the thought of you going to nightclubs, Dottie,' she said. 'There's a lot of funny people in nightclubs.'

'There'll be one more then if Dottie goes,' said Rita.

'Excuse me while I laugh,' I said.

'I'd really rather you just went to that café of yours,' said Mum. 'It's a lot safer.'

'I won't be on my own,' I said. 'I'll be with Mary and... a couple of boys.' Behind Mum's back Rita raised her eyebrows and made an 'I knew it!' face at me.

'Oh?' said Mum. 'What couple of boys?'

'Elton Briggs. He asked Mary to go. And I'll be with Ralph Bennett.'

'Who's Ralph Bennett?' asked Aunty Brenda.

'A friend I used to know from school.'

'She's got a boyfriend, Maureen!' said Aunty Brenda.

'No I haven't!' I said. 'We're just friends.'

'Oh yes? That's what Elizabeth Taylor said about Eddie Fisher, just before she pinched him off that lovely Debbie Reynolds!' said Mum.

'Hussy!' said Aunty Brenda. Rita nodded. I tried not to look at her.

'You don't mind if I go then, do you? To the club? We'll all stick together and I'll make sure we get the last bus back.'

There was a silence while Mum bit her lip and looked at me, and I knew she was thinking about what was the worst that could happen and imagining all sorts of catastrophes. 'What about all the smoke? You know you're not good with smoke.'

I thought that was a bit rich considering we practically lived in a semi-detached ash tray.

'Oh, let her go,' said Rita. 'She's got to grow up sometime.'

Flippin' heck. Was my darling sister on my side?

'See what your dad thinks,' said Mum.

I rolled my eyes and went into the kitchen and peered through the smoke until I located him. He was sitting at the table reading the sports pages, half an inch of roll-up between the yellow ends of two fingers.

I sidled up to him.

'Dad, you don't mind if I go into Brighton on Saturday night to listen to a band do you?'

'What does your mum say?'

'She said I was to ask you.'

Dad looked up at me.

'You're not going on your own are you?'

'No. I'm going with Mary Pickles and Ralph Bennett.'

'A boy?' said Dad. He's quick; you have to give him that.

'Yes,' I said.

'As long as you don't bring any trouble home,' he said.

I wanted to ask him what sort of trouble but thought I'd better quit while I was ahead.

I leaned down and kissed his forehead. He squeezed my hand.

'Thanks Dad.'

'You daft bugger,' he said.

I went back into the living room. Mum and Aunty Brenda were sitting on either side of Rita, looking over her elbows at the pictures in her magazine. *Sing Something Simple* was playing on the radio and Mum was absent-mindedly humming along with the music and swaying slightly.

'Dad says he doesn't have any objections to me going,' I said, 'as long as I don't bring any trouble home.'

'That's good advice,' said Aunty Brenda. 'Your poor mother doesn't want you bringing trouble to her door, especially with Rita's wedding coming up.'

'What trouble are you talking about?' I asked innocently.

Aunty Brenda shook her head and gazed up at me.

'Ahh, she's very immature, isn't she, Maureen?'

'Always was,' said Mum.

"Hello, I'm here," I thought.

'Haven't you told her about, you know what...?' Aunty Brenda asked in a knowing voice.

Actually I knew all about 'you know what', I mean I was seventeen for heaven's sake, but I didn't think that now was the time to tell them that I knew.

'I never got round to it,' said Mum.

'You should have done by now, Maureen. It's your duty as a mother. I bought our Carol a book with illustrations. That did the trick.'

While I was trying to keep a straight face, Aunty Brenda went all peculiar and started talking in a weird voice and slowly mouthing words at me as if I was deaf.

'You mustn't bring any unwanted babies to your mother's doorstep,' she said.

I decided to play along with it.

'I'm going to listen to a band,' I said. 'Where would I come across any unwanted babies? And even if I did, why would I want to bring them home?'

Aunty Brenda leaned round behind Rita's back and said to Mum: 'I'll give her a loan of the book.'

Later, Mary and me walked to the recreation ground and sat on the swings. All the little children had gone home and we had the place to ourselves. It was still warm; a gorgeous summer evening, all soft with little moths and the scents of the flowers in the gardens of the houses on the estate and the sounds of the families inside the houses coming out through the open windows.

That evening, on the swings, I told Mary all about the unwanted babies. After she'd stopped making the swing sway madly all over the place with laughing so much, she went into the 'How Babies Are Made' scenario again, which we both found slightly disgusting but which still had a sort of fascination that we couldn't resist. It was hard to keep off the subject when we were on our own.

'I can't see why anyone would want to do that,' I said, twisting the swing chains round and round. They were rusty and made my fingers red. 'Unless they wanted a baby.'

'Or they wanted to make someone jealous...' said Mary giving me one of her knowing little smiles.

'How do you mean?'

'Well, take Christine from the sack factory.'

'Take her where?'

'Very funny! Remember when she used to fancy Bruce Denny? The lad who worked in the arcade on the pier?'

'Yep.'

'Well he never even noticed her till she slept with that goofy-looking boy from the butchers, and then he asked her out.'

'But why would you go out with someone who only wanted you for one thing, I mean, that's not real love is it?'

'Oh Dottie, you are so square!'

'Round, Mary,' I said, 'round!' And we both fell about laughing again. We laughed all the time about sex, but really I found even the thought of it too embarrassing to be true.

When we were younger I asked Mum why Mary Pickles knew all about having babies and I didn't and she said it was something to do with keeping hamsters and having the *News of the World* on a Sunday. Sometimes I wondered if there was a big conspiracy to make us all believe that you had to do *that* to make a baby when really there was a much more sensible way of doing it. I thought I'd be hard pushed to do *that* with Paul McCartney and I really, really loved Paul McCartney.

For the briefest moment I wondered if I would ever *do it* with Ralph Bennett, and that thought made me feel a bit weird inside. I lifted my feet off the ground and let the swing spin back. It made me giddy.

'We'll have to buy some new clothes for Saturday,' said Mary dreamily.

'I haven't got any money.'

'You'll have to do something with the clothes you've got then,' said Mary.

'Like what?'

'I dunno. Hitch your skirt up or something. Make yourself look older, sophisticated. Like you go to clubs a lot.'

I smiled and slipped off the swing. It was still light and beyond the rooftops of the houses on the estate the sunlight was colouring the sea a bright red gold behind the tall grey chimneys of the power station.

'I can't wait for Saturday,' Mary said, jumping off her swing and falling into step beside me. 'It's time we spread our wings. We've already spent too much of our lives hanging around the estate. This could be the start of something fabulous.' She took hold of my arm. 'And I promise you that if we come across any unwanted babies lying around the place we'll just ignore them.'

'Absolutely,' I said linking arms with Mary and walking back towards the estate.

Dear Diary,

Me and Dottie are going to the Whisky A Go Go tonight to see Elton's band. This is going to be the start of my new life. I just know it is.

I've been watching the clock all day, wishing the time away.

I wish Dottie would stop worrying about stupid things like what if her breathing isn't so good. What if we miss the last bus home. What if. What if, what if.

Just relax Dottie, for gawd's sake.

I've got to look the best I've ever looked.

I've got to make Elton fall in love with me.

Will tonight ever come?

Tatty bye diary

Love

Mary Pickles (almost girlfriend of Elton Briggs)

Aged 17 years.

Chapter Eight

It was the Saturday that me and Mary were going to see Elton's band. I was pretty excited to be seeing Ralph again, but my excitement was nothing compared to Mary's, she was practically hysterical. She had been watching the clock over the cigarette counter all morning, as if staring at it was going to make it go any faster.

'I'm not going to look at it again until I've served five customers,' she said.

Two customers later I caught her looking at it again. I knew tonight was important to her, but I just didn't want her to be disappointed. The trouble with Mary was that she never did anything in half measures. It had been the same in school. She had to paint the best picture. She had to write the best story. She had to win the race. That's just the way Mary was. And now she had to get the boy.

When work finally (*finally!*) finished, we went back to Mary's house and her mum gave us some toast and dripping, which was all that was left after Mary's swarm of locusts brothers had been in the kitchen. Mary's mum ran herself ragged trying to feed those boys. There was always at least one of them in the kitchen rooting through the cupboards looking for something to eat. It used to drive Mrs Pickles absolutely to distraction. She used to chase them away, swatting them with a tea towel like they were stray cats or something! Mary said that if her mum wanted to save food, she had to hide it. That day we ate our snack at the kitchen table while the twins foraged around us, and after that we went upstairs to Mary's bedroom, the only brother-free place in the house.

It was only a tiny room, a box room really, and Mary's bed took up almost all the floor space. Above the bed was a picture of

Montmartre, which her old headmistress, Mrs Dicks, had given her. It showed all the artists painting around the church, with the city of Paris spread out below. Mary told me why it meant so much to her.

'Mrs Dicks told me to look at the picture, really look at it,' said Mary. 'She told me to imagine myself in the picture, sitting in front of an easel with a box of paints at my side. She said if I really wanted to be that girl in that picture, I could do it. I had the potential and the talent, but it was up to me to use it, not to waste it. She said it always feels like you've got as much time as you need to do all the things you want to do, but you'll be surprised how life has a habit of stepping in and interfering with those plans, and most importantly never settle for second best. That's what she said, Dottie. Never settle for second best. I didn't really understand what she was on about at the time because I was too young, but I do now.'

And that was why Mary decided not to apply to Brighton College of Art but to aim straight for the top, for L'Institut d'Art in Paris. Only thirty students were admitted each year, so there was massive competition for the places. Everyone said she was daft, as there was a perfectly good college of art right here in Brighton, but Mary was determined, and once Mary was determined you might just as well save your breath.

'I know I'm not ready yet,' said Mary. 'But I will be one day.'

And she would. Mary spent every free minute practising her drawing. She couldn't afford oil paints and canvases, not on her salary from Woolworths, but she could apply for the Institute with pencil drawings. If hard work could get Mary a place at that art school, then I had no doubt at all that she would get there.

Mary's bedroom was really tiny. You had to kneel on the bed to look out of the window and there was only room for one person to stand up at a time. Still, Mary and I loved it in there, with Mary's things all piled on the shelves above the foot of the bed.

I was really jealous of Mary having a room all to herself and not having to share with an annoying older sister like I did.

'Come on,' said Mary, tipping a box of make-up, brushes and ribbons onto the bedspread. 'It's time to get ourselves ready to spread our wings.'

I grinned at her and decided to stop worrying about all the bad things that might happen and join in Mary's excitement.

'We're going to look amazing, Dottie Perks,' she said. 'We are going to look so amazing that all the boys will be stunned and awed and unable to take their eyes off us for a single second!'

We spent ages backcombing our hair and changing our clothes. The window was open and all the outdoor noises from the estate came in; barking dogs and kids shouting and playing with home-made water-bombs and music. Mary's two oldest brothers, Winston and Warren, were outside trying to start the motorbike they kept in the front garden and spent all their lives playing with. Despite the attention, the bike never actually did anything apart from make screeching, coughing noises when the boys jumped on the pedal. It was nice being in Mary's bedroom listening to all those familiar sounds.

We had to take turns with the mirror. Mary went first. She told me that this was only fair, because it was her mirror and she wanted me to watch her so that I would feel brave enough to put on lipstick and mascara and blusher. She sat, cross-legged on the bed, and scrutinised her reflection as she tried to get the lipstick on just right.

'There's so much hairspray on this mirror that I can hardly see anything,' she complained, rubbing at the glass with her elbow.

'In my case, that's a good thing,' I said.

Mary cocked her head to one side and pulled a flirtatious face.

'I have to look my best, Dottie, because there's going to be lots of girls there tonight all vying for Elton's attention.'

Well, I wasn't sure I agreed with that, but I wasn't going to say anything.

'Do you think I look okay?' she asked.

'Yes.'

'No, really, *really* okay. The best I've ever looked?'

'Yes.'

'Dottie—'

'You look fab,' I said.

'Fab enough for Elton to notice me? Fab enough to stand out amongst all the other girls at the club? Because tonight is really important, Dottie. Tonight is my chance to impress the lead singer in a rock band! I mean, imagine that! Imagine me, Mary Pickles, going out with him, Elton Briggs. Imagine the band becoming really successful, like the Rolling Stones.'

'Imagine,' I said.

Mary sighed dramatically and clasped her hands to her heart. I rolled my eyes at her in the mirror.

'Hurry up,' I said, 'it's my turn!'

I tried to push past her, but she pushed her back onto the bed. Then she took a paper bag out of the pocket of her coat that was hanging on the hook on the back of the door and wiggled it in my face.

'Guess what I've got!'

'What?'

She opened the bag to show me.

'False eyelashes!'

'Are you sure you know how to put them on?' I said. 'Sally at work said they're really tricky.'

'It can't be that difficult, Christine was wearing some the other day.'

I turned over the packet to read the instructions.

'Mary, it says you need tweezers and a magnifying mirror and…'

'It'll be fine. I'll do yours first, then you can do mine.'

Putting on the eyelashes wasn't as easy as it looked. Mary somehow or other managed to put one of them on the wrong way up, so the lashes curled down over my eye, like a dead spider.

'I can't go to a club looking like this,' I said.

'You look fine.'

'No I don't. I look stupid.'

I went into the bathroom and managed to sort it out, but my eye had gone a bit pink and watery. I thought it would be best not to make a big deal of it. After that, I did Mary's eyelashes and made a pretty good job of it, even if I do say so myself.

We took it in turns to stand on the bed so that we could see ourselves in all our finery. Mum had slipped me some money to get something new for our evening out and I found a nice little blue top to go with my jeans. Mary was wearing a tight, pale green jumper and a skirt with a nipped-in waist. Her hair was held back with a ribbon and the eyelashes really suited her. They made her look much older and less innocent.

'Do I look nice, Dottie?' she asked for about the millionth time.

'You look fab,' I said.

Mary and I had arranged to meet the boys inside the Whisky A Go Go Club. It was famous, not just in Brighton but throughout the whole country, but it wasn't exactly what I'd expected. In my head I'd imagined bright lights and a glamorous entrance with swinging doors and rope banisters on the staircase, chandeliers and a red carpet like in a film. I thought everyone would be very glamorous too. Instead, it was down a side street and there were lots of rough-looking people hanging around outside, leaning on the walls and smoking and staring at us. The boys were mostly wearing T-shirts and had greased-back hair and tattoos up their arms and the girls were in very short skirts and were wearing sunglasses even though it was evening and the sun was close to the horizon. It made them look a bit sinister because we couldn't see their eyes. On the main street, we could hear the roar of motorbike engines as the rockers rode through Brighton with their cigarettes trailing smoke as they looked for girls and excitement and trouble.

Mary and I linked arms, which was always a bit difficult given the differences in our height, and we held onto one another tight. To get in we had to pay a tattooed man at the door, who squinted at us through his cigarette smoke and then pointed us through coloured plastic strips hung over the door frame down some very dark, narrow stairs with no banisters at all and something sticky on the walls. The club itself was smoky and far too small for all the people squashed inside it and so dark you could hardly see anything, which was a shame.

Everything smelled of hairspray and armpits and cigarette smoke and perfume. I could feel my lungs getting tight and I thought: 'Oh please God, don't let me have an asthma attack, not here, not tonight, not in front of Ralph Bennett.' I put my hand in my pocket for the millionth time to check that I had my inhaler, and it was okay, it was there.

Mary, being small, was able to squeeze her way through the crowd of people who managed to look cool despite being packed tight as sardines. They all seemed to belong and were smoking and laughing and talking in spite of the noise. I was holding onto Mary's elbow for dear life and following in her wake. She was determined to get to the front so she could get a good view of Elton, and I was determined too because I knew that's where Ralph would be and I quite liked the thought of saying I'd been to see a band with Ralph Bennett. I practised it in my head and it sounded romantic and special, the sort of thing a person would say if she had an actual boyfriend.

'Come on, hurry up!' said Mary over her shoulder. I could hardly hear her over the din of people shouting to make themselves heard over the music being played through the loudspeakers.

I was going as fast as I could, but unlike Mary, who was below head-height and sort of invisible, I had to keep apologising for bumping into people with my shoulders and hips and elbows and standing on their feet. As well as all this, I had the problem of not being able to see much anyway because my left eye was sore and the eyelid felt as if it was swollen. Not a great look for my first time in a nightclub.

''Scuse me,' I said, squeezing through the crowd.

We got as near to the front as we could; the stage itself was only about three feet high and the size of a paving slab, and crouching on the stage fiddling with some wires and plugs was Ralph. He was wearing slacks and a sweater and his hair flopped over his eyes and he looked… Well, he looked handsome. I watched him for a while and he didn't know I was there, and while I looked at him, the noise and the crowds and the smoke all seemed to fade away. It was as if Ralph and I were the only people in the club.

My heart beat a little faster and I felt a blush spread along my face and neck. It probably didn't matter because it was so dark. I played with the chain of my necklace. Then he looked up and caught my eye.

'Hi,' he said, squatting on his heels to smile at us. Well, actually at me, I think. Perhaps.

'Hi,' I said.

'Where's Elton?' asked Mary.

'He's backstage warming up.'

'Can I go and see him?'

'Not really,' said Ralph. 'It's only the crew that's allowed back there.' His eyes kept flicking to my face.

'Are you all right, Dottie?' he asked.

I knew he was looking at my eye, so I wafted my hand in front of my face.

'Gosh it's hot in here,' I said to change the subject.

'I'm going to get a drink before they start,' he said. 'Would you like one?'

'Thanks,' said Mary. 'Babycham for me.'

'Me too,' I said.

'That will be two orange juices then?' said Ralph, standing up and dusting his hands down the thighs of his trousers.

'We're nearly eighteen,' said Mary pouting.

And you look about twelve, I thought.

'He likes you,' Mary said once Ralph had gone.

'Does he?' I asked, feeling all warm inside.

Mary turned to give me a withering look.

'You'd have to be blind, or daft, or both, not to notice the way he goes all gooey-eyed every time he looks at you.'

'Really?' I said. And suddenly I thought that the Whisky A Go Go was the best club in the whole world.

'Yes, Dottie *really*.'

Mary peered at me.

'You don't like him the way I like Elton, do you?'

'How do I know which way you like Elton?'

'Well, I like him in a forever sort of way, I always have. I want to be with him forever, Dottie.'

'Well maybe that's how I like Ralph, but I'm not sure, I have to get to know him all over again, but for now, well, I think he's okay.'

'But he's a nobody, Dottie. He's going to be a plumber, for heaven's sake. If you end up with Ralph Bennett you'll never get away from the estate. Your life will be mapped out. Marriage, council house, kids. You'll never get away.'

'Who said anything about marriage? All I said was that he was okay.'

After what felt like forever, a fat man who was the warm-up act came onto the stage. He was a comedian and he told lots of not-very-funny jokes about his mother-in-law and his wife and Irish people. He was so hot that there were huge great circles of sweat under his arms and his face was all shiny and wet and he had to keep patting it with a handkerchief. Nobody took much notice of him and at last he left the stage and then there was a ripple of excitement and Elton's band came on.

They were very loud and very energetic and, much to my surprise, I thought that Elton was really good. It was quite a thrill to be there. The band covered some of the big hits, *Let's Twist Again*, *Sealed with a Kiss* and they did a brilliant rock and roll version of *The Locomotion*. But they also did some of their own songs. I didn't know if Elton had written them or was just singing them, but a couple of the songs were really good. Mary never took her eyes off the stage and at the end of every song she clapped like mad and shouted: 'Elton! Elton!'

Elton was the lead singer and there was no doubt in my mind that he was basing himself on Mick Jagger. He had the same way of coming to the front of the stage and pushing the microphone stand forward, and frowning at the audience. I had to smile, thinking what my dad would have made of it. I reckon that Elton thought he was the cat's whiskers, especially with Mary screaming like she was and setting some of the other girls off.

In the middle of one song, a cover of *Can't Help Falling in Love with You*, Elton came right over and crouched down in front of Mary and sang some of the words right into her face. The spotlight was picking out his face and hers and they were both staring into one another's eyes and I don't think I'd ever seen Mary look so happy!

After he moved away again, she turned to look at me and her eyes were bright and her cheeks were glowing. I was happy for her. But during the next song, Elton seemed to be singing to an older blonde woman on the other side of the stage. She must have been at least twenty-one. I hoped Mary didn't notice, but it was hard not to because Elton kept winking at the blonde and narrowing his eyes and pursing his lips when he sang to her.

Ralph somehow or other managed to squeeze his way back to us and gave us both our drinks. I sipped at the drink and it was sweet and very cold. Ralph watched me and I gave him a little smile over the top of my glass. He asked if we were enjoying the show so far and before I could answer, Mary said 'Yeah we're having a great time.'

'Are you all right?' Ralph said, smiling at me.

And I said: 'Yes, I'm fine,' but I wasn't really, because I was so squashed and there was a horrible tight feeling in my chest, and although I'd sneaked a puff on my inhaler I was still finding it hard to breathe and the smoke was making the inside of my lungs all itchy and, on top of that, my eye was sore. But it was all worth it, to be here, in this place, with Ralph.

Afterwards, Mary wanted to hang around the stage door and wait for Elton, but luckily there wasn't time. Instead, Ralph bought some chips and walked us to the bus stop. It was such a relief to be outside again, in the cool air. I almost wanted to cry with relief. I didn't even notice all the crowds around us, the sound of a police siren on its way to break up some fight, probably, and all the rockers and their girls showing off and bumping into us. Mary went on and on about what a brilliant evening she'd had, the best night of her life, etcetera. I kept eating chips and thinking how nice Ralph was and how I thought I liked him in exactly the same way that Mary liked Elton and that I didn't care what he did for a job. What was wrong with being a plumber anyway? I ate another chip. It was hot and salty. The whole thing made my head hurt.

When the bus came, Mary jumped straight on. I hesitated. I turned back towards Ralph.

'Thanks,' I said.

'What for?'

'You know. The drink and everything.'

Ralph smiled and looked at his feet and scratched the back of his ear. I wondered if I dared kiss him. Just on the cheek, just to let him know that I liked him, that I was interested in him, but before I could pluck up the courage, Mary noticed I wasn't on the bus and she'd turned round and grabbed hold of my arm. I never got to say goodbye to Ralph at all.

Mary and I sat on the front seat of the upstairs of the bus. Down below us Brighton slipped away and the estate arrived. Mary drew a heart in the grime on the window with her finger and she put an arrow through the heart and at the back of the arrow she wrote MARY and at its tip she wrote ELTON 4 EVER.

Then she looked at me and said: 'Your eye looks funny.'

'Tell me about it,' I said.

'I expect it will be all right by tomorrow,' she said.

'I hope so.'

'It was worth it though, wasn't it?'

'Was it?'

'Of course it was, we were the best-looking girls in there.'

I squeezed her hand and I thought how lucky I was to have a friend who cared about me as much as Mary Pickles did, and I hoped, I really hoped, that this time Elton would notice her and ask her to be his girlfriend. And the next time she asked me if I liked Ralph the same way she liked Elton, I would definitely tell her that he was much more than okay. As the lights of Brighton slipped past outside, I promised myself I would be true to my heart from now on, always.

Dear Diary,

Last night was stupendous, amazing, fantastic. Elton is the most dreamy boy in the whole world. He sang a song just to me. I have to try and play it cool. I think Elton likes girls that are cool.

I will do anything to get Elton, anything at all.

Love from

Mary Pickles (besotted of See Saw Lane)

Aged seventeen.

Chapter Nine

The morning after we'd been to Brighton to watch Elton's band, I was having a really lovely dream about me and Ralph skating round the ice rink. We had our arms crossed in front of our bodies and were gliding round, just the two of us, and never mind that in real life when I went skating the boots nearly always killed me because my feet were so big and I had to hang on to the side if I didn't want to spend the whole time on my bum. In my dream, Ralph was smiling down at me and I was staring into his eyes, which were, by the way, a very nice shade of darkish green, and I was feeling like I never wanted to stop, we were going round and round and it felt so easy and so right. Then suddenly the dream started to go wrong… I was bumping up and down, I was tripping over, I had lost hold of Ralph… I was falling… I opened my good eye and saw my sister who was holding a shoe about two inches above my nose.

'What are you doing?' I squeaked.

'Don't move, Dottie,' she said. 'There's a big black spider on your pillow.'

Don't move? She had to be joking. I've never moved so fast in my life. I sprang out of the covers and hid behind Rita as best I could. It was hard to get a good look at the spider on account of the rollers she puts in her hair every night. I don't know how she ever manages to sleep.

'I think it's dead,' she said.

I peered round her elbow.

Judging by the squashed mess on my pillow that spider must have been crawling round arachnid heaven a good couple of swipes ago.

'I hate spiders,' said Rita, shuddering inside her baby-doll nightie.

'So do I,' I said. 'But that's my eyelash you just murdered.'

Rita turned round to look at me with exasperation. She dropped the shoe onto the floor. It was one of her best stilettos, she must have been pretty scared of the spider to use that.

'You're such an idiot,' she said.

'Why am I an idiot?'

'Because you're supposed to take them off before you go to bed.'

'I couldn't take them off could I?' I said. 'They were stuck to my eyelashes.'

'And stop winking at me!'

'I'm not! I can't seem to open my left eye.'

'Oh you stupid girl! What have you done?'

She turned away from me and drew back our bedroom curtains. Daylight came flooding in, highlighting my tidy half of the room and Rita's messy one.

She came and looked at my eye again. 'I think it's infected or something. It looks awful.'

Rita picked up the clothes she'd dropped on the floor the previous evening and shook them out.

'Go and show Mum what you've done to your eye,' she said. 'You probably need ointment or something,' and she flounced out of the door and slammed it behind her. I heard her arrive at the bathroom door at exactly the same time as Dad and there was a bit of a scuffle before he gave in and left Rita to it. It was usually the best tactic when she was in one of her moods. Heaven help poor Nigel, I thought, but at least she wouldn't be *my* problem for much longer.

I sat down at the dressing table and leaned forward to peer at myself in the mirror. I looked like Dracula's sister; my left eye was all red and swollen with half a squashed eyelash hanging precariously onto the bottom lid; by comparison, the other eye seemed pale and bald, like a little naked kitten. I tried opening the shut eye with my fingers, but it was too sore. The only good thing about the scenario was that it was Sunday and I didn't have to see anyone or be anywhere.

I picked at the remaining lash for ages, until I heard Mum calling from downstairs, and from the tone of her voice it was obvious that Rita had come out of the bathroom and gone down to share the news with her.

'Dottie,' she shouted, 'come down here and show me what you've done.'

I sighed and put on my dressing gown and went downstairs. Clark was sitting at the kitchen table eating cornflakes; he winked at me.

'Very funny,' I said, but it's hard to be withering with one eye swollen up like a golf ball.

'Look at the state of you!' said Mum. 'You'd better sit down.'

She dipped some cotton wool into a saucer of warm water and started dabbing at my eye.

'Is that better?' she asked.

I tried opening it again but it still wouldn't budge.

'Not really,' I said. By now I was beginning to feel a bit panicky.

Just then, Aunty Brenda came through the back door without knocking, which was typical. Once she saw my predicament it would be all over the estate. I'd never get to live it down.

'Just thought I'd pop in with some dress patterns,' she breezed, plonking her bag on the table, causing some of the water to slop out of the saucer. She lifted the tea cosy and felt the pot with the back of her hand and had poured herself a cup of very stewed tea before she noticed me.

'Why is Dottie winking at me?' she asked Mum.

'She's not winking at you, Brenda,' said Mum. 'She's glued her eye shut, hasn't she.'

Aunty Brenda didn't appear to be surprised by this at all.

She put two sugar lumps into her tea and said: 'That happened to my neighbour Mrs Baxter, you know, her with the funny husband and the mock-Georgian door. You know the one, got a girl called Penelope with thin hair, about Dottie's age. Well anyway, she squirted glue in her eye instead of Optrex. That eye never saw the light of day again; they had to give her a glass one in the end.'

Disgusting! I thought.

'It was ever such a good match though,' said Aunty Brenda. 'Of course, you might not be so lucky, Dottie, what with you having such funny colour eyes.'

Rita had come in to the kitchen some time during this conversation. Her hair was still in curlers. She helped herself to a triangle of toast off the plate.

'Well, she can forget about being my bridesmaid,' said Rita. 'I'm not having her walking down the aisle with a glass eye.'

'Dottie won't need a glass eye,' said Mum, squeezing my shoulder.

'I wouldn't bank on it,' said Aunty Brenda, shaking her head.

'You'll have to go down the hospital,' said Mum, 'they'll know what to do. I expect they get this sort of thing all the time.'

Rita snorted.

'I can't go on the bus looking like this,' I said.

'Well not in your dressing gown, obviously,' said Mum. 'But how else do you think you're going to get there?'

'You could always call an ambulance,' said Clark, who was all for a bit of drama.

'Couldn't you call me a taxi?' I asked hopefully.

'You're a taxi,' said Clark.

'Very funny.'

'I know,' said Mum, who did sometimes have good ideas. 'Clark? Where's that patch you had to wear when you got hit by that cricket ball?'

'Upstairs, I'll get it!'

'Make sure you disinfect it,' I called after him. All in all I was feeling quite miserable.

I went back upstairs and got dressed and put Clark's patch over my eye and I looked really, really stupid. I thought all I could do was hang my head low and hope I didn't bump into anyone I knew. Sometimes I really wished I was small, like Mary. You could get away with things if you were little, but when you were the size of a house, like me, you tended to stick out at the best of times.

Back in the kitchen, Mum smiled at me and said: 'That's better, nobody'll notice now.'

Oh really?

'Would you like me to come with you?' she asked.

'No, I'll be fine,' I said miserably.

'Go on, let me. It'd get me out of this madhouse for a couple of hours,' Mum said quietly.

'Are you sure?'

She passed me my cardi and shouted to Dad, who was in the front room. 'Nelson! I'm taking Dottie to the doctor, she's glued her eye shut.'

'Pity it wasn't her mouth,' Dad said, and then started laughing his head off as if he'd said something funny, which he hadn't.

'It's your mouth that needs gluing up,' said Mum. 'Then you wouldn't be able to keep sticking all them fags in it. And you can do the washing up while I'm gone.'

'That told him,' giggled Clark, spraying cornflakes all over the table.

'And you can dry,' said Mum.

I sat on the bus thinking about the night before. The Whisky A Go Go hadn't been a bit like I thought it would be. It had been so crowded and dark and so full of smoke it put me in mind of our front room. If that's what spreading your wings is like, you can keep it, I thought.

Mary had enjoyed every moment of the evening and I knew she'd want to go there again. I wasn't so sure. I thought back to the café and how much I'd liked sitting and talking to Ralph and how he'd looked at me as if he'd really liked me. And do you know what? I thought, I think he does like me. I really think he does.

'Come on, Dottie,' said Mum. 'This is our stop.'

I followed her through the gates, past a lawn fringed with geraniums, into the hospital, feeling like a little kid. The waiting room was packed and I felt like a right lemon sitting there like Long John Silver; the only thing missing was the parrot. The waiting room was full of men who had obviously been in fights, old shaky-looking people and squealing toddlers with bright red cheeks and sweaty heads.

'Do you think they'll be able to fix it?' I said.

'We'll see what the doctor says,' said Mum quietly. She took hold of my hand and held it on her lap.

I loved my mum.

❊ ❊ ❊

Half an hour later I came out of the treatment room with the offending eyelash removed. I was relieved, but my eye did feel sore and I felt a bit sorry for myself. I put the eyepatch in the bin on the way out.

When we got home, Mary was in the kitchen looking at Clark's latest set of photographs. He stared at me when I walked in and said: 'Not a bad match, Dottie.'

I scowled at him. 'What?'

'Your glass eye, it's not a bad match.'

'Oh very funny, ha ha, you're a laugh a minute, Clark Perks.'

'Did it hurt?' asked Mary, blinking. Her eyelashes, of course, still looked fantastic. At least she actually cared. She was the only person apart from Mum who had actually considered *my* feelings.

'A bit,' I said. I didn't want her to feel bad, because although technically it was her fault, I knew she hadn't meant to hurt me. 'Not much,' I said and I put a big smile on my face.

'How come only one eyelash got stuck?'

'I dunno. The other one came off in the night.'

Clark added: 'And was bludgeoned to death in cold blood by Rita. Her trial comes up next week. We're all pushing for the death sentence.'

I thought that was really funny, Mum didn't though. 'That's a terrible thing to say about your sister, Clark,' she said.

'She's my sister?!!!!' screamed Clark and he grabbed his throat and made this choking sound and slid under the table. Mum was laughing now. We left them to it and went up to my bedroom. It smelled of Rita's perfume and hairspray. I opened the window to let a bit of air in.

'Where's Rita?' asked Mary.

'Her and the insurance man have gone to talk to the vicar this afternoon.'

'I wish it was me and Elton talking to the vicar,' said Mary.

Fat chance, I thought, given that once he'd sung that one song to her in the club, he'd barely looked at her for the rest of the night.

Mary sat on the edge of my bed. 'I know it's a bit of a long shot.'

'What is?'

'Me getting into the art school in Paris. They only take the best, but my drawings are getting better and better, I'm almost there, I'm almost ready to apply.'

'That's great, Mary. I mean, I don't want you to go because I'll miss you, I really, really will, but if you think you're ready then you should try.'

Mary frowned. 'I know.'

'What's wrong then?'

'I'll lose Elton.'

'Not necessarily.'

'Elton is really talented, there are people round him all the time, when I say "people", I mean girls. Specifically. There are a lot of girls and most of them are taller than I am. And better developed.'

Mary flopped back onto the bed with her arms stretched above her head. She stared up at the patch of mould on the ceiling from where there was a leak in the roof and she sighed dramatically. 'I need him to make some sort of commitment so that I know he will wait for me.'

'I'm not sure Elton is the waiting kind, or the commitment type come to that.'

Mary rubbed the bridge of her nose. 'That's why I need a plan. That's why I need him to fall in love with me. I know he likes me, but liking me isn't enough. He likes hundreds of people. I need him to fall in love with me and realise he can't live without me. I need him to wait for me.'

She turned her head to look at me earnestly.

'Oh,' I said.

'So how do I get him to do that, Dottie?'

'I guess it will just take time.'

'I haven't got time, not when he's out there singing with his band and all those girls are throwing themselves at him. I have to get him to want me now.'

I picked up the threadbare rabbit I'd had since I was a baby and turned it over and over in my hands. 'If you want to stand out from the crowd, you need to be different from the rest of them.'

'Yeah, I know. But how? It's not like I've got ages to think of a plan. What if Brainless become the next Rolling Stones and Elton becomes the next Mick Jagger? What if he goes to live in London? What then? He'll have models and actresses and all sorts throwing themselves at him and I'll have lost him forever.'

I personally thought this was a bit unlikely, but if Brainless did become famous, then it was possible that Mary's theory was right. Certainly, if Elton had a hit record he wouldn't think twice about leaving Brighton and never coming back. Maybe somewhere in Dartford, where Mick Jagger grew up, there was someone like Mary wishing she'd made her move a bit more quickly. Mary had obviously spent a lot of time thinking about this. She had a look of urgency in her eyes that I could not ignore.

'You have a point,' I conceded. 'But I don't really see what you can do about it, except maybe to play hard to get.'

'I think *he* has to be chasing *me* to play hard to get.'

'You'll just have to get him to chase you then, won't you?'

'How do I do that?'

'I dunno, play hard to get, I guess.'

At which point we both fell back onto the bed giggling.

Dear Diary,

I've been going out with Elton for three whole weeks. Three whole weeks. That's twenty one wonderful, amazing, mind blowing days!!! He came into Woolworths and asked me out. Dottie said I should try playing hard to get. She should try her hand at stand-up comedy. Why would I want to play hard to get? I want him to get me don't I? Dottie has a lot to learn about love.

Tonight me and Dottie, Elton and Ralph are going to the Miss Brighton contest at the end of the west pier.

Did I mention that Elton had asked me out? Well, he did.

Tatty bye diary

Mary Pickles (girlfriend of Elton Briggs. Rock star)

Aged 17 years.

Chapter Ten

It was the night of the Miss Brighton beauty contest and Mary and I were going to watch it with Elton and Ralph. It was a lovely evening and I was feeling happy. There were butterflies of anticipation inside me. It seemed to me as if I was standing on top of a diving board, about to jump off into the deep waters of the next stage of my life. I couldn't wait.

We were meeting the boys at the bus stop. Mary was almost beside herself with excitement because she was finally going out with Elton. He'd come into Woolworths late one Wednesday afternoon and was hanging around by the pick 'n' mix counter. I saw him before Mary did because the local school had just turned out and she was surrounded by a bunch of kids who were pushing and shoving each other out of the way trying to choose their sweets and get Mary's attention. Elton was wearing blue jeans and a black shirt with a black leather waistcoat over the top, it was easy to see why Mary was so attracted to him, it wasn't just the way he looked, there was something about him, something kind of cool and mysterious; definitely not my type, but I could see the attraction. I wasn't going to be busy for at least another hour, when the factory turned out, so I went across to Mary's counter. 'I think you've got a visitor,' I whispered. Mary was busy shovelling fruit salad chews into a paper bag.

'I haven't got time to see anyone now,' she said.

'I think you'll have time for this one,' I said, grinning.

Mary turned round and saw Elton. She went visibly pale and the fruit salad chews shot all over the counter.

'Don't worry,' I said. 'I'll take over here, tell Mr Rankworthy you've come over funny and you need some air.'

'Thanks, Dottie,' she said.

'Try playing hard to get,' I whispered.

Mary gave me one of her looks.

I watched her go over to Mr Rankworthy to plead her case, she looked up at him like a little puppy dog and you could see him melting like a slab of Neapolitan on a hot day. He put his arm around her shoulder and led her outside. I thought for one awful moment that he was going to stay with her, but after what seemed like an eternity he came back into the shop. I gave Elton the nod and he went outside to join Mary.

For the next ten minutes I was busy serving the kids, and as the last one went off clutching a bag of rainbow drops, Mary came back into the shop. She certainly wasn't pale now, in fact her face looked like the rising sun and she was grinning from ear to ear as she skipped over to me.

'Well?' I said, smiling at her.

'He asked me out, he actually asked me out.'

'What did he say?'

'He just asked me if I'd like to go out with him.'

'Nothing else?'

'Elton doesn't say a lot, does he?'

'When are you going to see him then?'

'Tomorrow, he's taking me to the Istanbul. That really cool club over the top of Dorothy Perkins.'

I gave her a hug, 'I'm really happy for you,' I said.

Mary was on cloud nine for the next few weeks. Her excitement was beginning to rub off on me and I hoped that maybe it would be my turn next.

We had arranged to meet the boys after work. It was one of those balmy summer evenings when you feel like anything is possible. It was lovely to see Mary looking so happy. I was feeling excited and happy about the evening ahead. I can't remember exactly what we talked about, Elton probably, and then he and Ralph walked round the corner. Well, Ralph walked but Elton sort of swaggered, he had slicked back his hair and he had that cocky, smiley way about him, and Ralph was sort of in his shadow. I quite liked that. I'd spent almost ten years of my life walking behind Mary. It was something Ralph and I had in common.

'Hello, gorgeous!' Elton said to Mary, taking the cigarette out of his mouth just long enough to kiss her. Ralph and I smiled at one another awkwardly while the two of them messed around. Mary was flirting like a professional. I didn't know where she'd learned to do that.

When the bus came, we went upstairs and Elton sat with his back to the window and his legs spread out on the seat in front of him. He pulled Mary down onto his lap and they snogged for a moment or two, then she climbed off him and came to sit next to me, in the seat behind. Ralph sat on his own. Smoke from Elton's cigarette was wafting over the back of the seat and into my lungs. It was making them feel a bit uncomfortable and tight.

I pushed open the window to let some air in and looked down on the families coming back from the beach; fathers in shorts, mothers in summer dresses and little kids in sandals with cardigans over their swimming costumes. The children were carrying buckets and spades and the mothers were carrying picnic bags and the fathers had newspapers tucked under their arms and were smoking cigarettes. Everyone looked tired and a bit sunburned but they were smiling.

Mary's elbows were resting on the back of Elton's seat and they were giggling and larking about. I sighed and leaned my forehead against the window and, in the glass, I caught Ralph's eye in his reflection. He smiled at me, and I smiled back, and then he came to sit in the seat behind so we could talk.

'Elton says you know someone in the contest,' he said.

I nodded. 'Sally from work.'

'Is she looking forward to it?'

I laughed. 'She said she needs as much moral support as she can get. She was so nervous yesterday she came over all unnecessary and had to sit down in the staff room while Mrs Burgess from Hosiery rubbed her shoulders and made her drink sherry!'

Ralph grinned and rubbed his nose. 'Why's she so nervous?'

I shrugged. 'She's worried she won't get any votes. But she doesn't need to because she's the prettiest-looking girl I've ever known, and one of the nicest.'

Ralph smiled at me. 'She sounds like you,' he said.

I could feel myself going red. 'Anyway we promised we'd turn up and cheer her on,' I said. 'So here we are.' Right at that moment Mary gave a delighted shriek and burst out laughing. I didn't know what to say after that so I looked out of the window again. The bus was making its way along Brighton seafront now. I watched the boys stacking the deckchairs and the ice-cream and hot-dog vendors packing up.

Actually, I'd been looking forward to the Miss Brighton contest for ages – it was one of the biggest things that ever happened down our way and people always talked about it for weeks afterwards. I'd been before with my family and it had been brilliant. It was a real show, with music and microphones and lights. The girls always looked so beautiful in their swimsuits and sandals with their hair all lovely, like princesses, and I'd wished, when I was a little girl, that I would grow up to be pretty enough to be in a beauty contest. When I'd told Dad my ambition, he'd said I was too good to be parading up and down in front of every Tom, Dick and Harry in my smalls. I think it was a nice way of telling me I was too fat.

'Oi, you, take your feet off the seat or I'll chuck you off the bus!'

It was the conductor, all red in the face and sweaty, and he was jabbing his finger towards Elton's chest.

'What, these feet?' said Elton.

'Those feet,' said the conductor.

Very slowly Elton took his feet off the seat, one leg after the other, all the time smirking at the conductor and blowing out smoke through his lips.

'And less of the bloody cheek, sonny,' said the conductor. 'Or else.'

As soon as he'd gone downstairs, Elton dropped the fag end on the floor and put his feet back on the seat. I looked at Mary. She looked a bit embarrassed.

Eventually we got off the bus and joined a stream of people going towards the West Pier. There was a real buzz of excitement in the air, everyone was talking and laughing. The air smelled of fried onions and candyfloss and cigarette smoke and the Pier was all lit up and the lights were making reflections in the black water below. You could see the lights of the Palace Pier further along the coast. I suppose we were lucky to have two piers, I shouldn't think many places did. And the big, fancy buildings that faced the seafront were lit up too, and their windows were open and you could hear the sea tumbling over the pebbles on the beach. I almost felt like skipping, it was so lovely, and then I felt something warm touch my hand and I glanced down; it was Ralph's hand. I smiled up at him and curled my fingers round his.

'Oh *come on,* you two!' Mary called impatiently.

Elton was carrying a black bag on his back.

'What's the bag for?' I asked.

'Elton's brought some drink,' said Mary.

'Just something to get us in the mood,' said Elton.

'In the mood for what?' Mary asked and then she went all giggly again.

'You don't have to have any,' said Ralph.

'I won't,' I said. 'My mum would kill me.'

'Oh Dottie, you're nearly eighteen! Who cares what your mum would say? Maybe it's time you let your hair down a bit,' said Mary.

'No thanks,' I said. 'My hair's perfectly fine as it is.'

The contest was being held in the concert hall at the end of the pier, so it was a bit of a walk to get to it, especially as so many people were all heading in the same direction. Everyone seemed to be in high spirits. There were lots of couples holding hands or leaning over the railings looking down into the water, and lots of separate groups of boys and girls eyeing each other up. The pier was made up of planks of wood with spaces between the planks so you could see the black water lapping away against the posts beneath. It made me feel a bit dizzy. Mary's stiletto heels kept getting stuck between the gaps and every time that happened we had to stop and wait for her to take off her shoe and free it, so it was taking us ages to get to the end. At one point both her heels got stuck at the same time and she was left rocking backwards and forwards like some demented children's toy. Mary and I both burst out laughing, but Elton wasn't amused.

'Bloody hell,' he said. 'I wanted a seat at the front but we'll never see anything at this rate.'

'She can't help it,' I said. 'Get on my back, Mary, I'll give you a piggy back.'

'Oh would you?'

Ralph stepped forward. 'Don't worry,' he said. 'I'll carry her.' Mary climbed onto Ralph's back.

When we reached the end of the pier there were loads of people milling around waiting to go into the theatre, or playing on the games machines. It was very noisy and very exciting. Ralph put Mary down and we headed for the ladies toilets as we always did whenever we went anywhere. We stood in front of the mirror to touch up our make-up.

'Were you and Ralph holding hands earlier?' Mary asked, her reflection glaring up at me.

'Yes,' I said.

'Oh, Dottie!' She shook her head at me in the mirror.

'Why does it bother you so much?' I said.

'Because you can do better than him.'

'I like him,' I said quietly.

'Well, it's your life,' she said. 'Just don't say I didn't warn you, when you end up married to a plumber with a load of ginger kids running round your ankles.'

'I like ginger kids,' I said.

Mary looked in the mirror and pouted. 'Do I look okay?'

'You look fab,' I said.

We came out of the toilets and found the boys, who were standing round the corner. Elton was smoking and drinking from the bottle. He was even more animated than usual and his eyes were very sparkly, so I guessed he'd had quite a lot already. Mary held out her hand for a drink and took the bottle and swallowed several mouthfuls. I didn't know what to do. She wasn't used to drink, but I couldn't really see how I could stop her. Elton grinned at her wolfishly and said: 'Wow! That's my kind of girl!' and he threw his arm around her shoulder. Mary almost fainted with joy. She immediately picked up the bottle and drank some more.

'Right,' she said, wiping her lips with the back of her hand and smearing her lippy. 'Let's go!'

She started squeezing herself through the crowd. The rest of us followed in her wake, apologising as we went, until we got into the theatre. We were lucky to find four seats together quite near to the front.

Almost at once the lights were dimmed and there was some music and then the curtains swished back and on the stage was a bloke who looked a bit like Cliff Richard. He had on a blue shiny suit with silver sparkly lapels.

'He looks a right idiot,' said Elton.

'I think he looks nice,' I said. I couldn't bear to agree with anything Elton said. He had the same effect on me as my sister.

The bloke told some jokes and sang *It's Now or Never* in a very melodramatic way which made Mary and me giggle. Then at last it was time for the beauty contest. One by one the girls came onto the stage and they walked up and down and did a twirl and then stood in a line in the light with one foot in front of the other and one hand on their hips. I thought they all looked lovely in their swimsuits. Elton started wolf-whistling and some people told him to shush. Sally's bathing suit was white and she had on these really high heels and her hair had been set. She didn't look a bit like the same girl who worked on the haberdashery counter in Woollies.

'Sally looks nice, doesn't she?' I whispered to Mary.

'Which one's Sally?' she said.

'The third one on the left, in the white swimsuit.'

'Gosh,' said Mary. 'I didn't even recognise her.'

Out of the corner of my eye, I could see Elton taking swigs out of the bottle in his bag, then he passed it to Mary. I was feeling really uncomfortable about the way things were going. I tried to concentrate on the beauty contest.

When it came to the 'personality' section, all the girls smiled a lot while they were answering their questions, and almost all of them said they wanted to get married and have children. One of them said she was going to university and wanted to work for the space programme in America and the presenter chuckled away and rolled his eyes at the audience and said: 'Oh my! Have you been reading about women's liberation, my darling?' and everyone laughed. Well most people laughed. I didn't and Ralph and Mary didn't either but Elton certainly did.

'There's nothing wrong with being a housewife, is there, girls?' the presenter asked the rest of the group and they all beamed back at him and nodded.

I was beginning to agree with Elton that the presenter *was* an idiot.

To be honest, I thought the whole thing was a bit boring, which was odd because every year up until then, it had seemed the most exciting and glamorous event in the whole world ever. I was glad when it finally ended. Sally didn't come first second or third, but she was in the last five, so I thought she had done pretty well. The girl who wanted to go into outer space came last.

Once it was all over, everyone stood up at once and started pushing towards the exit and as I was sitting at the end of the row, I sort of got carried along with them. It wasn't until I was outside that I realised I couldn't see the others anywhere. I hung around waiting, but they didn't come out of the exit I'd come out of. There were so many people everywhere, and I didn't know if they would wait for me at the end of the pier, or if they'd head back towards the seafront. I walked all the way round the pier twice hoping to find them but it was almost impossible. I knew they'd be looking for me too. We were probably following each other round in circles. I hung around for a bit longer then made my way to the bus stop, hoping to find them there. They weren't in the queue.

There was a wind coming off the sea and I was starting to feel really cold, my eyes started watering, then I saw Ralph running towards me.

'I can't find Mary and Elton,' he said. 'I thought you were with them.'

'I thought you were all together,' I said. I must have looked worried.

'They'll be fine,' said Ralph

'Well, I'm glad you found me,' I said, smiling.

'So am I,' he said.

The bus arrived. We climbed up the stairs and got a seat at the front. Ralph put his arm around me and I snuggled into him. I stared out of the window, feeling happier than I had ever felt in my life. Soon we had left Brighton behind. We passed the Rec where Mary and I used to play and where William and Wallace had given Mary's hamster a swimming lesson. Me and Mary were all grown up now and everything was changing. I wondered what had happened to Mary. I hoped she'd get home all right. I hoped Elton was looking after her.

Ralph walked me to my door and under the glow of the street lamp he held my face in his hands and kissed my forehead.

That night in bed I cuddled my pillow and remembered the feel of Ralph's hand in mine. It had felt like the beginning of something wonderful. I could hardly wait to find out what would happen next.

Dear Diary,

Last night under the west pier I was kissed by Elton Briggs. And just in case you didn't hear that, Elton KISSED me last night.

I think I might have died and gone to heaven.

I didn't play hard to get by the way.

Tatty bye

Mary Pickles (whose lips have been kissed by Elton Briggs)

AGED SEVENTEEN

Chapter Eleven

It was Monday again, one of those boiling hot, Indian summer days when there's not a breath of freshness in the air and all you want to do is lie on the beach and doze. It was only two days earlier, but already Saturday and the beauty contest felt like ages away. Mary and I were back at work. Woollies had this new brand of hair dyes in, with names like 'Bubbly Blonde', 'Ravishing Red' and 'Ardent Auburn'. The boxes had pictures of pretty girls on the front who would have looked good whatever colour their hair was. Mary and I had been unloading the boxes that had arrived that morning on the back of a lorry and were stacking them on the shelves.

'*We* ought to dye our hair,' said Mary, picking up a box that said 'Strawberry Blonde' on the front.

'What colour will it turn out though?' I asked. 'Because that's two different colours, isn't it?'

'You're so picky,' said Mary. 'It will be a blend of the two, won't it!'

'Do you want pink hair?'

'It won't be pink, it will be blonde.'

'Why call it strawberry then?'

'It sounds more sophisticated. It says here that blondes have more fun.'

'More fun than who? Us?'

'Than anyone!' said Mary, rolling her eyes up to heaven. 'Didn't you notice that most of the girls in that beauty contest had blonde hair? The girl that won had blonde hair, and the girl that came second.'

'Oh well, we'd better both go blonde then otherwise you'll be having fun and I won't,' I said cheerfully.

Mary glanced at me.

'What do you mean?'

'If you dye your hair blonde and I don't,' I said.

'Don't you ever take anything seriously?' Mary asked.

I thought for a minute then said: 'Probably not.'

She turned away from me and started straightening the boxes on the shelf.

'Is everything okay?' I asked.

'Why wouldn't it be?'

'It's just… I was just a bit worried about you… all that gin Elton drank on Saturday… and you had quite a lot and…'

'What?'

'I don't know. Sometimes when people have too much to drink they do things they don't mean to do.'

'I know what you're thinking, Dottie Perks.'

'Do you now?'

'You're thinking that we did it, aren't you? You're thinking that we did it under the pier and that's why we missed the bus.'

'Well, it was beginning to cross my mind.'

'Well we didn't. Happy now, dear?'

'I worry about you, that's all.'

'I know you do, but I've got a mother for that.'

'You will tell me, won't you?'

'For heaven's sake, Dottie.'

'But you will, won't you?'

'Okay, now stop going on.'

I didn't know why it was so important to me to know, because I didn't really want to know at all. It's just that I had a feeling that once she 'did it' things would change between us. When we were younger, Mary used to say that once you made love to a boy you became a woman and I used to have these visions of us suddenly turning into our mothers, which was a bit disconcerting because for a start I'd have to shrink about five inches. The whole thing was giving me a headache, so I decided not to think about it.

'Anyway,' said Mary briskly, holding the box up to my head so she could compare the colour of my hair against the model on the cover. 'I don't think you would suit blonde.'

'Why not?' I said. 'I want to have fun too.'

'I think you'd suit red,' said Mary.

'Red?'

'Well not exactly red.' She was rooting around in the boxes.

'Don't spoil my display,' I said.

'Like this one,' said Mary, handing me a box that said: 'Turn heads with Tantalising Tawny.'

I immediately had a vision of me walking around our estate through crowds of people with spinning heads.

'Will turning heads be as good as having more fun?'

'Of course it will. It means people will notice you.'

I wasn't sure that I wanted people to notice me. I had spent my whole life trying to get people *not* to notice me.

'Well, I'm going to go Strawberry Blonde,' said Mary. 'If you don't want to turn heads that's up to you.'

There was only one head that I wanted to turn and it was Ralph's. If I went red too, we'd be a matching pair.

'I think I'll stick to the colour I've got,' I said.

'Suit yourself,' said Mary. 'I'll be the one having all the fun.'

Okay, I thought, on your head be it.

❋ ❋ ❋

We didn't have a chance to talk again until it was time to go home. We were in the cloakroom putting on our proper clothes and brushing our hair when Mary asked: 'What do you want to do this weekend?' It wasn't at all like her to ask me my opinion with regard to planning our social lives.

'Don't mind,' I said.

'Good, 'cos we're going to the Whisky A Go Go.'

My heart sank.

'We're not going there again, are we?'

'Of course we are, that's where we hang out now, isn't it?'

'We've only been there once. I wouldn't call that hanging out."

Mary sighed, 'Oh Dottie, I thought we had already decided that that is where it's all happening.'

'I don't know,' I said.

'Oh come on. I can't go on my own, and I really, really, really want to see Elton.'

'You *are* still going out with Elton, aren't you?'

She shrugged. I thought: So *that's* what the matter is!

'He said he's not ready to go steady yet,' she said.

'Oh Mary!'

'He says he likes me though.'

'Well that's nice, isn't it?'

'*Nice.* I want more than *nice.*'

'Yea, well you would.'

Mary laughed. 'Patience has never been my strong point.'

'He likes you and that's a beginning.'

'It might be the beginning but it's not going to be the bloody end.'

I smiled. 'So how did you leave it?'

'He said he'd see me at the club on Saturday.'

'He'd see you?'

'Well he said he'd be there. Probably. If nothing else came up.'

I thought that was typical of Elton. Instead of making a concrete date, he'd made sure he left all his options open. I wondered how many girls he'd said he'd 'see' at the club.

'Doesn't sound like much of an offer to me,' I said, gently.

'It's not, is it?'

'What's more important to you, Mary, art school or Elton?'

'That's the bloody problem. They're both important to me.'

'Well I think you need to make up your mind, girl.'

'What about you and Ralph?' said Mary, changing the subject, just like she always did when she didn't want to talk about something. 'You seemed to be getting pretty cosy.'

'He walked me home,' I said.

'And?' said Mary.

'And nothing,' I said.

'I know you, Dottie Perks, you can't fool me. What else happened?'

'He kissed me,' I said shyly.

'That's it,' said Mary, going all dramatic, 'the beginning of the end, you might just as well go down the council and put your name on the housing list.'

'He only kissed me,' I said, giggling.

'You'll be sorry, mark my words.'

I looked at Mary Pickles, my very best friend in the whole world, and I knew that if I could be with Ralph, then I would never be sorry.

'Come on!' said Mary. 'Hurry up. We need to get to the record shop before it closes.'

I stood up, hung my work overall back on the hanger, put it in my locker and then I took Mary's arm and we went out of the cloakroom and clattered down the concrete steps that led to the staff door of Woollies. I offered Mary a piece of cherry-flavoured bubblegum and she took it. I didn't know what I could do to stop her hankering after Elton.

Mary pursed her lips and concentrated on making a bubble. She went cross-eyed watching it, which made me laugh, and then it burst all over her face. She picked at the bits and put them back in her mouth.

As it was payday, we went straight to the record shop, which stayed open late so the shop girls could spend their wages. Mary bought *Sweets for my Sweet* by The Searchers and I bought *She*

Loves You by The Beatles. 'Fancy going down the café tonight?'
I said as we walked back through the estate. There were loads of
kids running around chasing one another and the dogs were chasing the kids and it was all very, very noisy. We had to keep swerv-
ing to avoid bumping into children hurtling along the pavements
on home-made go-carts. In the gardens, washing hung flat on the
lines and babies cried in their prams. The ants were swarming, the
air was full of them, and you could smell the fat from all the chip
pans in all the kitchens.

'Maybe,' said Mary.

We got to the top of the twitten and stopped and Mary said:
'I'll call for you at eight and we can decide what to do.'

I picked some leaves off the privet hedge that was growing
beside the railings.

Mary stepped forward and kicked a ball back to two small
boys wearing just shorts who had come running into the alley.
Then she jumped up onto the railings and sat there swinging her
legs and chewing her gum.

'You really do like Ralph, don't you?'

She was staring at the ground, or her shoes, I wasn't sure
which. Suddenly she looked up.

'You won't forget me, will you?'

'How could I forget you, you daft thing.'

'I'll call for you at eight,' said Mary.

'Okay.'

'You never know,' said Mary, sliding backwards off the railings
and hanging on by her legs, 'they might both be down the café.'

And suddenly I felt sick and happy and excited all at once. I
ran down the twitten calling to Mary as I went.

'Mary.'

'Dottie.'

'Mary.'

'Dottie.'

When I got home I went straight into the front room to play my new record on the radiogram that was built into the side-board.

'What rubbish have you brought home this week?' said Dad who was sitting in his armchair reading the paper and smoking.

'*She Loves You,*' I said, 'The Beatles.'

'You're not putting that on while I'm in the room,' he said.

'Yes she can!' shouted Mum from the kitchen. 'Dottie is a contributing member of this family and she has as much right to play her record on that radiogram as anyone else in this house, and I'd like to remind you that it was my wages that bought that radiogram, not yours.'

Blimey, I only wanted to listen to a record and it was turning into world war three. I bet Mary was in her very own bedroom playing her record on her very own Dansette record player that she'd got for her birthday, without a care in the world. Lucky Mary.

'Got a new record?' Mum asked coming into the front room. I was kneeling down, blowing dust off the head of the arm of the record player. I loved the smell inside the cabinet; it was a smell of furniture polish and felt and rubber. I loved the noise the record player made when it was turned on, and I loved stacking the records and watching them drop and spin. Everything about it was exciting.

'The new Beatles one.'

'I quite like George Harrison,' said Mum. 'He used to look a bit like him,' she said, nodding over at Dad.

'I never looked like that pansy,' he said without taking his eyes off the paper.

'You might not have had the haircut,' she said, 'but you had his smouldering eyes.'

Dad looked up and smiled at her and it suddenly occurred to me that they actually liked each other.

'I can still smoulder when I want to, Maureen,' he said, wink-ing at her.

'Oh my God, stop, please! I'll play it another time,' I said. 'I have to get changed, me and Mary are going down the café.'

'Aren't you having your tea first?' asked Mum.

'What is it?'

'Goulash.'

Mum had recently discovered that one of her distant relations twelve thousand times removed had been Polish and had decided that we should experience some Polish culture in a culinary way.

'Don't worry,' I said. 'I'll get something down the café.'

'Make sure it's something nourishing,' said Mum.

I wasn't sure about it being nourishing, but there was a good chance it would be English. I went up to my bedroom and Rita's Prince of Wales check miniskirt was on the floor, so I picked it up and put it on. I was pleased to find that it was really quite loose on me now. I turned round and round in front of the mirror. I had definitely lost weight since leaving school. Mary said it was because I'd stopped eating all those stodgy school dinners. She was probably right because every lunch time I used to eat a big dinner followed by spotted dick or jam roly-poly pudding with custard, then when I got home Mum would feed me again. Now I just had a sandwich at lunchtime and as little of Mum's concoctions as I could get away with. Maybe with 'Tantalising Tawny' on my head and less fat on my body I might actually start resembling someone who looked reasonably normal. I began rummaging through the rest of Rita's things. I put on one of her Playtex bras and then put a pink sweater over the top. The effect was amazing. I looked a bit like Rita, like a woman. The clothes didn't just make me feel different, they made me walk differently and stand differently too.

By the time I got downstairs Mary was waiting for me.

'Wow!' she said. 'Look at you. Miss Glamour-puss! You look nice, Dottie. Is that Rita's skirt?'

'Don't tell her!' I said. 'Please, please don't tell her.'

'Do you know,' said Mum, 'you're getting a nice little figure, Dottie Perks!'

Mary and I giggled about this all the way into town.

Before we went into the café we went across the road to check our hair in the mirror of the Flick 'n' Curl and put on a bit more lippy. We knew by the smell of fish when we opened the café door that Christine and Angie were in there. They were playing on the football machine and Mary nearly squeezed the life out of my arm when she saw that they were playing with Elton and Ralph.

We went up to the counter and ordered two iced milkshakes, then sat down and sucked at the drinks.

Ralph looked across at us as we sat down. His face coloured and I could tell by the heat that mine did too. Angie scored a goal and jumped up and down cheering and Elton punched his arm, but he took no notice of either of them.

Ralph said something to Elton that I couldn't catch.

'Oh right, so I'm supposed to control the whole table on my own, am I?' asked Elton.

Ralph's eyes scanned the room.

'Mary!' he called. 'Come and be my defence!'

She couldn't have moved quicker if he'd asked her to marry him right there and then.

Ralph sat down at the table. I sipped at my drink and tried not to make a noise with the straw and pushed a bit of spilled salt around the tabletop with my fingernail. Ralph watched me with a little smile on his face. After what seemed like forever, he said 'I was hoping you'd be here.'

'So was I,' I said. 'I mean, I was hoping *you'd* be here, not that *I'd* be here.' I coughed, 'Obviously.'

'Dottie,' he said.

And at exactly the same moment I said 'Ralph' and we both laughed.

Ralph started fiddling with the sugar bowl. Spinning it round so that some of the sugar sprayed onto the plastic cloth that covered the table, then he said, 'Do you want to go out with me on Saturday?' The words tumbled out of his mouth like they had been sitting on his tongue for ages and needed to escape.

I smiled at him and then I remembered. 'Mary wants to go to the club on Saturday,' I said.

'Elton's got a date on Saturday,' he said softly.

'He's not taking her to the club, is he?'

'I expect he will,' said Ralph.

'But he said he might see Mary there.' I looked down. I felt furious for Mary, and hurt for her, and humiliated for her. Okay, she knew what Elton was like. He'd told her he didn't want to go steady, but that wouldn't have made any difference to Mary.

'Poor Mary,' I said.

Ralph didn't comment.

Suddenly things seemed awkward between us and I wasn't sure how that had happened, maybe he just felt bad for Mary.

'Elton likes Mary,' he said, 'he just doesn't want a permanent girlfriend.'

'I know,' I said, 'he told her, sort of.'

'How about Saturday then?' said Ralph, breaking into my thoughts. 'We could go for a walk on the Downs.'

'Could we make it Sunday?' I said. 'I think I should spend Saturday with Mary.'

'Sunday, then,' said Ralph. Then we just sat there looking at each other and smiling and all the ice melted into my milkshake, but I didn't mind. It was just like one of those dead romantic films.

Just then Mary and Elton walked past us. Elton had his arm around Mary's shoulder; she winked at me as they went out the door together. Maybe Ralph was wrong about Elton. Maybe he really did want to be with Mary. I crossed my fingers under the table.

Dear Diary,

I hate Elton Briggs

Oh Okay I love Elton Briggs but I jolly well wish I didn't.

He mucks me about all the time and I let him.

What's wrong with me?

It would be really nice if you could come up with the answer sometime. No pressure diary but any time soon would be good.

Mary Pickles

Aged seventeen and beyond fed up.

Chapter Twelve

Mary was really quiet at work on Saturday, which I guessed was because we weren't going to the club. I hadn't told her about Elton's date, I had just said that Elton wouldn't be there.

We were sitting on the steps outside the staff room eating our lunch in the sunshine and waving away the wasps that kept bothering us.

'We could go to the café tonight if you like,' I said, trying to cheer her up.

She started wrapping her sandwich back up in its paper.

'Not hungry?' I said.

'Not really,' she said, putting the sandwich back in her bag. 'Did Ralph say why Elton wasn't going to the club?' she asked.

I knew I was going to lie to her, I couldn't tell her the truth. I couldn't hurt her like that, and anyway Elton might change his mind one day and decide he did want to go out with Mary, and only Mary, so what was the point of hurting her now?

'No,' I said, crossing my fingers behind my back.

It was really warm on the steps. We were well into September but the sun continued to shine every day. Mary had taken her cardigan off, but I kept mine on because I didn't want the sun bringing out the freckles on my arms. Right now I wanted to look the best I could. I wanted to look the very best I could for tomorrow.

Some boys from the stockroom were kicking a ball round the yard, bouncing it off some empty crates that were stacked along the wall. I felt like getting up and joining in. I wanted to run about and be silly. I wanted to tell everyone about Ralph.

'The thing is,' Mary said, 'I never know where I am with Elton, sometimes he wants to be with me and then at other times he acts as if I don't exist.'

'It was the same at school though, wasn't it?' I said, taking a banana out of my bag and offering her half. She shook her head.

'I suppose it was,' she said.

'So he hasn't really changed, has he? Maybe he still has some growing up to do.'

'Do you remember that teacher that used to take us for History?' she said.

'Mrs Dicks?'

'No, Mrs Roberts. Do you remember that story she told us about a bloke called Achilles?'

'Vaguely,' I said.

'I've never forgotten that story,' she said. 'It was about this bloke who was really strong, except for his heel.'

'I remember,' I said. 'I thought it was a bit daft, I mean why would you be strong everywhere but your heel?'

'Well, I think I'm a bit like Achilles.'

'What, with a weak heel?'

And that made Mary giggle, which set me off. I was laughing so much I got a pain in my side, and tears were streaming down Mary's face.

'I'm serious,' said Mary eventually, wiping her eyes on her cardigan.

'Okay,' I said, trying to compose myself, 'I'm listening.'

'I think,' said Mary, 'that Elton is my Achilles heel.'

I had a feeling that actually Mary could be right, because in every other part of her life, she was brave and strong and funny, but where Elton was concerned she seemed to lose herself and quite frankly become a bit... strange.

'Still,' she said, sounding like the old Mary. 'What are you going to wear on your date with Ralph?'

'I haven't got a clue,' I said.

'Well, that's what we can do tonight,' she said, smiling. 'I'll come round to your house and help you choose an outfit.'

'Thanks, Mary,' I said.

'Come on,' she said, grabbing my arm. 'Let's give the boys a run for their money.'

We both jumped up and started wrestling the boys for the ball.

❋ ❋ ❋

When I opened my eyes the next morning I had this warm tingly feeling in my tummy. Today I was going to see Ralph. Today would be our first date, just us, the two of us, on our own, with nobody else to worry about. I snuggled back down under the covers, smiling. I wanted to bottle this feeling and keep it with me forever. I could hear Rita snuffling away in the bed next to me. She was lying on her back with one arm dangling down the side of the bed, she looked quite serene lying there. Pity she couldn't stay like that.

I pushed back the covers and opened the curtains. I wanted to make sure it wasn't raining; I needn't have worried, sun streamed into the bedroom.

'Bloody hell,' screamed Rita from the bed as the light fell across her face. 'Some of us are trying to sleep, you know!'

'Sorry,' I whispered, letting the curtain fall back. I took my dressing gown from behind the hook on the door and went downstairs. Mum was in the kitchen sitting at the table, a cup of tea in front of her.

'You're up early,' she said, smiling at me.

'I couldn't sleep,' I said.

'Cup of tea?' she asked, standing up.

'Thanks, I'd love one,' I said. I opened the back door and sat on the step. It was a perfect day. The sun was warm on my face and a soft breeze was rustling the leaves on the trees. There was a cool softness to the air and everywhere looked fresh and new. I know that spring is supposed to be a time of new beginnings, but for me, from now on, it would be forever autumn.

'Here you are,' said Mum, handing me a mug of tea and sitting down beside me. I pulled the sleeves of my dressing gown down over my hands and cradled the hot mug.

'Isn't it a lovely day?' I said, smiling back at her.

'And it's even lovelier having you all to myself,' she said, smiling back.

I took a deep breath, and turned to her. 'I've got a date today,' I said.

'That's nice,' said Mum. She didn't seem surprised. 'Who's the lucky boy?'

'Ralph Bennett,' I said.

'Have you known him long?' said Mum.

'I've known him forever,' I said. 'We were at school together.'

'So that's why you couldn't sleep,' said Mum, linking her arm through mine.

'He's nice,' I said.

'Has he by any chance got rather beautiful red hair?' said Mum.

'How did you know that?'

'Because he was always hanging around.'

'Where?' I said.

'Round the street,' said Mum. 'You know, cycling up and down outside the house.'

I couldn't believe what I was hearing. 'Really?' I said, smiling.

'Especially in the holidays,' said Mum. 'I said hello to him once. I've never seen anyone go that red, that quick.'

'That sounds like Ralph,' I said, laughing.

'My little girl is growing up eh?' said Mum.

'Not so little,' I said.

'Actually you're a lot littler than you used to be, I told you that puppy fat would drop off you.'

'Me and Mary used to laugh about that, imagining all the places where the fat could drop off,' I said.

'You and Mary Pickles,' said Mum. 'You've had a wonderful friendship, haven't you?'

'I've been lucky,' I said.

'You've both been lucky,' said Mum. 'Does she know about Ralph?'

'Yes,' I said.

'So she's happy for you then?'

'I think so,' I said, sipping at the hot tea.

'Things may start to change,' said Mum.

'In what way?' I asked.

'Well, if you continue seeing Ralph, things will be different between you and Mary, and that's normal.'

'I don't want things to change,' I said.

'You've got a big heart, Dottie,' said Mum. 'And there's plenty of room in it for both of them.'

'I hope so,' I said.

'When you were born,' said Mum, 'Rita was only three, so I made sure that my lap was big enough for both of you so that she wouldn't feel left out.'

'I'm not sure I want both of them on my lap,' I said, giggling.

'I think Clark got his sense of humour from you,' said Mum, smiling. 'Now why don't you have a bath, before Rita surfaces, you can use my Ashes of Roses bath salts.'

'Thanks,' I said, standing up. I bent down and kissed the top of her head.

It was lovely lying in the bath. The room was all steamy and it smelt lovely. I lay there wondering what our date would be like, what we would talk about and whether we might actually kiss. I stayed there dreaming until the water was cold and my fingers had turned into prunes.

When I got back downstairs, Rita was sitting in the middle of the kitchen with a towel round her shoulders staring into the mirror which was propped up on the sink. Mum was practis-

ing different ways of doing Rita's hair for 'The Wedding'. It was
the First Rehearsal at the church the next evening and we had to
practise walking down the aisle.

'Waste of flippin' time,' said Dad. 'I mean, how difficult can
it be, walking down an aisle? I know how to walk, I don't need
to practise.'

I agreed with Dad that having a rehearsal this far ahead of
the actual wedding was an awful lot of fuss and bother for one
day and also I agreed with Clark that it was really, really boring, and that made three of us who would be really glad when
it was all over. But another part of me was actually, secretly,
enjoying all the preparations. I was a bit excited about the day
itself and there was one thing that I was *really* looking forward
to. After 'The Wedding', Rita would be moving out, which
meant I could have a bedroom all to myself for the first time
in my whole life! I would finally, at last, have some privacy.
I would be able to have the dressing table all to myself! And
when Mary came round we could go up to my room without
Rita coming in and sneering at us for being immature. I could
hardly wait!

Mum ignored Dad as she quite often did. She had curled two
strands of Rita's hair so that they sort of twizzled down either side
of her face and if my big sister hadn't been scowling so much she
might actually have looked quite nice.

Mum stepped back to admire her handiwork.

'Oh, you look lovely!' she said. Rita peered at her reflection
this way and that.

'I don't know...' she said, pulling at one of the twizzles. 'It's
still a bit ordinary.'

'Flowers,' said Mum. 'Once we've got those plastic flowers in
your hair you'll look like a princess.'

I rolled my eyes and unfortunately Rita saw me in the mirror
and she pulled a troll face back.

'What about you?' she asked. 'What are you going to do with your hair?'

'Funny you should mention that, Rita,' I said 'because I'm thinking of dyeing it "Tantalising Tawny". It says on the box that it turns heads.'

'No you're not,' she squealed. 'She's not, is she, Mum?'

'Oh I don't know, it might be nice for Dottie to have a bit of a change.'

'Not on my wedding day she's not,' said Rita, glaring at me. 'If anyone's going to be turning heads it's me.'

'I expect you'll both turn heads,' said Mum, winking at me.

'This is the most important day of my life and I'm not having her ruining it.'

'She won't ruin anything. I'm sure you will both look lovely,' said Mum.

'Well I'm not having her spoiling the photographs with a tawny head.'

'I think it will bring out my eyes,' I said.

'Which one?' said Clark.

'Enough now,' said Mum.

Chapter Thirteen

Ralph and I followed a public footpath up through the Downs. It was really high up there and green and it seemed a million miles from anywhere. You felt like you could do anything you wanted to do, be anyone, go anywhere. Once we'd reached the top of the Devil's Dyke we could see for miles in all directions. The South Downs snaked away to either side of us, the whole of England was stretched out behind us and in front was Brighton and the sea, brilliant in the early autumn sunlight. It was really windy up there and the grass was moving, making the fields look as if they were doing some mad kind of dance. Seagulls swooped in the sky, and the leaves of the trees in the distance were showing the very first signs of changing colour for autumn.

I pulled the sleeves of my cardigan down over my fingers.

'Imagine living up here,' I said. 'Imagine seeing this every morning when you looked out of the window.'

'One day I'll build you a house,' said Ralph. I glanced across at him to see if he was being sarcastic. He was smiling. Ralph didn't know how to be sarcastic, he was just joining in a game.

'Just a little one,' I said. 'It doesn't have to be big.'

'With a porch. Like you see in all those American films.'

'And a rocking chair...'

'Two rocking chairs...'

'Of course! That's what I meant. Two rocking chairs.'

I smiled up at Ralph to let him know that I was with him in the game and that it didn't have to be just a game. Ralph walked away a few steps and stood gazing out over the cleft in the hillside. It was dotted with rather dirty-looking sheep. I'd pulled my cardigan tighter round me and shivered. The wind was blowing my hair all over my face. I walked a little way until I was standing just behind Ralph.

'Why do they call it the Devil's Dyke?' I asked.

He was still lost in thought.

'Ralph?'

'Sorry,' he said.

'The Devil's Dyke. Why do they call it that?'

'It's an old legend.'

I laughed. 'Not a scary one, I hope.'

'My gran used to tell me the story. She said the Devil wanted to flood the Weald but he was disturbed by an old woman putting a lighted candle in her window.'

'A candle in a window was enough to stop the Devil?'

Ralph laughed at this.

'It should be called old woman's dyke,' I said. 'Or candle's dyke. Or tiny-little-light-in-a-window's dyke.'

'The legend goes on to say that as the Devil escaped across the English Channel, a clod of earth from the dyke fell from his cloven foot and into the sea and that became the Isle of Wight.'

'My sister Rita's going to the Isle of Wight for her honeymoon,' I said and suddenly we both found this hilariously funny and ended up with tears rolling down our faces.

'I haven't laughed that much in ages,' said Ralph, wiping his eyes on his sleeve.

I stepped closer and slipped my arm through his. He smiled down at me.

'I'm glad he didn't flood it,' I said, looking out across the swaying fields. 'Because it's beautiful.'

Very quietly, Ralph said: 'So are you.'

I laughed. 'No I'm not.'

'You are to me.'

'You need glasses then.'

'Why are you always putting yourself down?'

I shrugged my shoulders. The truth is that I had never thought of myself as pretty. I mean, I didn't think I was ugly but I wasn't pretty like Mary and Rita, at least no one, up until now, had ever said I was. I was tall, almost as tall as Ralph, but I wasn't tall and willowy, I was kind of solid. Aunty Brenda said I was well-built, which wasn't exactly flattering. I had grey eyes, which I quite liked, and nice thick hair, okay it was a kind of mousy-brown colour but it was shiny and thick. So, to sum up, I was tall, well-built, I had mousy brown hair and grey eyes, and I wouldn't go down in history as one of life's great beauties.

'You are beautiful to me,' said Ralph, breaking into my thoughts.

I glanced up at him. Ralph was looking at me with a tenderness that I'd never noticed in anyone before. He meant what he said; I knew he did.

I couldn't speak. It was probably the nicest thing anyone had ever said to me, ever.

Then he said: 'Will you be my girlfriend, Dottie?'

No, *that* was the nicest thing anyone had ever said to me.

'Yes,' I said. 'I'd love to be your girlfriend.'

Then Ralph took off his jacket and laid it on the grass and I sat on it, holding my knees, and he bought me an ice cream from the van that was parked up on the top, then we just sat quietly holding hands, listening to the sound of the grass blowing in the wind and looking down the dyke towards the little village of Poynings nestling in the valley below us, and I felt like the luckiest, happiest, girl in the world.

❋ ❋ ❋

That autumn was the best autumn of my entire life. It was one of those beautiful autumns where the leaves change colour on the trees very slowly and the sunlight is always bright and you can see your breath in the air in the mornings. I noticed everything about

that autumn, things that were there before but that I'd never noticed, like the little spider webs caught in the leaves of the privet
hedges and the shine on the milk-bottle tops and the way the
aeroplanes on the way to Gatwick Airport made stripes in the sky
that slowly faded away to nothing.

For the first time since I was a really small child I *liked* getting
up in the morning. Before, I'd eke out every last second in bed
that I could. I'd hide my head under the sheets and pretend I
couldn't hear Mum calling, especially at that time of year when
the weather started to turn colder. Not any more! Now I was up
before Rita, who always got up early to nab the bathroom first. I
had so much energy, I couldn't wait to be washed and dressed and
out of the front door and walking up the twitten to meet Mary so
that we could walk to the bus stop together.

I saw Ralph at least three times a week, sometimes more than
that, and even when I didn't see him, he'd put little notes through
the door just saying he missed me and that he'd been thinking
about me and if I wasn't ready when he came to the house he'd
sit at the kitchen table and Mum would give him a cup of tea.
When he could, which wasn't often enough for me, he'd come
into Woolworths and take me out at lunchtime. The other girls
would tease me, they'd say: 'Oh here comes lover boy!' but I enjoyed the teasing. As soon as it was my lunch hour, we'd go and
sit on a bench and eat our sandwiches and he'd tell me about the
funny stuff that had happened to him in the morning and I'd tell
him about the mad customers we had.

'Does Ralph ever talk about me and Elton?' Mary asked one
afternoon. We'd finished work and had walked down to the seafront. A brisk wind was blowing in off the sea, and the few people
that were about were huddled inside their coats and hats. A woman pushing a pram was having trouble holding onto it as the wind
caught under the hood and tried to drag it from her. Down the
street an umbrella rolled on its own, spinning round and round. I

felt the first drops of icy rain sting against my cheeks. The sea and the sky were both grey and surly.

'Let's go into the café,' I said. I hoped to change the subject when we were inside. But once we'd ordered tea and buns, and sat down at a little table by the window, Mary started up again.

'I just wondered if Ralph had said anything to you about Elton saying anything about me,' she said, picking the currants out of her bun. I took a big bite of mine. The café windows were steamed up. Condensation was running down the inside, mirroring the raindrops that trickled down the outside of the glass.

I took a deep breath. I looked across the table at Mary. She was staring down at her plate and her shoulders were hunched. She wasn't at all like the cheerful, fun-loving girl I used to know. I was trying so hard not to be annoyed by her constantly going on about Elton, but, if I'm honest, it was beginning to get to me. She went round and round in circles, never going anywhere, never moving on.

'Why would he, Mary?' I asked as gently as I could. 'I don't think boys talk about things like we do. They're more direct than girls. You know that, you know what your brothers are like.'

Mary snorted. 'My brothers are Neanderthals.'

I scraped a bit of icing from the top of the bun with my finger and sucked it off.

'What I mean is... I think... Well, if Elton wanted to say something to you, he'd say it to your face. He wouldn't send a message through Ralph and me.'

'Mmm,' Mary said. 'Would you ask him? Ask Ralph if Elton's said anything?'

I sighed. I thought maybe it was time to take the bull by the horns. I thought it was time I gave her a little push away from him.

'Mary, there are plenty of other boys in Brighton apart from Elton, you know.'

'What would you feel like if you lost Ralph?'

Mary was right. It was easy for me to give out sage advice when I had the boy I loved.

'Sorry,' I said.

Mary rested her chin on her hand and stared out of the window to the sea.

❄ ❄ ❄

When I got home, Mum looked up from the sink where she was peeling carrots.

'You all right?'

'Yes,' I said. Then I pulled up a chair at the kitchen table and sat down. 'Actually, no I'm not really. I don't know what to do about Mary.'

'What's wrong?'

'She wants to be with Elton and it's not that he doesn't like her, I think he likes her, but he doesn't want to go steady with her. He knows she likes him, she makes that pretty obvious, but he's not careful about her feelings, he thinks it's quite okay to walk into the café with a girl on his arm even though he knows that Mary might be there.'

'And it's getting you down?'

'Yes, because she keeps getting hurt.'

Mum scraped away at a carrot.

'You can't really do much about it,' she said. 'It's between Mary and Elton, nothing to do with you.'

'I know.'

Mum smiled at me. 'Mary will be all right,' she said. 'These things have a way of sorting themselves out, you'll see.'

❄ ❄ ❄

The autumn wore on. A storm blew all the leaves off the trees and made the pavements slippery. People had fires in their back gardens and the air smelled of coal-smoke in the mornings. Our house was freezing cold except for the kitchen and the living room when the fire was lit. Aunty Brenda said it was the same round her house. I noticed her legs were all red and patchy from sitting too close to the fire. It looked as if she had some sort of deadly disease. Dad read something in the paper saying the council was going to put central heating in all their properties and he said about bloody time and if they didn't hurry up it'd be too late and we'd all be frozen to death. Mum rolled her eyes, but I had chilblains on my toes and Clark had a terrible cold. Rita and I took to wearing socks and jumpers to bed at night. The sight of one another wrapped up as if we were going on an Arctic expedition made us laugh.

On bonfire night, Ralph invited me round to his house for a party. I asked Mary if she wanted to come with us and she said she didn't. I thought that was a bit sad as the year before I remembered her running around our back garden holding a blazing Roman candle with her scarf trailing behind her, shrieking at the top of her voice. I wanted the old Mary back, even going out with Ralph wasn't making me feel any better about it, being so unsure about Elton was stopping her enjoying life.

When Ralph came to pick me up, I asked if we could just go round to Mary's to check on her first.

'I don't know,' said Ralph. 'My mum and dad are waiting for us to get back before they light the fire.'

'Please, Ralph,' I said. 'I'll only be a minute. I'll just knock on the door and make sure she's all right.'

'And what if she isn't?'

'I don't know,' I said, miserably.

So we walked up the twitten and I knocked on Mary's door while Ralph hung around out by the hedge. Mary's mum answered. She was looking pretty flustered, but then I expect most people would look flustered if several of their sons were having a jumping jack war in the street and somebody had just set a Catherine wheel off on the front door. I could tell because the paint – which wasn't in the best nick anyway – was now all dramatically scorched in a big circle.

'Hello, Mrs Pickles, is Mary in?' I asked.

'No, dear, she went out earlier,' said Mary's Mum. 'Have you seen the cat?'

'No.'

'Dear God, I fear for that poor animal.'

'Do you know where she went?'

'No, dear, she usually hides under the bed.'

'No, I mean Mary. Do you know where Mary went?'

'I thought she said she was going to your house,' said Mrs Pickles.

'Oh,' I said. 'Thank you.'

'If you see her,' said Mrs Pickles, 'throw a jumper over her and put her in a cardboard box and bring her home.'

Back out on the pavement, Ralph took hold of my hand. 'She isn't in,' I said.

'Well you can stop worrying about her now,' he said. 'She's probably with Elton.'

Actually, that was making me worry even more.

＊ ＊ ＊

When I got to Ralph's, I forgot all about Mary. His mum and dad were really friendly. His dad gave me a glass of hot toddy which he said would put hairs on my chest, and his mum gave me a hot dog, and it was a proper hot dog sausage out of a tin in a bread roll with ketchup, like the Americans ate in the films, and then we went out into the garden. Their garden was separated from its neighbours by a wire fence and all the neighbours were out in their gardens too, so it was like being at a very big, outdoor party.

Everyone had helped make the bonfire, which was amazing; it had tyres and all sorts on it, and even a guy. Ralph's dad sloshed it with petrol before lighting it and it went up with a great whoosh. Soon it was burning so fiercely that we had to stand back, and when I looked up at Ralph's face it was glowing orange in the light of the fire. He looked down at me and smiled, and squeezed my hand through my glove. We walked down the garden until we were out of sight of the others. It was a clear crisp night and the sky was full of stars, we stood together looking up at them.

'I love nights like this,' said Ralph. He was quiet for a while and then he said, 'See those three stars all in a row?'

'I'm not sure,' I said, gazing up at the sky.

'Just look for a while and you should see them,' said Ralph.

I stared at the hundreds of stars, trying to find three in a row and then I saw them, 'I've got it,' I said.

'That's Orion's Belt,' said Ralph.

'Just his belt?' I said, smiling.

'Just his belt,' said Ralph, putting his arm round my shoulder and laughing.

Suddenly one of the stars shot across the sky.

'Make a wish, Dottie.'

I closed my eyes and wished that this perfect night could last forever.

'Well?' said Ralph. 'What did you wish for?'

'I can't tell you that,' I said. 'It won't come true.'

'Technically,' said Ralph, 'it's not really a star.'

'What is it then?'

'It's a meteor.'

'What's that?'

'It's tiny bits of dust and rock called meteoroids that fall into the earth's atmosphere and burn up.'

'Are you telling me that I just wished on a lump of rock?'

'Looks like it,' said Ralph, laughing.

Then he leaned down and he kissed me. The kiss was gentle, as if a soft breeze had barely brushed my lips. We smiled at one another and I felt something change inside me then. I wasn't sure what it was. I'd never felt like that before, but the feeling was that I wanted to be with Ralph always, standing next to him, the two of us, together.

That night in bed I dreamt of a skinny red-haired boy cycling up and down outside my house and a kiss that tasted like a summer's day.

Dear Diary,

Sometimes Elton acts as if he doesn't even like me very much. Dottie and Ralph are all loved up and even snooty bloody Rita is getting married.

I wish Elton could be a bit more like Ralph (not that I fancy Ralph Bennett, god forbid, but at least he looks like he actually wants to be with Dottie).

What more can I do to make Elton love me the way I love him?

Bloody hell.

Mary Pickles (feeling unloved)

AGED SEVENTEEN

Chapter Fourteen

It was late November. The nights were closing in and there was a chill in the air. Wedding fever at our house had reached dangerous levels. Mum and Rita were strung tight as bows. They were both very emotional and the slightest little thing could set either of them off. For example, Dad moved his armchair closer to the wireless to listen to the football and where the chair had been was a stain. And when she saw the stain, Mum's eyes went all red and glassy and she had to fish for the hanky she kept up her sleeve, and she was dabbing at her nose and Dad said: 'For Dave's sake, what's the matter now?'

'How can you be so heartless?' said Mum tearfully.

Dad and I exchanged confused glances.

'Don't you know what that is?' Mum asked, pointing at the stain. Dad did his best. He racked his brains for a couple of moments and then shook his head.

'That's where our Rita threw up after her fourth birthday party!'

We both looked at her for further enlightenment.

'And now she's a grown woman about to go off and have a life of her own!' Mum said before collapsing into sobs.

Dad looked very uncomfortable but he did get up and pat her on the back and say, 'Glass of medicinal, love?'

Being with Ralph was easy, but at the same time it was exciting. When I knew he was coming over, my heart would speed up and I'd feel all full of energy, like I used to feel before Christmas when I was little. I would watch out of the bedroom window and, when I saw him coming along the road, I'd have a mad five minutes rushing between the bathroom and the mirror and the window, so that I was always out of breath and pink-cheeked when he arrived. And when I was with him, I still felt energetic and alive, but at the same time I felt calm, as if I was exactly where I was supposed to be in time and place.

The rest of my family behaved better when Ralph was there too. He got on really well with Clark. And Ralph and my dad were big supporters of Brighton and Hove Albion football club. One Saturday he and Dad went to the Goldstone ground in Hove to see them play a home match. Ralph was becoming part of my family and I liked that. Every moment together was precious, walking along the beach, throwing pebbles into the sea, or leaning on the edge of the pier looking at the ships going by on the horizon.

Eventually, after what felt like absolutely forever, and after more fuss and bother than anyone could possibly imagine, the dresses were finally finished the day before 'The Wedding'. It was a Friday and Ralph and I had been hoping to go out and do something on our own, but Mum said we couldn't until I'd tried the dress on. I was cross about having to stay in, but Ralph pointed out that it was only one evening out of our lives and what was one evening? Also, as he said, it meant a lot to my family that I tried the dress on to make sure it was perfect. He whispered in my ear that he wanted to see it too.

I didn't hold out much hope for the dress, which looked like a pink sack with a hole cut out for my head. I made a face when Aunty Brenda held it up and glanced over to Ralph.

'I'm not sure I want Ralph to see me wearing this,' I said.

'Don't be ungrateful, Dottie,' said Mum. 'Your Aunty Brenda has worked very hard on that dress. Ralph's going to see you wearing it at church tomorrow anyway. I'm sure it will look lovely once it's on.'

'On what?' said Clark. 'On fire?'

Me and my cousin Carol went upstairs and put our dresses on. Something happened when I slipped the dress over my head. It changed into something magical, something lovely that fitted me like a glove that slipped over my hips and finished just above my ankles. I turned this way and that in front of the mirror, and Carol, whose dress was too tight, looked at me in awe.

'Whoa!' she said. 'You look…'

'What?'

'Amazing!'

It was the only nice thing that I could ever remember Carol saying to me.

When we came downstairs Mum went all misty-eyed and Ralph stood up and looked at me with the widest smile I'd ever seen on his face. He held out his hand and I walked around the table and took it. He leaned down and kissed my cheek.

'You're beautiful,' he whispered and for a moment – oh I know I shouldn't have – but for one moment I wished it was my wedding in the morning. I wished I was going to be walking down the aisle and standing next to Ralph. I wished…

'Nelson!' Mum called. 'Come and see the bridesmaids' dresses!'

'Do I have to?' Dad called from the living room. He was doing the pools.

'Yes!'

We heard his slippers flapping along the lino in the hall and then Dad came into the kitchen. A fag was burning between the two yellow fingers of his right hand. He looked at me, standing there beside Ralph, and then he looked at Carol, and it was obvious he wasn't sure what he was supposed to say.

'They'll do,' he said.

'What do you mean, "They'll do"! Can't you be a bit a bit more enthusiastic about it?'

'What do you want me to say? They're dresses!'

'They are not just dresses, Nelson, they are bridesmaid dresses that Brenda worked her fingers to the bone to make for your daughter's wedding. Your daughter who is soon to be the wife of a man who is in the insurance business and they deserve more than a "They'll do"!'

'I wish you'd told me all that before I walked into the kitchen,' said Dad. 'I'd have a prepared a speech. Women, eh?' He winked at Ralph.

Mum opened her mouth to say something else to him and Dad backed off a bit but he was saved by Rita, who burst through the back door looking as white as a sheet and crying fit to burst.

She threw herself into Mum's arms and Mum rubbed her back and said, 'There there,' and mouthed to Aunty Brenda: 'Put the kettle on.'

'Sit down, love, whatever's the matter?' said Mum. She looked really worried.

'Has Nigel let you down, dear?' asked Aunty Brenda.

'No,' sobbed Rita.

Mum mouthed: 'Thank Heavens!' to Aunty Brenda and Aunty Brenda crossed herself and rolled her eyes skywards and filled the kettle with water.

'You're not in trouble, are you?' said Dad.

'Of course she's not in trouble,' said Mum. 'Not that it would matter if she was, she's getting married tomorrow. Make yourself useful and get the best cups out.'

Rita let out another wail and dropped her head into her arms on the table.

'Now come on,' said Mum. 'What's this all about?'

Rita raised her head. She looked terrible. Her hair was all over her face and there were great black mascara smudges all around her eyes.

'President Kennedy's only gone and got himself shot!' she wailed.

Beside me Ralph tensed. His hand squeezed mine even more tightly.

'Is he going to be all right?' I said.

'Of course he's not going to be all right! He's dead,' screamed Rita as if I should have known.

Aunty Brenda crossed herself again and lifted the kettle off the hob with a tea towel.

'That's terrible,' she said, shaking her head. 'Those poor little children!'

I was really shocked about President Kennedy getting himself shot, but I was even more shocked at Rita's reaction to it. I mean, when it came to Rita's milk of human kindness, it wasn't what you would call overflowing, but here she was being really very upset about it.

'And his lovely young wife,' said Mum. Tears were welling up in her eyes at the thought of the lovely Jackie Kennedy being widowed so young. 'Oh it's terrible,' she said. 'Terrible!'

That's when Rita blew the milk of human kindness theory out of the window. She stared from Mum to Aunty Brenda and back again. Her mouth was wide open as if she couldn't believe what they were saying.

'Never mind *them*!' she sobbed. 'What about *my* wedding?'

'What's it got to do with your wedding?' I asked.

Rita gave me one of her most withering looks. 'Everyone will be watching the news on the telly and no one will be out on the street watching me leave the house!' she said.

'She is such a caring girl,' said Clark. 'We are all so proud of her.'

'Shut up, brainless,' shouted Rita. 'What do you know about it?'

'Well, brainless I might be,' said Clark. 'But at least I've got a heart and not a swinging brick, and it seems to me that President Kennedy getting shot will come higher on people's list of priorities than your stupid wedding.'

Rita couldn't really argue with that so she came over all dramatic.

'I want to die,' she sobbed.

'Don't talk silly,' said Mum, struggling to banish the thought of the poor young widow from her mind. 'And anyway not everyone's got a telly. I'm sure some people will see you leave the house.'

'I'd be relieved if they didn't,' Dad mumbled. 'I'm not looking forward to walking down the path in a top hat and tails for all the neighbours to have a good laugh.'

'You don't have to give me away,' screamed Rita, 'I can easily get someone else to do it.'

'I'd give you away anytime Rita, just say the word,' said Clark.

'As if I'd let you walk me down the aisle! I'd rather go on my own.'

'That's silly talk,' said Mum, stirring about six spoons of sugar into Rita's tea. 'Every bride wants her dad by her side on her wedding day.'

'Why did they have to go and shoot him right before my special day?' said Rita.

'I don't suppose they knew it was your special day,' said Dad.

I thought that was quite a sensible comment but Mum said: 'Nelson Perks, get out of this kitchen before I say something I'll regret.'

Dad left and Mum pressed the cup of wet sugar into Rita's hands.

'Now dry those tears,' she said, smoothing Rita's hair like she was a little girl, 'And see how lovely Dottie and Carol look in their dresses.'

Rita looked at me and Carol and she actually smiled.

'They do look nice,' she said. 'Thanks ever so, Aunty Brenda.'

'That's all right, Rita,' said Aunty Brenda, but you could tell she was touched. It wasn't often our Rita said thank you to anyone.

Dad poked his head back round the kitchen door. 'Well, am I walking her down the aisle or not?'

'Out!' said Mum. 'Men, eh? We'd be better off without them.'

I glanced up at Ralph but he hadn't taken offence.

'But my Nigel's not like that,' Rita sniffed, wiping her eyes with the corner of a tea towel.

'Of course he's not, dear,' said Mum. 'He's cut from a different type of cloth altogether.'

'Is it all right if I go upstairs and get changed now?' I asked.

'I wish you would,' said Rita. 'I wish you'd change into someone normal.'

'If I had feelings I'd be hurt,' I said.

'Who's President Kennedy?' asked Carol.

Chapter Fifteen

The morning of the wedding found Mum, Aunty Brenda, Rita, Carol and me in the Flick 'n' Curl having our hair done. We took up the whole row of chairs in front of the mirrors. Three people worked there. The owner was called Mrs Mustoe and she was a bit of a scary woman with a big bosom and tall hair piled up on her head in a beehive. She wore high heels and she had big calves and lots of jewellery and smoked all the time. I knew she was sophisticated because she smoked menthol cigarettes through a pink cigarette-holder. She always had a slight sneer on her face and Mum said she ran the place with a rod of iron.

As well as Mrs Mustoe, there were two girls, Louise and Wendy. They were both very pretty and wore pink gingham nylon over-dresses. Mum and Rita had already had a long talk with Mrs Mustoe, so everyone knew what they were doing. Mum and Aunty Brenda were having a wash and set and the rest of us were having our hair put up with great big curls on the top. Rita said it was the height of fashion. I wasn't convinced.

'It will look lovely,' said Mum. 'You wait and see.'

She had been right about the dress so I decided just to let them get on with it. I wanted to look my best though. I wanted Ralph to be proud of me when I walked up the aisle behind my sister. I was still buzzing from the previous evening and remembering the way he'd looked at me when he'd seen me in the dress.

'Your sister's wedding, is it?' Wendy asked, winding my hair into big pink rollers. She pinned each roller so tight to my scalp that it hurt.

'Yes,' I said. I was staring at myself in the mirror. Behind, I could see Mum and Aunty Brenda's legs sticking out from beneath their pink gowns as they lay back with their heads in two neighbouring basins. I could see the shape of the sherry bottle in Aunty Brenda's handbag. Mrs Mustoe's cigarette smoke was already creating a sort of haze at head-height.

'I love weddings,' Wendy said, taking a couple of kirby grips out of her mouth and fastening another roller. I winced. 'I can't wait to get married.'

'Are you engaged then?'

She shook her head. 'No, but I've been seeing a feller for nearly three and a half weeks, so it's getting pretty serious.'

'Oh.'

'Yes, the longest I'd been out with anyone before him was seven days, and that was on holiday at Butlins. I never heard from the lad again. They can be like that, men, you know. They say women are flighty, but in my experience it's the men who are the worst.'

'But your new one is nice…? And you've been seeing him for nearly a month…' I prompted in an encouraging tone of voice.

Wendy stepped back to look at my hair and picked up a bottle full of spray. She began to squirt my hair from all different angles. The spray smelled of petrol and stung my eyes.

'Well I haven't actually seen him for the whole of the three and a half weeks, because he lives in Eastbourne and he only comes across at weekends, so technically speaking I've only seen him for six days.'

I didn't know what to say about that, except don't book the church.

'There,' said Wendy. 'All done. Now we just have to dry it.'

She put cotton wool over my ears, and fastened the whole lot with a hairnet and then pulled the pink dryer down and slid it over my head. There was a thrumming noise and I got very hot straight away.

'Here's the controls,' she mouthed, pressing something into my hand. 'If its gets too hot you can turn it down.'

I couldn't see the others now because if I turned sideways all I could see was the inside of the hairdryer. If I looked out of the corner of my left eye, I could see the café and I wondered if Ralph and Elton were there. I wasn't going to have a chance to talk to Ralph until the reception in the Co-op hall. Mary had been invited because she was my friend and also because Rita needed her portable record player so that Clark could play records. I wasn't allowed to invite anybody else because Dad said 'guests cost money' and money was limited, especially with Nigel having such a big family. Dad said it was bloody typical and he hoped when it was my turn I'd pick an orphan who didn't have any bloody brothers or sisters, cousins, aunties or uncles.

Clark, he said, could invite the whole street to his wedding if he so wished because Dad wouldn't be footing the bill and Clark said no fear, he was never going to marry.

An hour or so later, the inside of the Flick 'n' Curl had all but disappeared in a fug of cigarette smoke and hairspray. All the windows and mirrors were steamed up. Mrs Mustoe inspected us all and said: 'Hmmm,' and got Louise and Wendy to hold hand mirrors up behind us so we could see what we looked like from the back. Mum gave them all a tip and they said: 'Good luck!' to Rita and 'Hope it all goes well.'

We trooped out with bright red faces and very itchy necks and it was really nice to breathe fresh air again, even though it was a freezing cold day and the wind coming off the sea was making my ears sting. Rita, me and Carol had pink plastic roses stuck in our hair, which were awfully uncomfortable, but I had to admit they looked pretty nice. Best of all, Rita looked really happy, which boded well for the rest of the day.

When we got home, Dad and Clark were in front of the telly watching President Kennedy's assassination. Rita's face immediately fell. I think she'd forgotten about the tragedy in the excitement of being at the Flick 'n' Curl.

'Put that off, Nelson,' said Mum. 'It's not fitting to be watching that on Rita's wedding day.'

'It's history,' said Dad. 'You mark my words; people will still be talking about this fifty years from now.' But he turned it off.

'Thank you, Nelson,' said Mum.

'That's all right, love,' said Dad.

We were all in our finery in good time to get to the church and we were all feeling quite cheerful and excited. Even Mum had had more than a nip of the sherry.

As for Clark, well I'd never seen him look so clean. In fact I'd never seen Clark look like a proper person before.

'I feel a right plonker in this get-up,' said Dad, tugging at the collar of his shirt.

'I think you all look very nice,' said Aunty Brenda. She popped a mint into her mouth and offered one to Mum.

Then we heard Rita's footsteps on the stairs and a hush of anticipation fell across our living room.

The door swung open and there was a rustle and swish of fabric as Rita came into the room.

'What do you think of your daughter, Nelson!' said Mum.

Dad looked at Rita. We all looked at Rita, who was smiling fit to burst. She was wearing a long, white dress with three-quarter-length sleeves and a sweetheart neckline. Her hair was tumbling around her face. She didn't have a veil, instead a cloak was fastened around her shoulders and a big, fake-fur-lined hood slid between her shoulder blades. She was holding a posy of winter greenery.

Rita blinked her false eyelashes several times and Aunty Brenda said: 'Ahhh!'

Dad swallowed. 'She looks...' he said and then he got all choked up and couldn't carry on.

'For heaven's sake, Dad!' said Rita.

'Leave your dad alone,' said Mum. 'He's feeling moved by the occasion and it's not often your dad gets moved. It's a very proud moment for a father when his eldest daughter gets married.'

Clark took a picture of Rita standing in between Mum and Dad, then Mum looked out of the window and squeaked and wafted her hand in front of her face a few times to cool herself down, even though the room was icy cold. She turned and said: 'The cars are here! Come on everyone!'

She turned to Rita, and stroked her cheek. 'You look beautiful, Rita,' she said, her eyes welling up with tears.

'Don't you start!' said Rita.

'She looks just as beautiful as you did on our wedding day,' said Dad.

'I'll see you both at the church then,' said Mum, sniffing.

'For God's sake, Mum,' said Rita. 'Stop it. You'll ruin your make-up.'

'Sorry, love,' said Mum, dabbing her eyes and spreading her mascara all over her face.

'Come on, our Maureen,' said Aunty Brenda, putting her arm through Mum's. 'Gird your loins, girl. We've got a wedding to go to.'

After we'd been shivering for half an hour in the church porch, Rita and Dad finally showed up in a big black car with white ribbons on the front. I smiled at Dad and said: 'Your hat's all wonky.'

'Take it off, Dad,' said Rita. 'You're not supposed to wear it in the church.'

'What's the point of it then?' he asked.

'Don't start,' said Rita, sounding just like Mum.

'I could murder a fag,' he said.

'And I'll murder you if you have one,' said Rita.

Inside the church the music started. Me and Carol picked up the back of the dress and we all walked forward into the church.

Nigel stood at the altar looking like a rabbit caught in the headlights. He'd had his hair cut and his ears looked bigger than normal. I wondered if Rita might change her mind. I glanced around this way and that. Everyone had turned to look at us and they were all smiling. In the middle of the aisle I caught Ralph's eye and he grinned broadly and gave me the thumbs-up. He was looking very smart too. I thought he was the most handsome man in the church. I bit my lip and tried to stop smiling but I couldn't. I was the happiest girl in the world. I couldn't have been any happier if it had been my wedding day.

Everything happened very quickly. The service only seemed to last about five minutes and then Mum was crying and Nigel's mum was crying and suddenly it was all over and we were outside freezing cold again and having our photos taken by Clark.

'Where's Dad?' asked Rita. 'We need him for the family group.'

'I'll look for him,' said Mum.

'I'll come with you,' said Aunty Brenda.

'He's having a fag with the vicar around the side,' I said.

Mum and Aunty Brenda disappeared for a moment and returned with Dad. 'Can't you manage to behave halfway decent for one day?' Mum was shouting.

'I was only having a fag!' said Dad. 'I wasn't fornicating among the gravestones. Anyway, I've paid for this bloody wedding and if I want a bloody fag, I'll have a bloody fag.'

'Have you been drinking?' demanded Aunty Brenda, peering at him closely. I thought that was a bit rich given the amount of sherry she'd got through.

'I might have had a tot of whisky before I left home,' Dad said defensively.

'Well, all I can say, Nelson Perks, is that it's made you very brave, so now you can just shut up and behave yourself!'

'Sorry, Brenda,' said Dad.

'Okay,' said Mum. 'Now put your hat on and make Rita proud of you.'

'Right, love,' he said.

Mum always ends up forgiving Dad. She must love him, I suppose.

The wedding reception was at the Co-op hall next to the church.

'They've really done you proud, Maureen,' said Aunty Brenda, gazing round the room at the ribbons tied to the chairs and the balloons bobbing about at every table. 'Who would have thought that pink and purple would have gone so well together?'

'Rita chose the colour scheme,' said Mum with some pride.

'I expect that comes from mixing with a higher class of people,' said Aunty Brenda.

'Probably,' said Mum, winking at me.

Mary was there with her mum, but I didn't get much chance to talk to her because all the tables had been pushed together to make a big square with one side missing, and she was on the same side as me but there were quite a few people between us. Ralph was sitting next to me, and I was so proud of him. My aunties and uncles kept coming over and saying what a good-looking young man he was and he was charming with all of them, although I could tell he was finding all the attention a bit much. We ate cream of chicken soup, roast beef with all the trimmings and Arctic roll and then Clark played some records. Ralph and I danced to the song *Moon River* by Danny Williams and as we danced he sang the words into my hair. We were pressed up together very close and the feeling was so nice, so romantic and sexy that I could have stayed like that forever; for the rest of my life. I couldn't help thinking about all the other dances Ralph and I would have. For the second time I allowed myself a little private fantasy about the two of us being married. I imagined us choosing a song and dancing together on our anniversary every year, just Ralph and me and the music. But I couldn't dwell on this for anywhere near as long as I'd have liked to because I knew Mary was sitting at the back of the hall with her mum. After the dance, I kissed Ralph's cheek and went to sit with Mary who was looking very pretty. While we were talking, Nigel's brother came over and asked Mary to dance, and he was quite nice-looking, better than Nigel anyway, but she wouldn't.

'Go on,' I said. 'Why don't you? What's wrong with him?'

'There's nothing wrong with him, he's just not Elton is he?'

'I suppose not,' I said. 'I'm sorry I couldn't invite him, but Dad was having palpitations every time someone new was added to the list.'

'That's okay,' said Mary, 'it will give us something to talk about when I see him.'

'Don't you talk much then?'

'Not a lot,' said Mary, grinning.

The day ended with all of us trooping down to the bus stop to see Rita and Nigel off on their honeymoon. They were staying in a chalet on the Isle of Wight for a week. Nigel's parents were too tipsy to come with us and Aunty Brenda said they might live in a mock-Georgian house in Acacia Drive but that our family had made the better showing.

Chapter Sixteen

I woke the next morning to a strangely quiet room. Even when Rita was asleep she made this kind of snorty sound and it was strange not to hear it. It made the room feel kind of empty. I got out of bed and pulled back the curtains. There had been a heavy frost overnight and the garden looked beautiful. Bright sunlight streaked across the lawn and dappled through the trees and shrubs, making everything sparkle and glisten. It was lovely. Dad's new shed looked like a piece of art, covered in silvery spider's webs. The shed had been there for at least eight years, but Mum still insisted on calling it new. Dad says it's just to remind him that he burnt the old one down. I turned back into the room and looked across at Rita's empty bed. It was unmade, just as she had left it, the sheets and blankets tumbling onto the floor, the pillow smeared with Rita's trademark black mascara. To my utter surprise I felt a lump forming in my throat. Rita and I had shared this little bedroom for as long as I could remember and I had looked forward to the day when I had it all to myself. So why was the empty bed making me feel sad?

Just then Mum walked in holding a cup of tea. She saw the look on my face and said, 'I thought you might be feeling a bit lost.'

'I don't know what I'm feeling,' I said. 'It's not as if we ever got on, is it?'

'Feelings are funny old things,' said Mum. 'They catch us on the hop sometimes and they don't always make any sense.'

'Feeling sad about Rita's empty bed certainly doesn't make much sense.'

'You may not have got on with her, but you were used to her, and if it makes you feel any better, your dad couldn't eat his boiled egg this morning and it had something to do with not having to fight Rita for the bathroom.'

'And how about you, Mum?'

'Don't start me off,' she said and hurried out of the room.

I smiled to myself as I picked Rita's dressing gown off the floor and hung it on the back of the door. It seemed that Rita, with all her stroppy ways and her notions of grandeur, was going to be missed.

In the afternoon, Mary and I were sitting having a coffee in the café. She had been unusually quiet on the way there, not looking in the shop windows as she usually did, and now she was sitting staring into space.

'Penny for them,' I said.

'I'm not even sure they're worth that,' she said, sighing.

'Talk to me.' I said.

'Do you know, Elton never asks me about myself,' she said. 'I bet Ralph knows everything about you.'

'I don't know about everything, but I suppose we do share most things.'

'Elton doesn't even care about my dream of going to study art in Paris.'

'Maybe he's jealous.'

'Maybe.'

'What do you talk about then?'

'*Him*, we talk about *him*. *His* music, *his* dreams, *his* ambitions.'

I didn't know what to say. I didn't want to go on about how different it was with Ralph.

'And I'm not really myself when I'm with him,' she went on. 'I'm always frightened of saying the wrong thing, because if I do, then he sulks for days. That's not good, is it?'

I took a sip of my coffee; I was beginning to understand what she was saying. To be yourself, to make mistakes, even to be unkind, you have to feel loved. You have to know that however you behave that person will forgive you, because they care about you. A bit like your parents, I suppose. Elton's feelings for Mary weren't unconditional. They depended on how good she made him feel about himself. As long as she was bolstering his ego everything was fine, but as soon as she needed some attention he lost interest in her. Mary had pretty much answered her own question.

'When did you last see him?'

'I don't know, a week ago, I suppose.'

'Ralph said he'd see me here this afternoon, maybe Elton will be with him.'

'I'm tired of playing games, Dottie. I'm almost eighteen for heaven's sake and I'm still acting like the lovesick girl I was when I was twelve.'

Just then Ralph came into the café, followed by Elton, who had his arm around a pretty dark-haired girl. Ralph sat down next to me and Elton and the girl went up to the counter.

'She's just a friend of his, Mary,' said Ralph. 'We met her on the way here.'

'I've got to go,' she said, standing up.

'Sorry,' I said to Ralph and I followed Mary out of the door, almost running to keep up with her. We didn't speak till we got to the seafront. We sat in one of the shelters and stared out over the sea.

'I'm an idiot, aren't I?' she said softly.

I shook my head. 'Actually I think it's Elton that's the idiot, not you.'

'What the hell do I see in him? I mean, who but an idiot would put up with that? But I do, don't I? I just put up with it till he decides he wants to go out with me again.'

'I guess it's that Achilles heel thing that you were going on about.'

'Well I'm beginning to think it's my head that's weak not my heel.'

Mary's eyes were full of tears and she was swallowing hard to keep from crying.

'It's okay to cry,' I said.

Mary blinked furiously. 'I wouldn't give him the bloody satisfaction,' she said.

I squeezed her arm. 'That's my girl,' I said.

Later, me and Ralph were sitting on a bench in the park. I took his hand and held it on my lap.

'Has Elton spoken to you about Mary?' I asked.

'In what way?' said Ralph.

'Well, does he want to go out with her or doesn't he?'

Ralph took his hand back and put his arm around my shoulder.

'You don't like him much do you?' he said.

'It's not so much that I don't like him, it's more to do with not trusting him. If he doesn't want to be with Mary, why doesn't he just leave her alone? At least then she might find someone who *does* want to be with her.'

'You'd have to know Elton to understand it.'

'What is there to understand?'

'He doesn't like change and he doesn't like losing people. So even if he sees other girls, he won't want to let Mary go because he knows how she feels about him. When we were growing up and we fell out with each other, he would always be the first one to say sorry even if the row wasn't his fault. You say you don't trust Elton, but the truth is Elton doesn't trust *anyone*.'

'But why? I don't understand.'

'It's to do with his dad dying when he was so young. The only people he cried in front of were me and his mum. He's devoted to his mum but he's always worried that he's going to lose her.'

'That she'll die like his dad did?'

'It's not only that. She's had a couple of boyfriends, but Elton kicked up such a fuss that they never worked out. He's a bit complicated is our Elton.'

'But he does *like* Mary, doesn't he?'

'Well she's the only girl he keeps going back to, so he must like her.'

'But why walk into the café with another girl when he knows there's a chance Mary will be there? That's just mean, isn't it?'

'Elton's always been a flirt. He picks girls up and then he drops them, it's what he does. I can't say I approve of it, but it's never interfered with our friendship. What it *is* affecting is you and me because we seem to spend an awful lot of time talking about it.'

'I know we do. It's just that when Mary gets hurt and angry so do I.'

'Well I'm not Elton's keeper and you're not Mary's. Whatever we say or do, it isn't going to change anything is it? Elton will continue being Elton and Mary will continue being hurt, but she's not a child Dottie, she will do exactly what she wants to do whatever you say and however much you worry.'

'You're right. I know you're right.'

'So can we concentrate on our relationship and stop worrying about theirs? Because I'm pretty sure they're not worrying about us.'

True to form, the very next day, Mary and Elton were together again. Elton said sorry about the girl he walked into the café with and Mary, of course, forgave him. The four of us started to have fun together. 'Brainless' were getting quite a name locally and the three of us went to as many of Elton's gigs as we could. We went to Eastbourne and Hastings and, once, even as far as Croydon.

That time they were playing in a really nice hotel. Mary and I sat on a red velvet sofa in the foyer while the boys were setting up. We were dressed up to the nines and the people who had paid for tickets to the concert were milling around chatting and smoking and talking about the band. It was exciting being there and being part of the band's entourage. Mary was perched on the settee and she kept flicking her hair and checking her reflection in the mirror behind us. She pulled a face at me when I laughed at her.

'Well it looks as if all your dreams are coming true,' I said.

'What dreams?' said Mary as if she didn't know what I was talking about.

'*Your* dreams,' I said. 'You know, getting out of the estate and sitting in swanky hotels and going to fabulous places. Isn't this everything you ever wanted?'

'It's some of what I wanted. I wouldn't call Croydon fabulous,' she said. 'It's not Paris, is it Dottie? It's not Montmartre.'

'But one day it could be.'

'I wish I could be sure of that.'

I tucked my arm through hers and gave it a squeeze. 'Where's the old Mary gone, the Mary that used to say: "What's the point in doing something if you always know how it's going to turn out?"'

'When did I say that?'

'When you were eight.'

'Sounds as if I was wiser then than I am now.'

'You were barmier,' I said, smiling.

One night the four of us went to the fair at Southwick, a town just along the coast. We could hear the music as soon as we got off the train and the sky above the green was a blaze of light, orange and red and gold. As we got closer to the fairground we became part of a crowd of people, most of them our age, everybody all wrapped up in coats and scarves. Everyone was happy, everyone was laughing. There was a buzz in the air and the sugary-pink scent of candyfloss mingling with the frying smell of sausages. We stepped over the tangle of wires on the ground, walked past the noisy generators and the caravans all parked up round the outside with mean-looking dogs chained outside, and into the fair. It was a bright, noisy mix of music and shouting and people, all bumping and jostling and laughing. Ralph held my hand tight and I leaned closer to him. Mary could hardly contain herself she was so excited, her enthusiasm rubbed off on the rest of us, even Elton. We went on the waltzers, the four of us pressed up tight together as it spun. Mary's eyes were bright and shining and her cheeks were rosy. She hung onto the handle and screamed with laughter and Elton laughed with her. They were like two kids. And it was nice to see them like that, having fun.

'Let's do that again!' Elton said, but Mary said no. She was so giddy she wobbled on her feet when we climbed off the ride, and had to sit down on the steps for a moment or two with her head on her knees.

I rubbed her back. 'You okay?' I asked.

'I've never felt better!' she said.

Suddenly Elton held out his hand, 'Come on, Mary, you lightweight!' he said. 'Bet you're not man enough to join me on the bumper cars!' Mary was on her feet in an instant, running towards him saying she'd show him who was the best driver.

So Mary and Elton went on the bumper cars and Ralph and I watched; it was as if they were on a dance floor, circling one another. I noticed that Elton never took his eyes from Mary's green car. I saw how he wove amongst the other cars, waiting until he could drive towards Mary's, and bump her. The electricity flashed and crackled in the grid above them, and I wondered if maybe there was a future for Mary and Elton after all.

It was the old Mary, the Mary I loved, the feisty little girl who hung upside down on the railings. She was so happy. She wanted to go on everything. We followed in her wake as she ran towards the Switchback. We went on all the rides that evening, ending up on the Ferris wheel. Ralph and I sat cuddled up together in one seat while Elton and Mary were in the seat above us, we could hear her squealing as the wheel took us high above the crowds, it was windy up there and my hair was blowing across my face, I wanted to stop the clocks, I wanted that night to last forever, I was sitting on top of the world with the boy that I loved and my best friend was happy; I was happy too. I was so happy.

Dear Diary,

Last night I did a really stupid thing, I asked Elton if he loved me. How bloody uncool is that? Elton told me not to get soppy. I'm fed up of always necking on park benches and shop doorways and round the back of my house. It's hard to feel romantic when I'm always freezing bloody cold.

Then he said his mum had joined a bingo club and she would be out of the house every Thursday evening.

Does that mean we are going to do it?

Should I do it, diary?

Tatty bye diary

Love Mary Pickles (about to become a woman)

Aged seventeen.

Chapter Seventeen

Me and Mary were sitting on the swings down the park.

'You know I said I would tell you when we did it?' said Mary.

'You've done it?' I screamed. 'What was it like? When? How?'

'What do you mean, how?' said Mary.

'No I don't mean how, obviously,' I said, giggling, 'but when?'

'Well we haven't exactly done it yet but we're about to.'

'Really?'

'Elton's mum has joined a bingo club.'

I must have looked totally bewildered.

'Yes, that's how I reacted when Elton told me. It means the house will be empty every Thursday.'

'You're going to do it every Thursday?'

'Oh for heaven's sake, Dottie, I don't know. We haven't done it *once* yet.'

'Are you scared?'

'I am a bit.'

'You will be careful, won't you?'

'I'm not a complete idiot, Dottie Perks.'

'You can be, Mary Pickles,' I said, frowning.

'The thing is,' said Mary, 'I know things have been better between us, but I mean, even when we *are* together he's still eyeing up other girls.'

I'd already noticed that but I couldn't say it to Mary.

'I have to have some sort of commitment from Elton before I go to art school. If I don't, I'll lose him.'

'I don't want to put a downer on it, Mary, but it sounds as if it's something you've decided you've *got* to do, not something you *want* to do.'

'I have to do it, Dottie.'

'No, you don't.'

'Yes, I do.'

'You might not like it.'

'If I never try it, I'll never know,' she said.

'Huh?'

'That's what my mum always tells my brothers when they don't want to eat something.'

'I can't imagine your brothers ever not wanting to eat something. They'll eat anything.'

Mary laughed, and leaned back on the swing, tipping her head back, letting the ends of her hair brush the ground underneath.

'In a week's time I probably won't be a virgin any longer, Dottie. In less than seven days I will have crossed over to the other side, no longer a girl but a woman. And once I've crossed over, there will be no going back.'

'Do you think you'll feel any different? I mean, do you think you'll still want to hang around with me once you're doing it with Elton?'

I was tipped back now as well, mirroring Mary. We were both looking at one another from this weird position.

'Now you're the one who's being stupid,' she said.

And she smiled an upside-down sort of a smile.

Ralph and I had been going out together for five months by now. Mostly we just went for long walks over the Downs or along the beach. The council had put up some Christmas lights along the seafront, and we liked to walk there in the evenings, watching the lights reflected in the waves that came splashing over the pebbles. Nothing Ralph and I did was particularly exciting when I thought about it, but we both sort of knew without saying anything that it really didn't matter what we did as long as we were together. The more I got to know Ralph the more I liked him. He was sweet and kind and he made me feel special and safe. I trusted him; that was the thing. I knew he would never lie to me, or say mean things behind my back, or look at another girl any more than I would do anything to hurt him. It was strange at first, being part of a twosome, because the only twosome I had ever been part of was me and Mary Pickles, and yet in another way it didn't feel strange at all – it just felt right.

'I wish I'd told you when we were at school,' said Ralph one evening.

'Told me what?' I said.

'That I liked you.'

'You sort of did,' I said, grinning. 'I've always kind of hoped that it was you who sent me a Valentine's card. Am I right?'

Ralph laughed and squeezed my gloved hand. 'Quite the little Romeo wasn't I?'

'So it was you, then?'

'Guilty as charged.'

One evening when we were sitting on a bench down beside the lagoon and the moonlight was rippling on the water, and the snow was falling around us, we kissed and it was the sweetest kiss in the whole world and the kiss tasted of spearmint toothpaste and raspberry ice lolly. And something else. Ralph. It tasted of Ralph. The kiss went on forever. It was a grown-up kiss, a beautiful kiss. When the kiss finished, Ralph cupped my face in his hands and said: 'I love you, Dottie Perks, and I think I've wanted to tell you that for the whole of my life.'

Me and Ralph had always walked in Mary and Elton's shadows, maybe now the only shadows we would be walking in would be our own.

That Christmas was perfect. Ralph joined my family for Christmas dinner. We played daft childish games that had bored me the year before but seemed hilarious with Ralph there. I gave Ralph a snow globe. It had a little cottage inside and when you shook it the snow fell on the roof and on the hills around it. It was the cottage of my dreams, the sort of cottage that I dreamed Ralph and I would live in one day. Ralph bought me a beautiful silver locket. He hadn't put a picture inside but he had written 'I love you' on a piece of paper instead.

'I thought you could put your own photo in there,' said Ralph.

'I want one of you,' I said.

'Madwoman,' said Ralph, smiling.

'We can go to one of those booths and get some taken.'

'There's one on the pier,' said Ralph. 'We'll go there if you really want to.'

'I do,' I said.

❋ ❋ ❋

The four of us saw 1964 in together. We watched the fireworks exploding over the pier, sending sprays of silver and gold into the sea. Passing ships sounded their horns as midnight struck. It was magical. Mary was hanging on to Elton, her hair was blowing across her face and her eyes were shining with excitement. She looked across at me and smiled. It was one of the most loving and tender smiles I had ever known. That smile was to come back to me in the dark days that followed.

Ralph and I saw each other every day during January. He met me straight from work and usually we went to the café and sat together making one drink last as long as it could. He told me about his day and I told him about mine and gradually we learned little things about each other and everything I learned about Ralph made me like him more. After that, if the weather was cold, which it usually was, he would walk me home. We held hands, sometimes he put his arm around my shoulder and I liked the feeling of the weight of it; I liked the feeling of having someone care for me in the way that Ralph did, as if I were something precious.

'Don't you get bored of just sitting around doing *nothing* with Ralph?' Mary asked one day.

'We're not doing nothing. We're talking.'

'About what?'

'I don't know. Nothing.'

Mary rolled her eyes and I laughed and said: 'Okay, point taken!'

But she didn't understand and she couldn't understand how I felt about Ralph. I couldn't explain how things were changing between us, how I knew, without him having to say or explain, that he felt the same about me as I felt about him.

I had never been able to keep up with Mary, not properly, she was always the leader, but Ralph encouraged me to step forward. He asked me what I thought about things, he seemed to respect my opinion.

And those evenings, those January evenings when we walked home in the dark, I'll never forget them. I won't forget how Ralph held my hand or how he would stop when we reached a dark corner, and how he would press me back against a wall and tilt my face up towards his and kiss me. His face was cold and his hands were cold, but I was warm, I was burning up as he kissed me, and as the days wore on we got better at kissing, we were learning about each other, we were learning about desire.

I thought about him all the time; at work, at home, in bed. I imagined what it would be like to be married, to have a bed of our own, when we would be able to do more than kiss and do it as often as we wanted. I drove myself half mad thinking of how it would be to be in bed with Ralph. I think it was the same for him. I could feel it in the way he looked at me, and knowing how much he wanted me made me feel precious; it made me feel beautiful.

Mary still hadn't told me about her special night with Elton. It was weeks ago and she still hadn't mentioned it, so I just blurted it out one day.

'You haven't told me about the night Elton's mum went to the bingo.'

'And I'm not going to,' said Mary. 'It was too embarrassing for words.'

Seeing the look on Mary's face I knew better than to push it.

January turned into February. There was a Valentine's dance at the local Youth Club and we all had tickets. I bought a card for Ralph, nothing flash, just a red heart on a white background and the words *Be Mine* on the front. Mary bought a big card for Elton with a cartoon of two cuddling puppies.

'What do you think?' she asked and I said I thought it was lovely but I couldn't see Elton putting it up on his window ledge somehow.

We all went to the dance, everyone did. The Youth Club was just an old green tin hut in the middle of a field, but it had been decorated with hearts made out of crêpe paper and streamers and red balloons, fairy lights were strung across the stage and they twinkled in the darkened room, and as long as you didn't look too closely it actually looked quite glamorous for once.

Ralph and I danced five dances in a row. We were really into rock and roll and he was a good dancer, but after that we were very hot.

'Come outside to cool down,' he said and Elton made a jeering noise and raised his glass to Ralph and said: 'Good luck, mate!' and Ralph laughed and scratched his ear and said: 'Come on, Dottie, ignore him. He's jealous.'

I couldn't understand why Elton would be jealous when I knew Mary would have been out of the door with him in a flash if he'd asked her to step outside with him.

Ralph took my hand, and we walked through the room, out into the darkness. The air was icy, but it felt clean and it smelled of the sea. I leaned on the railings at the front of the club, and I took a few deep breaths and the next thing I knew Ralph's hands were on my shoulder. He turned me round to face him and he kissed me and I kissed him back and his hands were on either side of my head, in my hair, and he was pressed up against me and perhaps I was a bit dizzy with the dancing. Perhaps it was because it was Valentine's night, I don't know. But that night I put my hands underneath his shirt and I felt his chest, I felt how strong and broad it was, how warm and different to mine. I put my hands around him and then I moved them to the front, to the button of his trousers. My heart was racing and I was scared but I knew what I wanted. I'd always told Mary that I wanted to save myself for the right time, for when I was married, but suddenly I didn't care about all that, in fact, any morals I might have had about sex before marriage were about to fly out the window.

Ralph pulled gently away from me but held me close. His breathing was fast and although it was cold I could see beads of sweat on his forehead.

And then I asked him something that had been on my mind for a long time but had been too embarrassed to mention. 'Have you ever done it before?' I said.

'Not properly,' he said, breathing more easily. 'Just a few fumbles in the dark. What about you, Dottie?'

'The same,' I said, 'and always with the wrong boy.'

'So let's wait,' he said, 'let's make it special, not here, not in the car park outside a grotty club. How will that sound when we tell the grandchildren?'

I laughed. I pretended I hadn't noticed what he'd said about our future grandchildren. I pushed my hair back from my face.

'God, Dottie, you're so… so perfect!' Ralph said. He took hold of both my hands, held them tight. 'We can wait a bit longer, can't we?' he said. 'We've got all the time in the world.'

I smiled up at him. He tucked his shirt back into his trousers and smoothed my hair, and when we both looked respectable again, we went back into the club.

Everything looked the same, the lights twinkled and the music was soft and romantic. I looked across at Elton and Mary, they had their arms around each other and Mary was smiling up at him. Everything looked exactly the same, but I suddenly had this terrible feeling of loss, as if it was all too perfect, as if I needed to remember everything before it all faded away.

Chapter Eighteen

That was the year that we all turned eighteen. Mary's birthday was in February and mine was in June, and Ralph and Elton's birthdays were so close together in March that they decided to have a joint party. They hired the Co-op hall where Rita had had her reception. The party was booked for the last Saturday in March. A long cold winter was beginning to soften and turn into spring, and there was a sense of anticipation in the air. It wasn't just the primroses opening their little yellow faces in the park, or the birds singing in the garden, or the warmth in the air when we walked along the seafront. It was more than that. It was a feeling that we were all on the cusp of something: that something was about to happen, that our adult lives were about to start.

Mary and I were both looking forward to the party, but Mary especially.

'I know, I just know, things are going to change between Elton and me,' she said one evening when we were up in her bedroom.

I had to admit that things *were* better between them, but it was still pretty up and down.

'Oh yeah?'

'Yeah!'

She was standing, looking through the clothes that hung from hangers hooked over the picture rail. She turned and grinned at me.

'I'm going to make sure I look the best I've ever looked at this party. I'm going to make all the boys want me, and when Elton sees that I'm the best girl there *by miles,* he'll fall completely and madly in love with me.'

'Okay,' I said, trying not to feel hurt that Mary clearly thought she was going to look miles better than me too.

'I'm going to need something new to wear,' she said, 'something classy. Something… tight-fitting and glamorous. Like a film star would wear.'

'We could go shopping on Saturday,' I said. 'The new season's fashions are coming into the shops. There are some lovely things around.' I picked up a magazine and started to flick through the fashion pages.

'And I need to get Elton a really special present, something that will show him that I understand him, that I know what he really wants. What do you think I should get him?'

'I haven't got a clue,' I said.

'What are you getting Ralph?'

'Nothing much,' I mumbled.

'Go on. Tell me.'

I stared hard at the pages of the magazine. 'I've bought him a watch.'

'A watch! Wow!' Mary made her eyes big and round and bounced down onto the bed. I felt a bit embarrassed now. I'd been so pleased with the present. It had cost me a week's wages, but I knew Ralph would love it. Now I was worried that Mary would decide to buy Elton a watch too, and if she did, then Ralph would think we'd just teamed up as a pair to go shopping and that I hadn't put any thought into the present. And I had put thought into it, lots of thought. 'What sort of things does Elton like?' I asked quickly to take Mary's attention away from the watch.

She chewed on her nail.

'The only thing he's really interested in is music.'

'And women,' I said, grinning.

Mary pushed me back onto the bed.

'Not any more,' she said, batting her eyelashes at me, 'from now on I'm going to be the only girl in Elton Briggs's life. I'm going to make sure of it. You just watch me, Dottie!'

I picked up Mary's old battered teddy bear, it had seen better days and one of its eyes was missing. I turned it over in my hands but Mary snatched it off me and threw it into the corner of the room.

'So what am I going to buy Elton for his birthday?' she asked again.

'What about a record?'

'Too ordinary.'

'Let's go into town then, something might catch your eye.'

We had a lovely day trailing round the fashion shops in Brighton. In the last year a number of small boutiques had sprung up in the town. They were noisy and colourful and were named after their owners, who were called exotic names like Zita and Marlene. The shops stocked the same clothes that were in the London stores. They were expensive, but they were amazing and they were fun, not like the dull department stores where our mothers bought the clothes they didn't make themselves.

Mary and I tried on miniskirts and maxi dresses. We draped ourselves in feathers and furs, we danced around in thigh-high boots and shimmied in front of the mirrors in spangly, geometric dresses in oranges and purples and greens. We posed and pouted and put on hats and laughed at one another until our stomachs hurt. In the end Mary brought an amazing yellow and black tunic dress. It was very short and sleeveless with a cute little collar and three big, shiny black buttons at the back. I didn't buy anything. I'd spent all my money on Ralph's watch, not that I minded.

Mary bought a pendant for Elton. It was a silver-plated plectrum on a black piece of cord. Mary said it was perfect and I thought so too. It was kind of cool. After that we called into Woolworths to get some eye shadow to match Mary's dress and we saw Sally.

Mary showed her the dress and Sally was suitably impressed.

'That'll be perfect for Paris,' she said.

Mary looked at me and then back to Sally.

'Paris?'

Sally nodded. 'Yep. The management team has decided they're sending us all to Paris in the summer as a "thank you" for all the hard work we've put in over the last twelve months.'

'What, Paris France? French Paris?' Mary asked. 'French Paris where Montmartre is?'

Sally laughed. 'Yes, that's the one!'

'Oh my goodness!' Mary's eyes were wide and bright.

'But how come?' I asked. 'Normally we just go out for a meal.' Actually the previous summer we'd gone and played bingo. It had been really good fun and Mary had won half a crown. The Mecca hall seemed a long way from Paris.

'Our store made more profit than any other in England last year,' Sally said. 'This is our reward. We're going to go on a coach and stay in a proper hotel. We'll need money for extras, but that's all. There's a brochure in the staff room.'

Mary was beyond excited 'Can we have a look now?' she said.

'Of course you can.'

Mary and I ran to the back of the store and through the door that led up the back stairs to the staffroom. We poured ourselves a cup of tea from the urn, sat at a table and pored over the brochure. It was full of beautiful pictures of Paris, which it described as '*the most romantic city in the world*'.

'Imagine that!' said Mary. 'The most romantic city in the world. This is probably going to be the single most exciting thing ever to happen to us in our *whole lives!* Apart from Elton and Ralph's party of course.' She turned over a page in the brochure. There was a picture of Montmartre. It was a big, white church on the very top of a hill and all around it were little cafés and bars and squares where artists painted and singers sang and dancers danced. 'Look at that! That's where I'm going to be one day,'

Mary said. 'I'm going to be one of those artists painting at one of those easels. That's going to be my life!'

Mary sat back in her chair and closed her eyes.

'I can hardly believe it,' she said. 'I told you we were at the beginning of our lives and this just proves it. We're going to go abroad, Dottie, abroad, overseas, to a different country! To the *one single place I've always wanted to go to my whole life!* Isn't it the most exciting thing *ever?* I can hardly wait for us to get on that coach and drive out of Brighton. I wonder if we're allowed to take guests. Do you think we will be? I could take Elton and you could take Ralph. Can you imagine that? We can climb the Eiffel Tower! You can borrow your brother's camera and take pictures of me and I'll take pictures of you and…'

I loved seeing Mary so happy.

She studied the map on the back page of the brochure.

'This is where we will be going,' she said, tracing the journey with her finger. 'Coach to Newhaven then across the English Channel to Dieppe and then it will be Paris here we come! Ooh la la!'

She closed her eyes and I knew what she was thinking. She was imagining herself in her new dress, dancing through the streets of Paris with Elton at her side. She was thinking of her future, a future that would involve lots of travelling, lots of cities, lots of excitement and adventure.

In the staffroom at Woollies that afternoon, I looked at my friend's blissfully happy face and felt something I had never felt before. I realised that we wanted different things. I had always been happy to go along with whatever Mary wanted. When we were little, we'd fitted nicely into our separate roles. She had always been the feisty girl who made up the exciting games, I was proud to be her friend and to do whatever it was she wanted me to do. I never had to use my imagination because I was always swept up in Mary's. I'd never wanted to do anything other than what Mary wanted, because she was everything to me.

And now, now things were changing.

I was excited about Paris too, of course I was, although I'd never particularly wanted to go abroad. I didn't see the point when I had everything I wanted here, at home. I would go to Paris with Mary and we would have a wonderful time, but Mary's dreams were no longer my dreams because she was no longer everything to me. Now, I had a dream of my own to follow.

Dear Diary,

It was a bloody disaster, I have never been so embarrassed in my whole life.

I don't want to even talk about it. Not even to you.

Mary Pickles (wishing she could turn back the clock)

Aged eighteen.

Chapter Nineteen

Two days before Ralph and Elton's party, I got ill. It started with a cold and then it went on to my chest and I was struggling to breathe. I hadn't had an asthma attack for months and Mum was so worried she sent for the doctor.

'Will she need to go into hospital, Doctor?'

I knew she was worried sick because she was twisting her pinny round and round her hand. 'It's only a cold, Mum,' I said.

'Is it, Doctor? Is it just a cold?'

'You know that Dorothy always has to be aware that a cold can very often lead to an asthma attack, but if she stays in bed and rests she should be okay. I will call in again after evening surgery. If she gets worse and you are worried, then call an ambulance, but as I said she should be okay if she rests.'

'Well you won't be going to this party, Dottie,' said Mum, plumping up my pillows. I felt like crying. I had been so looking forward to it, but I knew she was right – I was going nowhere.

Mary came round in the afternoon. She sat on the end of my bed. I stared at her blearily through my runny eyes.

'You poor thing,' she said.

'I feel like a poor thing.'

'Will you really not be well enough to go?'

'Doctor's orders,' I said. 'So as far as my Mum's concerned, it's set in concrete.'

'Ralph's going to be gutted.'

'I know he is. I feel really bad about it.'

'It won't be the same without you.'

'You'll be fine,' I said. 'You'll be with Elton anyway.'

'Yes, but his band's going to be performing. I expect he'll be on the stage most of the time.'

'Well, you and Ralph will just have to look after each other, won't you?'

'I suppose so,' she said, making a face.

'Stop making me feel guilty, Mary Pickles,' I said croakily, although really I felt too ill to feel guilty.

'Sorry,' she said. 'Here, I've bought you something.'

She rummaged in a carrier bag and plonked a *Jackie* magazine down on the bed.

'Thanks,' I said.

Mary stood up and went across to the window; she seemed to be lost in thought. 'I've got a bad feeling about this party,' she said, suddenly turning round.

'Why? I thought you had a good feeling about it.'

'I did. But I haven't heard from Elton all week.'

'I shouldn't worry about that. He's probably busy planning it all. Ralph's been pretty tied up with the arrangements too.'

'Really?'

'Of course. Why? Do you think it's something else? Has something actually happened?'

'Elton never asked me to help. I'd have loved to help him get everything ready.'

'But you've been at work.'

'I know. But knowing Elton, the silence could be anything. It might be his way of saying he doesn't want to go out with me anymore.'

'Wouldn't he just tell you if he didn't want to go out with you anymore?'

'He's not that brave. I usually find out by accident, when I see him with another girl.'

It was still beyond me why Mary put up with him. He kept hurting her and she kept going back for more.

'I know what you're thinking,' she said.

'I just hate seeing you get hurt all the time,' I said gently.

Mary came back to the bed and sat down.

'I'm a mess where he's concerned. Sometimes I wish he was more like Ralph.'

'Ginger hair and all?' I said.

'Perhaps not the ginger hair,' she said, smiling, 'but you know where you are with Ralph.'

I knew what she meant. Ralph would never do that to me. I trusted him completely. I was lucky.

Mary picked up the magazine. 'How to get the boy of your dreams,' she read out loud. 'It should be me reading this, not you.'

'You could be worrying for nothing. Wait till he sees you in your new dress – you'll bowl him over.'

Mary was still looking pretty down. I propped myself up on my elbows and blew my nose. Then I said: 'At least you're *going* to the party. I'm going to be lying here thinking about you every moment and wondering what you're doing and thinking about how much fun you're having. I want to hear every single detail, so come round early tomorrow and tell me.'

Mary nodded. She looked at her watch. 'I should go; Winston's girlfriend is coming over to do my hair.'

'Just enjoy yourself.'

Mary looked back at me as she was going out the door and pulled a face.

'Go on,' I said. 'Have fun. Once Brainless start playing you won't even notice I'm not there.'

Ralph came round on his way to the party. He was wearing blue jeans and a purple shirt with a black stripe running through it. I thought he looked very handsome.

'I'm so sorry you're going to miss the party,' he said, sitting on the bed and reaching for my hand.

'Don't,' I said, 'it's all hot and clammy.'

'I'm partial to hot and clammy,' he said, grinning.

I leaned over the bed and took a package out of the cabinet.

'Happy birthday,' I said, smiling at him.

He held the present in his hands and started feeling it and turning it over. 'Can I rattle it?' he said.

'No you flippin' can't, just open it. Go on, tear off the paper.'

I wish I'd had a camera to capture the look on his face when he opened the present, because he was beaming. 'Wow,' he said, looking at the watch. 'It's great, thank you.'

'I'm glad you like it,' I said.

'I love it.'

'Good.'

'I just wish you were coming to the party.'

'Don't *you* start.'

'Why? Who else has started?'

'Mary.'

'So you want me to keep an eye on her?'

'Yes please,' I said, yawning.

'For you, anything. Now get some rest and get well. I'll call by tomorrow and tell you all about it.'

After he'd gone, I snuggled down beneath the covers. My head felt muzzy and I was hot and uncomfortable and achy. I must have fallen asleep because when I woke, it was dark outside. Nobody had come in to draw the curtains and all I could see was the blackness through the windows. I was cold now, cold and shivery. I pulled the blankets up to my chin, but they didn't help. I felt as if my blood had turned to ice. I felt as if something dreadful was on the other side of the window glass. I felt full of dread.

The next day I was feeling a bit better but not great, I was coughing for England and was still headachy and feverish. I was bored with being in bed. I'd read the *Jackie* magazine from cover to cover and when I did fall asleep I had this vivid dream of Mary's dad on stage with Brainless, dressed as Elvis Presley.

I'd been waiting all day for Ralph and Mary to come round and tell me all about the party. It wasn't until teatime that Ralph put his head round the bedroom door.

'How's the invalid?' he said.

'Bored,' I said, making a face. 'Where have you been all day? And where's Mary?'

Ralph sat down on the bed and held my hand. He seemed to have trouble looking at me.

'Well?' I said.

'I had a hangover,' he mumbled. 'I've only just got up.'

'Ralph Bennett!' I said, giggling, which started me coughing. Ralph handed me the glass of water that was beside my bed. 'I didn't think you drank much.'

'I don't, usually,' he said, looking sheepish.

'Is that why Mary hasn't come round? Did she get drunk as well?'

'Worse than me,' he said, 'I had to walk her home. Her dad was waiting up for her; he wasn't very happy about it.'

'Well tell me about it then. Was it a great party? Were there lots of people there? Did you enjoy it? Did Mary enjoy it?'

'I can't remember a lot.'

'Ralph Bennett,' I said, pulling myself up the bed, 'I've been waiting all day to hear about this party and you're telling me that you don't remember much about it?'

'I don't think Mary had a very good time. I remember that much.'

'Mary was right then, she said she had a bad feeling about the party.'

'Elton was flirting a bit, the way he does.'

I was feeling bad for my friend. 'I don't know why you go round with Elton Briggs,' I said sharply.

'Because he's my friend,' Ralph snapped back. 'And your friend Mary's no angel.'

I was a bit taken back. I'd moaned about Elton over the years but I'd never heard Ralph say a bad thing about Mary, or anyone else for that matter. Suddenly things felt awkward between us. I didn't know how to make it better.

'Look,' Ralph said eventually. 'We shouldn't be arguing about Elton and Mary; they're old enough to figure things out for themselves. We've got each other and that should be all that counts. I love you, Dottie, but I can't keep apologising for the way *my* friend treats *your* friend.'

'You're right,' I said, 'I'm sorry.'

'So am I,' said Ralph. 'Now give me a cuddle.'

'But I've got a red nose.'

'Didn't I mention that red's my favourite colour?'

Chapter Twenty

It seemed like forever, but it was actually only three days before Mary came round to see me. I was out of bed by then but the cold had really knocked me for six and I felt as weak as a baby. I was still off work.

I was helping Mum with the dinner when Mary knocked on the back door.

'At last,' I said, opening the door and hugging her.

'Off you go,' said Mum, 'I can manage here.'

Mary and I went upstairs to my room. I took hold of her hands and pulled her on to the bed. 'Tell me everything about the party,' I said, 'don't leave anything out.' Mary just stared at me, then she put her head in her hands and started crying. I immediately put my arms around her. 'What's wrong?'

'It was awful,' she sobbed.

'Oh Mary, why?'

'That girl was there, you know the one he walked into the café with. Elton was all over her all evening. He barely noticed I was there. How could he do that? How could he just ignore me? He just ignored me, Dottie.'

'Ralph said…'

'Ralph said what?' she snapped.

'That you didn't have a great time,' I said gently.

'He was right, I didn't.'

'I'm really sorry.'

'I hate him.'

'Do you?'

'I *want* to; it would be easier if I did.'

'I wish I'd been there.'

'*I* wish you'd been there. I wouldn't have felt so stupid. I felt like a bloody groupie. The daft thing is, I expect we'll be back together in a few days and what's even dafter is the fact that I'll be stupid enough to *take* him back.'

There was so much I wanted to say. I was so mad at Elton but I knew this wasn't the time, and anyway, I would only be telling Mary what she already knew. I didn't mention the getting drunk bit. She hadn't told me, so I guess she didn't want me to know.

'Did he like the pendant?' I asked.

'I haven't got a clue. I'm not even sure he opened it. I left it on a table.'

'I'm really sorry, Mary.'

'You and me both,' she said sadly.

❊ ❊ ❊

April was beautiful, with warm sunny days and long balmy evenings. Since deciding to get less involved in what Mary and Elton were doing, Ralph and I had time to just enjoy being together.

It was a perfect spring. A time of growing up and being in love.

One gloriously sunny day we took a picnic up onto the Downs. I just loved it there. It was so different from the narrow streets on the estate, there was room to breathe and dream and, well, just be. I liked the feeling of the breeze blowing through my hair. I liked seeing the butterflies dancing above the wild flowers and the birds wheeling in the sky. I loved watching the light on the sea in the distance, seeing Brighton all spread out below like a toytown; like somewhere a million miles away.

Spring had been unusually warm that year and the rolling fields were covered in daisies. We spread a blanket on the exact same spot where we had had our first date. We lay side by side looking up at the clouds scudding across the blue sky. I closed my eyes and thought about how happy I was.

'Do you know how happy I am?' I said.

'Let me guess,' said Ralph, spreading his arms out wide. 'This much?' he said.

I squinted my eyes up against the sun. 'More,' I said.

'How much more?' said Ralph, laughing.

'A million times more,' I said, kneeling up and staring down into his face.

'Is that all?'

'A billion times more. A trillion times more!' I shouted.

'Enough to stay with me forever?'

'And beyond,' I said, brushing the hair away from his eyes.

I had been making a daisy chain, pressing my nail into the tiny stem and threading the little white flowers through, one by one.

Ralph took the daisy chain from me and started winding it round my finger. He stared at me in a very intense sort of way.

'What?' I said, smiling at him.

'I'm thinking.'

'About what?'

I had never seen Ralph look so serious. He stood up and walked a few feet away. I got up and followed him.

The view from the top of the dyke was beautiful. The rolling hills of the South Downs, the Weald and, in the distance, the shimmering waters of the English Channel.

'There's something on your mind, Mr Bennett,' I said, slipping my arm through his. 'And I demand to know what it is.' I was joking with him, but when he turned to look at me he was still looking deadly serious.

'Will you marry me, Dottie?' he said.

The question seemed to come out of the blue, like he hadn't planned to say it.

'I haven't got a ring yet,' he went on, 'but I will, and then we can make it official.'

'I don't mind about the ring,' I said and I didn't, but something was bothering me and I couldn't put my finger on it.

He swallowed, and took a deep breath. 'I love you, Dottie,' he said. 'I always have. I always will. I will always, always do my best to make you happy. I will try never to hurt you. I can't promise that we will ever be rich, but I will take care of you and I will never let you down.'

His words came out quickly, almost pleadingly.

'I may have done this the wrong way round,' he continued, 'not getting the ring first, but I don't want to lose you.'

I reached my hand up to his face, put my palm against his cheek. He was frowning. If it hadn't been the happiest moment of my life, I'd have almost thought he was close to tears.

'You won't lose me,' I said very gently. 'Why would you say that? Why would you even think that?'

Ralph shrugged his shoulders. Then he put his arm around me and held me tight almost too tight.

'Dottie...? What are you thinking?'

I smiled. 'I'm thinking about what you just said.'

'And?'

'Don't rush me,' I said, teasing him.

He smiled then. The clouds blew away from the sun and the world lit itself up.

Then he started to tickle me. 'Say yes, or it will be death by tickling.'

'Okay,' I shouted between giggles. 'Yes, yes.' Then I looked into his eyes and very gently said, 'Yes, of course I'll marry you.'

I could see the tension leave his face. We lay side by side on the blanket, our fingers entwined. I had never felt so happy. 'I want to go home,' I said.

'But we haven't had our picnic yet.'

'I want to tell someone.'

'Tell the sheep,' said Ralph, laughing.

'I'm going to be married,' I shouted across the hillside. A few raggedy sheep looked at me and carried on snuffling away at the grass.

'I need to tell Mum and Dad.'

'Let's wait till I get the ring.'

'Okay,' I said. 'If that's what you want, but I'll have to tell Mary.'

'Why?'

'Because I won't be able to keep it from her. She'll know. We can read each other like a book.'

Ralph stared down at the ground.

'I won't tell anyone else,' I said. 'Just Mary.'

'Of course,' he said eventually. 'Of course you must tell Mary.'

❊ ❊ ❊

The next day was Sunday and I couldn't wait to get round to Mary's and tell her my news.

I knocked on the back door and went into the little kitchen. I could hardly believe what I saw. Mary was standing beside her mum, up to her elbows in cake mix.

'Can you believe this?' said Mary's mum.

'Not really,' I said, grinning.

'Mum said the way to a man's stomach is through his heart,' said Mary.

'Sounds painful,' I said, laughing.

'The other way round,' said Mary, giggling.

'Well, that's a relief,' I said.

'You look happy,' said Mary's mum.

'I am,' I said.

'I can finish this off,' she said to Mary.

'Fancy going for a walk?' I said.

Mary washed her hands, took her coat down from a hook behind the door and we headed for the seafront. Most of the shops in West Street were closed but we gazed into the windows at all the new fashions. Mary had her eye on a red checked miniskirt and black roll-neck jumper that was on one of the models in Hannington's window.

We walked down to the pier. There were loads of people around, even though it was a bit of a dull day that was threatening rain. We made our way onto the beach and sat on the pebbles with our backs leaning against the old stone wall. The sun was beginning to filter through the clouds. I closed my eyes, enjoying the warmth of it on my face.

I was bursting to tell Mary my news, but I suddenly felt uneasy about it.

'Well, spit it out then,' she said.

'Spit what out?' I said. I picked up some pebbles and let them fall through my hand.

'Whatever it is you want to tell me,' she said.

'How do you know I want to tell you anything?' I asked, playing for time.

'Because I can read your mind, Dottie Perks, now spill.'

'Ralph has asked me to marry him,' I said.

'Oh!' Mary looked at me. I couldn't read her expression but it certainly wasn't delight on her face. 'Oh,' she said again. Then she pushed herself up and stalked off down the beach. I ran after her. I caught up with her beside the groyne.

'Mary,' I pleaded, 'don't be like that.'

Her face was red and cross-looking.

'Like what?'

I stared at her. 'Like this.' I felt desperate and disappointed and… angry. 'I had a feeling you'd be like this,' I shouted.

'Why bother telling me then?' she shouted back.

'Because you're my best friend, that's why. Because I want to share it with you. Because I want us to look through wedding magazines together. Because I want you to be my bridesmaid. That's why.'

I left Mary leaning against the groyne and walked down to the water's edge.

There were two little girls running into the cold sea, shrieking and giggling.

Suddenly Mary was beside me.

'They remind me of us,' she said.

I smiled and linked my arm through hers.

'It seems like yesterday,' I said.

'Sometimes I wish it was.'

'Really?'

'Sometimes.'

We stood arm in arm watching the children playing, each of us lost in our own thoughts.

Mary nodded towards the little girls. 'They think it's going to be like that forever, don't they? Playing on the beach all day, then going home for their tea. No worries, no regrets.'

'What do you mean?'

'Oh, I don't know. Life was simpler then, wasn't it?'

'You're not going to lose me, you know. If that's what this is all about? Because if it is, you couldn't be more wrong. Marrying Ralph doesn't mean the end of our friendship.'

'You say that now.'

'I'll say that forever, because however much I love Ralph, I wouldn't be me without you.'

'Really?'

'Absolutely, always, forever, infinitely.'

'I'm a cow aren't I?'

'Yes, but you're my cow, Mary Pickles.'

Dear Diary,

Ralph asked Dottie to marry him and instead of being happy for her I was angry, like really angry. She forgave me, she always does. Dottie is a better person that I am. I don't like myself at the moment.

Mary Pickles (bad, bad, friend)

Aged eighteen.

Chapter Twenty-One

June was glorious. The days were long and warm. Ralph and I spent a lot of time down on the beach. We'd spread a blanket over the pebbles and just sit quietly watching the tide chasing pebbles and seaweed backwards and forwards over the stones. I used to lay back with my arms behind my head and close my eyes and enjoy the feeling of the sun on my face and Ralph beside me.

We started to talk about our future.

'We'll have to rent somewhere to start with,' said Ralph.

'That's okay.'

'But it won't be forever. Once I'm a qualified plumber I reckon we can think about buying somewhere.'

'It all sounds very grown-up and serious,' I said, smiling.

'I want you to be happy.'

'I'll be happy wherever we live.'

'So will I, but it's good to have something to work towards and I want the roof over our head to belong to us.'

'Do you enjoy plumbing?'

'I worked for the railways when I left school but there were too many chiefs and not enough Indians. That's when I decided that I would be happier working for myself. Plumbing seemed like the obvious choice. I've always liked fixing things and I actually love it.'

'More than you love me?' I said, teasing him.

'I'd choose you over a leaky tap any day of the week,' he said, grinning.

Ralph was saving up for a ring. We spent some happy times gazing in jewellers' windows. Once, we went into a shop, the girl came out onto the pavement with us so that we could point to the rings we liked. Back inside, she got a little key from under the

counter and opened the back of the window. She took out two
black velvet cushions with a selection of rings on them and even
though we told her we were only looking at the moment, she
made me feel special and let me try on a selection of them.

The only thing that was spoiling these dreams was Mary. She
wasn't herself at all. She was moody and sullen, which was odd,
because her and Elton were getting on okay. She had seemed to
accept my marrying Ralph. I could tell she wasn't completely
happy about it but she seemed to be resigned to it. It didn't help
matters when I told her I wouldn't be going to Paris with her on
the work trip. We were in her bedroom playing records when I
broke the news.

'What do you mean, you can't go?' she screamed.

'I would if I could,' I said, wanting desperately for her to understand, 'but we're saving up for a wedding. I can't expect Mum
and Dad to pay for it all.'

'I knew this would happen,' she said, glaring at me, 'I knew
that everything would change.'

I didn't know what to say. I hated arguing with Mary.

'This has been our dream, since we were children, you and me
travelling the world, getting out of the estate, having a better life.
It's been our dream!' Mary cried.

'*Your* dream, Mary,' I said as gently as I could. 'It's *never* been
mine.'

'So you're happy to settle for married life, a load of kids and a
council house?'

'I love Ralph, I want to marry him, it doesn't feel like I'm set-
tling for anything. It's what I want.'

Mary stood up and stared out of the window, not speaking.

I stood beside her and leaned on the window ledge. 'You'll
have a great time,' I said. 'You can tell me all about it when you
come back, it will almost be as good as going myself.'

'Bloody Ralph Bennett,' she muttered.

'I want you to be happy for me, Mary,' I said, linking my arm through hers.

'Well, I'm not feeling happy for you right now.'

'I know, but you will, won't you?'

'I haven't got much choice, have I?'

❊ ❊ ❊

As June gave way to July things got worse. Mary was pulling away from me. She stopped coming over to my counter for a chat. She found excuses not to see me. I couldn't remember the last time we'd gone to the record shop together, or sat in her bedroom doing our hair and trying out new make-up. She hadn't said anything about being ill but she was taking odd days off work. I didn't know what to think. We had always shared everything. I had always known just how to help Mary and how, if she was in a sulk, to win her round, but for the first time ever, I didn't have a clue.

'You go round and see her,' said Mum.

'But I don't think she wants to see me,' I said sadly.

'When has Mary Pickles not wanted to see you?'

'I don't understand what's going on.'

'That's why you have to talk about it,' said Mum. 'You're not going to solve anything sitting here worrying about it, now get yourself round there and sort it out. When I got to Mary's house that evening, her third brother, Wesley, and her fourth brother, Wayne, were in the front garden messing about with the motorbike. There was nothing unusual in that; what was unusual was that they hardly looked up from what they were doing when I arrived. Normally they would joke with me; that day they pretty much ignored me. In fact, I got the impression they were pretending they hadn't seen me.

I stood for a moment and still the boys said nothing. The awful feeling in my stomach got worse.

'Is everything all right?' I asked.

Wesley grunted.

'Is Mary all right?'

'I think she's in her room,' mumbled Wayne.

I knocked quietly on the door and Mrs Pickles answered it. She looked even more anxious and worried than usual. I stepped into the house. Mr Pickles was sitting at the kitchen table, but he didn't look up either.

By now I had a feeling of absolute dread in my stomach.

'Is Mary all right?' I asked again. And with that, Mr Pickles banged his fist on the table and walked out. I just stood there not knowing what to do.

'Mary's in her room, Dottie,' said Mrs Pickles, picking up the chair that her husband had knocked over. 'You can go up if you like.' I looked closely at Mary's mum and I could see that her eyes were all red and her face was blotchy as if she'd been crying.

'Is she in bed?' I said.

'No Dottie, she's not in bed,' said Mrs Pickles quietly. She picked up a dishcloth and turned her back on me and began to dry the dishes that were draining on the sink.

I walked up the stairs and tapped on Mary's door. There was no answer. I put my ear against the door but I couldn't hear anything; she wasn't playing her records.

'Mary it's me, Dottie,' I said. 'Can I come in?'

There was still no answer so I pushed down the handle and opened the door. Mary was sitting on her bed. She was very pale and she was crying, quietly. It broke my heart to see her looking so sad. I sat down next to her and put my arm around her. She didn't snuggle into me like she normally did, but sat stiff and rigid, holding a hanky to her nose.

'Has someone died?' I asked, because that was the only thing I could think of that made any sense.

'No,' she said, but she said it so softly I could barely hear her.

'Please tell me what's wrong, Mary.' I wiped a tear from her cheek with the back of my finger as gently as I could.

She shook her head and swallowed.

'I can't, Dottie.'

'Have I done something?'

'Of course not.'

It was then that I noticed the picture of Montmartre. It was screwed up on the floor. I picked it up. 'Why have you done that?' I asked, trying to smooth it out.

'Because I'm not going to need it any more,' she said.

'But why?'

'Because I won't be going there,' she shouted, 'Ever.'

'I don't understand.'

Mary sniffed and wiped her eyes with the handkerchief. She took a deep breath.

'I'm going to have a baby,' she said and she burst into tears again.

I couldn't take in what she was saying.

'Are you sure?' I said.

'Of course I'm sure. Do you think I'd make it up?'

'I didn't mean that,' I said, 'it's just that…'

'It's just that what?' said Mary, standing up and walking across to the window.

'Have you told Elton?' I said.

Mary shook her head.

'He'll have to marry you. He'll have to do the right thing,' I said.

'That's what Mum and Dad keep saying.'

'Of course they do,' I said. Mary walked back to the bed and sat down. 'Have you told them whose it is?'

'No,' she said miserably.

'They don't know about Elton?'

'No.'

I put my arm around her shoulder.

'How can I tell them, Dottie? My brothers would kill him if they knew and…'

'And what?'

'It wasn't really his fault.'

'Well, he certainly had *something* to do with it.'

Mary put her head in her hands.

'You'll have to tell them eventually,' I said.

'I know,' she said, and then she turned away from me and sobbed into her pillow as if her heart was breaking.

I sat there for a while rubbing her shoulder.

'It's not the end of the world,' I said gently. 'I know it's going to be difficult, and I know it will be a bit of a shock for Elton, but once he gets used to the idea it won't be so bad and you'll get to marry him and…'

Mary pushed my hand from her shoulder.

'It's what you always wanted,' I said. 'Elton and…'

'Don't!' said Mary. 'Don't say anything else.'

'All right but…'

She sat up and wrapped her arms around herself.

'Go away,' she said. 'Please go away. I want to be on my own.' When I didn't move, she said, '*Please*, Dottie!' Her voice was desperate. I kissed the back of her head, and left her and went back downstairs.

Mrs Pickles was sitting at the kitchen table with her hands around a cup of tea.

'Goodbye, Mrs Pickles,' I said. I wondered if I ought to say I was sorry or something.

She looked up at me. 'Did she tell you what's happened?'

I nodded. 'Yes.'

'I suppose it's that boy she's been seeing.'

I thought of Elton and his sparkling eyes and slicked-back hair. I imagined his face when he found out. It wasn't up to me to break the news. It wasn't my news to break. It was up to Mary.

'I don't know,' I said.

She stared into her tea as if it could solve all her problems. She looked very old, all of a sudden, and broken.

I walked back home in a state of shock. Me and Mary had always told each other everything, I just couldn't believe that she had kept something like this from me. Once again, I felt the familiar pangs of guilt. I'd been so wrapped up in Ralph I hadn't even noticed Mary was expecting a baby. She must have been worried sick, but she'd carried that burden all by herself. Poor Mary. She must have felt so frightened, and so lonely. And it was probably going to get worse before it got better.

I walked round a dog that was sniffing in the hedgerow. Maybe it would all turn out all right in the end, when the dust had settled. Mary wasn't the first girl to get caught like this and she wouldn't be the last. Maybe when Mary and Elton were married he'd grow up a bit and be a proper husband and father. He'd probably have to give up his dream of becoming a rock star. He wouldn't like that but he'd get used to it. It might be the making of him. I knew Mary would never have wanted it to happen this way, but it was what she had always wanted: to be married to Elton.

I reached our house and pushed open the back door. 'Tea's nearly ready,' said Mum in her normal, cheerful voice. She was stirring a pan of mince and onions on the hob and a big pan of boiled potatoes was bubbling nearby. Her sleeves were rolled up and her face was ruddy, shining with sweat. She'd made some scones earlier and they were cooling on a wire rack. They smelled delicious, but I couldn't have eaten a thing.

I would have liked to rush towards Mum and have her scoop me up and hug me like she used to when I was a child. I didn't even know how to begin to tell her about Mary. It was too much. I had to get used to the idea of her being pregnant in my own mind first before I could start talking about it with Mum.

'Did you sort it out?' she said.

'It was nothing I'd done,' I said.

'Well there you go then,' said Mum, smiling, then she looked at me more closely. 'Is it something you can talk about?' she said gently.

'Not yet, Mum.'

'I'm here if you need to.'

'I know.'

I went up to my bedroom. I sat on my bed and gave way to the tears that were threatening to choke me. At least with Rita gone I could cry in private. How could Mary be having a baby? She might have been eighteen but she still looked about twelve. How was she going to look after it? And what would everyone say? What would Elton say when he found out he had to let go of his dream and marry Mary? I couldn't imagine Elton doing anything he didn't want to do, whatever anyone said.

There was only one person I wanted to see, one person I wanted to tell. It was the person who would know best how Elton was likely to react. It was the person who would be there to support him, and me. It was Ralph.

My heart wasn't in dressing up to go out that evening. My face was pale, my eyes swollen from crying. I met Ralph in the usual place and he hugged me and asked if I was all right. I kept my face hidden by my hair and we started walking down to the café.

I was pleased to see him, to be with him, but I didn't know where to start to tell him everything that had happened in the previous two hours. I was shivering, really cold, and he put his arm around me and held me tight.

'What's wrong?' he asked. 'Something's wrong! Tell me what it is.'

'I don't know how,' I said.

He stopped, and made me look up at him.

'Whatever it is, it can't be that bad.'

'It is,' I said.

We went into the café. I sat down at one of the tables and waited for Ralph to get the coffees. I pushed a little pile of sugar around the tabletop with my fingernail.

'Do you want some records on?' he asked, putting a cup of coffee down in front of me.

'No, thanks,' I said.

He sat down beside me and put his hand gently on my arm. He leaned down to try to catch my eye but I wouldn't look at him. I still didn't know how I would find the words to tell him.

'Come on then out with it,' he said. 'It can't be that bad.'

I'd been thinking of nice ways to explain, adult ways, ways that would make it sound less shocking, but I still couldn't make myself actually say the words. I watched the steam curling from the surface of the coffee. I watched the pattern of the milk, still swirling on the top, and I listened to the buzz of the voices of the other people in the café.

Ralph spooned sugar into his coffee. He stirred it. I was on the point of telling him, I was just about to say something, when the café door swung open and Elton came in. He had the usual swagger about him, the usual half-smile. He did a mock salute when he saw us and sauntered over to our table, as if he didn't have a care in the world.

'No Mary?' he said, pulling out a chair and sitting down, 'I thought she'd be with you two.'

By the look on Elton's face it was obvious he knew nothing. Now I felt a kind of anger towards him. He should have been there for Mary when she needed him. He should be with her now. Still I didn't look up. I made the sugar on the table into a letter 'M'.

'When did you last speak to her?' I asked.

Elton shrugged. He had a cigarette packet in his hand. He turned it over on the table, flipping it with his fingers and then catching it. 'I dunno,' he said, 'a couple of days ago.'

'You need to speak to her, Elton,' I said.

He caught the packet, flipped it again. His legs were stretched out, getting in people's way. A girl climbed over his ankles to get to the door and frowned at him. He didn't notice. 'Why?' he asked.

'You just do,' I said. I could hear the urgency in my voice, a kind of panicky shrillness that wasn't usually there.

Ralph heard it too. 'What's wrong, Dottie?' he asked.

I didn't know what to do. I didn't know what to say. It was up to Mary to tell him, but now they were both looking at me waiting for an answer.

I should have said something vague. I should have hinted or implied or just said that I was worried, but before I could stop myself the words came out.

'Mary's pregnant,' I said.

'She's what?' said Elton.

'She's going to have a baby.'

There was a moment's silence. A moment of absolute shock when it felt as if time stood still and nobody breathed. All I could hear was the deafening sound of my heart pounding in my chest.

I looked up then. I looked at Elton and I held his eye. I could almost see his brain working, hearing, but not understanding; trying to make sense of what I'd just said and then immediately going on the defensive. The cigarette packet dropped onto the floor and he left it there.

'Well don't look at me,' he said angrily. 'Is she saying it's me? Is she trying to pin it on me?'

'Well, who else would she be trying to pin it on?' I asked.

'You tell me,' he said. His eyes were wide and angry, and something else, something I'd never seen in Elton before; he was frightened. He pushed back his fringe with his hand, leaned down to pick up the cigarette packet, tapped it on the table. 'It wasn't me,' he said. 'If it's true that Mary's pregnant, then it's nothing to do with me.'

I was now totally confused. My heart was beating faster and faster. I wanted to be angry with Elton, I wanted him to face up to his responsibilities and be a man and do right by Mary, my best friend, but there was something in his eyes that made me believe him. 'It *must* be you,' I said.

'Well it's not,' said Elton, 'and do you want to know why it's not? Because we've never done it.' He was leaning forward. He was tapping the cigarette packet on the table; he was pale and he was frightened but he was sincere. I noticed how thin his wrists were, and his fingers. I noticed the hairs on his wrists where they emerged from the cuffs of his jacket. I noticed that Elton was vulnerable. He was like a rabbit in the headlights.

I stared back at Elton. 'But what about when your mum went to the bingo and Mary came round to your house? I thought...'

'Mum went with a neighbour. The neighbour got a headache. They came back early. We never did it.'

Then I remembered asking Mary about it and her telling me it was too embarrassing to talk about. I thought she was talking about the sex, but perhaps she wasn't. She hadn't wanted to tell me that nothing had happened, that her great passionate love affair hadn't exactly been that.

Elton pushed back his hair again. His chest was flushed, and his neck. I felt a stab of pity for him.

'If it wasn't you... then who?'

If it wasn't Elton, then it meant that Mary had cheated on him. If it wasn't Elton, then who on earth was it? She'd never mentioned anyone else to me. She'd never breathed a word about anyone else. Elton and I stared at one another in mutual horror as we both realised that Mary must have lied to us both, if not directly, then by omission. We were so wrapped up in one another, so frantic were our thoughts, that neither of us had paid any attention to Ralph. It was only when I heard him scrape back his chair that I looked up.

He was standing beside the table, as white as a sheet.

He rubbed his forehead with the palm of his hand, then he looked at Elton. 'I'm sorry, mate,' he said. He had tears in his eyes as he turned to me. 'I'm so sorry, Dottie,' he said.

And it was then that I knew.

Dear Diary,

Don't ask. Just don't bloody ask.

Mary Pickles (trapped.)

Aged Eighteen

Chapter Twenty-Two

Mary and Ralph were married on a rainy August morning at Brighton Town Hall.

Since learning the truth about Mary and Ralph I was all over the place. I couldn't eat. I couldn't sleep. I couldn't bear to have the radio on. The only place I felt safe was in my room. I felt so empty inside and so hurt. I still couldn't believe what they had done to me. I would have trusted them both with my life, but they had ruined my life. I hadn't only lost the boy I loved; I had lost my best friend. If ever I had a problem, no matter how small, I could talk to Mary about it. We would talk it through and somehow make it all right.

Time meant nothing to me. I'd spend hours staring out of my bedroom window, not seeing anything, just going over and over what had happened. Reliving all the wonderful times I'd had with Ralph. Remembering Mary and our lives together. Tormenting myself with it all. It was like having a tape recorder in my head that just kept going round and round.

Ralph had asked me to marry him knowing what he had done with Mary. How could he have done that? I went from being so angry I wanted to kill them both and then myself to missing them so much that I could hardly breathe. I wanted so badly to hate them and there were times when I almost convinced myself that I did. But how do you stop loving someone? How do you switch off love? The truth is you can't.

I hadn't spoken to Ralph or Mary. In my heart I knew that they would be missing me as much as I was missing them. I knew they would be wanting to see me, to try and explain why they had done what they had done, but I wasn't going to let that happen. I would make them suffer as I was suffering. I wasn't going to make it easy for them.

On the morning of the wedding I was lying on my bed in a kind of stupor. I'd woken early and as soon as I woke up the tape in my head started again. I was literally driving myself mad. I couldn't bear it. I knew this was going to be the hardest day of my life. I buried my head in the pillow and cried and cried.

I heard my bedroom door open and felt someone sit down on the bed. They didn't speak, they just gently rubbed my back. It felt good, nice. I thought I hadn't needed anyone, but this human contact made me feel I was not alone. I didn't have to go through this alone.

'Mum sent this up,' said Rita eventually.

'I don't want anything,' I mumbled.

'Come on, sit up,' she said. 'You can't spend all day in bed.'

I pulled myself up the bed and Rita handed me a cup of cocoa. I sipped the hot sweet liquid and it felt nice.

'What are you going to do?' said Rita.

'There's nothing I *can* do, is there?' I snapped back.

'Well, you could have a bath for a start.'

'And that's going to solve everything, is it?'

'No, but at least you'll smell better.'

'That bad, eh?' I said.

'Worse,' said Rita. 'It's beginning to smell as if someone died in here.'

I took another sip of cocoa and smiled.

'Well that's a start,' she said.

'They're getting married today.'

'I know,' said Rita. 'Mum said.'

'I don't know how I can get through it.'

'Well, if you can't do it for yourself, do it for Mum; she's worried sick about you.'

'Okay,' I said begrudgingly, 'I'll have a bath.'

'It won't last forever, you know,' said Rita.

'What won't?'

'The pain you're feeling now. It won't last forever.'

'How do you know?'

'His name was Clive. He went to the grammar school. He was my first boyfriend and we loved each other, or at least I thought we did.'

'What happened?'

'His family emigrated to Canada. He said he would write but he never did.'

'I don't remember that.'

'Well, you wouldn't, would you? You couldn't see left or right of Mary Pickles.'

'Sorry.'

'It was a long time ago,' said Rita. 'I was only sixteen.'

I had a vague recollection of Rita wandering round the place like an Anna Karenina cut-out, but Rita was always being dramatic about something, so I don't suppose I took much notice.

The sweet cocoa and listening to Rita was beginning to have an effect.

'Perhaps you should go the wedding,' said Rita.

'Why on earth would I want to do that?'

'Because it might be better than mooching around here all day, imagining the wedding to be all hearts and flowers and happy ever afters. Because that's not how it's going to be, is it?'

'Isn't it?'

'Of course it's not. They don't love each other, do they?'

'No.'

'When Clive went to Canada I imagined him doing cartwheels over the Rocky Mountains and having the time of his life.'

'And wasn't he?'

'No, they had a rotten time. They came back after a year and by then I'd got over him.'

'Maybe you're right.'

I dragged myself out of bed. I felt light-headed and my legs felt heavy, as if I was getting over a long illness. I ran the bath and as it was filling up I cleaned my teeth. My face in the mirror above the sink was white, with dark smudges under my eyes.

I stepped into the tub. The warm water on my body felt comforting and I was beginning to feel a bit more human.

By the time I got back to the bedroom, Rita had laid some clothes out on the bed for me. I barely registered what she had chosen; I just put them on. I was dressing to go somewhere I didn't want to go, and I didn't care what I wore.

We went together, me and Rita and Mum, and we stayed out of sight until everyone had gone in. Ralph arrived first, with his parents, then Mary with hers. Only the twins out of all of Mary's brothers were there, and I thought that was sad.

We waited until the wedding before Mary's was over. That looked as if it had been quite a jolly affair, because a load of people came tumbling out onto the wet pavement. They were all laughing and talking, and the men were slapping the groom's back and the groom was wearing a Beatles suit and the bride really was blushing, wearing a flowery dress and carrying a bunch of pink roses. They kissed as they came out and they looked so happy. I wished I could go with them, wherever it was they were going.

Once we were sure they had all gone in, we slipped in the back of the room.

There weren't many people at Mary and Ralph's do. They hardly took up any space in the room; they just filled a few of the padded seats at the front. I sat between Mum and Rita. It was nice having them warm on either side of me. It made me feel safe.

Ralph and Mary stood at the front, like naughty children who were about to be punished. I was staring at Ralph's shoes that were brown and very shiny. It made me feel sad to think that he had polished his shoes so that they looked nice even though I knew in my heart that he didn't want to be there.

The registrar was a small, thin chap with a receding hairline. He was wearing a brown, badly fitting suit and his shirt looked as if it was in need of an iron. He spoke so softly it was hard to hear him and he didn't smile once. It was more like a funeral than a wedding. Once Ralph and Mary had said their vows, Rita and Mum and I left. We went outside and we stood there, huddled together.

It was still pouring with rain. People tramped past in raincoats and umbrellas, and the buses sprayed water with their wheels.

'I've got to get back to work,' said Rita.

'You took time off work?' I said.

'Well you don't have to sound so shocked,' said Rita, going all huffy. 'Contrary to popular belief, I do have some feelings, you know.'

'Sorry, and thanks for today.'

'You're welcome,' said Rita.

Mum and I watched Rita totter off in her Stead and Simpson's stiletto heels. Then Mum turned to me. 'What about you, love?' she asked. 'What do you want to do?'

'Would you mind if I just had a bit of time by myself?'

Mum put her hand on my cheek. 'No,' she said. 'Of course I wouldn't mind. Take as long as you want. When you come home I'll have something nice ready for your tea.'

She kissed me goodbye and she went one way and I started walking in the opposite direction downhill towards the sea. When I got to the promenade I couldn't find a dry bench to sit on so I leant over the railings. The tide was in, the sea looked grey and cold and it was bashing and splashing against the wall. It reminded me of when me and Mary were kids, how we used to love it when it was stormy and the sea was rough and angry-looking. We would stand at the railings and wait for the waves to hit the wall, then we'd run back screaming as the spray crashed over on to the prom. I stood looking out over the water. You couldn't even see the horizon; there was just greyness where the sky met the sea.

In my whole life, I'd never wanted to run away from home before, but now I did. Everywhere I went, I was reminded of Ralph, or Mary, or both of them, and I didn't think I could bear it. I wanted to be a million miles away. Mary and I had walked every single pavement on the estate where we both lived. We'd been in every shop in town, we'd ridden every bus route. The places I hadn't been with Mary, I'd been with Ralph. He and I had walked up to the Downs so many times while we were making plans for our future. We'd been to the beach, dawdled on the pier, walked home from the cinema together, his hand holding mine, our shoulders bumping together. Now all the friendly places, the happy places, the places I thought would become part of our history had changed their temperament. I'd imagined telling our grandchildren fond stories about the places Ralph and I had visited while we were courting. I'd imagined saying: 'This is the bench where we sat; holding Granddad's coat over our heads to protect us from the rain,' or 'This is where the seagull swooped down and stole Granddad's ice cream.' Now it hurt to remember the good times and every time a thought or a memory flashed into my mind, it was like being stung and the stings didn't get better, they just accumulated until I felt as if I was carrying a huge, lead ball of hurt around inside me. I had never been so lonely. Never.

Dear Diary,

Yesterday was the worst day of my life. I married Ralph Bennett.
I feel like I've been trapped in a box and someone has closed the
lid and locked me inside with Ralph bloody Bennett and I'm stuck in
here for the rest of my life. I don't love him and he doesn't love
me, he loves Dottie and I love Elton.

I'll never marry Elton now. We'll never go travelling together. I'll
never sleep beside him on a plane or climb the Eiffel Tower or visit
New York.

I'll never live in Paris and be an artist. Instead I'll be living in a grotty
flat on a grotty estate with Ralph Bennett and a baby. A baby!!!
I don't even like babies. I'm going to be living the life that Dottie
dreamed of living.

And worst of all I have broken my best friend's heart. I am so
sorry, Dottie, I am so very sorry. I don't think I can do this without
you.

Bye bye diary.

Mary Bennett (prize idiot)

Aged eighteen.

Chapter Twenty-Three

Mary's life more or less mirrored mine and I couldn't avoid seeing her pretty much every day. We were both still working at Woolworths and, according to Mum, Mary was still living at home

All this meant that we still had to travel the same routes, we still had to see one another at work and, sometimes, when I was walking along the pavement towards home, I'd look up and there would be Mary coming the other way.

It was awful. It was really awful.

When I saw her I was so full of anger that part of me wanted to go up to her and shake her and hit her and hurt her to give her a tiny taste of how much she had hurt me. I hated her sometimes, I really did. She'd taken something she knew I loved, not because she wanted it, but just because she could. She'd taken away my future. I should have been the one carrying Ralph's baby, I should've been the one planning a future with him. He should have been mine!

But there was another part of me that, even while I was hating her, still loved Mary. She had been my best friend for most of my life. She knew me better than anyone else in the world and I missed her so badly.

When we saw one another in the street, either she would turn around and walk away from me, or she'd pretend to drop something, or turn her face away, anything to avoid having to look at me or talk to me or so much as catch my eye. I was the same. If I saw her before she saw me, I'd go the other way. I didn't want to have to speak to her. I didn't want to look at the lump that was forming beneath her clothes.

It was more difficult at work. On the days when we were busy it wasn't so bad, but on quiet days it was hard to avoid one another completely. Once, when I was in the stockroom looking for a box of pocket mirrors to restock the shelves, I saw Mary come in. She looked around but couldn't see me because I was crouching down. She came in and shut the door and I heard her sit down and sigh, and then she started to cry, quietly. I held my breath and didn't move and I listened to her sobbing and I felt as if my heart was breaking. And at the same time I wanted to go over to her and slap her face and say: 'Shut up! It's your own fault you're in this mess!' I squeezed my hands tightly together and dug the nails of one into the fleshy part of the other to try to stop myself from screaming at her. The other part of me wanted to put my arms around her and promise her that everything was going to be all right.

After a few minutes the door opened from the outside and Sally called out 'Mary, are you all right?' and Mary made a sort of hiccupping noise and replied 'Yes, fine, I'm just coming.'

I counted to forty after she'd left before I went back into the shop with the box in my arms. I walked straight past her and did not look at her puffy face or the blotchiness around her eyes. How could I say anything to Mary when I couldn't sort my own feelings out, when I couldn't tell the difference between love and hate, when I was so mired in grief for the future that Mary had stolen from me?

One Saturday lunchtime when I had nothing to do – I never had anything to do any more – I walked down to the café, and I sat in a seat by the window and watched the drops of rain chasing each other down the windowpane.

'Is anyone sitting here?'

I turned and there was Elton. He looked tired and awkward, but I couldn't be bothered to ask if he was okay. So I just shrugged. He pulled out the chair and sat down. He hunched over the table and made a big performance of stirring sugar into his coffee then he pushed a plate towards me and said: 'Do you fancy a chip?'

I gave him a little smile and took one and dipped it into the puddle of ketchup on the side of his plate.

'Ralph's desperate about you,' Elton said. I didn't answer. I ate another chip. Water was dripping off Elton's leather jacket on to the top of the table and he smelled very strongly of aftershave. 'He's eaten up with guilt.'

'That's hardly my problem, is it?'

'No,' Elton said. 'It's not. But I thought you ought to know.'

'I don't care.'

I ate another chip.

'He was out of his mind at that party, you know.'

I didn't respond.

'I've never seen him so drunk. He didn't know what he was doing.'

'He's an idiot, then.'

'Yeah, but...' Elton sighed. He took a packet of cigarettes out of his pocket and began to play with it, turning it over and over between his fingers. 'You ought to talk to him, Dottie.'

'No,' I said.

'Just give him a chance to explain.'

'No.'

'I think... I think I am partly to blame for what happened,' he said, taking another chip and blowing on it. 'Mary wanted to know what I was doing all the time. I told her I didn't want to go steady but she kept acting as if we *were*. I was fed up with it. I wanted to have fun at my party, and Gemma's fun.'

'Is that the girl you came into the café with?'

'I shouldn't have done that, I suppose.'

'You hurt her,' I said, 'you kept hurting her.'

'Yeah, well, I didn't mean to, so it doesn't count.'

'Are you going out with Gemma?' I said, glaring at him.

Elton shook his head. 'Look, Dottie,' he said, 'I'm not going out with anyone. I don't want to do the going steady thing, that's what Mary didn't understand. I mean I told her often enough, but she saw you and Ralph and wanted the same, but I'm not Ralph. I want to make a go of my music. Mary was fun to be with, at least she used to be, but I don't want to be tied down to anyone. Is that such a crime?'

The café had started to fill up. Elton and I sat miserably, sharing the bowl of chips. I was aware of sounds around us. The hiss of the frothy coffee machine and the ding of the cash register. Someone had put a Billy Fury record on the jukebox, all familiar sounds from a million years ago when we were happy.

'He's working at the cake factory,' said Elton suddenly. 'He had to give up his apprenticeship. They need the money.'

I couldn't take any more. I pushed back my chair and stood up. I fastened the buttons on my coat with shaking fingers.

'At least give me a message to give him,' Elton said.

I picked up my bag and hooked the strap over my shoulder.

'You can tell him I hope it was worth it,' I said. And then I walked out of the café.

* * *

Mary had grown so big that she couldn't do her job properly and she left Woolworths at the beginning of October. I thought this would make things better, but in a weird way it made things much worse. However much I had made it my daily business to ignore her, I had known she was there. I could see she was all right. Seeing her every day had been a pain, but it was a pain I'd grown used to, like a sore tooth that you can't help poking with your tongue. Not seeing her and not knowing how she was doing was like losing her all over again.

It was Wednesday and my day off. I lay in bed with no plans. It was windy outside and the rain was batting the windowpane. If Mary had been around we would have gone down to the seafront. We loved watching the sea when it was wild and crazy. We didn't mind when it sprayed over the promenade soaking us, it was something we had never grown out of. But there was no Mary to share things with any more; I couldn't even remember the last time I had been to the record shop and bought a record. I did try once, but hadn't even got as far as the counter before walking back out.

I decided to go for a walk anyway, because I knew that I would drive myself mad if I stayed in again. I got washed and dressed. I opened the drawer to get my scarf and there were the letters, Ralph's letters to me, a great bundle of them, all of them unopened. They had come regularly, every week, for the past three months. I didn't want to read what he had written. There was nothing he could say that would justify what he had done or make me feel any better about it. I went downstairs, picked up my coat from the hook in the hallway and went into the kitchen.

'You're never going out in this, are you?' said Mum, reaching for the kettle and filling it with water.

'Thought I'd blow a few cobwebs away,' I said, smiling at her.

Just then Aunty Brenda came bustling through the back door, she was drenched through and her hair was sticking to her forehead. She took off her coat, leaving a puddle of water on the kitchen floor, and then she proceeded to rub her glasses on the sleeve of her jumper.

'They ought to invent windscreen wipers for people who wear glasses,' she said. 'I nearly walked into a lamp post just now. You're never going out in this, Dottie?'

'She needs to blow away a few cobwebs,' said Mum.

'She'll blow away more than that,' said Aunty Brenda. 'Is that kettle boiled?'

'Nearly there,' said Mum.

Aunty Brenda hung her coat up on the back of the door. 'Our Carol's still in bed,' she said. 'Reckons she's got the flu. Funny how she only gets the flu when it's raining.'

'I'm off then,' I said.

'Aren't you going to have some breakfast?' said Mum.

'I'll get something when I'm out.'

'You should eat something,' said Aunty Brenda, shovelling two heaped teaspoons of sugar into her tea. 'There's nothing of you. You used to be quite podgy, but you're turning to skin and bone. It's not good for the system, losing all that weight, it'll play havoc with your bowels, you mark my words.'

'I think her bowels will be all right, Brenda,' said Mum, winking at me.

The rain stung my face as I walked through the estate and the wind took my breath away. I cut across the park. I wished I'd worn boots, as my shoes were sinking into the soggy grass. The duck pond was wild and splashy, water flopped up onto the path that ran around the edge and the wind moaned through the trees.

I walked on through Kemp Town. There weren't many people around, certainly no one who was just walking for the hell of it like I was. Most of them were scurrying between shops or sheltering in doorways. I walked on down to the seafront and leant on the railings. The sea was strangely calm, not as wild as I had expected. In fact it looked as if it was biding its time and at any minute it would do something stupendous. The seafront was almost deserted, there was just a lone figure huddled up on a bench in the shelter. It was Mary.

I didn't even think about it. I walked across and sat down beside her. Tears started running down her cheeks, mirroring the rain running down the sides of the shelter. We sat, side by side, staring out over the sea. And then very softly, so softly I could barely hear her, she said, 'Dottie.' I closed my eyes and said, 'Mary,' again she said, 'Dottie.'

I reached across and held her hand and whispered, 'Mary.' She glanced at me and then her fingers closed gently around mine. It felt like a coming home. I could feel the bitterness that had rendered me numb all these months melting away. I didn't know what the future held, or how I was going to deal with what had happened, but in that moment, on that bench, I didn't care. We had found each other again. Me and my friend Mary Pickles.

Dear Diary,

My life has gone completely down the drain but Dottie has forgiven me (again) so maybe now I will find a way to cope, because Dottie will be there with me.

I don't deserve her friendship but I will try to make it up to her.

I will. I really will.

Mary bloody Bennett (best friend of Dottie Perks)

Aged eighteen.

Chapter Twenty-Four

It was late November and Mary and Ralph were still living separately and neither of them seemed in any hurry to change the arrangement. This made things easier for me because it meant I could go round to Mary's, just as I always had done. If it wasn't for Mary's huge stomach, things were pretty much as they always had been. Me and Mary would go up to her room and sit on the bed and I'd tell her about work and she'd tell me about her brothers and the snooty looks she got from some of the women on the estate and we'd laugh almost like we used to laugh in the old days, except that it wasn't the old days, was it?

I think Mary would have been quite happy to have the baby and carry on living in her room. Her dad, on the other hand, had had enough of the situation.

'Me and your mum might not have had much money,' he'd said, 'but at least we lived under the same roof. Get yourself down the council and tell them you're having a baby and you need somewhere to bring it home to.'

On my next afternoon off me and Mary headed for the council offices. It was a grim-looking building, all concrete and bars over the windows like they were trying to keep people out. We went through a big door into a reception area. Wet footprints were smeared all over the lino and the place had an institutional kind of smell, like a school or a hospital.

'Where are we supposed to go?' Mary asked in a very quiet voice.

'I'm not sure, let's ask *her*,' I said, nodding towards a girl sitting behind a glass partition filing her nails.

'Excuse me,' Mary began tentatively.

'Repairs, complaints, housing or rents?' said the girl, without looking up. She turned her hand over and blew on the ends of her fingers.

'Pardon?'

The girl gave a long-suffering sigh. 'Repairs, complaints, housing or rents?'

'I'm not sure,' said Mary.

'Well, I can't direct you to the relevant office if I don't know what you want, can I?'

'She wants somewhere to live,' I said.

'Housing,' said the girl. 'Third door down on the left.'

'Blimey, who rattled her cage?' said Mary.

We found the right door and went in and immediately wished we hadn't. The room was full of kids and they all seemed to be screaming or crying or running round. Big metal radiators blasted out heat beneath the tall windows. It was hot as anything and there was a steaming smell of nappies. Long wooden benches were filled with people who looked as if they had been there for weeks and lines of people queued in front of a glass partition that ran the length of the room.

'I want to go,' said Mary.

'We're here now,' I said. 'So we might as well stay.'

I couldn't imagine that it would be any less hectic at any other time and I really didn't want to come back if we didn't have to. We chose the shortest queue and stood behind a very fat woman who was holding a baby who was in desperate need of a hankie. She also had a toddler hanging off her skirt. I tried to keep Mary's attention off the baby because it was so ugly and snotty that I thought it would put her off the idea of being a mother even more. The baby yawned and rubbed its face with its fists smearing snot everywhere. It was even making me feel a bit sick. Every so often the person at the front of the queue would move away and we'd all shuffle forward a few paces. Two chubby little girls who were chasing one another kept bumping into us. I told Mary to sit down and that I'd save her place, but she didn't want to leave me. I didn't blame her. I thought we were the only two normal people in the place. Then I thought we were two naïve young girls, and one of us was pregnant and married to someone she didn't love and the other was heart-broken. There wasn't much that was normal about us either.

Eventually the woman in front of us reached the front of the queue and straight away she started shouting at the boy sitting behind the counter. He only looked about the same age as Mary and me. He had spots around his chin and soft downy hair under his ears. He fidgeted with his collar and listened patiently to the woman.

'If you don't give us a bigger house I'm going to the papers, we'll see what they've got to say about it,' she said, jabbing her finger at the boy's face.

He looked down at the packet of papers in front of him on the desk.

'Madam,' he said politely, 'you already have a four-bedroomed house, we do not have any houses with more than four bedrooms on our stock.'

'I might have a four-bedroomed house, sonny,' she said, 'but I've got eight bleeding kids and my old man is havin' to forgo his conjugal rights because our Gloria's havin' to share our bedroom. I ask you: is that right and proper?'

She said this so loudly that the rest of the room suddenly went quiet. There were murmured mumblings of support from the benches.

'I'm sorry about your predicament,' said the boy. 'But…'

'Oh, are you now? Well, you don't look sorry. How would you like it if you weren't getting your oats cos you had our Gloria in the room?'

'This is better than the pictures,' Mary whispered.

'Shush,' I said.

'You are coming between a man and his rights!' the woman went on.

The boy sighed deeply and shuffled his papers. 'Madam, I can only reiterate what I have already said and that is that we cannot offer you alternative accommodation that is any larger than the house you already occupy. There aren't any.'

The woman suddenly turned round. 'Get off me bleedin' skirt!' she shouted at the toddler. 'It'll be round me arse in a minute!'

Then she put her face closer to the window until she was nearly touching the glass. 'So what do you suggest I do then, clever dick?' she asked the boy.

'Get rid of four of the kids?' Mary suggested.

'Shush!'

'The only advice I can offer,' said the boy, 'is that you put your concerns in writing and send it to our head office.'

The woman snorted. 'I've a good mind to bring our Gloria down here and let *you* find her somewhere to sleep.'

'If you did that, madam, we would have to inform the NSP-CC.'

'You can inform who you bloody well like, you spotty little runt. Who do you think you are, anyway? I've got knickers older than you.'

Beside me, Mary was shaking with laughter.

The boy went visibly pale at the thought of the woman's knickers. 'I'm sure you have, madam,' he said with the utmost politeness. 'Now, if you have finished, there are other people who are waiting to be seen.'

'Well, you haven't seen the last of me!' said the woman, hitching the baby further up her ample breast till it was nearly hanging over her shoulder. Dragging the toddler behind her, she stalked out of the room. The baby watched us over her shoulder as she made her exit. It had the saddest, bluest eyes I had ever seen.

The boy was by now sweating profusely. He took a drink of water from the glass at his side, and one of his colleagues, a short man with a moustache, came over and patted his shoulder and said something in his ear. It was probably some sort of pep talk. I bet they all dreaded getting that woman at their window.

Mary and I stepped forward and both gave him our sweetest smiles and he relaxed a little.

'Can I help you?' he croaked.

'I need a council house,' said Mary. Then she added: 'Please.'

'Right. How many children?'

'Sorry?'

'How many children do you have?'

'I haven't got any,' said Mary, holding up her hands to show they were empty.

'Dependants?'

'Sorry?' said Mary again.

'Do you have anyone who depends on you for accommodation?'

'I don't think so,' said Mary 'Do I, Dottie?'

'Only the baby,' I said.

'So you *do* have a child?' said the boy. 'How old?'

'Eight months.'

'You have an eight-month-old baby?'

'Well, I haven't actually got it yet.'

The boy put his pen down. He looked very close to tears.

'I don't want to appear rude,' he said, 'but to say that you are confusing me is an understatement.'

'Sorry,' said Mary. She gave him an apologetic smile.

'Let's start again, shall we?' said the boy.

'Do we have to?'

'We have to,' said the boy. 'Now think carefully before you answer. Do you have any children?'

'No.'

'So you do *not* have an eight-month-old baby?'

'Of course I have,' said Mary. 'Otherwise I wouldn't need a council house, would I?'

The boy turned to me with a look of deep despair on his face.

'She's pregnant,' I said. 'Eight months.'

'Bingo!!!' he said.

'So I need to get a council house to bring the baby home to.'

'Are you a single mother?'

'No, I'm not,' said Mary, looking offended.

'They were done at the Town Hall,' I said.

'Okay, I just need a few details. Firstly can I have your name?'

'Mary Pickles,' said Mary. The boy started to write it down.

'Bennett,' I said.

'What?' said Mary.

'Your name's Mary Bennett.'

Mary gave a sigh. 'Bennett,' she said.

'Are you sure?'

'Of course I'm sure.'

'Father's name?'

'George.'

'It's Ralph, Mary,' I said.

'He asked my father's name.'

'I think he means the baby's father.'

'That's right. So it's not George?' The boy's pen hovered over the page as if he was reluctant to write anything down.

'No, it's Ralph.'

'It *is* Ralph,' I said.

'So can I have a council house then?' said Mary.

'I'm afraid not,' said the boy.

'Why not?'

'Because you don't qualify for a house, you don't have enough points.'

'What sort of points?' I said.

'You get points per child, points for dependants, points for a disability…'

'So she can't have a house then?' I said.

'She can't have a house, no, but she does qualify for a flat,' he said. He was quite good-looking when he smiled. We both smiled back at him.

'A flat would be nice, Mary,' I said.

'We'll take it,' said Mary.

'Oh, that it was as simple as that,' said the boy. 'I'm afraid you have to go on a waiting list and when a flat comes available we will inform you.'

'How long's that going to take?'

'How long have you got?' said a lone voice from the benches.

'And you will need to fill in a form. Here you are,' he said, giving Mary a wodge of papers. 'Just pop it into this office when you're ready and we will go from there.'

'Okay,' said Mary. 'Thanks very much.'

We were just about to walk away from the counter when Mary, who was born with a faulty valve between her brain and her mouth, said, 'Doesn't it do your head in, working here?'

'Every day,' he said mournfully, 'every day.'

Dear Diary,

Me and Ralph Bennett are moving into a flat together

Can you believe that? Me and Ralph Bennett

how embarrassing is that?

I hate my life.

Mary Bloody Bennett

Aged Eighteen going on ninety

Chapter Twenty-Five

Mary heard from the council after only two weeks, probably because she was so far gone with the baby. She and Ralph had been offered a flat on the other side of the estate.

It was my day off and I said I would go with Mary to look at it.

When I got downstairs Clark was tucking into eggs and bacon. Rita was sitting at the kitchen table with a tea cup between her hands and she was moaning – again. It was all she seemed to do lately. I thought maybe marriage would improve her, but if anything she was worse. When she wasn't moaning, she was bragging about her new semi-detached house and her new fridge and all the other new things which she and Nigel had bought. It was a nice house on an estate that was so new they were still building it. The house had a big picture window at the front, and central heating, all the mod cons in fact. As Rita kept saying, there were a lot of things that still needed doing, like putting turf in the garden and buying a twin tub, but Nigel spent most of his free time decorating and there was always something new to see. Once a month we all had to traipse round for Sunday tea to admire it all.

'I'm not going there again,' Dad said after our last disastrous visit. 'Half a tomato, that's what was on my plate. Half a bloody tomato. Who gives anyone half a tomato?'

'Okay, Nelson,' said Mum. 'We get the point, our Rita gave you half a tomato. Get over it.'

'And one measly slice of ham. I call that mean.'

'I thought the Swiss roll was nice, though,' I said.

'What there was of it. And I had to take me bloody shoes off. Whoever heard of that? If you ask me...'

'And no one is,' said Mum.

'Our Rita's getting too big for her boots.'

'She'd just had that lovely shagpile fitted, she didn't want your great clod-hopping boots walking all over it.'

'Don't you start getting any ideas, Maureen,' said Dad.

'You're just fed up cos you had to smoke out in the garden,' I said.

'Well, I'm not going again,' said Dad, 'and that's that.'

'You *are* going again, Nelson Perks, if I have to drag you round. She's your daughter.'

And now the said daughter was sitting at our kitchen table moaning, when she could have stayed at home and done it at her own house, surrounded by all her nice things.

Mum lifted the biscuit tin off the shelf, pulled up a chair and sat down next to her. She took the lid off the tin and offered it to Rita, who took out a custard cream, put it down in her saucer and stared at it miserably.

'What's the matter, love?' said Mum. 'You don't look very happy. Is everything all right with you and Nigel?'

'Of course everything's all right with me and Nigel. Whatever do you mean?'

'Well, you know…'

'No, I don't actually.'

'In the bedroom…' Mum whispered under her breath.

'That's my business,' said Rita. Then she burst into tears.

'Come on, love, whatever it is, you can tell your mum.'

Rita sniffed. 'I think there's something wrong with me.'

'That's got to be the understatement of the year,' said Clark, smothering his egg in Ketchup sauce.

'We don't seem to be able to make a baby,' she sobbed. She wiped her eyes with her fingers and mascara smudged on her cheek.

'Clark, upstairs,' said Mum.

'But I'm eating my breakfast.'

'Take it with you.'

'Why?'

'Because we are talking women's problems.'

'How come no one talks about men's problems?'

'Men don't have problems. The last time your father had a problem was when he dropped his fag down the toilet.'

Once Clark had gone, Mum put her arm around Rita's shoulder.

'Things like that take time, my love. It doesn't always happen right away, even if you want it to.'

'But why not?' said Rita. 'Betty Green at work got pregnant on her honeymoon and Eleanor McDonald is expecting twins and she got married after me.'

'It'll happen,' said Mum, 'when the time's right.'

'Even Mary bloody Pickles is pregnant and I bet she doesn't even want it. It's not fair.'

'Mary was unlucky,' said Mum gently.

'Unlucky?' screamed Rita. 'Mary Pickles is a tart.'

'She *is not!*' I said.

'Oh shut up, you,' said Rita.

'It's going to be hard for Mary,' said Mum.

'Oh, poor Mary,' said Rita sarcastically. 'My heart bleeds for her.'

'Just because Mary doesn't live in a semi-detached house with a shagpile carpet and a toaster doesn't mean she hasn't got as much right to have a baby as you,' I said.

'Babies need a proper home,' said Rita. 'I bet that Mary Pickles doesn't even have anywhere to live yet.'

'Well, that's where you're wrong!' I shot back. 'Because they've just been offered a council flat.'

'Why am I not surprised,' said Rita, screwing up her face as if she had a bad smell under her nose.

'Actually, I'm going round to Mary's now, and we're going to have a look at it. And you can stop calling her Mary Pickles. Her name is Mary Bennett. *Mrs* Mary Bennett.'

'Why are you looking at flats with her anyway, after what she did to you?'

'It's called forgiveness, Rita,' said Mum.

I smiled gratefully at her, grabbed my coat and went out of the back door.

It was still freezing cold outside. There was slush on the pavements that made my feet wet and put me in a worse mood.

Bloody Rita, I thought, walking up the twitten. She was turning into a right snob. What gave her the right to look down on Mary? I'd hoped things would have got a bit better between Rita and I once she moved out, but we still managed to wind each other up. I guess that's just the way we were. Then I remembered how she was there for me when Ralph and Mary got married and something inside told me that however much we argued, she would always be there for me.

Was Rita right? Had I forgiven Mary too quickly? Why was I going to look at the home that her and Ralph were going to be sharing? The truth was that I couldn't understand it myself. I knew that people thought I was being brave but I wasn't, It would have been braver to have walked away from them both, but the thought of not having them in my life was something I couldn't even think about. Not brave at all. Part of me knew that my behaviour was odd, but right now it was the only thing I could do. I just hoped to God that Mary was right when she said that Ralph wouldn't be at the flat, because I'm not sure what I would do if he was.

Mary's front door was on the latch when I got there, so I tapped on it and walked in. The cat rushed in after me in a rush of ginger hair.

'Hello-o!' I called.

'Is that you, Dottie?' called Mary's mum. 'I'm in the kitchen, come through. Mary will be down in a minute.'

The kitchen was warm and cosy. It smelled of baking. Mrs Pickles was bent over, putting a tray of cakes into the oven. She closed the door, stood up and rubbed the hollow of her back.

She looked at me and smiled. 'I just want to say thank you, Dottie. What you have been able to do has made a huge difference to Mary. No one would have blamed you if you had turned your back on her, but you haven't and I know it can't have been easy.'

'Not easy, no.' I said. 'But I missed her, you see.'

She wet a cloth under the tap at the sink and wiped down the counter, which was covered in flour.

'Anyway,' I said, 'it's kind of exciting that she's getting a flat. I'm looking forward to seeing it.'

'And it's a nice one, according to the letter, only one previous tenant,' Mrs Pickles said. 'It's got a bathroom and everything. When we started out, there were no luxuries like that.'

'Mary's worried about furniture,' I said.

'Well, she doesn't have to be. The boys are all working now and they said they'd help out.'

'That's nice of them.'

'They're good lads.' Mrs Pickles washed her hands at the sink. I heard Mary's footsteps on the stairs and then she pushed open the kitchen door.

'Everything's too tight on me,' she said, pulling at the waistband of her skirt. 'I feel like a sack of potatoes.'

I could see what she meant. Even the flowery maternity top she was wearing was tight on her. It was odd to see Mary in clothes that were too small for her, normally she had the opposite problem. Mary sighed and sat down. She put her head in her hands. 'I hate all this,' she said.

'But aren't you excited about the apartment?' I said.

'Apartment?' said Mrs Pickles, laughing.

'That's what they call them in America.'

'Dottie, this is Brighton,' said Mary, 'not America, and it's going to be a grotty flat on a grotty estate.'

Mrs Pickles rolled her eyes. I guess she'd heard this complaint a thousand times before.

'But you can make it nice,' I said encouragingly. 'Your mum told me your brothers are going to help out.'

'I know,' said Mary. She smiled. 'Sorry. You must think I'm an ungrateful cow.'

'Nobody thinks anything of the kind,' said her mum. 'I thought you two were going to go and have a look at the flat. You might be pleasantly surprised.'

'And pigs might fly.'

Mary stood up and reached for her coat. 'Come on Dottie, let's go and see this apartment,' she said.

We walked along the road, arm in arm, with me taking special care that Mary didn't slip. Occasionally a car went past and black spray came up from its wheels.

We had to walk past our old primary school, so we stopped and looked through the bars on the big metal gate that led into the playground. The boys were haring around playing British Bulldog in the middle and the girls stood in little huddles round the edges playing clapping games or skipping. Their gloves hung out of their coat sleeves. Their socks were round their ankles and their legs were all red with the cold. A fierce-looking woman with a whistle on a ribbon round her neck was supervising.

'Seems like a long time ago,' said Mary. There was a wistful tone in her voice. 'I wish we were still there.'

'Really?'

'Everything seemed a lot easier.'

'I suppose it did,' I said, fishing around in my bag for my gloves. 'But I prefer having a job and earning my own money. I thought you did too.'

Mary went quiet, then said: 'At school, I got to see Elton every day.'

I should have realised that stopping at the school would have brought back memories of Elton. I slipped my arm through hers and said: 'Let's go and see this apartment, eh?'

'Yes, let's!' she said, giving me a watery little smile. We turned away from the school and walked on.

The block of flats was called Westland Court. There was a large green in front of it with children's swings and a slide.

'It doesn't look too bad,' I said, looking up at the building. Some of the windows had white net curtains strung across. Others were decorated with window boxes that would be full of flowers in the summer and some flats even had little balconies. 'It's okay, isn't it?' I repeated. 'In fact, it's quite nice.'

'The jury's out till I see what it's like inside,' said Mary. 'What number is it?'

Mary took an envelope out of her bag. There was a key inside that was hanging from a tag that said number nineteen on it. Along the front of the building was a series of arches but we couldn't see any numbers. We walked through the nearest arch and found ourselves in a kind of quadrangle. It was full of clothes lines that were strung between concrete posts. Nappies were pegged to the strings of some of them; I couldn't imagine that they'd ever get dry in that weather, but I don't suppose there was anywhere else for people to put them. The quadrangle was surrounded on all four sides by the flats. Just then a tall girl walked into the square pushing a pram.

'Blimey,' said Mary. 'It's Beverly Johnson from school, isn't it?'

'Mary Pickles!' said Beverly. 'And Dottie. What are you doing here?'

'We've come to look at a flat,' said Mary. She peered into the pram. 'Is that yours?'

'No it flippin' isn't!' said Beverly. 'It's my sister's.'

Mary stared at the baby and the baby stared back. I couldn't tell what either of them was thinking, but after a few moments the baby turned its face away and made some whimpery noises like it was about to cry. Mary wrinkled her nose. She didn't look particularly impressed.

'We're looking for number nineteen,' I said.

Beverly jiggled the handle of the pram to keep the baby quiet. 'It can't be far away. Do you know what block it's in?'

'Maybe it says on the envelope.'

Mary fished the envelope out of her bag again.

'Oh yes, it does. It's in Nightingale block.'

'All the blocks are named after birds,' said Beverly. 'My sister's in Swallow.'

'Could have been worse, I suppose,' said Mary. 'It could have been blue tit.'

It was nice to see that Mary hadn't lost her sense of humour. Beverly showed us where the block was and we went in. All the doors were the same colour green and they were all in lines. Mary turned right and I turned left.

'It's not down here,' I shouted.

'Nor here,' Mary shouted back. 'Let's try the next floor.'

There was a set of concrete steps leading to the next landing and that was where we found number nineteen. It had a green door just like all the others, and next to the door was a window, but you couldn't see through it because the curtains were drawn. A little boy on a tricycle pedalled up and down the landing, staring at us. I smiled at him and he stuck his tongue out.

'Go on, then,' I said, nudging Mary in the back. 'Open the door, or are you waiting for me to carry you over the threshold?'

We were giggling and fiddling with the lock when the door opened.

I stepped back and looked up and for a moment I thought my heart would stop beating.

I found myself staring up into Ralph's beautiful, sorry green eyes.

Chapter Twenty-Six

Ralph was as shocked to see me as I was to see him. He stood there with his mouth open, but I wasn't looking at his mouth, I was staring at the bunch of pink carnations in his outstretched hand. All I could think was: Ralph has bought flowers for Mary! He thought he was opening the door to Mary. The thought hurt me. Really, I felt as if somebody had punched me in the stomach.

He had never bought flowers for me. Not once.

Ralph followed my eyes down to the flowers and then looked back up at me again. He had gone a little pale. His hand dropped to his side. He looked as if he'd like to hide them behind his back, or put them straight in the bin or something. He held my eyes and said quietly 'It was my mum's idea. She thought they would cheer Mary up.'

'Oh great, thanks,' said Mary, taking my hand and pulling me past him into the flat.

I felt sick and dizzy, my chest was tightening up, I wanted to run, I just wanted to get away but Mary was still gripping hold of my hand. Why had I come here? What on earth was I thinking?

We went along a very small, narrow corridor into quite a nice, big room at the other end. It smelled a little musty, but not too bad. There was a picture window which made the room feel really airy. There were floral patterned curtains hanging at the window and the nets were already up. The carpet was brown and there was also a very old-looking sofa, a sunburst clock on the wall, and an empty cigarette packet on the hatch that led through to the kitchen.

'I'm not sitting on that old thing.' said Mary looking at the sofa.

'It'll do until we get something better, won't it?' said Ralph.

'No it won't,' said Mary, making a face. 'You'll have to phone the council and get them to collect it.'

'Okay,' said Ralph.

This exchange shocked me. I hadn't expected Ralph and Mary to behave like a couple, but that was exactly what they *were* doing. Something felt very wrong, as if I was in a play and everyone else was reading off a different script. This wasn't how it was meant to be.

'Well, it's better than I thought it would be,' said Mary, looking around. 'And that's something.'

I could feel, rather than see, Ralph standing behind us. My neck was burning with embarrassment and shame. He was still holding the flowers.

'I'll see if I can find something to put these in,' he said. 'Before they die.' I heard him leave the room and I let out my breath, which I hadn't realised I'd been holding.

We heard the sounds of cupboard doors opening and closing in the room next door.

'I'm sorry,' Mary said. 'He told me he couldn't come till after work. Pretend he isn't here.'

But when I looked over, I could see his black jacket lying on the back of the settee. I had rested my cheek against the shoulder of that jacket. I knew what it smelt like, I knew what it felt like, sort of rough and masculine. Sometimes I missed feeling the weight of Ralph's arm around me so much that it was like an actual pain.

I could manage if I didn't see him. I could put him out of my mind, but I couldn't do that when he was just a few feet away from me. Being so close to him hurt, it really hurt.

Ralph came back into the room. He kept his eyes down. He looked handsome. He looked more grown up. The flowers were in a blue mug.

'Put them on the window ledge,' Mary said. He did.

'Listen,' he said, 'I'm going to go. I'll let you two have a good look round on your own. You can talk about furniture and where the…'

He had been going to say 'where the baby's going to sleep.' I could tell by his face.

'I'll see you later,' he said and he picked up his jacket.

My first thought was one of immense relief. Thank goodness he was going! But then I realised that it wouldn't be right.

Ralph and Mary were husband and wife. They were having a baby. This was to be their new home. He had left work early to meet her here. He had bought her flowers. This was their life; they had to start living it.

'No,' I said. 'No, you stay, Ralph. I'll go.'

'Dottie…' they both said together.

I shook my head and did my best to smile. Both their faces were anxious. They were worried about me, and my feelings. I loved them both, I really did, but this was awful. I had to get away.

'I've got things to do,' I said. 'I'm going to meet someone.'

'Who?'

'Sally,' I said. I looked at the clock on the wall. 'I'll see myself out.'

'Don't go!' Mary said, and I knew she was worried about herself as well as me. She didn't want to be left in the flat with Ralph, on her own. She didn't want to have to discuss the things they needed to talk about. She didn't want to make plans with Ralph.

She would have to manage though. She would have to get used to him. That was one thing I couldn't do for her.

I waved my fingers at them, and left the room, closing the door behind me.

I noticed the tiny little kitchen next to the living room. The other doors were open off the corridor too. There was a bathroom on one side, and an empty room which was the bedroom on the other. I knew it was the bedroom because there was a big dusty oblong on the carpet where a bed had used to stand. A double bed.

I opened the outer door and went back outside into the cold air.

As I walked away from the flats, I knew they were watching me. I imagined them standing side by side watching me go, and I wondered if they had found anything to say to one another yet, or whether they were holding hands. I listened to the sound of the soles of my feet on the wet pavement and I walked faster and faster and as soon as I was round the corner, out of sight, I started to run. I ran through the green, past the swings, I ran and I ran and the wind was in my face and my lungs were bursting. I knew I should stop but I kept on running.

Chapter Twenty-Seven

By the time I got to the park I could hardly breathe, so I sat down on the first bench I came to. I knew I shouldn't have run like that. I put my hand in my pocket and took out my puffer, thank God I had it with me. I breathed the medicine down into my lungs and waited for it to work. I wanted to cry so badly it hurt, but there were people everywhere. How could life be going on as normal when all I wanted to do was die? I closed my eyes and swallowed on the lump in my throat that was threatening to choke me.

The only way I had been able to get through the pain of Mary and Ralph's marriage was because I knew that they didn't love each other. Somehow in my head that had made it okay. I don't know what I had expected at the flat, but it wasn't what I had just witnessed, but what the heck else could I have expected? That they would live in separate rooms and not speak to each other forever? What I had just seen at the flat were the beginnings of a life together. I had been the biggest fool. Mary and Ralph were married. They were going to have a baby. Ralph wasn't mine any more and he never would be.

I looked up and saw a figure running across the park. It was Ralph. I started to get up but something made me stay.

'I hoped you'd be here,' he said. He was panting and trying to catch his breath.

'I must be getting old.'

He sat down beside me, neither of us knew how to start talking, but talking was what we had to do. This was the first time that we had been together since everything had happened.

He was running his hands through his hair. 'Sorry isn't enough, is it?'

'How could you have done that to me, Ralph? How could you?'

'I could try to make excuses.' He shook his head as if he was trying to clear it. 'But nothing can excuse what I did to you. We were both drunk…'

There was anger boiling up inside me. 'So drunk that you both forgot about me? Would you ever have confessed what you'd done if you hadn't been found out? You had plenty of time to tell me, months, but you didn't say a word. In fact, you had the nerve to ask me to marry you.'

'I just knew that I wanted to marry you. I don't know what I was thinking.'

'I do. You had your bit of fun and you hoped that I would never find out about it. You both made a fool of me. The two people I am closest to in the whole world made a fool of me. Maybe you laughed about it together, maybe you did it again.'

'No we didn't, we didn't. We were idiots, we felt ashamed and wretched, we could barely look at each other. We never did it again, I promise you we never. And we didn't laugh behind your back, Dottie. I know what you must think about me now but we never meant to make a fool of you. We were the fools, not you. Never you.'

I looked into Ralph's eyes and I knew that he was telling me the truth. He wasn't a bad person. He just wasn't the person I thought he was. I wanted to hate him, I needed to hate him, but I couldn't.

Tears were rolling down my face, 'You broke my heart.'

'And I broke my own.'

There was nothing more to say, talking hadn't helped. I couldn't change what had happened.

We sat in silence for what seemed forever. Couples were walking hand in hand through the park, kids were playing with toy boats on the lake. Life was going on, but mine had ended.

Eventually Ralph got up. I looked at the boy I loved, as he stood staring down at me. He looked lost. I could have saved him, but instead I straightened my back and said, 'Mary will be waiting for you.'

I closed my eyes, I didn't want to watch him walk away.

I don't know how long I sat on that bench, mourning what I had lost and then allowing myself to remember the wonderful but short time that Ralph and I had spent together, even managing to smile when I thought of our first date up on the Downs and the moment when Ralph asked me to be his girlfriend, and then his wife. I thanked God I hadn't known then what was about to happen.

I felt different, better in a way, because I was now ready to let something go; I *had* to let it go. Maybe I had grown up a bit or maybe I had just accepted that it was time to go forward and to stop looking behind me.

I hadn't really lied to Mary and Ralph when I said that I was meeting Sally. She and another couple of girls at work had been asking me to go out with them for ages but I had always said no. Tonight they were going into Hove and had asked me along. I said I'd think about it, even though I had no intention of going. I'd got it into my head that they were only asking because they felt sorry for me, but standing there in that flat with Mary and Ralph I realised I would have to make a life of my own now and it was going to have to be a life that didn't revolve around Mary Pickles. She would always be my friend, but it was time to take a step back. If this really was a proper marriage then I had to let them get on with it. Once I had made that decision, it was like a ton of bricks had been lifted off my back.

I got up from the bench and walked across the road to the bus stop and I was soon sitting on the number six bus that would take me into Hove. I rested my forehead against the glass and watched the familiar roads go by; the houses with their yards and chimney pots, the boys on bicycles and the women queuing at the bus stops. Everything looked the same, but somehow it looked different. I was seeing it all through new eyes.

I didn't go home first. If I went home I knew I wouldn't go out again. Sally had said they were going to a café in George Street straight from work, I just hoped they hadn't changed their minds. I felt quite nervous as I climbed down the steps of the bus, but also excited. I checked my appearance in the shop windows as I walked along George Street and I thought I looked quite nice.

The café was called the Ballerina. Its windows were all misted up, so I couldn't see if the girls were inside. I stood there for a bit, not knowing whether or not to go in. I wasn't used to going places on my own. I felt like a baby just learning to walk. Several people walked past me and into the café and I was beginning to feel conspicuous. 'For goodness' sake, Dottie,' I said to myself, 'what's the worst that can happen? So what if they're not there? You just walk out again and get the bus back home, the world won't end.'

I took a deep breath and opened the door. It was pretty packed inside with people sitting at tables. Two girls were dancing round their handbags. *Johnny Remember Me* was playing on the jukebox. There was a good deal of noise, the music and chatter. It was bright and cheerful with red cloths on the tables and fairy lights round the walls; in fact, it made our café look pretty dull. I spotted Sally, Kate and Liz straight away, they were sitting at one of the tables with a couple of boys. Sally looked up and saw me and she smiled.

'Dottie! Hi!' she said, beckoning me over. I walked across and sat down. Everyone smiled and raised their hands to greet me.

'I was just saying to Kate I bet Dottie won't come. And here you are.'

'I nearly didn't come in,' I admitted. 'I was standing outside for ages.'

Sally laughed. 'You daft cow!' she said.

'I know,' I said.

Sally put her hand on my forearm. 'If you were worried, you should have said, we could have all come together.'

'I kind of decided at the last minute.'

'Well you're here now,' said Sally. 'What do you think of it?'

'I think it's fab,' I said, and I meant it. Already I was having fun. I'd missed that over the last few months.

'This is Dave and Steve,' said Sally. 'They're brothers.'

'Hi. I'm Dottie.'

'We haven't seen you here before,' said Steve.

'I've never been here before,' I said. 'But I'll definitely come again, it's really nice.'

'Steve and Dave work at Butlins,' said Sally.

'Bognor Regis,' said Dave.

'What do you do there?'

'We're redcoats,' said Steve, smiling at me.

'That's how Cliff Richard started!' I said.

'That's right,' said Dave. 'And if he can get discovered so can we.'

'Do you sing then?'

'We both do,' said Steve.

'And one day we're going to be famous!' said Dave.

'In your dreams,' Liz laughed.

Steve winked at me. 'Oh ye of little faith,' he said.

'So what do you do in between seasons?'

'Whatever we can get,' said Steve. 'We're working in the arcade on the West Pier at the moment. That's about the only sort of job we can get because we can only work till May when the season starts again.'

'So not many places want to take us on,' said Dave. 'But the arcade's okay. It's great for pulling.'

'Pulling what?' I asked.

Dave put his head back and laughed. 'Girls,' he said.

'Dave fancies himself as a bit of a ladies' man,' said Steve. He winked at me. I felt my cheeks grow hot. There was something nice about both boys, the way they talked like one person, the way they smiled and laughed. And they were nice-looking, both of them. Steve chewed a drinking straw and I felt his eyes on me.

'Me and Kate are thinking of joining them next season,' said Sally.

'What, at Bognor?'

'No, Minehead. That's where they're going next.'

I'd never heard of Minehead.

'Where's that?' I asked.

'It's in Somerset,' said Steve. Then he put on a funny accent like a farmer. 'Where the cider apples grow!'

'I can't imagine living anywhere but where I live now,' I said. 'The farthest I've been in my whole life is Chessington Zoo and I went there with the school when I was ten.'

'Then it's time you lived a little,' said Steve, smiling. He wagged his straw at me.

'No,' I said. 'I couldn't be a redcoat. I'm not any good at things like that.'

'Have you tried?' said Steve.

'I got highly commended in a talent contest once,' I said. 'I sang *The Merry Merry Pipes of Pan*.'

Steve laughed, but it wasn't in an unkind way, it was friendly.

'There you are then,' he said. 'You can sing!'

'I thought I could at the time, but I think I was deluding myself.'

'The judges must have liked you.'

'They probably felt sorry for me.'

I realised that Steve had moved his chair round so that he had his back to the others and it was just him and me talking to each other. Kate and Liz were up at the jukebox and Sally was laughing at something Dave had said.

'Anyway there are other things you can do at Butlins, you don't have to be a redcoat. Where do you work now?'

'At Woollies.'

'There are two big stores on the camp selling gifts and stuff. You could do that easily.'

I smiled. 'I don't think I'm brave enough for that,' I said. 'I know I couldn't go on my own.'

'Well I think Sally and Kate have almost made up their minds to go, they've sent for application forms. You could go with them. Think of the laughs you'd have! It's great there, honestly, Dottie! Everyone's on holiday so they're all out to have a good time. Everyone takes the mickey out of everyone else, we're all like one big team, all friends. And you have to come to some of the staff parties! They're the best!'

'It sounds brilliant,' I said.

'It is! And you get all your board and lodging, and you get paid on top of that!'

'The thing is, I'm kind of needed here at the moment.'

His face fell. Then he shrugged and smiled.

'Well, if you change your mind the season doesn't start until May.'

I nodded.

'I'll think about it,' I said, but I knew in my heart I couldn't go away, not with Mary having the baby. And in that moment I realised that however much I wanted to move on, I knew that I couldn't bear to be that far away from Ralph either.

'Penny for them,' said Steve.

'Sorry?'

'You look sad.'

'Long story,' I said.

I Remember You by Frank Ifield was playing on the jukebox; Sally and Dave were dancing to it.

'Fancy giving it a go?' asked Steve, holding out his hand to me.

'Why not?'

I took his hand and we walked onto the little dance floor. It felt strange being in another boy's arms. Steve was shorter than Ralph and I guess we fitted together pretty well. He didn't smell the same as Ralph either but he smelt nice, kind of musky and sort of manly, not that I had much experience of what boys smelt like. Steve's arms tightened around me and I let my head rest on his shoulder.

'That's nice,' he whispered in my ear.

When the song finished, Steve kept hold of my hand and we walked back to the table. Sally winked at me and I smiled back at her. I was having a great time and I hadn't expected to. Steve was nice. He wasn't Ralph, but he was really nice. I had a warm feeling inside me. It was a feeling I wanted to hold on to for as long as possible.

'Can I see you again, Dottie?' he asked.

'I'd like that,' I said. And I meant it.

Dear Diary,

Is it possible to get any fatter? When I look in the mirror I see someone I don't recognise.

It's awkward living with Ralph. He's not unkind to me, but it's obvious that he doesn't want to be here with me anymore that I want to be here with him.

I hate sharing the bed with him. We sleep as far away from each other as we can.

This is the pits.

Mary Bennett (the elephant)

Aged eighteen.

Chapter Twenty-Eight

It was mid-December. The baby was due at any time. Mary was so big it looked as if she was about to burst. She felt tired all the time, her ankles were swollen and she complained about her breasts hurting and stuff that I didn't really want to know about. It was hard to explain, because Mary was my best friend, and I didn't want to be anywhere else but with her, but it just wasn't much fun anymore, and nothing she was doing seemed to have much to do with me. I supposed it would be different when the baby came along and she had more energy again. I honestly thought she would be happier then.

And then there was Ralph. I seemed to spend my life avoiding him. When I was at the flat I was continually worried that he would walk through the door.

I became even better friends with the girls at work and I went out with them every weekend and sometimes in the week. Christmas was not far off and everyone was enjoying the buzz. The shop windows were decorated and Woolworths was full of selection boxes of chocolates and fairy lights and tinsel. Christmas trees were leaning against the wall outside. The smell of pine reminded me of happier times when I was a child. Without noticing, I began to enjoy myself. I was beginning to feel a kind of freedom. I hadn't stopped loving Ralph, that wasn't going to happen overnight, and I still missed my old life with Mary dreadfully, but I'd stopped feeling anxious all the time. I laughed more. It was a kind of moving on, and although there was a part of me that wanted nothing more than to live on the edge of Ralph and Mary's life, I knew that in the long run I would lose myself, and I wasn't going to let that happen. I would find the strength from somewhere and I would make a life of my own.

I could tell that Mary didn't like it very much that I was having a life that didn't involve her at all, so although I was having a great time I played it down. When I was with Mary, I didn't mention the boys, or how nice they were, and how we would spend hours in the arcade with them relentlessly teasing us and slipping us piles of pennies so that we could have extra goes on the machines. I didn't mention the plastic mistletoe hung over every table in the café or my invitation to the Festive Frolic party night at the Regent ballroom. I didn't say anything about that to Mary as she sat in the little flat, with her feet up to try to reduce the swelling and her hands resting on her belly, which was getting very round and which I found a bit frightening. It seemed strange, to me, that Mary's body could change so dramatically without her really having anything to do with it. She was becoming a mother whether she liked it or not.

You would never know Christmas was coming in Mary's flat. I bought a couple of strings of tinsel for her as a present. I stuck the tinsel around the mirror in the front room of the flat, but it didn't make it feel any more festive.

'What's the point?' she asked. I couldn't think of a good answer.

Mary sighed a lot, and I fetched her drinks that she never finished, and sometimes she closed her eyes and seemed to disappear into another place altogether. I always made sure I was gone before Ralph came home from work.

Once she said to me: 'This isn't the life that I expected to have.'

'I know.'

'I wanted more than this, I wanted us both to see the world, now I'm going to be stuck here forever in a council flat with a bloke I don't even fancy. I wanted fabulous and I've ended up with ordinary.'

I didn't know what to say to her, because to be honest I thought she was probably right.

'What did you do last night?' Mary asked. 'I called in at your house on the way back from the shops and you weren't there.'

'Oh nothing much,' I said. It was a lie. I'd been on the pier with Steve. I'd had a fantastic time. I'd laughed so much my sides had hurt. We'd had a go on some of the fairground rides and I felt so happy with the wind in my face and Steve's arm round my shoulder, the world spinning as the waltzer travelled round, Steve pressed against me. And then we'd eaten peanut toffee and drunk steaming cups of mulled cider. I'd watched Steve on the grabber. He was an expert on that machine and he always gave me the little gift that he'd won. My bedroom window ledge was lined with little teddy bears and cigarette packets. I gave the fags to Dad, but kept the packets. After we'd been in the arcade, we went to the café and danced until it closed. We'd held hands and kissed under the mistletoe.

I smiled at her. 'I didn't do anything interesting,' I said.

'Never mind,' said Mary, with a little sigh. 'I'll be able to come out soon. When the baby's born. We can take it out in the pram. We'll be able to go for walks along the seafront and things like that.'

'Yes,' I said as enthusiastically as possible. 'Yes, of course we can.'

I *did* miss Mary. I missed being with her all the time and having her with me to laugh at things and share every single tiny part of my life with. I wanted to tell her about Steve and how much fun we were having. I missed everything about Mary.

But, at the same time, in a strange and amazing way, I felt like I had been reborn. I was no longer 'Dottie who tags along with Mary Pickles', I was just 'Dottie'. It took a while before I felt able to express an opinion of my own without agreeing to everything that was said to me, but it happened. And people actually seemed interested in what I had to say. I always just used to leave the talking up to Mary. Perhaps Mary did Ralph's talking these days.

Ralph still went out with Elton sometimes, but Mary wouldn't see Elton. She wouldn't let Ralph invite him round to the flat because she said she didn't want him to see her looking like the size of a house.

'Do you still like Elton?' I asked her casually.

'What does it matter whether I like him or not?' she said. 'He wouldn't want me now, would he?'

'I'm sorry,' I said.

'It's not your fault, is it? It's all mine.'

'My mum says you were unlucky. I mean there's our Rita trying really hard to have a baby and she can't do it and you only did it once. I'd definitely call that unlucky.'

'Or stupid.'

'Let me help you with this ironing,' I said.

A heap of it was piled up in the linen basket that was on the floor in Mary's living room. I put up the ironing board and plugged in the iron. It was a smart, new one that one of Mary's aunties had given her. I didn't mind doing the ironing for Mary. It was quite soothing really and while I ironed she sat in the chair watching me. I could see Mary twice, once in real life and once reflected in the tinselled mirror. In both she looked sad. Now all the furniture was in, the room seemed quite small. It felt as if we were playing at being grown-up.

'Have you thought of any names for the baby?' I said, to change the subject. I passed Mary one of Ralph's shirts. She laid it out beside her on the settee and folded the arms in.

'Ralph likes Caroline. If it's a girl.'

'Caroline's nice.'

'I think it sounds a bit posh,' said Mary.

'What about Helen? After Helen Shapiro.'

'I don't like Helen Shapiro.'

'You used to.'

'Well I don't now.'

'How about Sandra then? After Sandra Dee.'

'Will you shut up about names, Dottie? I don't care what it's called, okay? And what if it's not a girl?'

'I don't know,' I said. 'I've just always thought it would be a girl.'

'Well it's probably going to be a boy,' said Mary. 'An ugly little boy.' And then for good measure she added, 'With ginger bloody hair.'

I sighed. That was what it was like at the time. I was lying to Mary about my life without her, and when I was with her she was miserable and I was bored. It wasn't exactly ideal.

Mum seemed to know how I was feeling.

'It's difficult for you, isn't it, love,' she said as I got ready to go and see Mary one evening. 'It must be ever so hard, going round to the flat.'

'It's okay,' I said, with a shrug. 'It's how it is, isn't it? I can't change it.'

'It's very good of you, to be so loyal to them both,' Mum said. 'Wouldn't you rather be going out with Steve?'

I shrugged again.

'You do like him, don't you?' Mum asked. 'He seems a very nice young man to me.'

'He is, and yes I do like him.'

'But he's not Ralph?'

I looked at my mum and my eyes went all hot. How could she tell?

'I don't think I can ever feel the same way about Steve that I do about Ralph,' I said.

'You don't have to,' said Mum. 'Don't go putting pressure on yourself thinking you ought to feel this or you ought to feel that. Give it time and just enjoy his company.'

'Okay.'

'You never forget your first love, Dottie,' she said. 'But you do learn to love again. It's just a different kind of love, a deeper love.'

'Was Dad your first love?' I asked her.

'No, he wasn't,' she said. 'His name put me off for a start, can you imagine what it was like going out with a boy called Nelson? My dad took the mick out of him something rotten.'

'You still went out with him though?'

'Only because he never gave up. He was like some annoying little insect buzzing round me. Every time I turned round he was there.'

'Mum,' I asked. 'If it wasn't Dad, who was your first love?'

Mum sighed and a dreamy look came over her face.

'It's a long time since I've thought of him. His name was Jack. He lived next door to me when we were growing up. Everyone knew we would end up together; we were inseparable. People used to say, if you want to find Maureen just look for Jack.'

'So what happened? How come you married Dad then?'

'Jack got killed in the war, Dottie. He was only gone a week and he was killed.'

She turned to me and smiled wistfully and I saw something I'd never seen before in her eyes. I saw a glimpse of the young girl she used to be.

I took her hand. 'Mum, that's awful. What did you do?'

'I wanted to die too. You see, I couldn't remember a day in my life when Jack wasn't there. I did a lot of crying and I wouldn't go out and I made everyone around me miserable. And all through that time your Dad used to come round the house, you see he was Jack's best friend. I used to make my mum say I was out. Then one day she said she'd asked him in and he was sitting in the front room and I had to go downstairs and tell him myself that I didn't want to see him because she was fed up of making excuses for me.'

'Did you go downstairs?'

Mum smiled. 'Not right away, no. I shouted at my mum and said that I would only ever love Jack and I wouldn't ever go out with anyone else for the rest of my life.'

'What did she say?'

'She said my name was Maureen O'Connell not Greta Garbo and that Jack was dead and he wasn't coming back and there was a perfectly nice young man sitting downstairs in our front parlour who was daft enough to want to go out with me.'

Mum smiled and squeezed my hand. The look was gone; she was back to her old self again.

'And you fell in love with him?'

'Not right away, but he never rushed me. I think if he'd tried to rush me, it wouldn't have worked out. He made me feel safe and he let me talk about Jack, because you see he missed him too. I suppose you could say he grew on me and I missed him when he went off fighting. One day I realised that if I ever lost him, it would be as bad as losing Jack. That's when I knew I loved him.'

'That's so romantic, Mum.'

'It seems like a long time ago.'

'So you think I should give Steve a chance then?'

'You're still young, Dottie, and this Steve might not be the one for you, but yes, give him a chance, enjoy his company and see where it takes you.'

It felt strange talking to Mum about being in love and learning about Jack. Somehow you don't expect your parents to have ever felt the way you do. In fact, it's hard to imagine that they were ever young at all. I wondered if Mum had told Rita about Jack.

I was still thinking about all this when I ran up the flight of stone steps that led to Mary's flat, clutching a tin of mince pies Mum had baked for her. At least now we had something to talk about, but when I knocked on the door nobody answered. I tried to look through the window, but I couldn't see anything. I

knocked again. I lifted up the flap from the letter box and shouted: 'Mary! Are you all right?'

Then the girl from the next flat came out.

'She isn't there,' she said, leaning against the door.

'Oh,' I said. 'Do you know where she is?'

'They've taken her off in an ambulance.' The girl picked at her
nail. I felt my heart hit the floor.

'What's wrong? Is she having the baby?'

The girl shrugged. 'I dunno. She was screaming her bleedin'
head off, so I went down to the phone box on the corner and
called an ambulance. Didn't know what else to do.'

'Was Ralph with her?'

'Who?'

I was breathless with frustration. 'Ralph! Mary's husband!'

'I don't know about no husband. She was on her own.'

Poor Mary! She must have been so scared, all on her own in
pain. I wished I hadn't spent so long talking to Mum. I should
have been there earlier. I should have been with her! I didn't know
what to do. I thought I ought to fetch Ralph. I decided to get her
mum.

'What hospital have they taken her to?' I asked the girl.

'Didn't say.'

Silly cow! I thought. I ran back down the steps just as Beverly
Johnson walked into the square. I'd never been so pleased to see
anyone in my life.

'Beverly!' I said. 'I need you to go round to Mary's house and
let her mum know she's just been taken into hospital. Could you
do that?'

'Course I can.'

'Thanks Beverly. Tell Mary's mum that I don't know which
hospital they've taken her to, she'll have to find that out herself.
Oh, and tell her I'm going to the bakery to get Ralph.'

'Don't worry, I'll be as quick as I can.'

I ran to the bus stop and caught the number two that stopped right outside the factory. The journey seemed to take forever, with loads of people getting on at every stop. I thought I was never going to get there. I went in the main door and up to the reception. It was decorated with tinsel and Christmas cards. There was a girl sitting behind a desk. 'I need to see Ralph Bennett,' I said. 'His wife's been taken into hospital.'

'I'll take you to the manager's office. He'll know which department he's in.'

I followed her down several corridors till we got to a door marked 'Manager'. The girl explained about Ralph then left.

'You'd better sit down, young lady,' the manager said. 'You look as though you've had a shock.'

I sat down while the manager made a phone call to locate Ralph.

'He'll be with us in just a minute,' he said.

When Ralph first walked into the office I wasn't even sure it was him. He had a hat on his head that covered his hair and his face was completely white, even his eyebrows and eyelashes were white.

'Dottie, what are you doing here?' he asked.

'Mary's in the hospital!' I said and burst out crying. Ralph immediately came over and put his arms around me. It was so nice to be looked after that I sank into them. I relaxed against him. I was so relieved.

'It's okay,' he said. 'Everything's going to be all right.'

I looked up at him through my tears.

He should have been saying those words to Mary, not me.

'Which hospital have they taken her to?' asked the manager. He was a tall, thin, balding man. If you just looked at him you would have thought he was quite severe, but actually he was nice. He spoke calmly but gently, like there was nothing to worry about it.

'I don't know,' I sniffed.

'Don't worry, I'll get my secretary to make a few calls, we'll soon find her.'

I nodded. The manager took a clean white handkerchief out of his top pocket, passed it to me and left the room.

'Thanks,' I whispered, dabbing at my eyes.

'You're shaking,' said Ralph, taking hold of my hand.

I swallowed. 'She was in pain, Ralph, she must have been in awful pain because the girl next door said she was screaming, and she was all on her own.'

Ralph nodded. He bit his lower lip.

'She'll be okay. Please stop worrying. We know she's being taken care of now.'

I think he was trying to reassure himself as much as me.

The manager came back in to the room. He was smiling.

'She's in Buckingham Road Maternity Hospital, and by the sound of things, you had better get there pretty sharpish.'

'Is she having the baby?'

'Looks like it,' he grinned. He patted Ralph's shoulder. Ralph stood up. He looked very pale underneath all the flour and his eyes were wide and terrified.

'My pushbike's outside,' he said

'I'll take you,' said the manager. I thought that was very nice of him. 'Get out of those overalls,' he told Ralph. 'Don't want you getting flour all over my leather seats.'

Ralph was so nervous he made a right meal out of getting out of the overalls.

'Right,' he said at last. 'Thank you.'

'Give her my love, won't you,' I said, standing up.

Ralph stood in front of me, staring at his hands. I took the crumpled overalls from him. I wanted to hold him. I wanted him to hold me.

'Excuse me,' said the manager, 'but don't you have a birth to attend?'

'Just get to that hospital,' I said. 'Go on.'

Ralph started to go out the door then stopped and came back. He kissed me on the cheek.

I followed him out of the factory and watched him drive off like a film star in the back of a big, fancy black car. I smiled to myself and tucked the overalls under my arm.

The day had warmed up, the sun had broken through the clouds, so I didn't bother with the bus. I felt like walking. I made my way home, climbing up the hills, through Kemp Town, towards the estate, but it was a lot further than I thought, so I stopped off at the park and sat on a bench and watched the little kids playing in the sandpit. They were all wrapped up and their cheeks were rosy with cold. Mary Pickles was about to be a mother; in fact the baby might already be born. It was such a strange thought – Mary being a mother! I just couldn't picture her with a baby somehow. She never was very interested in babies. I wondered what Ralph must be feeling. I expect he'd be over the moon. I suddenly felt very alone. This really was the beginning of their new lives, their new family. I stayed for a bit longer, watching the kids playing on the swings, then made my way home, holding tightly onto the floury overalls that smelt of cakes and bread and Ralph.

'What's happened to you?' Mum asked when I walked into the kitchen.

'What?' I said.

'What's that you've got all down you? It's not snowing is it?'

I looked down at my coat and it was only then I realised that I was covered in flour. I put the overalls on the counter and dusted myself down a bit.

'I thought you were meeting Steve this evening?' Mum said. 'I wasn't expecting you back this early.'

I had forgotten all about Steve. I sighed. There was no point going now, I would be hopelessly late. I hoped he hadn't waited too long. I hoped he wouldn't be upset, or worried. He wasn't the sort to be angry.

'What is it?' Mum asked gently.

'Mary's having her baby,' I said.

'Oh love, come here!' said Mum. She gave me a hug and kissed the top of my head.

'Sit down,' she said. 'You sit down and I'll put the kettle on and you can tell me all about it.'

Dear Diary,

They actually had the cheek to tell me that I'd had a natural birth, well there was nothing natural about it. It was like passing a block of flats, I was in bloody agony. Some old cow of a nurse told me to stop screaming. And she called me mother. 'Now, mother,' she said, 'we don't want baby upset do we?'

Right at that minute I couldn't have cared who I upset, least of all the baby. All the baby had to do was come out, and it was taking its bloody time doing that.

It was a girl, but it could have been anything, it was all red and screwed up. It looked like Winston Churchill, all it needed was a cigar. I told that to the nurse, who looked like she could have happily throttled me in the bed. Like I cared.

Now I'm supposed to bond with it (whatever that means).

Mary Bennett (mother of the year)

Aged eighteen.

Chapter Twenty-Nine

Mary didn't have a little lamb, she had a little girl. Her mum came round to tell us the same evening the baby was born. Mary's mum was wearing her best coat and hat and she was all pale and shaky. She said she had come over all faint.

'It must be something to do with being a grandmother,' she said.

Mum made her sit down in the best chair and she poured them both a schooner of sherry from the bottle that wasn't supposed to be opened until Christmas Day. Mum asked me if I wanted some, but I shook my head. I didn't like the taste. I appreciated being treated like one of the women though. I was grateful that I was included in their circle.

'You see,' Mary's mum said, 'it's just not how I had it all worked out in my head. I thought it'd be one of those big boys making me a grandma first, not Mary.' She shook her head. 'Not our little Mary.'

'What's the baby like?' Mum asked in an encouraging voice. 'Does she have hair? Who does she look like?'

'She's beautiful,' said Mary's mum. 'Absolutely beautiful. And our Mary did ever so well. Screamed the place down, mind, but she did ever so well.'

She glanced over at the door to check that Dad and Clark weren't around.

'Only six stitches!' she said with some pride.

'My!' said Mum.

Mary's mum and my mum both nodded sagely. I was thinking: Stitches? Why would Mary need stitches? Had she fallen off the bed or something?

'They're ever so good in there,' Mary's mum said. 'Brought Mary a lovely roast chicken dinner, boiled potatoes, sprouts, gravy. And bread and butter. She said she wasn't hungry, but I told her she had to eat to bring the milk in.'

'Why did she have to bring the milk in?' I asked. 'Don't they have people to do that at the hospital?'

'I'll explain later,' Mum said, touching the front of her breasts with her fingers. I understood then. It made me feel a little queasy.

'I said you'd go and see her tomorrow, Dottie,' Mary's mum said. 'They only allow two people at a time during visiting hours. Ralph's one, obviously, but Mary's ever so keen to see you and show you the baby.'

'All right,' I said. But I didn't want to go. I didn't want to see the baby that Ralph and Mary had made.

'Dottie…' Mum was giving me an encouraging look. 'That'll be lovely.'

✳ ✳ ✳

Next day, during our lunch hour, Sally helped me choose a card for Mary and Ralph. It had a picture of a stork carrying a baby wrapped in a pink blanket in its beak. The baby's little arms and legs were waving out of the blanket and it said: 'Congratulations on your Bundle of Joy'. Then we went to the florists and the girl made me up a little basket of pink- and cream-coloured flowers. Back at Woollies, we put together a whole big bag full of pick and mix sweets because we knew Mary would prefer those to chocolates.

I caught the bus to the hospital straight from work and got there at 6 p.m. just as visiting time started. There was a queue standing in the dark outside the maternity ward, they wouldn't let anyone in early, and as soon as the doors opened we trooped in. Ralph wasn't there yet, he wouldn't finish work until a lot later.

The maternity ward was a longish ward with beds on either side. It was very clean and tidy with a tiny little Christmas tree at one end. The women were in the beds, propped up with pillows, and beside them were little see-through boxes on wheels. Babies were in those boxes. Mary and Ralph's baby was in one of those boxes.

I walked down the centre of the ward looking for Mary. My heels clicked on the shiny brown lino. Visitors dropped off on either side and there were kisses and whispers and cooing. Everybody was trying not to wake the babies.

Mary was in the very end bed.

I almost didn't recognise her, because she wasn't sitting up like the other women, she was lying on her side with her back to the ward. She was wearing a hospital gown and her hair was spread all over the pillow. I thought she must be sleeping, so I crept closer as quietly as I could. She had her back to the box beside her bed.

I put the flowers and the sweets and the card on the table at the foot of the bed, then I looked into the box. Looking back up at me was the tiniest little baby, like a person in miniature. She had one eye open and the other closed and her fists were scrunched up by her cheeks. The open eye was dark and beady and her lips, tiny little lips, were moving, as if she were telling herself a private story. Every now and then the tip of her tongue tapped against her lips. She was tucked in by a pink blanket right up to her chin, and most of her head was hidden by a knitted bonnet, tied with a pink ribbon. The baby looked at me with her one open eye and I looked back and it was as if we understood one another. There was a bond between us. And at that moment I stopped resenting the baby, and I knew I could never again be sorry that Mary and Ralph did what they did, because if they hadn't, she wouldn't have been here. She was, quite simply, the loveliest thing I had ever seen.

'Hello,' I whispered. The baby tried to open her other eye but couldn't get the co-ordination right. I smiled. 'Hello,' I said again. 'I'm Dottie.' The baby put one fist against her mouth and began to worry at it. I put my finger down to help her, and immediately her lips fastened around the tip of my finger and she sucked. I felt this tug in my stomach as she sucked, like she was telling me she needed me. It was amazing and I smiled down at her, and it was only then I noticed that Mary had turned over and was looking at me. I felt sort of guilty. I took my fingertip out of the baby's mouth and turned back to my friend.

'Oh, Mary!' I said, and leaned down to hug her.

'Careful,' she said. 'I hurt all over.'

'Was it that bad?'

She hitched herself up the bed. I could tell she was in pain.

'It was like passing a block of flats,' she said.

I smiled and passed her the presents.

She took a Black Jack out of the pick and mix, unwrapped the paper and put it into her mouth. She sucked the sweet and I stood beside her.

'How long do you have to stay in hospital?' I asked.

'Ten days,' she said. 'But that's all right, I like it here. They do everything for you.'

'Oh, good.'

Beside us, the baby made a little mewing noise, like a kitten. She was trying to put her fist in her mouth again.

'Can I hold her?' I asked.

'If you want.'

I leaned down and picked the baby up very carefully. She was tightly wrapped in her blanket and I held her like a parcel. She turned her face towards me and nuzzled into my chest.

'Oh Mary,' I said, 'she's lovely.'

Mary rummaged in the bag of sweets and took out another Black Jack. She concentrated very hard on unwrapping it and not looking at the baby.

'She's so beautiful, Mary.'

'If you like that sort of thing,' she said.

❋ ❋ ❋

Later, when I told my Mum about Mary and how down she seemed and how uninterested she was in the baby, she told me not to worry.

'It's a very big thing, having a baby,' she said. 'Mary's body is having to get used to not being pregnant, and her mind's having to get used to the fact that she's a mother. When you have your first baby it's a shock to the system... all the responsibility and that. But she'll get used to it. We all do in the end.'

'Was Rita a shock to your system?' I asked.

'She was.'

'She'd be a shock to anyone's system,' said my brother. 'It's amazing you ever had another child.'

Mum laughed.

'Anyway' – she squeezed my shoulder – 'Mary's lucky, she's got you to help her. Just try to make her look on the bright side.'

I nodded.

Mum looked at me.

'What?'

'I'm so proud of you, Dottie Perks.'

I smiled.

'But listen, I know you'll do your bit, but that baby is Mary and Ralph's responsibility, not yours. Don't you go letting it take over your life.'

'I won't.'

'Good girl,' said Mum. Then she said: 'Hadn't you ought to be getting ready?'

'Ready for what?'

'To go and apologise to that nice young man of yours for standing him up last night!'

I gave Mum a hug.

'You're right!' I said and I ran upstairs to change.

Dear Diary,

Having a baby is the most natural thing in the world isn't it?

Millions of women have babies every day. It's supposed to be the best thing that ever happens to you, the most fulfilling, the most bloody rewarding, and I'm trying, I'm really trying, but it isn't like that for me.

I do love Peggy, I really do, but I'm so tired. Sometimes I think I would give her to a passing stranger just to get a few hours' sleep.

Sometimes I dream about how my life could have been. I see a room on the top floor of a house. There is a little bed full of beautiful soft pillows and cotton sheets and a patchwork quilt. My room is in the eaves and there is a square window that looks out over Paris. In my dream I smell linseed oil and turpentine. My easel is under the window and stacks of finished canvases lean up against the wall. Then I wake up and I'm in this dingy flat on a dingy estate in Brighton. There is no colour here, the only smell is misery. My life has shrunk to these four walls.

I'm not sure that Dottie likes me much anymore. I see her expression when she looks round the flat. I hear her tut when Peggy has a wet nappy. I hear her sigh when she picks up the dirty washing. I hear her and Ralph laughing together when I am in bed. I need her help but lately I just wish she wasn't there.

I don't want to feel like this. She is my best friend and when I look back on my life I realise that she was the most important person in it. All of my most precious memories I have shared with Dottie. Sometimes between waking and sleeping I remember. Moments caught in time, like snapshots in my head. Those long summer days. Standing at the edge of the sea, screaming as we run into the water, clinging to each other as the freezing cold spray takes our breath away.

Sometimes I want to go back, sometimes I want to start again.

Tatty bye diary

Mary Bennett

Aged eighteen.

Chapter Thirty

Mary didn't seem to take to motherhood. She didn't seem very well and she certainly wasn't enjoying her life. She hadn't really picked up since Peggy was born. That's what they called the baby, Peggy. I didn't know what to think. It was like she had switched off. She was pleasant enough, but you got the feeling that when you spoke to her she was only half listening. She wasn't interested in anything. I didn't know what to do. I didn't know how to reach her. I told her mum that I was worried about her and she said that Mary just needed to rest.

'She'll be right as rain once she's rested,' said Mary's mum. 'It's not unusual, you know, for young mums to be exhausted.'

She slept whenever she didn't have to be awake. By the end of January, Mary's tiredness was worrying everyone around her and eventually her mum took her to see the doctor.

'I'm low on iron,' said Mary the next time I went round. 'He's given me some tablets. He says it can happen when you've had a baby, so hopefully I'll soon be better.'

I wanted so much for Mary to get well and I really wanted the tablets to work. I wanted my friend back.

Not long after, I went round to the flat to find Mary in floods of tears.

'She won't breastfeed,' she sobbed. Peggy's face was all red and sweaty, screwed up like a fist and she was screaming her head off.

'Maybe she's not hungry,' I said.

'Of course she's hungry,' shouted Mary. 'She's always bloody hungry.'

I picked Peggy up and held her against my shoulder. I whispered to her as I walked around the rooms in the flat and gradually her crying eased off; she was still hiccupping and trying to catch her breath but she had stopped screaming.

'Why don't you have a lie down, Mary?' I said.

'I think I will,' she said. 'I just wish I wasn't so tired all the time. Those tablets haven't made any difference at all, except that now I'm bloody constipated.'

'It'll get better,' I said, not really knowing if it would.

Mary didn't try to breastfeed Peggy again; she put her on the bottle. Sometimes, if I was there at the right time, I took a turn giving it to her. I loved it. I loved the way she stared up into my face as she sucked, the way her tiny lips locked onto the rubber teat, the look of utter contentment on her face as her tummy filled. She was intensely fascinating to me. I loved to hold her, and bathe her and walk around the flat, holding her to my shoulder. I could not understand how Mary could be so disinterested in this beautiful, amazing little creature with her tiny pink fingernails and her lovely, inquisitive eyes.

I knew it was easier for me. I could come and go as I pleased. I wasn't responsible for Peggy every second of every minute of every day. I could bathe her in the little plastic tub in front of the gas fire in the flat's living room, pat her dry, powder her, put her into clean clothes, feed her and leave her. After I'd done all that, I could go down to the café to meet Steve and I could laugh and dance and sing and be free. It wasn't me who was being woken three or four times a night by Peggy's screaming. It wasn't me who had to pace the floor with her, singing interminable lullabies, to stop her crying from disturbing the neighbours.

I understood all that, but I still couldn't understand how Mary could have disassociated herself so completely from her baby. I was only her mother's best friend, but I still wanted every face Peggy saw to be a smiling face. I wanted to fill her days with flowers and toys and her evenings with lullabies and cuddles. I wanted her to always have a nice full tummy, and warm, clean clothes. Looking after the baby did not seem, to me, to be a chore. It was hard for me to keep my patience with Mary, who acted as if she didn't care. But how could I judge her? I didn't know what it felt like to be responsible for another little life.

There were times when I caught myself thinking that Mary had only herself to blame for the position she was in. It wasn't like her life was anywhere near as terrible as she made out. She had a nice home, a nice husband, a beautiful baby… I'd have swapped my life for hers any day – only I'd have made the most of it! After thinking these thoughts I felt disloyal, I felt like a bad friend and I was determined to help her all I could.

'Look at her,' I said to Mary. 'Look at her little face! See how she's trying to smile, you can see how hard she's trying! She's moving her arms up and down as if that will help her face! She's so gorgeous.'

I turned around and saw the distress on Mary's face, and of course I couldn't be angry. I swallowed my resentment, put the baby down on her blanket on the floor, and put my arms around Mary. She began to cry.

'I didn't want it to turn out like this,' she said. 'This isn't how it's supposed to be. I was supposed to be having the time of my life, wearing nice clothes, going to parties, having fun and instead I'm stuck here in this flat with a husband I hardly know and a baby that doesn't like me.'

'Of course she likes you! You're her mother!'

'She doesn't. I'm useless with her. I couldn't even breastfeed her.'

Mary cried and I sat and hugged her and kissed the top of her head and assured her that everything was going to be all right.

We had that conversation, or one like it, over and over again.

Nothing I said cheered Mary up, she refused to look on the bright side, she was adamant that Peggy didn't like her, and I found the way she seemed to blame the baby very hard to deal with. I couldn't tell Mary anything about my life without it prompting in her either tears of self-pity or the kind of comments that made me feel guilty about enjoying myself while she was imprisoned in her life. She resented me because I was free, she resented the baby because she thought Peggy hated her, and she resented Ralph for going off to work while she was stuck in the flat.

My feelings towards Mary were so mixed up. It had never been like this, we had always been able to tell each other everything, but now I was hiding my thoughts from her, I was resenting her and that was wrong. I must try to help her more. I started going to the flat every night after work and only seeing Steve at weekends. The flat was a mess and it was beginning to smell bad because of all the dirty nappies left all over the place. I couldn't understand why Mary had become like this, it just wasn't her, it wasn't the Mary I knew. So I would go there every evening and clean up and play with Peggy. Mum said I was spending too much time there and that Peggy wasn't my responsibility and I should let them get on with their lives, but she didn't know what it was like, she didn't see the state of the place and she didn't see that Mary wasn't looking after Peggy properly. Mrs Pickles went in every day and helped Mary as much as she could but she had six boys and a husband to look after. She always put her coat on as soon as I got there so we didn't really talk.

I had been avoiding Ralph by leaving the flat early, but one evening I lost track of the time. Peggy had a cold and I couldn't settle her and I was still there when Ralph came home. At first it was awkward, we didn't know what to say to each other so we both busied ourselves with the baby. After that evening I started staying later so that I could see Ralph. I started looking forward to seeing him. Mary was nearly always in bed, so we'd sit and have a cup of coffee and we'd talk about ordinary things, like my work and his and we'd talk about Mary, about how she wasn't coping, about the fact that she wasn't bonding with the baby like she should be. We laughed about silly things just like we used to. These times became precious to me.

Dear Diary,

Ralph is kind and patient with me, he doesn't judge me. He is so gentle with Peggy. I lie on the couch and watch them together, her eyes light up when she hears his voice. I want to be a better mother, I even hope that one day I can be a better wife. I used to wonder what Dottie saw in him but now I understand. Ralph Bennett is a good man. Mum said that maybe in time we could learn to care about each other. He's not Elton, I can't feel the same way I feel about Elton, but we are friends and that's a good start.

Yesterday was Christmas Day. The three of us spent it quietly on our own. It was nice. Ralph bought a pink rabbit for Peggy, she loved it. She held it up to her face and rubbed her nose in it, it made us laugh. Then Ralph gave me a parcel wrapped in red paper, it was tied up with a green satin bow. I tore it open, it was a sketch pad, a big block of good quality cartridge paper, better than anything I have ever had before, and a box of pencils, a rubber and a sharpener. I laid them all out on the living room floor. Ralph said it's not Paris but it's the best he could do. I truly loved him in that moment.

While Ralph is at work I sketch the baby. I have started to draw rough sketches of her sleeping, waking lying on her back or on her stomach, waving her little arms around. I am improving. I've done close-ups of her ears, her eyes, her darling little hands. I don't show my drawings to anyone. I keep them hidden under my bed.

Did I tell you that Peggy's eyes are the darkest blue? Did I tell you that her hair is the most beautiful shade of red? And did I tell you that I wouldn't want it to be any other colour?

Tatty bye diary

Mary Bennett (artist extraordinaire)

Aged Eighteen

Chapter Thirty-One

Christmas came and went. It used to be my favourite time of the year but this year my heart just wasn't in it. Aunty Brenda, Uncle Eddie and Carol came round as usual and in the evening Rita and Nigel came round for their tea. I joined in a game of charades and played Ludo with Dad, but inside I was wishing the day away. Steve bought me a big brown teddy bear and I bought him the latest Eddie Cochran LP. I didn't go round to the flat, I just couldn't bear to see Mary and Ralph playing happy families on that day. I waited until it was all over before I went round. One afternoon, having finished work at lunchtime, I stopped off at the shops and bought a present for Mary and Peggy. Peggy didn't have any toys of her own, only second-hand things that Mary's mother had given her, and most of those were boys' toys. She was now two months old and I'd noticed that she had started to reach out for things, her chubby little fingers curling round my hair when I bent over her, and she was sucking the edge of her blanket. I decided on a soft pink rattle shaped like a teddy that chimed when you shook it. For Mary, I bought some magazines, a bag of sweets and a tube of lipstick. I hadn't seen her wearing make-up since the baby had been born. I thought that might cheer her up.

When I reached the flats, I could hear Peggy crying from the bottom of the steps. I let myself in with the key hidden under the doormat and called Mary's name but there was no answer. The baby was in the front room in her basket, she was screaming and her face was all red and sweaty. I picked her up. She was wet through and she reeked of urine. As soon as she was in my arms, she began to calm down; the screaming subsided into gulping sobs that made my heart ache.

'Poor baby,' I cooed, kissing the silky top of her head. 'Poor little Peggy, don't worry, Dottie's here now. Mary?' I called again but louder this time. Mary came out of the bedroom rubbing her eyes.

'What?' she asked.

'Oh, Mary!' I was angry and frustrated. 'Didn't you hear her?'

Mary yawned. 'I was asleep.'

'Peggy's soaking wet. Don't tell me you didn't hear her crying!'

'Well obviously I didn't, did I?' said Mary. 'Give her to me I'll change her.'

'Are you sure you know how to?'

'What's that supposed to mean?' she said, glaring at me.

'You don't do it very often, do you?'

'You do it then,' Mary said. 'You're right. You do it better.'

I felt bad then.

'I'm sorry Mary, I didn't mean to say that. I don't do it better than you. I was just…'

'I only meant to lie down for a minute or two,' said Mary. There was a sob in her voice. 'I didn't mean to go to sleep.'

'No of course you didn't. It's all right,' I said. 'Don't get upset. I'm here now.'

Mary sat on the sofa watching as I changed Peggy.

'Who's a nice clean girl now then?' I said, tickling her under her chin. Peggy giggled so I tickled her again.

'She likes you more than she likes me,' said Mary.

'Of course she doesn't.'

'She does,' said Mary. Then she sort of stared at me before saying 'You know she does.'

'Mary, you have to stop being like this. I haven't seen her for more than a week. She's only smiling at me because I'm smiling at her. She just likes the attention. Here, why don't you hold her?'

'No,' said Mary, pulling away from the baby I was holding up to her. Her baby. 'It's okay.'

She leaned back against the sofa and closed her eyes. She looked like a little girl, a frail sad little girl.

'Have you been eating properly?' I asked. 'Because you look as if you've lost weight.'

Mary sighed and shook her head. 'I don't seem to have much of an appetite. I'm too tired to eat. I'm tired of everything.'

'Perhaps you should see the doctor again,' I said.

'That's what Ralph says.'

I always got a kind of hot feeling in my stomach when Mary referred to Ralph in that way, like they were a family, like they made decisions together. I knew I was being mean and jealous but I couldn't help it.

I put a fresh sheet in Peggy's basket and laid her down. I sat next to Mary on the sofa and took hold of her hand. It seemed even smaller than usual and it was cool.

'I think Ralph's right,' I said.

'He says he'll make an appointment,' said Mary. 'If he could just give me a tonic or something to make me feel less tired then I'm sure I could look after Peggy better.'

'Yes.'

'I do try, Dottie, but everything I do just wears me out, so it's easier to let Mum take over, or Ralph or you. I know what you all think of me, you think I'm a lazy cow and a bad mother.'

'Of course we don't,' I said. But I knew there was part of me that did.

'And do you know what, Dottie?' she said. 'I don't care, because I'm too tired to care.'

'I bought you a present,' I said. I passed her the paper bag containing the lipstick. She took it out, took the lid off and pushed up the tube to look at the colour. It was a paleish peach that I knew would suit her. She looked at it for a moment, then put it down.

'Don't you like it?' I asked.

'It's lovely. Thank you,' she said, in a tone of voice that made me realise she would never wear the lipstick.

'Shall I make you a sandwich?'

'No thanks, I think I'll just go back to bed for a bit now that you're here. Perhaps you could take Peggy for a walk or something. She's supposed to have fresh air. It's supposed to be good for her.'

Mary walked over to the basket and looked down at the baby.

'I'm sorry, little one,' she said. 'Sorry I'm so useless. Dottie should have been your mother. She'd have made a lot better job of it than me.'

I tried not to be irritated by that remark, really I did, but it annoyed me and it upset me and it hurt me. It wasn't just the pathetic self-pity in Mary's voice, when nobody had made her go out and sleep with Ralph, nobody had made her go and get pregnant. It wasn't just that. Mary was right, I *should* have been Peggy's mother. If anyone was going to have a baby with Ralph Bennett, it should have been me! And if it had been me, then I would have loved that baby with every inch of my being and I'd have looked after her and made sure she was always clean and dry and happy and I would never, never in a million years have gone to sleep and left her screaming with her bottom all sore from lying in a nappy soaked with her own wee. And if I had, which I never would have, I'd never have felt sorry for myself about it. Those were the unkind thoughts that were in my head, thoughts that I was ashamed of thinking.

I could hardly look at Mary.

I waited until she'd gone back into the bedroom and closed the door and then I picked Peggy up. Her eyes were beginning to droop. I gently traced the outline of her face with my finger, she was such a beautiful baby.

It was hard work bumping the pram from the front door of the flat down the steps, difficult for me and I was healthy and strong, impossible for someone as weak and tired as Mary. Once I'd got it to the bottom, I went back up to the flat and fetched Peggy. I tucked her in and set off. It was a bit windy but dry. I was wearing my navy duffle coat and green matching scarf and gloves that Aunty Brenda had made me for Christmas. Peggy stared out at me from a red fluffy bonnet; she looked warm and cosy.

We walked to the park where we sat on a bench overlooking the boating pool. There were people playing with motorised boats. They were crouched at the side of the water controlling the boats with little black boxes and the air was filled with the acrid smell of petrol. I put the hood of the pram up because I was worried about the fumes. People smiled at me as they walked past and sometimes they stopped to look in the pram to compliment Peggy on her bonniness and her beauty. I knew that they thought I was her mother and I didn't do anything to put them right.

I stayed out with Peggy for hours. I didn't see the point of taking her back to the flat, and if I'm honest, I didn't think I could bear another session of misery with Mary. I'd brought a bottle with me, wrapped in a towel in the bottom of the pram, and although it wasn't quite as warm as it should have been, Peggy didn't seem to mind. I fed her at a table in one of the cafés and at the same time I had a frothy coffee and a Chelsea bun. One wall was covered in posters and there was one about a mother and baby group. It was being held in a local church hall. I asked the girl behind the counter for a pen and wrote down the number. I would give it to Mary. It might help her to meet other young mums. I felt increasingly annoyed by Mary. She hadn't even *tried* to be a good mother. She hadn't put any effort in at all. She'd just given up. There were times when I thought I would be a better mother to Peggy, that I would love her more than Mary did. There were times when I thought Mary wouldn't care if Ralph, Peggy and me ran away together. There were even times when I wished that my best friend Mary Pickles would just disappear. Most of all I was worried about Peggy, and the fact that Mary hadn't heard her crying even though I could hear her from outside.

It had started to rain, so, reluctantly, I headed back to the flat. I left the pram at the bottom of the steps, picked Peggy up all bundled in her blanket, and went up to the flat. Mrs Pickles was waiting at the door.

'Oh thank God you're back,' she said. 'I was worried sick.'

'Mary asked me to take Peggy out for some fresh air,' I said a bit defensively.

'I know, dear, I know. But let me take her now.'

'What's wrong? Has something happened? Is Mary okay?'

'No, Dottie, she's not. I'm very worried about her, so I'm taking her and Peggy home with me.'

I followed Mrs Pickles into the front room. Mary was sitting on the couch, she looked even smaller and paler than she had when I'd left her. She had her coat on over her nightie. I sat down beside her and took her little hand, it felt kind of damp and clammy and there was a funny smell about her that I hadn't smelt before. She didn't smell like Mary. I thought she probably hadn't had a proper bath for weeks. Her hair was lank and greasy and her skin was awful.

She did her best to smile. 'Will you wait for Ralph to come home, Dottie, and let him know we're at Mum's? He shouldn't be long.'

'Of course I will.'

'I don't know what's wrong with me, Dottie.'

'Nothing's wrong with you,' I said cheerfully. 'A few days with your Mum looking after you and you'll be right as rain!' It was the kind of thing everyone kept saying.

'I'm scared.'

'There's nothing to be scared of,' I said.

'You will come over, won't you?' said Mary. 'Once you've told Ralph?'

'I can't,' I said, 'I'm meeting some friends.'

'Oh.'

Mary's mum gave me an odd look but she didn't say anything.

'Maybe later?' said Mary.

'I'll try,' I said.

Chapter Thirty-Two

Once Mary and her mum had left I started cleaning up the flat. I washed the dirty dishes that were stacked in the sink and got on my hands and knees to clean the kitchen floor. I scrubbed every inch of the bathroom. Then I went into the bedroom.

I picked up the unwashed clothes that Mary had simply dropped on the carpet. I tried not to, but I couldn't help being disgusted by her slovenliness. There were soiled baby clothes as well as Mary's dirty underwear and creased nighties on the carpet, and that was covered in a layer of hair and dust. She had spent so long in the bed that the sheets were dampish and musty, blooming with faint, pinky stains. They were still warm and had that same strange smell about them, a smell of sweat and unhappiness. I put the blankets and quilt in the corner and took off the sheets, balling them into the dirty linen pile I'd already made. I'd take the washing down the launderette later. It took me a while, but I heaved at the mattress until I managed to turn it, then I fetched some clean sheets from the airing cupboard in the bathroom. I remade the bed, smoothing the under sheet, taking care with the coversheet. Mum had taught Rita and me how to do hospital corners, because she said there was nothing nicer in life than a well-made bed.

I walked across to the window and opened it wide to let in some fresh air. It had stopped raining and everywhere smelt fresh and new. The flats backed directly onto the Downs. I leant on the window ledge and stared out at the hills. They were green and gentle, wrapped around Brighton like a giant pair of arms, protecting the city. Above the hills, white clouds were drifting lazily through a perfect blue sky.

Spring was just around the corner, but it wasn't a spring I was looking forward to.

I remembered going up onto the Downs with Ralph for our first date. I remembered sitting beside him on the grass, and how his hand had felt when it first touched mine. I felt a tightening in my throat; I felt as if I couldn't breathe and then I started to cry, great gulping noisy sobs that filled the flat; it felt as though every part of my body was crying, as if my eyes alone couldn't hold all the tears that were threatening to choke me. I cried for me, for Mary, for Ralph, for what could have been and never would be. I didn't know he was there until he spoke.

'Don't, Dottie,' he said. 'Please don't.'

He had come into the room behind me and he was standing there now, just a few feet away from me. I thought of all the things we should have said and done together, the life we should have had, everything that I had lost, that had been taken from me.

His voice seemed to trigger something in me and I started screaming at him. 'How could you do that, Ralph? How could you?' and I found myself hitting out at him. He didn't even try to defend himself; he just stood there looking helplessly at me.

'Haven't you got *anything* to say to me?' I screamed.

'I'm sorry,' he mumbled, 'I'm so sorry.' He took a step towards me, held out his arms, tried to hold me, but I wouldn't let him. I pushed him away as hard as I could. For a few moments we stood staring at one another, me panting and sobbing, him pale and subdued. I tried to contain my anger. I swallowed it down. I wiped my nose with the back of my hand.

'Sorry isn't good enough, Ralph,' I said. 'You've ruined everything. You slept with my best friend, for God's sake. Do you really think I am going to settle for sorry?'

Ralph sat down on the newly made bed. He ran his hands through his hair till it stood up at odd angles. 'I wish there was something I could say that would make you understand,' he said, 'but there isn't, because I don't understand it myself. I don't understand how I could have done that to you, or to us.'

I sat down beside him. I held my hands between my knees. 'You have to try, Ralph. I know there is nothing any of us can do to change things, but I need some answers, I want to know what happened.'

Ralph squeezed his eyes shut as if he was trying to remember that night. 'Elton was flirting all night with Gemma,' he said. 'Mary was drinking everything she could lay her hands on. I was drinking as well, probably more than I would have done if you had been there. Towards the end of the evening I noticed that Mary was missing. I assumed she had gone home, but I thought I had better make sure, so I went looking for her. I eventually found her in a dressing room at the back of the stage. The bass player from Elton's band was all over her so I told him to leave her alone, that she was drunk. We had a few words and then he went off. Then…'

'Tell me.'

'Well, Mary was laying back on this pile of old curtains, and she smiled up at me and said something about how she didn't think I had it in me to be such a man. I said I would walk her home, but she asked if I'd stay with her for a few minutes, and I said I would. So I sat down next to her and we talked, stupid talk. We were both so drunk. And next thing…' he looked away from me, towards the wall.

'What?'

'Next thing we were kissing and… It happened so fast. I don't know how it happened. And afterwards, as soon as we'd done it we were both… well… I couldn't believe what I had done; neither could Mary. We both sobered up pretty quickly and then I took her home.'

I shook my head and tried to take in everything he'd said. I had hoped for something else. Something that would have made it easier to forgive him.

'So that's all it was?'

'That's all it was. It was quick and it was pointless and afterwards I thought if I didn't think about it, it would just go away, that you would never know, that it wouldn't affect you or hurt you.'

The truth wasn't dramatic or exciting. Ralph and Mary hadn't been covering up a secret passion, or anything like that. The truth was mundane and dull and sad. All that had happened was that they had both got drunk. That didn't excuse what they'd done, but they hadn't done it to hurt me.

I wasn't angry any more, just terribly sad.

I reached my hand across the bedcover and put it on Ralph's. 'I don't know what to do and I don't know how I'm supposed to feel.'

'I love you,' he said. 'I never stopped loving you.'

I took his face in my hands and kissed him. He looked surprised but then he started kissing me back, so gently, so sweetly and lovingly that I felt the kiss all the way from my lips down to my toes. And I had a feeling in my stomach, something I'd never ever felt before, but it was irresistible, it was urgent, like being dreadfully thirsty and seeing a glass of water in front of you, like kissing the boy I loved, and knowing I was a heartbeat away from having all of him.

Beside me the curtains drifted in the breeze. I felt Ralph pulling away from me.

'Where's Mary and the baby?'

I was confused; what was he talking about? Why was he talking at all?

He put both hands on my shoulders. 'Dottie, where's Mary and Peggy?'

Of course, he didn't know where they were. Ralph was looking at me, waiting for an answer. 'Dottie?'

What had I been thinking? Had I really been about to make love to my best friend's husband? I pulled myself together. I pictured Mary sitting on the couch, so thin, so pale. 'Mary's mum has taken her home, she's ill.'

He shook his head and rubbed at his forehead with the back of his hand. He stood up. 'I have to go.' He leant down and kissed my cheek.

As he got to the bedroom door he turned around.

'None of this is your fault, Dottie.'

'Just go,' I said. 'Just go.'

❊ ❊ ❊

When I got back, Mum was in the kitchen cleaning the oven. When she saw me she straightened up and rubbed the small of her back. I looked down at my feet. I thought she might be able to tell what I'd just done by looking at me. 'Have you been round Mary's all this time?'

I didn't answer her directly.

'Mrs Pickles has taken Mary and Peggy round to her house. They're going to stay there for a few days until Mary feels a bit better,' I said.

'So how is she?'

'I don't know.'

'What do you mean?'

'I didn't go back to their house with her.'

'So what did you do then?'

'Well, I had to wait for Ralph, to let him know where they were.'

'So Ralph's gone round there, has he?'

I was so relieved that that she hadn't suspected anything that I let my frustration with Mary spill out.

'You don't know what it's like round there!' I said. 'Mary's neglecting that baby. She spends all her time on the couch or in bed and she doesn't *do* anything, Mum! Honestly, the flat is disgusting. There were dirty nappies and knickers and stuff all over the bedroom. I cleaned it up.'

'Oh,' said Mum, sounding not the least impressed. 'Doesn't it worry you that Mary is so tired all the time? Don't you think that something might be wrong?'

I shrugged my shoulders and didn't answer.

'Or does it suit you that Mary's not well?'

I could feel my face going red.

'What do you mean?'

'I mean that Mary not coping gives you a reason to be angry with her. A reason, even, to hate her.'

'I don't *hate* her! I just...' I ran out of words. I stared at the ground. All the anger and frustration drained out of me. 'How can I hate Mary?' I pleaded. 'She's my best friend!'

'I know,' said Mum. 'That's why you feel so passionately about her. That's why all this is affecting you so much.'

'But they don't love each other.'

'Are you sure about that, Dottie? Because love comes in all different forms. Is Ralph supporting Mary? Is he helping with the baby?'

I thought about how patient he was with Mary, I had never heard him say a bad word against her, and he was very sweet with Peggy.

'Yes, yes, he's very good.'

'Mary and Ralph are married, Dottie, and whether or not they love each other is no business of yours. I know it's hard, but it's true.'

'It *is* my business!' I shot back. 'I'm the one who has to sit there and listen to Mary going on and on about how miserable she is and how useless she is and how unhappy she is...'

'Mary is your dear friend and you are letting her down.'

'I'm helping her.'

'No, you're not, my love. You're judging her and you're blaming her and it's not doing Mary any good, and it's certainly not helping you. It's got to stop.'

This was hard to hear from my mum, but I couldn't ignore what she was saying. She was the wisest person I knew and I had always respected her judgement.

'What if Mary isn't just wallowing in self-pity? What if she is ill?' Mum asked.

I didn't know what to say. I went slowly upstairs, my legs suddenly felt like lead. I sat down on the bed. Everything felt wrong and I couldn't get Mum's words out of my head. I knew, deep down, that she was right. I trusted my mum. She'd always given me really good advice and now I had disappointed her. I lay down on the bed with my arms behind my head and stared at the damp patch on the ceiling. I wanted to think about Ralph, about what had just happened. I closed my eyes and tried to bring back all the feelings. The way that kiss had made me feel, the way he smelt, how he made me feel beautiful and precious, but I couldn't. All I could think of was how I had betrayed Mary. It wasn't just what I had done, it was what I had wanted to do, before Ralph pulled away. When I closed my eyes again I saw Mary leaning over the basket, talking to Peggy.

Dear Diary,

I like being back in See Saw Lane. I like being in my own little bedroom. I am happier than I have been for a long time. The flat has never felt like home. I lie in my bed and listen to my brothers thumping around the house, they sit on my bed, they make me laugh, they bring life into my little room.

Ralph and mum are taking care of Peggy. They bring her to me clean and fed, she lays on the bed beside me. Ralph, Peggy and me are being cared for, we are loved.

I don't know what's the matter with me. I am so tired. I am just so tired.

Tatty bye

Mary Bennett (at home)

Aged eighteen.

Chapter Thirty-Three

After work the next day I went back round to Mary and Ralph's flat to finish tidying up. The bed was still dishevelled from where we had sat and kissed. I started to remake it. I smoothed out the sheets and tucked in the blankets, that's when I noticed the book, peeking out from under the bed. I picked it up and slowly turned the pages. Peggy's eyes looked back at me, the lashes so intricately drawn they looked real. Every drawing was perfect. Peggy's eyes, her nose, her mouth. A drawing of her chubby little hand with tiny creases of fat circling her wrist and then pictures of Ralph. Ralph holding Peggy on his lap, laughing down at her. Ralph asleep with the baby on his chest. Ralph posing, looking slightly embarrassed, a half smile on his face. Mary had been drawing her family and part of her family was Ralph.

I thought back to last night, I didn't want to but I had to. Ralph had pulled away from me, he had, he had pulled away from me. He hadn't wanted to make love to me. I felt sick and embarrassed and ashamed. I closed the book, put it back under the bed. Mum's words came back to me. 'There are different kinds of love, Dottie.'

When I got home, Mum was sitting at the kitchen table. I didn't want to talk to her. I didn't want to talk to anyone, but she said, 'Sit down a minute, love.'

'Can we talk later?' I said, hanging my coat up behind the door.

'Sit down Dottie, I'll make us a cup of tea.'

I sat down and waited.

It was strangely quiet in the kitchen, neither of us saying a word. There was just the hiss of the boiling kettle, the sound of the water being poured into the cups, the rattle of the spoon against the china as Mum stirred in the sugar. I waited.

Mum put two teas on the table, then she reached across and held my hand.

'Mary is in the hospital,' she said.

I was finding it hard to concentrate on what she was saying. I could see her lips moving but I just couldn't take anything in, it was as if my hearing had gone. All I could think of was the drawings and Ralph pulling away from me. I wished Mum would just shut up.

I shook my head trying to clear it. 'Mary's where?'

'She's been taken to the hospital in an ambulance. Warren came round to let you know.'

'That's good, isn't it? They'll keep an eye on her in there. She can have a proper rest. She won't have to lift a finger there.'

Mum sighed. 'She hasn't gone to hospital for a rest, Dottie.'

'What then?'

'She had a nose bleed. She lost a lot of blood. Mrs Pickles tried to persuade her to go to hospital straight away, but she wouldn't, not until Ralph got home from work.'

I felt confused. I could hear the words Mum was saying, but they didn't seem to make any sense. I tried to ignore what she'd said about Mary wanting to wait for Ralph.

'But a nose bleed isn't serious,' I said. 'Everybody has nose bleeds. Clark used to have them all the time.'

Mum shook her head. 'Sometimes nose bleeds are a symptom of something else.'

'Like what?'

I glared at Mum. I felt horribly angry, not with her in particular but with everyone, with the world.

'The doctors want to do some tests,' Mum said. 'It might be nothing but...'

'She can't be ill. She's just tired, that's all,' I said. 'You told me, her mum told me, everyone said that people are tired when they have babies.'

Mum smiled at me. 'That's probably all it is. It's probably nothing to worry about. At least she's not on her own, Ralph is there with her.'

I groaned.

'Dottie?'

Mum stood up and came round the table. I couldn't look at her. I had to squeeze my eyes shut and bite my fist to stop myself from sobbing or screaming or something.

'Oh Dottie, love!' Mum gently moved the hair out of my face, and stroked my cheek with the back of her hand. 'Try not to worry. I'm sure Mary will be fine.'

'Where's Peggy?' I whispered. 'If Ralph and Mary are both at the hospital…'

'I expect she's with her grandma.'

Now I started to cry, big, wet, snotty sobs.

Mum wrapped her arms around me, cradling me to her as if I were a small child. She let me cry for a while, and when the crying had eased a little she said: 'Things will sort themselves out, you know. It might all seem wrong at the moment but…'

I shook my head. 'No,' I said. 'Nothing will ever be right again.'

Mum sighed. 'We've all been expecting too much from you,' she said. 'You've been through such a lot, haven't you? You were badly hurt but you couldn't do anything about it, because the people who hurt you were the two people you loved.'

I hung onto Mum and she rocked me back and forth against her.

'So you had all this anger and all this pain but no one to be angry with, because it wasn't really anyone's fault. And we all expected you to get on with it, to support Mary all the same. You had to watch her marry Ralph, you helped them get a flat, you've looked after that baby. What you have done has been brave and loyal and strong.'

Mum kissed my head and held me so tight, and I wanted to tell her everything, but I couldn't, I just couldn't.

I swallowed my guilt and wiped my eyes.

'Mary will be all right, won't she?'

'Fingers crossed,' she said.

'Mum?'

'I'm sure she'll be fine.'

Dear Diary,

They have taken me to the hospital, don't worry I've taken you with me. I don't really mind being here. I want the doctors to find out what is wrong with me. Hopefully they can give me some pills to make me better. Everyone is being lovely to me, I am being spoiled.

All of my brothers have been in, looking clean and smart in their best clothes. I bet my mum made them dress up, I can't think that it was their idea. They come in ones and twos. Looking out of the window, leaning against the wall, thumbing through magazines they don't want to read. They look awkward and very young.

Winston stood beside my bed with his head bowed as if he was in a church. Bloody hell boys, lighten up. I'm not dying you know, I'm just not feeling that great.

The doctor is here so I have to go. He looks like Steve McQueen. This place is getting better by the minute.

Tatty Bye.

Mary Bennett.

Aged eighteen.

Chapter Thirty-Four

I hardly slept that night and the next day, I felt exhausted. I went to work but my heart wasn't in it. I hid myself away in the stockroom, tidying the boxes and the shelves. I wanted to be alone, without anyone talking to me. I needed to think.

Sally realised that I needed to be somewhere quiet. I didn't want to talk to people about lipstick and eyeshadow. I didn't want to look over at the sweet counter and remember Mary making funny faces at me over the pick and mix. Sally let me be alone with my thoughts and when anyone else came in to fetch something, they didn't bother me either.

At eleven o'clock Sally put her head round the door and called me into the staffroom. She told me to sit down at a table and brought me a cup of coffee.

'Is Mary going to be all right?' she asked, putting the coffee on the table.

'I hope so,' I said, 'but I don't really know, no one knows much yet.'

'Is she allowed visitors at the hospital?'

'Yes.'

'What time's visiting?'

'Two till three and then this evening.'

'When were you planning to go?'

'I haven't planned anything.' I picked up my coffee cup and blew across the surface. I hadn't looked Sally straight in the eye. I was afraid she might see something in my expression, some badness.

Sally stirred her own coffee. 'Why don't you go to see her this afternoon?'

'Could I?'

'We're hardly run off our feet. You'll feel better once you've seen her.'

'Thanks,' I said, 'you're probably right.'

She smiled. 'It's difficult, isn't it, when somebody you care about is in trouble? The closer you are to a person, sometimes, the harder it is to know what to do for the best. But for now I guess the only thing you can do is be there for her.'

'Yes,' I said.

'Do you fancy a Club biscuit?'

'No thanks, Sally. I'm fine.'

I spent the rest of the morning helping the lads in the stock-room, but by twelve o'clock I couldn't stay any longer. The smell of frying fish wafting down from the canteen was making me feel sick. I felt as if I had a stomach full of frogs.

I caught the bus to the hospital. I sat on the top deck and looked out of the window. When the bus stopped I climbed down the steps, jumped off and walked towards the building. I was far too early for visiting hours but I hadn't wanted to go home. I hadn't wanted to face Mum again.

I sat on a bench in the hospital garden and watched a grey squirrel ferreting round amongst the fallen leaves at the base of a beautiful chestnut tree. I had a tight feeling in my chest, I tried to breathe through it, but I knew it wouldn't go away until I could admit to myself that what I had done to Mary was wrong. I closed my eyes, looked into my heart and didn't like what I found there. It wasn't only that Ralph and me had kissed, it was that I had wanted more, I had expected more, like they both owed it to me. On top of all that I had judged her, just like Mum said I had, and I had done it in the cruellest of ways; I had done it to make myself look good in Ralph's eyes. I hadn't been there for Mary when she needed me most. I should have been more concerned that she was tired all the time, instead of just deciding that she was lazy. I shouldn't have cleaned the flat all the time making Mary feel useless. I should have sat with her and listened to her worries and fears. What did it really matter if the flat was a tip? I had been a bad friend and I was ashamed of myself; now all I wanted was the chance to make it up to her.

The squirrel must have sensed I was there and abruptly stopped what he was doing, he stared at me and then he turned and raced up the tree, disappearing into its branches. I sat on the bench until it was time for me go in. Once again I queued with the other people outside the doors, only this time it wasn't the maternity hospital, it was the Royal Sussex County, a large forbidding-looking building. I had to walk miles and miles through long corridors with brown lino on the floor. The corridors were lit by bare bulbs and every so often I'd come to a junction and there'd be another ward, but the ward Mary was in was right at the very end.

It was a nice, bright ward, much smaller than maternity, but it was quiet, too quiet, and the women in the beds weren't rosy, milky new mothers, but pale, exhausted creatures like people from another planet. Their visitors looked as washed-out as they were, and the nurses who tended them walked softly and spoke gently. The smell was awful. There was the normal odour of polish and disinfectant, but beneath that was the scent of something unfamiliar and frightening; a sweet smell that stung the back of my throat. It made me feel panicky.

Mary was in a bed at the furthest end of the ward. She seemed to have shrunk. Had all the blood bled from her, I wondered. Was this all that was left?

All the things I'd been feeling that morning – the guilt, the shame, the fear and the embarrassment, they all vanished. All I felt was a rush of love for Mary. All I wanted was for her to be back to herself again, for her to be well.

She turned her head towards me. Her face was ashen, her lips dry, her skin a palish grey colour and I realised then that she wasn't just tired; she was ill.

'Hi,' I said. I sat down on the chair beside the bed and smiled at her. She smiled back. Her lips moved but she did not make a sound. I reached out and took hold of her hand. It was tiny and cool, like a fragile little creature.

'Are you all right?' I asked. She blinked slowly and tried to speak, but I could see that the effort was too much for her.

'Oh, Mary…' I said. I felt a little pressure from the tips of her fingers on my hand.

She swallowed, and winced, and then her lips made the shape of the words: 'I'm scared.'

'I know,' I said. 'I'm scared too but you're in the best place now, with people to look after you. They'll have you better in no time.'

'I'm so tired, Dottie, I feel as if I could sleep for a hundred years.'

'Like Sleeping Beauty?' I said, smiling.

'I'm not sure about the beauty bit.'

'You look okay to me,' I said.

'You would say that,' she said softly, so softly that I could barely hear her.

I took a deep breath and from somewhere deep down inside me I found some strength. I leaned closer to Mary, and I made myself smile as if everything was going to be fine, and I looked right into her eyes and I said: 'It's okay, Mary, because whatever happens from now on, it will happen to us together, just like always.'

'Just like always,' she whispered and then she closed her eyes.

I sat by the bed watching her, now and then her eyelids flickered and I wasn't sure if she was asleep or just resting, and as I sat there, I realised that this girl lying on the bed beside me was the most important person in my life. She always had been. I heard a bell go off in the distance, alerting everyone to the fact that visiting time was over. I leaned across the bed and kissed her cheek, 'I'll be back,' I said.

Mary didn't open her eyes but she smiled and said, 'You'd better.'

❊ ❊ ❊

The next weeks went by in a blur. I stood behind the cosmetics counter in Woolworths and I talked to the customers as I normally did. I recommended the right colour lipsticks to go with their outfits and chatted about the weather, the news, the Beatles, Marianne Faithfull. I liked being busy; it meant I didn't have time to think about Mary or Ralph. After work, I walked home through the streets, through the estate and everything was the same but everything was different. At home I sat at the table with my brother and my parents and I ate my dinner and then I went upstairs to my room and I lay on my bed and I stared at the ceiling.

I actually missed Rita. I missed having her there to talk to me. I wondered about going round to see her, but I didn't.

When I thought about Mary, I tried to be positive.

So she was in hospital having tests. So what? That was a *good* thing wasn't it. That was what doctors and hospitals were for. That was the whole point of them, so that when people were ill they went to the hospital and the doctors found out what was wrong and made them better.

And it wasn't like Mary was a sickly person to start with; Mary had never been ill. She was the least ill person I had ever known. She hardly ever even caught colds. So how could she be seriously ill now? It was probably just some kind of deficiency or something. Maybe having the baby had depleted her, somehow. It was bound to be something that was easy to fix, *bound* to be.

Visiting times in the evening were from six until eight, so I started to go to the hospital straight from work, and on my days off I went in the afternoon. Sometimes she would be sleeping and I would pull a chair up close to the bed and just hold her hand for an hour. At other times her bed would be empty when I arrived and the nurse would tell me that Mary was having tests, and then I would stand at the window watching the world go by, until she was brought back into the room in a wheelchair. Nothing much else happened until two weeks later when the test results came back.

Mary had leukaemia.

Dear Diary,

I wish you could speak, because I know that you would tell me what's wrong with me. We tell each other everything don't we? But you're as much in the dark as I am.

Perhaps if I asked them they would say. If I asked them they would have to say, wouldn't they?

Mum and dad were in earlier. Mum looked as if she'd been crying. I don't think I'll ask. I'm too scared to ask.

It's my birthday today. Happy birthday to me.

Tatty Bye

Mary Bennett (coward)

Aged nineteen.

Chapter Thirty-Five

I met Steve in a café on the seafront. It was a lovely day. A warm breeze fluttered the flags strung between the old lamp posts that ran the whole length of the promenade. When you have always lived in one place, you don't always notice how beautiful things are because they are things that you have looked at for the whole of your life. Since Mary had got ill, my senses seemed to have heightened. I looked at things in a different way. Maybe I appreciated everything more, maybe I just appreciated being young and healthy on this beautiful sunny day in the town where I had grown up.

Now as I looked at the intricate designs on the ancient structures, I thought that they were quite beautiful. They were the colour of the sea, a kind of washed-out green, peeling in parts where the salty sea air had battered them over the years.

I think Steve knew what I was going to say to him, I thought he looked a bit sad as he sat down at the table. I had already ordered two coffees, putting a saucer on top of his cup to keep it warm. This wasn't a café I had ever been to before and the coffee was more froth than coffee.

Steve lifted the saucer off the cup. 'I haven't seen you in a while,' he said. 'Is everything alright?'

'My friend is sick.'

'Oh, I'm sorry.'

'So I can't see you any more.'

'You can't see me because your friend is sick?'

How could I explain to him how I was feeling? How there was no room for him, in this life of mine that had narrowed down to a young girl in a hospital bed.

I took a sip of froth, Steve pointed to my upper lip. I wiped the froth away with the back of my hand.

He reached across the table and touched my arm. 'It's okay,' he said. 'You don't have to explain, I can see you're really upset.'

'I'm sorry.'

'Can I send the odd post card from Butlins?'

'I'd like that,' I said.

* * *

Outside the hospital, life carried on as normal. Spring slowly turned into summer. The days began earlier and finished later, the air grew warmer, the flowers in the gardens of the houses on the estate came into bud, the men began to cut their lawns. Inside the hospital, nothing seemed to change. The faces were different, but nothing else; not the smells, not the temperature, not the awful sense of hopelessness. Every day I hoped for some good news, for something better, something to look forward to. And at last, one day, something *was* different. For the first time in a long time, the nurse at the desk smiled at me, not a sad, pitying smile, but a big grin.

'Go on through,' she said. 'Mary's been waiting for you.'

I ran through the ward and when I reached the room, Mary wasn't in the bed but sitting in a chair by the window. The light was falling on her face, and when she turned to smile at me I realised how small she was, and how fragile, like a bird. Her skin was stretched over her bones as if she were made of something precious and delicate. But she was sitting up, and smiling. I lay the flowers I had bought on the bed, and then I leant down and kissed her cool cheek.

'Look at you!' I said.

'Yes, look at me! Sitting in a chair today, and if I have my way I'll be roller-skating tomorrow.'

I laughed and pulled up the other chair so that I was sitting opposite her, our knees touching.

'Are you feeling better?' I asked.

She nodded. 'They gave me a transfusion and they did a good job. I feel like a ten-year-old again. I was even hungry this morning. I haven't felt hungry in ages. I had two pieces of toast and some scrambled egg.'

'Maybe the blood came from some big handsome man with a big appetite.'

'Maybe. Our mum's had all my brothers giving blood. She said if they were going to fill me up with blood, she'd rather keep it in the family. I told her they gave me Pickles blood to keep her happy, although when they fetch a packet out the fridge it doesn't have the donor's name on.'

I smiled. 'I don't care where it came from, it's just lovely to see you out of bed.'

'I really hope this is the start of me getting better,' said Mary. 'If they can keep giving me new blood, and I can keep eating and doing a bit more each day, there's no reason why I shouldn't be well enough to come home soon, is there?'

I hoped that was true. I hoped that was true with every inch of me. I took Mary's hand and held it and for a few moments we sat in silence, both of us planning the things we would do together when Mary recovered enough to leave hospital.

'What would you like to do first?' I asked.

'I think I'd like to go on to the pier and eat an ice cream,' said Mary. 'Not a cornet but one of those blocks of ice cream that you eat between two wafers. They're the nicest.'

'Okay,' I said. 'We'll do that first.'

'And then I'd like to go dancing. I'd like you and me to dress up really nice and have our hair put up and go out on the town.'

'We could wear false eyelashes.'

Mary giggled. 'Yes, definitely. And I'd like to have the last dance, the one that counts, with Elton. I'd like to know what it feels like to be in his arms again. I'd like him to hold me close and look into my eyes and perhaps kiss me.'

I rolled my eyes.

'What?'

'He'd have a job looking into your eyes, he's a foot taller than you.'

We were both laughing when Mary's laugh turned into a horrible cough. I gently rubbed her back until it passed. Her eyes went all watery and pink and we both remembered that she was still very ill. For a while we sat quietly. Mary closed her eyes and leant her head back against the chair. I covered her over with a crocheted blanket her mum had left for her. A nurse brought me a cup of milky tea and I sipped it, trying not to make a noise with the cup and saucer. Mary, suddenly, opened her eyes and looked at me again.

'I'm glad you're here,' she said.

'Where else would I be?'

'I can hardly remember a time when you haven't been here for me.'

I could hardly look at Mary, because it wasn't true. When Mary needed me most, I wasn't there at all. When Mary needed me most, I was kissing her husband. I am a bad friend, but I will make it up to her. She's all that matters now.

She sighed. 'Would you mind helping me back into bed? If we're going to go dancing I'm going to need my beauty sleep.'

'Too right,' I said.

I helped her out of the chair and into the bed, lifting her legs up for her, covering her over like a little child.

'Do you want a drink or anything?'

She shook her head, rested back into the pillow.

I sat back in the chair and watched Mary breathing; her breath was shallow and sounded sort of bubbly. It was so quiet that the noise seemed to fill the little room, and although part of me wished I was anywhere but here in this hospital, it was only there that I felt truly at peace, because as long as I could see her chest rising and falling I knew she was still with me. Some people had loads of friends, like the girls in the sack factory, and some people didn't have any, like my sister Rita, but I had always had Mary and I knew that if she left me I would be lost.

I stroked Mary's forehead very gently until she closed her eyes.

It was warm and peaceful in Mary's hospital room. A bee was buzzing at the window, trying to find its way out. I stood up and went to help it, guiding it to freedom with the magazine. It spiralled away without a care in the world. It seemed so wrong that a little insect could leave, but Mary couldn't. She couldn't go anywhere.

I sat down again and the cushion of the chair made a little *whoosh* noise beneath me. I rested my cheek on my hand and I closed my eyes.

❄ ❄ ❄

Mrs Pickles came into Woolworths to buy more nappies for Peggy. She said she couldn't be doing with washing and drying the dozen she had, not with having to fit in all the visits to the hospital and still looking after the baby.

I said: 'How was Mary today? She looked lots better last time I saw her.'

Mrs Pickles rummaged in her purse. 'She has good days and bad days, love,' she said.

That was all we said about Mary. After that Mrs Pickles stood in front of the cosmetics counter with the pram beside her and a bundle of new nappies tucked under her arm and carried on telling me how difficult it was to keep on top of the laundry and I stood beside the counter and listened and sympathised.

We were all the same. None of us told the truth – that what was upsetting us was that Mary was so ill. Instead we complained about little things: the buses always being late, barking dogs, the unseasonal heat, the nappies soaking in the bucket.

Peggy was in the pram, fussing. She was sitting now, propped up against the pillows. I wanted to pick her up, but I didn't think I should. It wouldn't have felt right. I looked at her though. I looked at her nuzzling at her fist with her mouth, and her hand all wet where she had been trying to suck it, and I noticed how she had rubbed away the hair at the back of her head so there was a bald patch, and I saw that her eyelashes were growing, and that she was bigger than she had been the last time I saw her. I had missed seeing her.

'She's a good girl,' said Mrs Pickles. 'She's no bother, that one.'

We smiled at Peggy and, delighted by the attention, she grinned a wide, gummy grin back up at us.

On my next day off, I went to the corner shop and bought a bag of pear drops for Mary, and a magazine. It was good for me not to have to rush for once. I knew I'd be able to sit with Mary for longer than usual and, even if she was sleeping, we'd be together.

I didn't really expect her to be interested in the magazine, but it seemed wrong to turn up with nothing. And if she was sleeping, at least I could look at it.

When I reached the ward that day Mary wasn't in her bed. She was sitting in the day room at the end of the ward wearing a pink dressing gown and fluffy slippers, looking out over the garden. Perhaps she was going to get better after all.

I skipped into the room and hugged her. And she felt thin and fragile beneath the winceyette gown, as if her bones were not joined together, but she had a colour to her cheeks and her eyes were bright, like they used to be.

'You're looking better,' I said.

'I'm feeling better,' said Mary. She looked at the paper bag in my hand. 'Please don't tell me you brought me grapes. People keep buying me grapes and I keep throwing them away. I never want to see another grape as long as I live.'

'I bought you pear drops,' I said.

'Good,' said Mary. She smiled at me and I smiled at her.

'So what's new?' I said.

'My pills,' said Mary. 'They're trying me on some new ones.'

'They seem to be working.'

Mary nodded. 'The doctor said they've got high hopes for them. They might turn out to be some kind of...'

'What?'

I sat down in the chair next to hers. She looked up at me and her eyes were bright and shining.

'Some kind of cure, they don't really know because they're so new and everything, but they've been using them in America and the results have been, oh what was the word they used?'

'Miraculous?' I asked hopefully.

'No,' Mary shook her head. 'Promising. They said the results were promising. But that's good, isn't it? That's a lot better than nothing!'

'It is!' I said. 'It's fabulous!'

My heart was beating more strongly than it had for weeks. I hadn't let myself think about a future since Mary became ill, because I could not bear to think of a life without her. For the first time since her diagnosis, I felt hope. It pulsed through me, in my veins. I allowed myself to imagine Mary might get better. This awful illness of hers might not be all that was left for her. It might be the beginning of a new stage in her life.

'So it's not the end of Mary Pickles yet!' Mary said. 'Watch out Brighton, I'll be back before you know it!'

There was something about the bright way she said this, something that made me think she did not quite believe it herself.

'You have to be positive, Mary,' I said. 'For Peggy's sake. For mine.'

'Yes,' Mary said, but she did not look at me.

I followed her gaze through the window. There was a very small but pretty garden beyond. A nurse was pushing the handles of a wheelchair. A very old man was wrapped up in blankets inside the chair. Beside them was a little girl picking daisies from the lawn. She had beautiful, strawberry blonde hair, just like Peggy's. I glanced across at Mary, and she shot me back a too-bright smile. I felt something break deep inside me.

Mary sniffed and wiped her nose with her forefinger.

'You'll never guess who's in here too!' she said.

'Who?'

'Louise Morgan! You remember Louise? She was at school with us. She was always being sick!'

'What's wrong with her this time?'

'No she's not a patient, she's a nurse!'

'That figures,' I said, 'she's had all that experience of hospitals.'

'It was nice to see her again,' said Mary. 'We were talking about old times. She told me...'

'What?'

'That you were always very kind to her.'

I laughed. 'I barely remember her.'

'You were nice to everyone.'

Mary picked at her fingernails. 'I'm sorry, Dottie. I'm sorry I hurt you.'

I shook my head.

I reached over and took hold of her hand. 'It doesn't matter any more,' I said and it didn't. All that mattered now was Mary.

Chapter Thirty-Six

Mum had cooked some chips to go with our Spam for tea.

'It's nice to see you've got your appetite back,' she said. 'You've been eating like a bird these past weeks.'

'Like a very big, fat bird,' said Clark. I stuck my tongue out at him. He kicked me under the table. Dad told us to grow up. It was just like the old days.

'Mary's on some new tablets,' I said. 'From America. She looks about a million times better.'

Mum paused with her vinegar bottle halfway over her chips and looked at me.

'Oh, Dottie!' she said.

'She's one of the first people in England to have them,' I said. 'They don't know for sure what will happen, but at least...'

I was going to say, at least they hadn't given up on Mary, but I couldn't get the words out. Mum put the vinegar down and Dad made a funny sort of sniffing noise.

'Does that mean she might not die after all?' Clark asked.

I nodded.

'She might get better?'

'Yes.'

Dad blew his nose loudly.

'Just for once,' he said, 'can we not talk about hospitals and tablets at the dinner table?' He pushed back his chair and got up from the table.

I looked at Mum and she looked back at me.

'We all have to deal with it in our own way,' she said.

For a week or so, Mary did seem to get better. Visiting the hospital became less of a tragic event, and more of a social one.

The ward always seemed to be full of Mary's brothers, those boys with their big feet and their noise and their smells of petrol and sweat and outdoors. Everyone liked having them there, all those pale, exhausted women seemed to come back to life a bit when the boys were walking down the aisle between the beds. They said 'hello' to everyone, they gave a bit of banter. It was almost fun when the boys were there. It meant everything started to feel normal.

Then one day, I came in early and I saw the pram at the end of the ward, beside Mary's bed and a black jacket hooked over the handles. I turned round at once and hurried back up the aisle, but at the swing doors at the entrance to the ward, I found myself face to face with Ralph. He was carrying Peggy in one arm and a vase full of water in his other hand. When he saw me, it slipped from his hands and the vase bounced once on the lino, spilling the water all over the floor.

'Christ!' Ralph said. 'I'm sorry!' He passed Peggy to me and leaned down and began to mop at the water with his handkerchief. The nurse at the desk picked up the vase and waved us away.

'Leave it, leave it!' she said. 'I'll sort it out.'

Ralph and I stood and looked at one another. Peggy was a warm, heavy, solid little bundle against my chest. I felt a lurch deep inside me. I breathed in the scent of her, the soap and milk and soft-haired essence of the baby. She grunted a little and smiled up at me. It was lovely to hold her again.

'Oh God,' I whispered. 'I've missed you so much.'

Ralph breathed in, and then slowly out.

'I've missed you too,' he said.

'I didn't mean…' I stopped. I did not know what to say to him. I didn't know what to do. Ralph didn't either. He scratched behind his ear.

'Mary's sleeping,' he said. 'She's not quite so good today.'

'I'll come back later then,' I said, but I held onto Peggy. She was wearing a little summer dress, patterned with daisies that I had not seen before and a white knitted matinee jacket. Her chin was wet and a little red.

'She's teething,' Ralph said. 'Her mouth's sore.'

'Poor thing.'

'I was going to take her out. For a walk, I mean, while Mary's sleeping.'

'Good,' I said. 'I'll stay here then, while you're out, in case Mary wakes up.'

Still I held onto Peggy.

Ralph sighed. 'Could we go outside together for a minute?'

I couldn't think of any reason not to.

Ralph fetched the pram and I lay Peggy in it. She fussed at first, but we walked out of the hospital and into the gardens. I pushed the pram along the path, smiling down at the baby, talking to her so I did not have to say anything to Ralph.

After a while her eyelids grew heavy and she yawned like a kitten, and then she fell asleep, and there was no reason not to sit beside Ralph on a bench in the shade of the horse chestnut tree and to watch the sparrows and wood pigeons pecking amongst the dappled shadows on the lawn.

For a moment or two, neither of us said anything, and then Ralph started to talk as if he couldn't get his words out quickly enough.

'I know you think this isn't a good time and maybe it isn't, but I don't think there will be a good time, I don't think there will be a good time ever again,' he said, 'and I need you to hear me because I can't sleep and I can't eat and I'm supposed to be strong for Mary and look after Peggy and…'

Ralph put his head in his hands and suddenly his whole body was heaving with sobs.

I hesitated for a moment, then tentatively I put my arms around him. I was overwhelmed by a wave of feelings, and I gave in to them. I held onto Ralph, my cheek against his hair, until he had calmed down. I held onto him. For a few moments it was just the two of us in the world.

When he calmed down I passed him the hankie that I kept up my sleeve and he rubbed at his face.

'I don't know how to do this,' he said. 'Any of it.'

I pushed his hair back out of his eyes. I wanted to kiss away his pain. I wished there was something I could do to make it easier for him.

'None of us do,' I said. 'We're all just making it up as we go along.'

'I hurt you again, didn't I?'

'I think it was me that hurt me, but it doesn't matter now.'

'Doesn't it?'

'No, not now.'

We sat for a while, and it was all right, it was not difficult being so close together, with the people walking past, the nurses coming off duty, the visitors clutching carnations wrapped in paper and baskets of fruit. It wasn't difficult sitting beside Ralph at all.

Chapter Thirty-Seven

Summer was here properly now. The schoolchildren were wearing their summer clothes, the beaches were busy every afternoon and Brighton had put on its bright, cheerful summer face.

Down the ward I could hear coughing and the rattle of the tea trolley, murmurs of conversation, laughter. There was a nice lady who brought round tea and biscuits every afternoon. She had a way of finding something funny and cheerful to say to everyone.

'The tea's on its way,' I said, 'could you manage a custard cream?'

Mary smiled or grimaced. I'm not sure which. The edges of her lips twitched. A white crust had formed at the corner of her mouth.

'So thirsty,' she said in a hoarse whisper.

'Would you like some water?'

'Mmm.'

I moved onto the bed and gently lifted Mary until she was propped almost upright against the pillows. Her skin was faintly blue, as if it were changing into water, or sky. Mary was fading; she was literally fading away.

I poured some water from the metal jug into the glass, and held it to Mary's lips. The water tipped into her mouth and most of it dribbled out again and ran down her neck and her chin, soaking the top of her nightdress.

'Oh, Mary, I'm sorry!' I cried.

Her mouth was open again, she was leaning towards the rim of the glass.

'Thirsty,' she whispered, and we tried again.

This time I managed to get it right and Mary took tiny sips of water, then she shook her head.

'Want to have a little sleep?' I asked, putting the glass back on the table. She nodded her head and already her eyes were closing.

I walked over to the window and stared down at the garden, it looked so peaceful. I desperately wanted some of that peace, even if it was only for a moment. I turned away and looked back at Mary. Suddenly she opened her eyes and stared at me.

'What?' I said.

'Do you think I'll see Harold?'

For a second I couldn't think what she was talking about. 'Harold?'

'My hamster, do you think Harold will be in Heaven?'

'I don't see why not,' I said, smiling at her, 'but that won't be for a long time.'

'Good!' she said and closed her eyes again.

Mary's hamster, Harold Pickles. I smiled. Mary had been given Harold for her ninth birthday. We used to spend hours teaching him how to jump over matchboxes. I remembered the day I heard about Harold's accident.

I was standing at the bus stop waiting for Mary. This was unusual because she was always there first. Mary timed how long it took her to get from her house to the bus stop and every morning she tried to break her own record. I thought I'd have to go on the bus by myself and I'd have no Mary Pickles to stand up for me when Dominic Roberts volunteered to rearrange my face. Then she came round the corner, and she was crying, and her face looked all pitiful and tragic, and I started falling over backwards trying to make her feel happy again. I hated it when Mary cried.

'Whatever's wrong?' I asked, putting my arm round her shoulders.

'It's Harold Pickles,' she said.

'What's happened to him?' I asked, fearing the worst.

'Well,' sniffled Mary, 'the twins gave Harold a swimming lesson in the boating lake last night and he drowned.'

'Which one?' I said, amazed, because both the twins are really good swimmers.

'Not the twins,' yelled Mary. 'Harold Pickles, and now he's dead!'

'Oh Mary,' I said, 'I'm really sorry.'

'Thanks,' she said, wiping her eyes on the sleeve of her blazer.

Mary was very quiet all the way to school, so I just sat next to her and held her hand. When the bus stopped everyone was pushing to get off and I accidentally banged into the back of Fiona Ferris, who had three ballet lessons a week and ate sandwiches with the crusts cut off and who Mary called Finicky Ferris.

'Watch who you're shoving,' said Fiona. 'I'm going to be a famous ballerina one day, and you might damage my legs, and my legs are my fortune.'

'Good job they are,' said Mary, 'because your face wouldn't open a Post Office account.' Fiona walked off in a huff.

Mary and I linked arms and I promised her one of my banana sandwiches at lunchtime.

'I really am sorry about Harold,' I said. 'He was ever so talented.'

'I know he was,' said Mary. 'There'll never be another hamster like him.'

'What have you done with him?' I said.

'I've wrapped him in cellophane and put him in a shoe box. I'm going to bury him after school. You can come if you like.'

'I'd love to,' I said, thinking what a waste of time all that training had been.

When I got home from school that afternoon, Mum was in the front room reading her latest library book.

'I'm home, Mum,' I said.

'Are you, dear?' she said barely looking up.

'What are you reading?'

'It's called *Arabian Passion*.'

'What's it about?' I said, twisting my neck round trying to look at the cover.

'It's about this handsome sheik who kidnaps a beautiful servant girl and takes her off to his harem in the desert.'

'What's a harem?'

'Well, it's a sort of big tent.'

'I'm going round to Mary's,' I said.

'That's nice, dear,' said Mum, burying her head back in the book.

I went into the kitchen for a glass of water just as Clark barged through the door.

'Is tea nearly ready?' he said.

'I shouldn't think so for one minute,' I said. 'The handsome sheik is just about to take the cleaner camping.'

'You're round the twist,' he said.

'Better than being round the bend I suppose.'

'Please tell me I'm adopted!'

'You're adopted.'

Just then Rita came through the back door. She had had an audition at school for *A Midsummer Night's Dream*. 'I've got Hippolyta,' she announced, draping herself against the door frame.

'And the first symptom of this deadly disease,' said Clark, 'is a swollen head.'

Rita glared at him. 'You are really not as funny as you think you are, Clark Perks,' she said.

'And you are really not as important as you think you are,' said Clark.

Actually I thought my little brother was hilarious. I left them to it and ran round to Mary's.

Mr Pickles was in the front garden pulling up weeds as if his life depended on it.

William was kicking a ball around and Wallace was swinging off the gate, he jumped down. 'We're being treated like mass murderers,' he said.

'Well, it was a pretty daft thing to do,' I said.

'We didn't know he'd sink,' said William.

'Harold was a hamster, William,' I said, 'not a cross-Channel swimmer.' And I walked round the back of the house. Mary's mum was in the kitchen, mixing something in a bowl.

'Hello, Dottie,' she said. 'Come for the funeral?'

'Yes, Mrs Pickles,' I said.

'You'll need some clothes then,' she said.

'Pardon?' I said.

'Clothes for the funeral,' she said.

'Oh,' I said, 'I hadn't thought of that.'

'Would you mind just taking a mug of tea out to Mr Pickles first?'

'Of course not,' I said.

'He's had some bad news, he always does the garden when he's upset. God forgive me, but there are times when I wish he'd get upset a bit more often, it's the only time it gets done.'

'It's nothing serious, is it?'

'Tommy Dorsey just died.'

I waited for her to enlarge on it, but she just handed me the mug of tea. I carried the tea outside and went up to Mr Pickles. 'I've brought you some tea,' I said.

Mr Pickles stood. 'Thanks, Dottie,' he said, taking the mug.

'I'm sorry about your friend.'

'What friend?' said Mr Pickles, wiping the sweat from his forehead with the back of his hand.

'Tommy Dorsey,' I said.

'Oh he wasn't a friend, no, I never met him, wish I had though, he'll be a great loss. He was only fifty-one, Dottie, and that's no age at all.'

'No age at all,' I said as solemnly as I could.

I walked back into the house feeling confused. Mrs Pickles looked up from her mixing bowl and wiped her hands down her apron.

'Now about those clothes,' she said.

She left the room and came back with one of Wayne's coats. 'Now we just need something for your head.' She rummaged in a drawer and took out a brown tea cosy. 'This should be all right,' she said, smiling. I put on the coat, then put the tea cosy on my head. It was shaped like a cottage and it had a chimney sticking out of the top.

Just then Wesley came into the kitchen, he scooped up some of the cake mix and said: 'Love the outfit, Dottie.' I could feel myself going red, so I went down the garden to find Mary. She was standing in front of a newly dug hole in the ground, wearing her old witch's fancy-dress outfit.

'What's that on your head?' she said, laughing.

'A cottage,' I said.

'We're ready, Mum,' she yelled up the garden.

I could hear Mary's mum rounding up the boys.

'I hate to think of Harold lying in the ground,' she said, looking sad.

I put my arm around her. 'He was a good friend,' I said.

Just then the back door opened and all Mary's brothers started walking slowly down the garden. They came down in twos, balancing a Freeman, Hardy and Willis shoe box above their heads. They laid the box at Mary's feet and Mary placed it in the hole. Then they gathered around the grave with their heads bowed.

'I thought we would sing *All Things Bright and Beautiful*,' said Mary, sniffing.

'Good choice, Mary,' said Warren.

I thought the funeral was very dignified, as befitted a hamster that could nearly jump over five matchboxes.

I went back to the house to take off the clothes, then Mary walked me back to the top of the twitten.

'Who's Tommy Dorsey?' I said.

'He's a band leader, my dad's really upset that he died, he's got all his records.'

Now it made sense. I ran down the twitten and we called to each other until I was at the other end.

'Mary.'

'Dottie.'

'Mary.'

'Dottie.'

Chapter Thirty Eight

I became very superstitious. I would not walk under ladders, I threw salt over my shoulder, I touched wood, I said 'good morning' to magpies and kept my fingers crossed. I made little one-sided bargains with God. I said: *You make Mary better and I'll never complain about anything for the rest of my life.* I would not let a bad thought into my mind. I would not allow myself to imagine, not for a single moment, what the world would be like if Mary died.

And on the surface, at least, things seemed to be going well.

The new tablets seemed to be working but there were side effects. Sometimes Mary was nauseous. Her face puffed up, and her skin became very dry and flaky, but she was cheerful. She had definitely put on a little of the weight she had lost and she was 'sick and tired' of being in the hospital.

Mary told me she had heard the doctors talking. They didn't think she understood, but she was not stupid. She knew that her body wasn't responding as well as they'd hoped. She knew they were worried.

One day, while we were there together, just the two of us, I was telling her about all the girls on television screaming at the Beatles and she said: 'It's not fair! I'm not an old lady, I'm a teenage girl. I want to have fun too.'

'Hmmm,' I said. Then I leaned towards her and whispered: 'Are you actually allowed out of here or do we have to set up an escape committee?'

Mary narrowed her eyes and glanced from side to side in a dramatic fashion.

'There are spies everywhere,' she whispered. 'We may have to tunnel our way out.'

'We could start digging under your bed.'

'And fill our pockets with soil and shake it out in the garden when nobody's looking.'

'And once the tunnel's long enough we'll wriggle through and emerge on the other side of the fence.'

'We'll need false documents. And disguises.'

'And a motorbike.'

'Oh yes, and a motorbike.'

'Has Winston fixed the one on your front lawn yet?'

'I can ask.'

'But if we're caught, the punishment will be severe.'

'Terrible.'

A nurse came in just then with a small glass of water for Mary, and some pills in a little plastic beaker.

'What are you two plotting?' she asked, passing the pills to Mary.

'How we're going to get me out of here,' Mary said.

'It's not a prison,' said the nurse with a smile. 'Let me have a word with the doctor and we'll see if your friend can't take you out for some fresh air some day soon.'

I went back to the hospital every day that week, and me and Mary were back to how we used to be. We didn't *need* anybody else; we were enough, just the two of us, Mary and me. In a strange, distorted kind of way, that was one of the best weeks of my life. It was almost as if I had never met Ralph or that Mary had ever lusted after Elton. Somehow it didn't matter anymore, none of it mattered anymore.

My world was a young girl in a hospital room and I didn't want to be anywhere else.

I'd forgotten how much fun it was being with Mary. And there were plenty of things in the hospital to make jokes about; the arrogant consultants with their long noses and their spectacles and the way everyone else treated them like gods; the other patients with their funny sayings. One woman's catchphrase was: 'Oooh! Me hip!' Another's was: 'Have a heart, won't you?' We teased Mary's brothers when they came to visit, reassured her parents and renamed the nurses after famous people; there was Ursula Andress, Audrey Hepburn, Marianne Faithfull, Cilla Black and Hattie Jacques. The handsome young doctor who let his white coat flap around his thighs and winked at Mary every time he went past was Steve McQueen. We pretended we were part of this made-up world, and Louise, who was in and out all the time, was part of it too. Mary, of course, was the star and I was her servant and Louise was the straight man. I was happy for Mary to be the star. She loved it, she loved lying back on her bed and snapping her fingers and giving me stupid orders: 'Fetch me my bedpan, girl!' she would say. 'And hurry! Mr McQueen is due any minute and I want to look my best for him!' We laughed so much that the nurses used to have to keep telling us to be quiet.

Only sometimes, all of a sudden, a cloud would pass over Mary's face and her eyes would slide closed. It was like somebody had switched off a light inside her. At those times I learned to make her comfortable, and cover her over to keep her warm, and then I would just sit with her, holding her cool little hand between mine.

One day, Mrs Pickles and I went together. She struggled on the bus with Peggy and the pram, and I never minded going with her. Looking after Peggy made me feel as if I was doing something, however small, to atone for what I had done to Mary. I didn't mind listening to Mrs Pickle's endless stream of complaints about the hardness of her life. I could see she was exhausted and I knew she couldn't say any of this to Mary.

It wasn't one of Mary's good days. The curtains were pulled around her bed when we arrived. The nurse at the end station told us the doctor was with her, and we had to wait until he had finished before we went to see her.

It was the tall, thin doctor, the one who rather scared me. He came through the curtains with a flourish, as if he were walking onto the stage of a theatre, and the trainee doctors followed behind. The doctor saw Mrs Pickles and me waiting at the end of the ward, and he strode towards us.

'Well there's good news and there's not so good news!' he said cheerfully. I felt my stomach lurch. I saw Mrs Pickles reach out her hand and hold onto the handle of the pram for support. 'The good news,' said the doctor, 'is that we're going to give Mary a room of her own. That'll be nice, won't it? You'll be able to stay with her as long as you like then. We'll move her as soon as we can find somewhere suitable.'

He beamed at the two of us, rubbed his hands together, and strode off through the double doors and out into the corridor. The younger doctors scuttled after him, the heels of their shoes clicking on the lino.

Mrs Pickles stared at the floor.

The doctor hadn't told us the not so good news. He didn't have to.

We sat with Mary until she slept and then Mrs Pickles went off to find a cup of tea.

I stayed with Mary, lying Peggy on my lap so that she was facing up at me, with her head on my knees, and playing with her fat little legs. Her teeth were still giving her trouble and she gnawed at her rattle constantly. I didn't hear anyone come towards me, until I felt a gentle hand on my shoulder. I looked up, and it was Rita. She smiled down at me. Nigel was standing a few paces behind her wringing his hat in his hands and looking wan.

Peggy wriggled in my lap.

'How is Mary?' Rita asked.

'She's sleeping,' I said. 'They're…'

'What?'

'They're going to move her into a private room.'

Rita sighed.

'Sit down if you like,' I said.

Rita perched on the chair beside mine. She reached out and tickled Peggy's chin. Peggy grinned up at her and made some gurgling noises.

'She's gorgeous, isn't she!'

'Yes,' I agreed. 'Do you want to hold her?'

Rita's face lit up. 'Can I? Do you think that would be all right?'

'Of course,' I said. 'I'd be glad. She's getting a weight now, I've lost all the feeling in my legs!'

I passed Peggy to my sister. Rita took her a little gingerly, but Peggy was so confident, beaming into Rita's face, that she relaxed almost at once. She held the baby on her lap, and Peggy bounced up and down on her legs, pulling at the collar of Rita's dress.

Rita looked at Peggy with adoration in her eyes, and behind Rita, Nigel watched them both, and I thought: this is what happens. Nobody's life turns out how they imagined it would. Things go wrong, and all any of us can do is make the best of it.

It's all we can do.

Dear Diary,

They've given me a room of my own, so I guess things must be pretty bad. I know that there is something wrong with my blood, but I won't think about that now.

My room overlooks the gardens, there is a big tree outside that taps against my window in the wind. I like the sound it makes. Tap, tap, tap, it goes, as if it's asking to come in. It lets me know that it's alive, that's what I want now. I want life, I want beginnings. Peggy is my beginning, my blood runs through her veins, but it's good blood, not bonkers blood like mine.

I'm tired.

Tatty bye.

Love Mary Bennett

Aged nineteen.

Chapter Thirty-Nine

I was sitting on a bench beside the boating lake. I had taken to going to the places that Mary and I used to go to when we were kids. It made me feel closer to her somehow. It was one of those perfect days, the sun was shining and there was a warm breeze that rippled the water and fluttered the flags on the little motor boats. There was so much to remember about our childhood, so many mad, barmy situations that Mary led me into. I was always happy to follow where Mary led, it wasn't until I was in the middle of one of Mary's bonkers escapades that I started having second thoughts.

There was the time when she'd made me pretend to faint in assembly so that she could get out of school to take me home because she wanted to catch a glimpse of The Beatles who were coming to play at the Dome and I'd bumped my head on the door as they were carrying me out and ended up with a black eye. And there was the time she'd convinced me it would be a good idea to let the photographer from the Argus take a picture of us on the beach 'because we looked so gorgeous' and he made us sit on the donkeys and I looked like an elephant. And the time she made me enter a talent competition because Elton was entering it and she wanted to get to know him better. I ended up singing *The Merry Merry Pipes of Pan*, dressed in a striped beach towel. Not my proudest moment. But Mary was fun to be with and she made my life more fun; she made my life better.

That was the Mary I knew, that was the Mary I remembered. The girl who passed the eleven-plus but refused to go to the grammar school, even though most people said she had to. The girl who took my hand and made me believe that I could be brave just like her. The little girl who hung upside down and saw the world and all its wonderful possibilities in a way that most little girls don't.

She had been lost for a while and I could have found her but I didn't. She would have found me if I had lost my way, I know she would.

My friend Mary Pickles was special and I would remind her of that every day of her life.

I got off the bench and headed for the hospital, because today I had something very special to do.

I was at the hospital exactly on time. Louise was waiting for me at the nurses' station by the ward doors.

She took both my hands in hers and squeezed them.

'She's all ready!' she said. 'Wait until you see her!'

We went together through the ward and down a small passageway that led to Mary's private room. The door was ajar, and we heard laughter from inside.

Mary was not only out of bed, she was dressed in proper clothes, sitting in a wheelchair, with her hair curled and wearing make-up.

'Blimey,' I said. 'Look at you!'

Mary patted her hair. 'Gorgeous, aren't I!'

'And modest with it,' said Nurse Brigitte Bardot. She was about sixty and had bad breath, but she looked as proud as if she were Mary's mother.

'I'll be all right, nurse,' Mary said. 'My driver will look after me now!'

The nurse tucked a blanket around Mary's knees and squeezed her shoulder.

'You look after her, mind,' she said to me. 'No matter what she says to you, don't let her get out of that wheelchair. If she overdoes it, she'll be in all kinds of trouble.'

'I won't,' I said. I smiled at Mary. I felt proud of her. And at the same time there was a prickly, hot feeling at the back of my eyes. It wasn't the blanket round her legs; it was the toes of her shoes sticking out beneath its hem. They were the same shoes Mary had worn the day she married Ralph, only now they were all scuffed and the leather was worn. I thought of all the life that had happened to all of us since Ralph and Mary's wedding. I tried not to think about it.

'Come on, Dottie, hurry up and get me out of here before they change their minds!' Mary ordered.

'Okay,' I said.

'Where are you taking me?'

'To the pier, m'lady,' I said.

It took me a while to get used to pushing the wheelchair. It was heavy, and although it was all right going in a straight line, as soon as we had to go round corners, or up and down steps, I ran into problems. Mary kept up a commentary on my bad driving, which amused her no end. People turned to stare at us.

We went to the end of the pier, and because it was a beautiful sunny day, it was packed. I got very hot under the armpits manoeuvring the wheelchair through the crowds and round people's legs. In the end we parked it behind a stack of deckchairs.

'I want to get out,' Mary said.

'You can't. The nurse said under no circumstances…'

'She's not here. You don't have to tell her!'

'Mary!'

'Oh come on, Dottie, help me out. It's the least you can do!'

I rolled my eyes, but at the same time I was laughing. I helped Mary to her feet, and she leaned into me as we went into the arcade. Music was blaring out of the jukebox and there were lots of young people all dressed up and chewing gum, dancing and shouting and having a good time. I could see from the light in

Mary's eyes that this was exactly where she wanted to be. Part of me was worrying about her doing too much. I knew she shouldn't be out of the wheelchair, I knew she should be keeping quiet and sitting down, but I'd told Louise what I'd planned and she'd agreed that Mary's happiness was the most important thing now.

And Mary was happy, I knew she was. There was no way I was going to deny her that.

She played a few of the slot machines while I held her up and then we headed for the ice cream bar, and we were in the queue when somebody tapped Mary on the shoulder and said: 'Hello, you!'

Mary turned slowly and looked up from under her fringe. 'Hello, Elton,' she said.

Elton swallowed. I could see the tension in his skinny neck. He was holding a hat in his hands, some kind of cap; it was the fashion. Elton had nice eyes, I realised. He was an arrogant so-and-so, but he had a kind face. And Mary's face was lit up like the seafront at Christmas.

'You look nice,' Elton said.

'Thank you,' said Mary.

Without being prompted, Elton took hold of Mary's arm. She steadied herself against him.

I stepped away from her a little, to watch. She held onto Elton's eyes, and of course this was all she'd ever wanted, and Elton Briggs was looking into Mary's eyes as if she was the only girl in the world.

He pushed the gum he was chewing into the side of his cheek. 'Listen, Ralph told me… I'm sorry…' he said. Mary gave the tiniest shake of her head and she smiled at Elton. She smiled her best, most alluring smile, the one she'd practised for hours in front of the mirror. And before, when she'd done it, she'd always looked like a child pretending to be grown up. But now, now she looked like a woman. A beautiful woman. Elton saw it too. He gave the smallest bow, and took her free hand in his.

'Would you like to dance with me, Mary?' he asked.

'I'd love to dance with you,' she said.

So for the first and last time, Mary Bennett, née Pickles, and Elton Briggs danced to Cliff Richard singing *The Young Ones*. Elton held Mary in his arms, and her head was against his chest; they moved very slowly, and though there were dozens of other couples on the dance floor, it was as though they were the only two people in the world.

I sat on a stool and watched the dance for a moment or two, but watching felt wrong. This was their time; their only time. I wandered over to the railings, and leaned on them, and stared down at the sea as it rose and fell and splashed against the barnacled legs of the pier.

When the song was over, I went back inside and I saw the tiredness come into Mary's eyes again, like a curtain closing, and Elton saw it too. He didn't make a fuss, he just picked her up in his arms and followed me out to where we'd left the wheelchair. He kissed the top of Mary's head and then he put her down, gentle as anything, and I covered her with the blanket. She was trying to put on a brave face, but it was a struggle.

Elton stood there for a moment, looking awkward.

'Well, I'll see you around,' he said to Mary.

'Yeah,' she said. 'See you around.'

Then he looked at me and smiled. His eyes were glassy and for a moment, I saw the boy that Mary had always wanted him to be.

I mouthed 'Thank you' and he gave a slight nod of his head. I had been afraid Elton wasn't going to turn up, but he had. He'd done exactly what he'd promised he'd do, and I would always be grateful to him for that.

Mary watched him walk away. She watched him until he was a tiny speck in the distance. She watched until even that part of him was gone. I bit my lip, and stepped on the wheelchair brake to release the wheels.

I pushed Mary back down the pier, the wheels bumping on the joins of the planks. Her skin had faded to a frightening colour, paler than white, it was the colour of water, the colour of the skin of the dying people on her ward at the hospital.

'Mary,' I whispered and it was a kind of a prayer, 'Mary, hold on there, it'll be okay, I'll get you back to the hospital, you'll be fine, you'll see.'

She didn't answer. Her eyelids flickered every now and then, but she didn't move. We had to stop at the traffic lights to wait to cross and I leaned down to straighten the blanket, and I noticed, although she was sleeping, that there was the faintest smile on her lips.

Chapter Forty

I didn't go to the hospital on Friday. Mary's Aunty and Uncle from Worthing were coming over for the day and Mrs Pickles was worried there would be too many people in the room. And when I turned up on Saturday morning, I wasn't allowed to see Mary. A nurse I didn't know was on the desk and she wouldn't tell me what was going on.

'Is she dying?' I cried out and the nurse held her finger to her lips and said: 'Shhh! You'll upset everyone!' and ushered me out of the ward as quickly as she could.

I saw Ralph before he saw me. He was standing in the shade of the big horse chestnut tree, rocking the pram. He was wearing his black jacket, and his hair was longer than it had been, curling over the collar. Most of his face was in shade, but the sunlight was bright on his neck, his ear, his shoulder. He was holding the pram handle with one hand, pushing it forwards and backwards, but he wasn't looking at Peggy. He was staring at the ground, completely lost in thought.

I sat down on the bench. Eventually he noticed me. We smiled at each other and then he sat down beside me. The leaves were turning from green to brown and the grass beneath the tree was spotted with fallen conkers, the glossy brown nuts spilling from their green cases. He reached across and rested his hand on mine. We stayed like that until it was time to go back to Mary.

I walked through those days. I functioned, but I wasn't really existing, I was in limbo. I was exhausted but it was hard to sleep. I lay on my bed in the dark, and thoughts of Mary filled my mind. When I did doze off, my sleep was shallow, interrupted by dreams of Mary. I dreamed she was running along the beach, weaving in and out of holidaymakers, waving and laughing. I'd run after her, but I could never quite reach her, and by the time I reached the pier, she had disappeared. There were other dreams, where I could hear her voice across a room, but I couldn't get to her, because people kept getting in my way. I woke feeling hot and panicky.

I was worried that Mary would die while I was sleeping, on her own. And while the good, grown-up part of me wanted to be there with her when it was time, the frightened, child part of me was terrified of how it would be. I had never seen anyone die. I did not know what to expect. I didn't really want to be there.

Mary's little room in the hospital was now the only place I felt at peace. I felt safe there, and contained. My world had become focused on that room, That bed, Mary's breathing. I felt solid there, stable. I liked the smells and the regimentation of the daily routines. I knew that there, Mary and I were surrounded by people who were used to death and dying. They knew what to do. It did not frighten them and their kindness calmed me. I knew they would look after me as they looked after Mary. The hospital was the place where I belonged as much as Mary.

One evening I was a bit early, and Mary's family were with her, so I went down to the beach and sat on the pebbles. The sun was sliding towards the sea and the sky was giving its daily light show, changing colour, being glorious. I watched the starlings flocking in their thousands over the Palace Pier, and listened to the city preparing for the evening's fun and entertainment.

After a while I heard footsteps crunching the gravel behind me and I looked up and it was Mary's older brother, Wayne.

'Hi,' he said.

'Hi.'

Wayne sat down beside me. His legs were very long and skinny in his jeans. He took a packet of Embassy out of the pocket of his leather jacket, tapped out a cigarette, put it in his mouth and lit it.

'Are you all right?' I asked.

'Fine,' he said.

'How's Mary?'

'Same.'

I sighed.

'Doesn't it seem wrong to you that everything outside the hospital is still carrying on as normal when everything inside is so…' Wayne said. It was one of the longest speeches I'd ever heard him make.

'I know what you mean,' I said.

I could not quite understand how the lights were still reflected in the sea, how the moon still rose in the sky, how people were still going to pubs and amusement arcades and chip shops as normal when nothing could ever be normal again.

'Is your mum still in with Mary?' I asked.

He nodded. He offered me the cigarette but I shook my head. He took a deep drag and leaned back his head and blew out the smoke, his hair falling back down his shoulders. The smoke hung in a little cloud above us.

❄ ❄ ❄

The children went back to school after the long summer holidays, and the weather turned cooler.

I went to the hospital after work, and arrived just as the tea trolley was going round. It was one of the best times to be in the ward. Patients and nurses were relaxed, and talking to each other. I walked through the ward, and into Mary's room.

For the first time in days, Mary was propped up against the pillows.

'What do you think of this, then?' said Mary's mum. She looked as pleased and proud as if Mary had just won an Oscar.

'I can't believe it!' I said. I walked over to the bed and leaned down and kissed Mary's forehead. 'Hello, you,' I said.

'Hello, Dottie,' she whispered. Her voice was so faint I could hardly hear her.

Mary's mum stood up. 'I'll be off then,' she said. 'Ralph's bringing Peggy up later. See you in the morning, love.'

Mary nodded.

I perched on the bed beside Mary. I could hear a faint, rattly noise coming from her chest when she breathed out. I did not like the sound of that noise. It was only tiny, but it seemed ominous. It was like the change you can feel in the air when a storm is on the way.

I smoothed Mary's cheek with the back of my hand, very gently.

'How are you feeling?' I asked.

'Like I want to say something to you.'

She swallowed and rested for a moment. I thought perhaps she might fall asleep, but she opened her eyes again, and her chest rose and I heard the rattle as she exhaled and I wanted to tell her to stop breathing like that. I didn't want the sound of that noise in my mind.

'I want you to promise me something,' she whispered.

'What?'

'Promise first.'

'But what if it's a promise I can't keep?'

'*Promise*,' said Mary.

'Okay, I promise, what is it?'

'I want you to move away from Brighton, away from the estate. You can do better than Woolworths. I want you to visit the places that I will never see. I want you to lie on golden sands under palm trees. I want you to swim in water that's as warm as a bath. I want you to be my eyes, Dottie.'

'Don't worry about all that,' I said, reaching for her hand.

She pushed my hand gently away and opened her eyes. 'I haven't finished,' she said. She took a deep breath. 'And one day, I want you to stand at the top of the Eiffel Tower with the boy you love.'

I didn't know what to say.

'Dottie?'

'Yes?'

'If that boy is Ralph then it's okay with me.'

'Please, Mary…'

'I want you to know that it's okay with me… I mean I don't mind if you want to be together… you know… after.'

'You're not going anywhere,' I said.

'Oh Dottie!' she said. 'We both know that's not true. I can see it on everyone's faces. I hear the doctors when they think I'm asleep.'

Tears were running down my face now. I knew I shouldn't be crying. Mary's mum said that it would frighten Mary if she saw us in tears, but I couldn't help it.

'I don't want to be with Ralph,' I said. 'The only thing in the world I want is for you to be back to how you were and for everything to be normal again, like it used to be.'

Mary blinked slowly.

'Maybe you don't want to think about that now but you might later on and I just wanted you to know that it's okay with me… I won't mind. You are the girl that Ralph loves, not me.'

'You mustn't give up, Mary. It sounds as if you're giving up.'

'Not giving up, Dottie, just accepting it.'

'Well, that sounds like giving up to me, and I won't let you. What about Peggy and your mum and dad and everyone who loves you? And what about me, Mary? How am I supposed to go on without my best friend in the whole world?'

She looked at me and smiled. She breathed out and it seemed to me that the noise in her chest was a little louder, a little more persistent with every breath.

'Perhaps Heaven will be fabulous,' she said, and then she closed her eyes.

'It will be if you're there,' I whispered. I held Mary's little hand and cried as if my heart was breaking.

Dear Diary,

It's time to go now. I am so tired, so terribly tired. People want me to stay. They hold tightly to my hands, as if by holding me they can keep me here. I want them to let me go.

Goodbye Peggy, I love you very much baby girl. I wish that I could have been a better mummy.

Goodbye Dottie, my forever friend.

Goodbye diary.

Love

Mary Pickles

Aged only nineteen xxx

Chapter Forty-One

Ralph came later. He brought Peggy and sat her on the bed beside Mary. She looked down at the baby and she smiled.

As it grew dark outside, I held the baby on my lap and gave her a bottle. And Ralph sat on the other side of Mary and talked to her about his work, and Brighton, and things he had heard on the radio. He made her smile. He made her calm. I realised that he understood her; he knew what to say to her.

He was a good husband to her.

One of the nurses put her head around the door.

'Everything all right?' she asked.

I smiled at her, and nodded. 'We're all fine,' I said.

I changed Peggy on the bottom of the bed, and put her nappy to soak in the basin in the bathroom beyond. Then I laid her in her pram, and Ralph and I sat on either side of Mary's bed, each of us holding one of her hands until she fell asleep.

It was a small room, just room for the bed, and two chairs, and a chest of drawers. It was my world. One hour went by, and then another. It was hardly ever just me and Mary in the room any more. Mary's aunties and uncles and cousins came in to say goodbye. Sally came in, and the next-door neighbours. When the doctor came in, he didn't even use the stethoscope to listen to Mary's chest any more. He just smiled and said: 'Good, good.'

Sometimes I slept with my head on the bed; mostly I stood quietly by the window so as not to get in the way of Mr and Mrs Pickles and Peggy. I watched the leaves falling from the horse chestnut tree. I watched the wind riffle through its branches, and pick up a handful of leaves, and let them drift amongst the hospital buildings.

I watched the children collecting the conkers.

I was warm in the room, listening to Mary's breathing.

I was where I wanted to be.

At four o'clock one afternoon, the priest came to Mary's room. I waited outside in the little corridor. It didn't take long for him to say what he had to say and then the door opened again, and the priest came out. He smiled at me and said: 'You can go back in now.' He smelled of peppermint. He said: 'God bless you, child.'

I went back into the room.

Mary's family and Ralph were gathered around the bed like people in a painting. Some of her brothers were in the room and a couple were in the corridor. Winston had gone outside for a cigarette. Ralph was at the top of the bed. He was looking down at Mary. He didn't look up at all.

Peggy was lying on the bed beside Mary, sucking her fist and kicking her fat little legs and making happy, gurgling noises. Everyone was looking at Peggy. There were two circles of red on her cheeks, because of the teething. She looked like a doll. And we all watched Peggy, and smiled at her, and none of us noticed, at first, that Mary had stopped breathing. I heard Mary's mother cry out, as if in pain, and then I knew. Peggy realised too. She must have noticed the expression on the faces of the adults and she stopped gurgling and held up her arms to be picked up. Mary's father picked up the baby and held her to him, her head cradled in his big hand.

The nurse came in. She said: 'Excuse me,' and she made her way through to the bed. She picked up Mary's wrist and held it between her fingers. She stayed like that for a moment or two, and we all watched her, hoping, I suppose, that she would say something reassuring, hoping she would find a pulse. But then she lay Mary's hand gently down on the cover again. She said: 'I'll just get the doctor,' and she left the room.

'Why's she getting the doctor?' asked William. 'Can they bring Mary back?'

Mary's dad said: 'No, son. No one can bring her back now.' He grabbed hold of the boy and pulled him to him with his spare hand and William threw his arms around his father's waist and sobbed as if his heart were breaking. Wallace had turned his back to the room and was staring out of the window.

I looked up and caught Ralph's eye. He gazed back at me, for a moment, and then he stepped forward to comfort Mary's mother.

I didn't know what to do, my first instinct was to get out of that room, but I knew that wouldn't be right. Everyone around me was crying but I just felt numb, I wanted to cry, but the tears wouldn't come. I felt breathless and dizzy. I leaned against the wall for support. I had never fainted in my life but I would almost have welcomed it, just to get away from this terrible emptiness. My head was telling me that my best friend was dead. Mary Pickles was dead, but my heart could not accept it. I could hardly breathe, it was as if my body had forgotten how to. I should be crying – why wasn't I crying? I almost envied the others the release that I knew their tears would bring.

Just then a doctor came into the room followed by the nurse. He walked over to the bed. I looked away. I hadn't been able to look at Mary since the moment she had stopped breathing.

'She was a very brave young girl,' he said quietly. 'I'm so sorry.' He left the room.

I wanted more; this was too final. We had been watching Mary dying for months, and now there was nothing left, there should have been more. Didn't that doctor know how important this was? Didn't he know that we couldn't go on living? He was a doctor; he should have told us how we could go on living. I wanted more.

The nurse walked over to Warren. 'Would you like to take your mum and the family into another room and I will bring you all some tea.'

Warren nodded his head, he was glad to be able to do something. 'Come on, Mum,' he said gently, and then he took her arm and guided her out of the room. The others followed but I couldn't move. I felt as if a part of me was missing and if I tried to walk I would fall. Ralph looked back at me.

'Dottie?' he said.

'I'm coming.'

I was too frightened to look at the bed. I walked across to the window and looked out on the street below. It had started to rain. The leaves on the horse chestnut tree were glistening and water was trickling down the window pane. Mothers pushing prams were hurrying to get their children home. A man was holding a newspaper over his head. They didn't know that Mary was dead. I watched Wayne as he walked over to Winston who was sitting on the bench in the little garden. I watched as he looked up at Wayne then put his head in his hands. I turned away from the window, took a deep breath and looked across at Mary. I wasn't frightened any more.

I stepped forward, closer to the bed. I leaned over and kissed her cheek.

'I'll keep my promise,' I said. 'I'll go to all those places, just like you want me to and I'll carry you with me every step of the way.'

I looked at Mary's lovely little face.

'Thank you for being my friend,' I said. I gently brushed her hair out of her eyes. 'You look fab,' I whispered.

A nurse came into the room. She handed me a book.

'Mary asked me to give you this,' she said.

I took the book and walked out of the room. Mary Pickles wasn't there any more, and I needed to find her.

I hurried along the seafront towards home. The rain was now a soft drizzle that cooled my face. I cut through Kemp Town and on towards the estate, then I started to run, I ran until I was at the top of the alley. It was only then that I felt her near me, and it was only then that I allowed myself to remember the way we were, me and my friend Mary Pickles. I could almost hear us calling to each other.

'Mary.'

'Dottie.'

'Mary.'

'Dottie.'

❄ ❄ ❄

I opened the book at the first page and began reading.

This book belongs to Mary Pickles

46 See Saw Lane

Brighton

The world

My eyes filled with tears. I closed the book and put it down on the ground.

I sat on the top bar of the railings and held on tight, and then I closed my eyes and slowly let myself slide backwards. 'You'd better be watching!' I shouted, as I let go of the bars and suddenly I was hanging by my legs. I opened my eyes and for the first time in my life, I was seeing the world from an upside-down sort of a place.

Epilogue

There are six hundred and seventy-four steps to the second level of the Eiffel Tower. I know because I counted as I climbed and I dedicated each step to my friend Mary Pickles.

It was a bitterly cold day, February. Paris was ice-cold, stone-cold, everything grey and hard, even the pigeons that fluttered from the eaves were grey, as if they had been carved from concrete.

After I left the hotel that morning, I walked through the city streets, along wide grey pavements, weaving amongst people wrapped up in coats and fur collars, hats pulled over their ears and scarves wrapped over their mouths and noses. It was a cold unlike any cold I'd ever felt in Brighton. There was something exhilarating about it. It was different. Everything was different in this city of dreams.

I saw a man with an organ grinder and a monkey. I saw a woman lean over the railings of a bridge and throw roses into the water below. I saw a man on a bicycle with a trombone strapped to his back. *Mary would have loved this,* I thought, and I smiled and I tucked my hands into my pockets and my chin into my collar.

The light from the cafés and bars was warm golden-yellow. It spilled on the grey, ice-cold pavements, and through the windows I could see waiters carrying trays at shoulder-height and serving coffee and pastries to the men and women who sat at the tables. The grey-blue smoke from their cigarettes curled through the warm colours inside the café, through the mirrors and the chandeliers, the reds and the golds and the greens of the paintings on the walls, ornate and gorgeous in their gilt frames.

I noticed everything. I tried to remember everything. I put it safe in my heart, for Mary.

I walked through those wide streets, past those grand, tall buildings with their little wrought-iron balconies, I walked along the side of the Seine, grey and oily, to the Eiffel Tower. And then I climbed the six hundred and seventy-four steps to the second stage.

Up there the air was even colder. Up there I felt a million miles from home. I felt as if I could stretch out my arms and take a deep breath and fly; I would fly away. I would fly to Mary.

The city lay beneath me, neatly laid out as if somebody had drawn it on a sheet of paper, the river winding through, the islands and the church towers, the squares and parks, the magic of the place.

I walked around the second level, buffeted by a rough wind. I saw Paris from every angle, and then I got into a little creaky lift and a man in a uniform cranked the door closed and took me up to the top. The lift cage rattled and creaked as it climbed. I thought of the chains and wheels pulling me up in the little cage. I thought of the wind that blew through across the city. I thought how little control we had over any of it. There was nothing we could do but accept what came to us.

The top of the Eiffel Tower is smaller than you'd imagine, a balcony that runs around the top of the tower, but oh, the views! The gardens below stretching out into the distance and the streets that run parallel. In the far distance, the city meets the clouds at the horizon. In the end, I thought, everything goes to where it is supposed to be. My breath shrouded my face. I held onto the railings and I gazed out.

This had been Mary's dream, not mine. It was Mary who had always wanted to come to Paris with the boy she loved. It had been Mary who wanted to climb to the top of the Eiffel Tower, Mary who wanted to see what I was seeing, to do what I was doing, to live the life I was living.

This had never been my dream. All I had ever wanted was to marry Ralph Bennett and for us to have a family together and to grow old with him in our council flat in Brighton.

I missed Mary so badly I felt as if my heart was breaking. I gazed out at the sights she would never see and I thought of how it would be if she was here.

'This is all for you, Mary,' I whispered.

I imagined her hand on my arm, I imagined her smile, and for a moment it was as if she was there, beside me, looking at the view with me.

'Wow,' she whispered, in my mind, 'isn't this fab! Isn't it just simply as absolutely incredibly amazingly fabulous as I told you it would be?

Fighting back the tears I looked out over Paris.

'Yes my dearest friend, this is as absolutely incredibly amazingly fabulous, as you told me it would be.'

LETTER FROM SANDY

Thank you so much for reading my book *The Girls from See Saw Lane*. Brighton in the 1960s was truly amazing. It was a wonderful time to be a teenager. It was a time of coffee bars, frothy coffee, the Beatles, the pier, and the pebbly beach. I hope that my story has given you a sense of that time and that place.

I wrote about friendship because all my life my friends have been so important to me, and still are. I hope that you have grown to love the characters of Dottie and Mary as much as I do.

If you have enjoyed it, can I ask you to leave a short review? As a new writer it would be really helpful. If you would like to know what happens next, the sequel to *The Girls from See Saw Lane* is entitled *Counting Chimneys* and will be out in Spring 2016.

To keep right up-to-date with the latest news on my new releases just sign up here:

www.bookouture/sandy-taylor

Thank you for reading my book. I hope that you have enjoyed reading it as much as I have loved writing it.

Sandy

ACKNOWLEDGEMENTS

So many people to thank: my amazing children and grandchildren, Kate, Bo, Iain, Kerry, Millie, Archie and Emma, for all the joy and love they give to me. My brothers and sisters, Margaret, Paddy, John and Marge, for always being there and being proud of my writing. All my friends, for their encouragement and belief that I would one day get a book out there.

Louie and Wendy, with love always. My talented friend Lesley for her ongoing support and help. Richenda Todd, for her invaluable insight and help in the early drafts of this book. The team at Bookouture: my publicist Kim Nash, thank you for your warm welcome to the Bookouture family, and my lovely editor Claire Bord, for taking this book to the place where it needed to be. Last but not least to my amazing agent Kate Hordern for seeing something in my little story and taking a chance on me (bad grammar and all). You are not only a wonderful agent but a friend. Thank you.

Made in the USA
Middletown, DE
28 April 2023

29651675R00195